Praise for Helen Warner

'A thought-provoking novel' *Heat*

'A page-turning good read' *Star*

'Four women, one wedding and unexpected results.
Great good fun' *Woman & Home*

'There's lots of bitching and a few tears in this fizzing read'
Woman's Own

'As bubbly as a glass of wedding Champagne' *Cosmopolitan*

'Action-packed' *Daily Telegraph*

'A ridiculously romantic story written from the
perspective of four women as they gear up for a wedding
that will have repercussions for them all' *Heat*

'The kind of book ... holidays were made for' *RED*

'Helen Warner paints a complex picture of
friends and lovers' *Star*

Helen Warner is Director of Daytime for ITV where she oversees a wide range of programming from *This Morning* to *The Chase*. Previously, she was at Channel 4 where she was responsible for shows including *Come Dine With Me*, *Coach Trip* and *Deal or No Deal*. She lives in Essex with her husband and their two children and she writes her books on the train to work.

Also by Helen Warner

RSVP
Stay Close to Me

with
or without
you

HELEN WARNER

London · New York · Sydney · Toronto · New Delhi

A CBS COMPANY

First published in Great Britain by Simon & Schuster UK Ltd, 2014
A CBS COMPANY

1 3 5 7 9 10 8 6 4 2

Simon & Schuster UK Ltd
1st Floor
222 Gray's Inn Road
London WC1X 8HB

www.simonandschuster.co.uk

Simon & Schuster Australia, Sydney
Simon & Schuster India, New Delhi

A CIP catalogue record for this book
is available from the British Library

Paperback ISBN: 978-1-47110-061-1
Ebook ISBN: 978-1-47110-062-8

Typeset by M Rules
Printed and bound by CPI Group (UK) Ltd, Croydon, CR0 4YY

with
or without
you

Chapter 1

'Jamie!' yelled Martha, as she raced down the stairs wearing only a pink bra and mismatched red knickers, her long hair still wet. 'Have you ironed my dress yet?'

She scuttled into the kitchen, which was a scene of early-morning chaos. The ironing board was up, the television was blaring out the breakfast news, and Jamie, in just a pair of boxer shorts, was running from the toaster to the table with a plate in one hand and the iron in the other. At the table, Mimi and Tom were arguing loudly over who had flicked a blob of marmalade onto the computer screen, resulting in Jamie, who rarely raised his voice, shouting that they would both be banned from 'screens' for a week if they didn't stop fighting.

'Here,' Jamie said in a softer voice, handing Martha her favourite dress, a stone-coloured, fitted shift. He watched with an amused expression as she clambered into it, before turning around and contorting her body so that she could zip it up at the back.

'How do I look?' She threw the question expectantly over her shoulder.

1

'Gorgeous,' he replied dutifully, bending to kiss the top of her head, before she scurried off in the direction of the front door. 'But I think you'd benefit from some shoes?' he added.

'Oh shit!' cried Martha, running up the stairs once more.

From the kitchen she heard Mimi's voice, 'Muuuuummm! Enough of the bad language! You're always telling us not to swear.'

'Aaarghh!' grumbled Martha to herself, as she knelt down in front of her wardrobe and rummaged through the pile of shoes in search of a matching pair. Eventually she located a pair of gold platform sandals that were more suited to a party than an interview, but with time running out she would just have to make do. She couldn't be late today, it was too important. Scrabbling to her feet, she stepped into the sandals, instantly growing in stature by four inches. She glanced at herself in the full-length mirror on the wall, before running out of the bedroom as quickly as the sandals would allow, only dimly registering that something wasn't quite right.

'Jamie! I'm off!' she shouted, snatching up her oversized leather satchel and opening the door. 'Bye, kids! Love you both, have a great day!' she added.

'Bye!' they chorused back. 'Love you!'

Jamie padded out of the kitchen, still wearing just his boxer shorts and looking, she thought, more handsome than he had any right to at such an early hour. 'Hey, don't forget your breakfast.' He smiled and handed Martha some buttered toast, wrapped in a piece of kitchen paper. 'And good luck!'

Martha grinned and reached up to kiss him. Even in her

high heels he was still taller than her. 'Thank you,' she mouthed, taking the toast. 'Love you, miss you, mean it!' she called out in a cod American accent as she finally left.

'Love you, miss you, mean it!' he replied, mimicking her accent and laughing as he watched her from the doorway. It had become their private joke, ever since a holiday in Florida a few years back when they had heard an earnest couple saying it to one another as they parted at the airport.

'Get inside!' she shouted as she unlocked the car and dumped her bag on the back seat. 'You'll give Mrs Moffatt a heart attack!'

Jamie beamed and stretched languorously, knowing full well that the gesture showed off his toned stomach. 'Ah, it's probably the only excitement she gets,' he protested. 'I'll put the bins out later too – she loves that!'

'Show off!' Martha shook her head and smiled as she climbed into her beloved Fiat 500 and started the engine. Their 75-year-old neighbour had lived alone ever since her husband Alfred had died almost four years previously, and she adored Martha and the children. But she especially adored Jamie. He had recently helped to set her up with a computer so that she could Skype with her son, who lived in Australia. Martha wouldn't have had a clue where to start, but Jamie was patience personified when teaching her how to use the laptop her son had bought her.

Martha took a deep, calming breath as she drove the familiar route to the train station. She switched on the radio and quickly became absorbed in the easy banter of the Radio 2 breakfast show, glad to have the company as she munched her toast. It was cold and the butter was congealed but she was grateful for it; it would be lunchtime before she got another chance to eat.

She knew she was lucky. Ridiculously lucky. She had two gorgeous, happy, healthy children, a husband who was her soulmate, and an exciting, high-profile job as a showbiz interviewer. Over her fifteen-year career, she had met just about all the major film and TV stars on both sides of the Atlantic, and was on first-name terms with several A-listers.

She had become the first port of call for all the big PRs, on account of her reputation as a writer who never veered into the realms of personal bitchiness like some other reporters; she always seemed to get to the heart and soul of her subjects. She had an innate ability to draw them out and get them to reveal things that they had previously managed to keep to themselves.

She had started out as a news journalist but had fallen into showbiz reporting by accident, when she was sent to interview a top female TV presenter for a magazine. During a searing interview, the presenter had broken down and admitted that she was an alcoholic, taking herself by surprise as much as Martha. As she wrote up the interview a few days later, Martha had called the presenter and offered to leave out the revelation, worried about the impact it might have on her young family. Martha had held back from telling her editor about the scoop for that very same reason. But the TV star had insisted that she was relieved to have finally admitted it, and that she had already enrolled in AA, determined to get help.

4

The interview made all the national newspapers, as well as being the main topic on a number of radio and TV discussion shows. It also propelled Martha into the spotlight and instantly made her a favourite with celebrities, who felt that they could trust her, even though, ironically, they always ended up revealing more to her than they planned.

For Martha's part, she loved her job, but she knew full well she wouldn't be able to do it without Jamie's support. He had been a journalist himself when they got together, but had given up a staff job on a broadsheet to look after the children full-time when Martha's career really took off. She often had to travel abroad, and without Jamie it would have been impossible to accept most of the assignments she was given.

Jamie never complained about putting his career second to hers, although she knew sometimes he found it difficult that she was the main breadwinner. He still earned some of his own money by writing freelance articles; they weren't big money-spinners but they gave him a certain amount of independence and helped his self-esteem. He was also working on a children's book, which Martha felt would be huge if he could get some interest from an agent.

But for the time being, his main role was looking after the children and he did it magnificently. He was very involved with their school, where he was chair of the PTA, and he spent hours each day playing with them, talking to them, taking them on trips and igniting their interest in everything from trampolining to astronomy. Unlike many of the school mums, he didn't find the daily grind of looking after children boring. On the contrary, he seemed to find them inspiring and was never happier than when it was just the three of them out on their bikes together, exploring. Martha had often thought that he did a far better job than she could ever do if their roles were reversed.

Pulling into the station car park, she punched the air with delight as she found a parking space in a prime position close to the exit and leapt out, wobbling slightly on her heels as she did so. She grabbed her bag from the back seat and raced for the platform of the small country station, mentally thanking her lucky stars that the train to London left from the nearest platform, rather than the one opposite, which involved a heart-attack-inducing race up a steep flight of stairs, a trip across a footbridge and back down the other side.

Sure enough, the train was already pulling in as she arrived, out of breath. Several other commuters looked at her curiously and she smiled to herself, delighted that even at thirty-six, she still had the ability to turn heads. She proudly shook her long, chestnut hair, which was dry by now and which she knew was her crowning glory. She never did anything with it except for washing it each morning, yet it was glossy and thick enough to appear in a shampoo commercial.

She found a seat beside a large, pink-faced woman, who had already marked her territory by placing her arm fully on the rest that separated the two seats. Martha raised an eyebrow, knowing that for the hour-long journey there would be a battle of wills over who eventually got the armrest. It annoyed her when other people did it but she had to admit she was one of the worst culprits if she got there first.

6

She plugged in her headphones, earning herself a scowl from the woman which she swiftly deflected with a beaming smile, and pulled out her cuttings on Charlie Simmons, the actor she was meeting that day. It was to be the first of a number of meetings, as she had been assigned to ghost-write his memoirs. It was the first time she had been asked to write a book and she felt uncharacteristically nervous; it was one thing to do an in-depth profile, but it was a much bigger leap to write a life story. The book had been commissioned after Charlie's Oscar nomination for his most recent film, in which he had played a very famous interviewer, and he was tipped to be the 'next big thing' in Hollywood, the latest British export to hit the big-time.

But Martha had heard that he could be tricky when it came to journalists. Usually, she never worried when she was warned that someone could be difficult; she quite often thought that she would be difficult herself if someone wrote horrible things about her. And judging by his cuttings, there was plenty for Charlie Simmons to be upset about, but if she was going to be spending a lot of time with him, Martha needed him to warm to her and, more than that, she desperately wanted to do a good job. This assignment could lead to a whole new career for her if she did it well.

Martha's father had been a newspaper editor, as well known for his violent temper as he was for his brilliance. He had inspired Martha to become a journalist in the first place, but she had never forgotten him telling her that every morning he got up and looked in the mirror, thinking that today would be the day he finally got found out. It was something she constantly experienced herself. She couldn't believe she'd made it so far without any of the problems that seemed to dog many of her female contemporaries, who were unhappily single or whose careers had been held back by their over-reliance on alcohol. She had managed to combine a very stable, happy home life with a successful career.

Martha looked out of the train window at the lush patchwork of green and yellow countryside flashing by in the early morning June sunshine and thought about her father's words now, wondering if this assignment would be the one where she finally fell flat on her face. The one where she finally got found out.

Chapter 2

After waving Martha off to work, Jamie joined Mimi and Tom at the kitchen table, where they were still finishing breakfast.

'Yuk, Dad, put some clothes on!' Mimi frowned as she took a bite of her toast. 'It's *gross* being naked at the breakfast table!'

'I'm not naked,' Jamie protested, 'I've got boxer shorts on. And this isn't a breakfast table, it's just a table. An ordinary, bog-standard table.'

Mimi smiled. At eleven years old, Jamie knew she loved these silly exchanges. The three of them regularly had heated debates about the most stupid of things.

'I would say . . .' Tom began in a considered voice that belied his eight years, 'that it could be classed as a breakfast table, if you're eating breakfast from it.'

Mimi glanced at her brother suspiciously. He didn't usually agree with her in these debates. 'Yes,' she said carefully. 'That's right. And if you're eating dinner, it becomes a dinner table.'

'Aah, but what if you're eating an apple? Or some grapes?'

Jamie cut in. 'Does it therefore then become an apple table? Or a grape table?'

'No, because that's not a proper meal. You only name the table after proper meals.' Mimi nodded slightly as she finished speaking, causing her long blonde hair to pool around her shoulders.

'And does it depend on what the meal is?' Jamie looked up at the ceiling, as if he was giving considerable thought to the issue. 'For instance, does it become a curry table if one is eating curry? Or a—'

'Yuk,' interrupted Tom, wrinkling his pert little nose. 'I hate curry. It's *never* going to be a curry table.'

'No,' Mimi said decisively, getting up from the table as if to emphasise that the debate was at an end. 'It makes no difference what the content of the meal is, it's the *time* of day that it's eaten that determines what the table is called.' She loaded her plate and bowl into the dishwasher. 'To name it after the individual food that's eaten at the table would be time-consuming and, frankly, a bit stupid,' she finished.

'I'd still like to make the case for it sometimes being called a snack table,' Jamie said. 'We eat an awful lot of what could only be described as snacks around this table. What do we call it at these awkward, in-between times?'

'I think we can agree that depending on the time of day, there will be a suitable name for the table,' Mimi said, washing her hands at the kitchen sink. 'Let's say that up until eleven a.m., it's a breakfast table. From eleven a.m. until, say, five p.m. it's a lunch table and—'

'That's a dangerously long lunch though?' Jamie protested.

'I think we can live with it,' Mimi replied curtly. 'And from five p.m. onwards, it's a dinner table.'

'Okaaaay,' Jamie agreed reluctantly, pursing his lips and shaking his head.

'Dad, we need to go to school,' Mimi said in a stern voice that always reminded him so much of Martha. 'We don't have time to continue this extremely important debate now. If necessary, we can return to it after school.'

'Around the table that is yet to be named?" Jamie countered.

'Grow up, Dad,' Mimi replied, coming over to kiss him before heading upstairs to brush her teeth.

'OK, buddy,' Jamie said, turning to Tom and ruffling his blond mop. 'Time to brush those teeth.' Tom pulled a face but trudged reluctantly towards the stairs.

Jamie watched his son's retreating back affectionately. Tom was a good kid but he would happily never shower or brush his teeth if he was left to his own devices. Jamie couldn't be cross with him as he knew he'd been much the same at that age.

After he had cleared away the breakfast things, Jamie set about making the children's packed lunches. He had got into the habit of putting little riddles and notes into each of their lunchboxes and it was becoming an increasingly elaborate process. To begin with, he used to scribble something silly on a bit of scrap paper. Now he found himself planning in advance what he was going to do and would print it out the day before. Sometimes, if the children couldn't figure out the answer, the three of them would work on it after school until they came up with the solution. Martha laughed at him for making such a big deal out of it, but Jamie loved challenging them and it gave him a small purpose each day.

His role as a stay-at-home dad was the obvious solution for the Lamont-Smith family. Martha earned considerably more than Jamie would if he worked full-time, and she got to spend more time at home between assignments than he would have done, so it made perfect sense. They had agreed early on that they didn't want to employ a nanny while they both worked because they wanted the children to have at least one parent at home. And as they lived an hour outside of London, meaning a long commute, and both worked odd hours, it would have been impossible with a nanny anyway unless she lived-in, and neither of them wanted that invasion of privacy.

Over time, they had found a way to make it work, but it hadn't been easy. In the beginning, Jamie had felt emasculated and impotent earning so little money and having to rely on Martha. But Martha had made it easier by setting up a standing order so that half of her money was paid directly into Jamie's account each month, meaning he could take responsibility for paying the household bills.

Jamie was therefore in charge of the family's finances, which helped him to feel more in control. For her part, Martha struggled being away from him and the children, so he wanted to do all he could to make it work for her. He never called her when there was a problem, unless absolutely essential, like the time he had had to take Tom to hospital when he thought he had meningitis, and he never let her know if the children cried because they were missing her.

In return, Martha had learned not to complain that the

house was a mess or that the children had had pizza again for their dinner, because all that really mattered was that they were happy and healthy. And they were, Jamie thought proudly now, as he put their lunchboxes in the hall beside their book bags. They were such interesting, intelligent and well-balanced children, and he knew that he had played a major role in making them that way. Whatever else he achieved in his life, nothing would compare with making a success of bringing up his children; he had a bond with them that he knew was rare and was borne of spending so much time in each other's company.

Mimi was the first to come down the stairs, now wearing her regulation summer uniform of navy blue skirt and pale blue polo shirt. Her long hair was loose and in her hand she clutched her favourite silver scrunchie and a large hairbrush. 'Will you do my plait, please, Dad?' she asked, handing him the brush and scrunchie and spinning around so that she had her back to him.

'You betcha!' Jamie grinned at her and thought, just as he did every day, how very beautiful she was becoming. He brushed through her hair and deftly tied it into a thick plait. 'How's that?' he turned her so that she could look at herself in the large hall mirror.

'Fab, thanks, Dad,' she replied, bending to pick up her lunchbox and book bag. 'See you later, love you – oh, and do put some clothes on,' she added, kissing him on the cheek, before setting off in the direction of the school, which was just five doors down the street.

Jamie watched her go, smiling to himself. She was so like

her mother. He and Martha had met fourteen years previously when they had both been taken on as trainees on a national newspaper. Jamie had fancied Martha immediately, but she wasn't so easily won over. She had a boyfriend from her university days, and although she seemed to like Jamie and was friendly towards him, she appeared to be impervious to his charms.

As a tall, handsome, Scandinavian-looking blond, Jamie was used to women falling at his feet, and so it came as a shock when Martha resolutely refused to do so. He tried absolutely every tactic, from trying to make her jealous by getting off with the editorial secretary at the Christmas party, to taking her out and getting her drunk, but nothing seemed to work. The boyfriend was apparently there to stay.

In the end, deciding he had nothing to lose, Jamie got drunk himself and declared his undying love for her, asking her outright if she would leave her boring boyfriend and go out with him instead. To his astonishment, Martha told him in a very matter-of-fact way that she had already finished with her boyfriend because she had fallen in love with Jamie, and that if he asked her again in the morning when he had sobered up, the answer would be 'yes'. The next morning, in between bouts of retching and endless cups of black coffee, Jamie repeated his declaration and asked her again. True to her word, she said 'yes', and they had been together ever since.

Their relationship had worked so perfectly from the start that it was clear that they were meant to be together. They rarely argued and were both placid and easy-going personalities, but there was also an intense, enduring passion between them. Even after two children, their sex life was as strong as ever and Jamie still found himself hardening at the merest thought of Martha naked. She had an incredible body, with surprisingly large breasts and a perfectly rounded bottom, despite her slenderness. Her long, dark hair and flawless skin meant that she turned heads wherever she went and Jamie always felt proud that this gorgeous creature was his wife.

'Bye, Dad!' called Tom, interrupting Jamie's lustful musings, as he came down the stairs in his uniform. Tom grabbed his bags before cheerfully making his way down the road after his sister, his messy blond hair glinting in the sunlight.

'Bye, Tom. Love you!' called Jamie, earning a scowl from his son, who pretended to despise any such public displays of affection in front of his friends. 'To infinity and beyond . . .' he added, just as he always did.

Jamie closed the front door and took a deep, contented breath. He loved the children's company, but he also loved being at home alone. It meant he had a whole, inviting day stretched out ahead of him. It also meant he had ample opportunity to have uninterrupted sex with his mistress.

Chapter 3

Charlie Simmons was woken by the sound of his mobile on the bedside table. He squeezed his eyes tightly shut to make sure that he wasn't still dreaming, but the phone continued to vibrate angrily and play the theme tune to *The Sopranos*. He tried to swallow as he reached for the handset but his throat was too dry.

'Hello?' he rasped, silencing the noise.

'Charlie, it's me . . .' said an unfamiliar voice.

Charlie shook his head to try to wake himself as he bunched the soft, goosedown pillows into a pile behind him and sat up. 'Who's me?'

There was a dry, husky laugh. 'Well, I guess I sound as bad as I feel if you don't know my voice.'

Recognition dawned and Charlie smiled to himself, groping with one hand for the bottle of mineral water he had half-drunk the night before. 'Hi, Louisa. You sound bloody terrible,' he said, taking a grateful gulp.

'I know. You don't sound great yourself. Anyway, look, I'm

really, really sorry but I feel like shit. I'm not going to be able to come this morning.'

'What's this morning?' Charlie closed his eyes again and rested his throbbing head against the headboard. He had drunk way too much last night, but he couldn't remember why or what the occasion had been.

'It's the first interview with Martha Lamont. You know, the one I've lined up to ghost your memoirs?'

'Oh, right.' Charlie tried to recall whether Louisa had told him about this and he had forgotten, or whether she hadn't told him in the first place. He must have forgotten, he decided. Louisa was a brilliant PR and ruthlessly efficient. There was no way she wouldn't have told him about the interview, and equally there was no way she would miss it unless she was feeling really ill.

'Don't worry, I'll deal with it myself,' he said. 'What time, and is there anything I should or shouldn't do?'

'Eleven o'clock. Don't sleep with her,' Louisa managed to croak, before descending into a coughing fit that sounded as if she was about to die right there on the end of the phone. Eventually the cough receded and Louisa came back on the line. 'Sorry,' she gasped. 'Got to go.'

'Get well, sweetie,' Charlie replied, before hanging up.

He sat in the gloom of the blacked-out hotel room, his eyes gradually becoming accustomed to the darkness. He wondered what time it was and pressed the home key on his mobile. 09:34. Immediately he calculated eight hours back, to work out what time it would be in Los Angeles, just as he always did whenever he looked at a clock. It would be 01:34 and his son,

17

Felix, would be asleep in his vast bedroom at the home he and his mother shared with her boyfriend.

The ache Charlie felt whenever he thought about Felix had not lessened in the four years since his mother had taken him to live on the other side of the world, and Charlie had realised long ago that it never would. Losing his beautiful, angelic boy, who looked so much like him, was a pain more devastating than any other heartache he had ever experienced – even that of losing his wife to another man.

He flew to LA as often as he could and he spoke to Felix most days on Skype, but it wasn't the same as spending day after day with him, doing all the normal things a dad does with his son. Charlie had spent the first two years of Felix's life looking after him full-time, so the bond they had was closer than most and made the wrench of losing him that much worse.

He groped for the lamp switch and clicked it on. The room was bathed in a soft tangerine glow and Charlie sighed heavily as he looked around indifferently at the splendour of his surroundings.

He was living in the hotel at the moment, having finally sold the little cottage in Surrey he had shared with Felix's mother. He hadn't got round to buying anywhere new yet, as he had resigned himself to the fact that his next home would need to be in Hollywood if he wanted to be closer to Felix. And he *did* want to be closer to him. He had had enough of being a long-distance dad and had started to investigate the possibility of applying for custody. He knew he wouldn't have a hope if he stayed in the UK, but if he lived in Los Angeles, he couldn't see any reason why Felix shouldn't live with him. His mother had had it her own way for long enough.

He had several meetings lined up in LA the following week, which would confirm his next role, and with it his permanent move to the US. He very much hoped his days of being an occasional father were finally coming to an end.

Charlie swung his legs over the edge of the bed and stood up, his feet sinking into the plush pile of the carpet as he did so. Stretching and yawning, he walked to the window and pulled back the heavy blackout drapes, flinching as the bright morning sunshine seared his eyes. From his vantage point overlooking Hyde Park, he could see people already out enjoying the warm weather. Mothers and nannies pushed achingly trendy prams between the over-flowing flowerbeds, while joggers and skaters did their best to dodge them. Usually, Charlie liked to go for a run first thing, but with this journalist due to arrive soon, he didn't have enough time today. Giving himself a shake, he picked up the phone and dialled the number for the hotel kitchen.

'Good morning, Mr Simmons,' said the voice of Sara, one of the girls who worked there.

'Call me Charlie, I keep telling you,' he smiled despite his inexplicable feelings of irritation.

'OK, then, Charlie,' Sara began, and Charlie could detect the note of amusement and mischief in her voice. 'What can I do for you? Are you going to be joining us again this morning?'

Recently, Charlie had begun to cook for himself in the hotel kitchen, much to the bemusement of the staff. He wanted to explain to them that he missed preparing meals for himself, that living in the hotel made him feel rootless and he yearned for a real home again. But there was no point. He would only sound spoilt and ungrateful. So instead, he just let them think he was an eccentric control freak.

'Not this morning,' he said. 'More's the pity.' Instead he ordered a room service breakfast of porridge and toast and lay back down on the eight-foot bed, staring up at the ornate ceiling.

He was dreading the arrival of this wretched journalist, Martha Lamont, and was regretting that he had ever let himself be persuaded to do his memoirs at all. He knew that Louisa wouldn't have lined the woman up if she didn't trust her implicitly, but Charlie still had an innate mistrust of all journalists, having been badly bruised by some of the things that had been written about him in the past.

Louisa had convinced him that it would be a chance to tell his side of the story and rectify some of the lies that had been printed about him. But the clincher for Charlie had been when she suggested that all proceeds could go to charity. His grandfather had died of Alzheimer's the previous year and, ever since, Charlie had done anything he could to raise money for research.

So here he was ... and he would have to open himself up entirely to this woman if she was to have any chance of doing his memoirs properly, meaning he would have to relive the pain of losing Liv and Felix all over again.

He wanted to hate Liv, but not only could he not do that, he couldn't stop loving her either; he had never met anyone he felt as connected to as he had with her. Before their split they had been everything to each other, and he still missed hearing her girlish laugh or watching her sleeping with her thumb resting on her lower lip like a child.

He had had plenty of offers and even a few brief relationships but, for him, no other woman had ever come close to her, and he had resigned himself to being single for the rest of his life. He would devote himself to his son instead.

Taking a deep breath, he thought about cancelling the interview, saying he wasn't feeling well. But Louisa would be furious with him if he did and he didn't want to upset her when she was feeling so ill. He got up and headed for the shower, his shoulders hunched with a feeling of impending doom. But maybe, he told himself, this Martha Lamont would be different to all the other journalists he had met. Maybe she would be the one to prove him wrong about her profession.

Chapter 4

As usual, the train into London arrived late, so Martha ended up racing to the hotel where she was supposed to be meeting Charlie Simmons. By the time she got there, she was sweating profusely, out of breath and desperate for a wee. She wasn't overly concerned though; she knew from long experience that celebrities were rarely ready on time. She would have a chance to visit the ladies and sort herself out before being called to his room.

But to her dismay, the receptionist greeted her with a dazzling smile and told her that 'Mr Simmons is ready for you now,' directing her to a room on the eighth floor. Martha hesitated. Should she risk incurring Charlie Simmons' wrath by being late, or should she use the loo? By now she was really desperate and worried that she might actually wet herself. She took a deep breath and decided that she couldn't be late. She would get to the room and immediately excuse herself to use the bathroom.

The lift chugged listlessly to the eighth floor. When the doors opened, Martha was surprised by the old-fashioned chintziness of the décor. She knew that this particular hotel charged in the region of £5,000 per night, so she would have expected it to look a lot more glitzy. But then, she reasoned, walking along the corridor towards the room number she had been given, maybe the people who could afford it liked this type of faded English splendour.

As she arrived at room 802, she knocked on the door and pasted on her brightest smile, despite the fact that she was now having to hop up and down on the spot to distract herself from her insistent bladder.

Then the door swung open and to Martha's intense shock, there stood Charlie Simmons himself. She had been expecting Charlie's PR, who had booked her. 'Oh!' she exclaimed, her heart hammering at the sight of him and her desperation to use the loo momentarily forgotten. Martha was used to meeting handsome film stars and she rarely found them attractive, but Charlie Simmons really was breathtaking in the flesh. He was well over six foot, with unruly dark curls that framed his slightly stubbled square jaw and eyes that seemed to her like deep pools of dark chocolate.

'Hello! I was, er, expecting Louisa . . .?' she tailed off, feeling herself redden as the desperate urge to use the loo returned.

'Louisa's sick,' Charlie said, proffering his hand, which Martha took and shook as firmly as she could, to compensate for what she knew would be horribly sweaty palms. 'So I'm afraid you've just got me.'

Martha blanched slightly at his tone. 'Sorry,' she muttered, 'I should have introduced myself. I'm Martha . . .'

'... Lamont,' he finished the sentence for her, standing aside to allow her into the room. 'Great name,' he added. 'Sounds like you should be an actress yourself.'

Martha beamed despite herself. She had always loved her name and hadn't changed it when she got married, protesting that Jamie's surname, Smith, was far too boring. Their children had subsequently taken both names in what her mother always referred to witheringly as a 'trendy double-barrelled surname'.

Charlie closed the door behind him and followed Martha into the suite, which was as big as Martha's entire house. In the reception room there were several pale blue over-stuffed sofas arranged around a heavy stone coffee table. On the table sat two silver pots, some china cups and a plate of freshly baked croissants. The smell of the fresh flowers that were stuffed artfully into over-sized vases on every spare surface combined with the aroma of coffee to make Martha feel light-headed.

She turned to face Charlie. 'I'm really sorry,' she began, feeling herself turn a deeper shade of red as she looked up at him with what she knew must be a pleading expression, 'but can I use your loo before we start?'

'Er, I guess so,' he said, his eyes moving down her body and settling somewhere around her midriff.

Oh shit, thought Martha, realising with a dull horror that Charlie now suspected her of being a cokehead. He couldn't even meet her eye. 'It's not to go and snort coke!' she blurted, acutely aware that her sweaty appearance and red-faced breathlessness must look like she was about to do *exactly* that.

Charlie bit his lip, as if he was making an effort not to laugh. His gaze was still fixed on her stomach for some reason. 'I should hope not,' he murmured in his deep, velvety voice that contained the merest hint of a Welsh accent. 'It's the second door on the left.'

Martha frowned, then dashed gratefully towards the door, suddenly concerned she might not make it. She slammed the door shut behind her and sank down onto the seat, exhaling with relief as she was finally able to let go.

Standing up to wash her hands afterwards, she gazed at her reflection in the mirror. She looked flushed and there was a faint sheen of sweat on her face. She splashed cold water over her cheeks and patted them dry before running her fingers through her hair to straighten it out. As she did so, her dress rode up slightly and she could finally see why Charlie had been staring at her midriff and why she had been getting so many 'admiring' glances all morning. There, outlined in glorious burnt technicolour against the pale beige of her dress, was a perfect iron-shaped hole, through which the top of her red lacy knickers was clearly visible.

'Oh shit!' she wailed, suddenly wanting to cry. How could she possibly go out there and interview the most famous film star in the world right now with a hole in her dress and her knickers visible? There was nothing for it. She would have to stay in the bathroom. She dropped the lid and sat back down to think through her options.

After a while there was a tentative knock at the door. 'Er, hello?' said Charlie's unmistakably gravelly voice. 'Are you OK in there?'

25

'No!' Martha shouted back. 'I've got a massive iron-shaped hole in my dress!'

There was a snort of laughter from outside the door, followed by a long pause, as Charlie apparently composed himself. 'Sorry,' he said in a slightly strangled tone. 'I won't laugh again. It's hardly noticeable ...' His words were swallowed up by another bout of laughter.

Sitting on the loo, staring down at the gaping hole in her dress, Martha felt the beginnings of a smile tugging at her lips. It was quite funny, she supposed. She would probably laugh about it herself one day. But not yet. It was just too bloody embarrassing.

'Look, do you want to borrow something of mine?' came Charlie's voice from the other side of the door after another couple of minutes had elapsed. 'Maybe some sweatpants and a t-shirt?'

Martha took a deep breath and looked down again at her exposed midriff. 'That would be great,' she admitted meekly.

After another pause she heard a swish as something was dropped at the door. 'There you go,' he said. 'I'll wait in the bedroom. Let me know when you're ready.'

'Thanks.' Martha waited until she heard his footsteps retreating, before opening the door and scooping up the clothes he had left there. She whipped off her dress and deposited it into the bin with a mournful stare. She knew that it was unsalvageable, but was nevertheless reluctant to let it go. Then she dressed quickly in Charlie's clothes, trying not to notice the faint scent of expensive cologne that still clung to the navy blue t-shirt, even though it had been laundered.

Feeling idiotic in her over-sized outfit, she emerged from the bathroom and cleared her throat loudly. 'Er, I'm ready!' she called out into the empty space.

There was a click as the bedroom door opened and Charlie appeared, all dark curls and handsome amusement.

'Sorry about that,' Martha smoothed herself down in an attempt to look briskly assured. 'Now, shall we finally get down to business?'

Charlie threw her a sideways stare and nodded warily. 'Sure. Those sweats look great by the way. Who knew they could work so well with gold platform sandals?'

Chapter 5

'Sweetie, eat your cereal,' entreated Liv, as Felix sat with his head bowed and his shoulders hunched over the games console in his hand.

Felix looked up at her in surprise, as if he'd forgotten she was there. 'Oh, sorry, Mom,' he said, giving her a conciliatory flash of his gap-toothed smile. Liv gazed across the table at him, wondering how it was possible that he could look so much like his father at such a tender age, with his dark eyes and curls and wide, cheeky grin.

Liv took a sip from her cup of English Tetley tea, several boxes of which her mother had brought over with her on her last visit. She couldn't function in the mornings until she'd had at least three cups. Danny laughed at what he called her 'quaint English habits', but she didn't care. For her, the American obsession with coffee seemed just as strange.

In the background, Radio 1 burbled out from the laptop on the steel work surface. It was another way for Liv to connect with home, even if it did mean listening to the afternoon show at breakfast time due to the time difference between LA and the UK.

A tiny hammer pounded against the inside of Liv's skull. She got up and walked over to one of the over-sized, sleek white cupboards and retrieved a packet of Paracetamol. She popped two pills out of the blister pack and put her mouth under the running tap to swallow them quickly. As she stood up, she caught her reflection in the gloss surface of the cupboard and instinctively pulled her fingers through her messy sheet of gold, wavy hair. The eyes that stared back at her were indistinct, but their shadows occupied a disproportionate area of her tiny, heart-shaped face. She blinked and looked away from her ghostly, shadowy self.

Felix galloped through his cereal at an alarming speed, gulping and crunching with the energy only small children can bring to any task. As he crossed the finish line and triumphantly dropped the spoon into his empty bowl with a nerve-jangling clatter, his head tipped upwards towards Liv with a beseeching expression.

Liv smiled, unable to resist. 'Go on, then. You can have fifteen more minutes playing on your computer before we have to leave for school.'

'Aw, thanks, Mom, love you!' he cried, hopping down from the table and racing towards his bedroom.

'Love you too,' Liv murmured to his retreating back, but he was gone and her words carried themselves in a circle around the cavernous space, before returning to her own ears.

She picked up her iPhone, which was never more than an inch or two away, and checked for emails from her PA, Carrie.

Sure enough, there was a message notifying her of a couple of appointments over the next few days. She tried to ignore the fact that there were fewer appointments and requests than there used to be.

Liv put the phone down and picked up Felix's bowl, which she placed into the dishwasher, before putting on the kettle in preparation for her second cup of tea. She could have left it for Juanita the housekeeper, but that was something Liv had never quite got used to; she always felt guilty just leaving stuff for her to clear away. 'It's her job!' Danny would say. He never seemed to experience the same sort of embarrassment at having staff, but Liv still preferred to do some things for herself and that included clearing away her son's breakfast things.

She knew that she was an exception among the all-American moms of Felix's classmates. Almost all of them had at least two nannies taking care of their children full-time, so that they could either work on their latest movie role or album, go shopping or have lunch at their leisure. But while Liv had a nanny who worked for her when she was shooting a film, she already felt terrible enough that Felix lived half a world away from his beloved dad; she wasn't going to let him have an absent mother too.

At the end of each school day, Liv usually found herself standing alone in the playground, waiting for Felix. The army of nannies who were also there weren't unkind or bitchy towards her, but they weren't friendly either. They knew they would have nothing in common with her. Liv was a rich, famous film star, with an even richer, more famous film star for a boyfriend. She could know nothing of their lives and they could know nothing of hers. Ironically, Liv often thought that each and every one of those nannies was probably happier than she was.

Although she had devised ways to cope with her homesickness, it still dogged her every move and she sometimes wondered how much longer she could stay in LA without losing it completely. But while Danny's career went from strength to strength, there was no way he would consider relocating to London, and with Felix so happy with his LA lifestyle, she knew that for now she was stuck here.

Felix emerged from his bedroom twenty minutes later, looking for all the world like a true American boy, his baseball glove in one hand and his basketball in the other. 'Remember I'm going to PJ's after school, Mom?' he said in the Californian accent he had developed and which still took Liv by surprise.

'I haven't forgotten, sweetheart,' she replied, scooping up her bag and heading for the garage, where there were three cars waiting for her to choose from. She glanced knowingly at Felix before unlocking her original black Fiat 500, which Danny had had refurbished and shipped over to LA for her not long after they got together.

'Aw, Mom, do we have to take that one?' Felix groaned, looking longingly towards the black Range Rover parked beside it.

'There's nothing wrong with FiFi!' Liv protested, but she was already fishing in her bag for the Range Rover keys. Felix was at an age where he didn't want to stand out from his friends and she didn't want to embarrass him.

On the way back from dropping Felix off, Liv called in at Bristol Farms, the upmarket grocery store in Beverly Hills. Juanita did their grocery shopping as well as their cleaning, but Liv had got into the habit of dropping in herself, mainly because she didn't want Juanita to know what she was buying. Juanita was a devout, teetotal Catholic, and Liv suspected she would disapprove.

When Danny was home, alcohol was never an issue because she could pretend that they were both drinking, but with him away on a shoot, as he was right now, she had to be a little more resourceful. It wasn't even as if she drank very much. It was just that she found that a few glasses of wine helped ease her loneliness a little.

She was aware that she was getting some curious glances as she pushed her cart up and down the carefully lit aisles. Back in Britain she had often been recognised, but the British public never approached her in the way the Americans did. In LA it seemed as though everyone was connected to the film industry and felt the need to say so whenever they met anyone remotely famous.

Sure enough, as she headed for the tills, having selected four bottles of white wine and a bottle of vodka, a tall, dark-haired man darted towards her and put his hand on her arm, forcing her to stop. 'Hey, Liv!' he cried in that over-familiar way that Liv had never quite got used to. 'Left Danny at home today?'

Liv smiled a tight smile. 'Something like that,' she said, making a point of manoeuvring her cart in the opposite direction. The man didn't get the hint. 'So . . . what movie are you working on at the moment?' he persisted, falling into step beside her. 'Only, I'm an actor myself and I—'

'Sorry . . .' Liv interrupted him with another forced smile. 'I'm in a bit of a rush. Excuse me.' She walked as purposefully as she could towards the till, where the girl on the checkout greeted her with a grin of recognition.

'Hi again. That must get a little tiresome,' she said, as she began to scan Liv's bottles.

Liv blinked back at her, making a mental note to vary the stores she shopped in. 'No, really, it's fine,' she lied, thinking how very British she sounded.

The girl gave her a sideways look, before pausing with a bottle in her hand and peering at her screen.

'Problem?' Liv's voice had become higher suddenly and her heart gave a nervous flutter.

'No . . . just checking I'd scanned them all,' the girl said distractedly, tearing her eyes from the screen and back up to meet Liv's.

Liv noticed that two strawberry-coloured patches had appeared on the girl's pale, freckled cheeks. She took the final bottle from her and placed it beside the others in the cart, trying and failing to stop the accusatory sound of glass hitting glass.

As she drove up Coldwater Canyon towards home, already anticipating her first sip of chilled white wine, Liv's cellphone rang.

'Hello?' she shouted, inclining her head towards the hands-free speakers, even though it wasn't necessary.

'There's no need to shout!' said her agent, Jonathan.

'Sorry, darling,' Liv cooed, switching automatically from harassed mother mode into smooth, movie star mode. 'What news?'

There was a pause and Liv frowned at the phone console, wondering if the line had disconnected. 'I'm sorry, Liv,' he said at last, 'but the part's gone to Sadie Roberts.'

Liv reached out and held her hand over the speaker for a second as she digested the news, fearful for a moment that she might start to cry. She had really felt that the role was hers. This movie could have been the breakthrough she so desperately needed and she just *knew* that she would have been perfect in the lead role. But Sadie bloody Roberts had beaten her to it. She wasn't even a very good actress, thought Liv mutinously, after she had bid Jonathan a curt goodbye and hung up.

She arrived home and mooched into the vast hangar of a kitchen, opening the cupboards one by one and suddenly feeling desperately in need of a drink. She checked the large clock and saw that it was 10.40 a.m. Was that too early? She listened carefully to the sounds of the house and could hear Juanita's vacuum cleaner whining from a distant bedroom. Quickly, she unscrewed the lid of one of the bottles and took a long swig. Only as the liquid hit her empty stomach did she notice that it was the vodka she had opened. She replaced the cap with a guilty shudder and put the bottle in the cupboard under the sink behind the cleaning products. No-one ever looked in that cupboard. Juanita had a whole utility room where she kept her own supplies.

Liv stood up, suddenly light-headed. She needed to eat but

she had no appetite. Listlessly, she put a piece of white, sliced bread into the toaster and took the Marmite out of the fridge. Marmite on toast was like an edible comfort blanket to her whenever she was feeling low, but she only ever ate it when Danny was away, as he always moaned about the smell.

She made herself another cup of tea and perched at the steel island in the middle of the kitchen to eat the toast, staring out of the plate-glass doors at the infinity pool glinting turquoise in the sunlight above the dusty Hollywood Hills.

She felt bitterly disappointed that she hadn't got the part, but more than that, she was nervous about telling Danny. She couldn't shake the fear that he was losing interest in her now that she had started to drop down the Hollywood pecking order. And she was finding it increasingly hard to ignore the rumours that constantly circulated that he had been linked to a number of his other leading ladies. 'Ignore it, baby,' he would laugh, whenever she brought up the subject of the latest salacious headline. 'It's just crappy journos trying to fill the pages of their crappy little rags. Anyway, I'm not screwing Tatiana Brown because she has extremely bad breath thanks to that stupid high protein diet she's on.'

Liv would laugh then too. She loved it when he slagged off the gorgeous superstars he worked with, claiming variously that they had BO or bad breath, that they talked incessantly about themselves or, her particular favourite, that they were thick as two short planks. Liv knew that wasn't an accusation that would ever be levelled at her, as her first-class honours degree in English from Oxford meant she was considered something of a freak compared with the usual Hollywood bimbos.

But as Danny's career continued unabated on its upward trajectory, she was spending an increasing amount of time on her own at their sumptuous, high-tech home in the Hollywood hills, meaning that she had an increasing amount of time to get on the Internet and Google herself and Danny. She knew she shouldn't do it. Knew she should resist the temptation. But it was becoming like a drug and she found herself unable to kick the habit.

Liv managed two bites of her toast. She looked again at the clock. It was still only eleven and the day seemed to stretch out before her like a carpet of loneliness. Felix's playdate after school meant he wouldn't be home until much later, and she cursed herself that she hadn't arranged to meet anyone for lunch, or booked in for a session with her masseur Carlos, who seemed to work magic on her always-tense muscles.

She abandoned her toast eventually, finding herself inexorably drawn towards her office yet again, where her MacBook was waiting, calling for her to open it.

She tucked one leg underneath her, noticing with some satisfaction as she did so how thin it looked, and sat down in the soft leather chair in front of her desk. She automatically went to the MailOnline site first, which seemed to have become her default setting. She missed Britain terribly, especially her mad, outrageous mother and her lovely older sister, and somehow surfing MailOnline made her feel less homesick. She read idly through various stories about public sector strikes, a tragic suicide plot between two teenagers who had hanged themselves, and finally a story bemoaning the fact that this had been the wettest June on record.

Liv tutted despondently to herself and looked out of the large, plate-glass window at the powder-blue sky and relentless sunshine. She even missed the rain, and suddenly felt a deep yearning to go out and get absolutely drenched in a downpour – not that there was much chance of that here. She and Charlie had both been winter people, happiest when it was cold outside and they could snuggle up together on the sofa in front of the blazing fire at their sweet little Surrey cottage.

Charlie. She wondered what he was doing right now, eight hours ahead of her in the UK. They spoke all the time on the phone and by Skype because of Felix, but their conversations were never very long or overly friendly. She could well understand his coldness towards her. She deserved it. She had humiliated him and, worse, she had broken his heart when she took his son to live thousands of miles away from him. But it still stung Liv when he made it clear he didn't want to speak to her.

He was the toast of Britain right now, and if the stories were to be believed, he would soon become the toast of Hollywood too, thanks to the recent Oscar nomination. A big part of her was pleased for him and proud of him, but a smaller, meaner part of her was secretly glad that he hadn't actually won the Oscar, although she suspected that it was only a matter of time. She felt jealous and a bit embarrassed at their extreme reversal of fortunes. Now it was his career that was on the up, while hers floundered.

Sighing deeply, Liv typed 'Charlie Simmons' into the search box. Immediately, pages and pages of sites appeared.

She scrolled casually through the regular fan sites and Twitter stories, then frowned and squinted as a new story caught her eye. It was freshly posted, featuring a picture of Charlie. In it, he could be seen leaving his London hotel with a very attractive woman, who was obviously wearing his t-shirt and sweatpants, along with a pair of perilously high gold platform sandals. They weren't holding hands or showing any obvious signs of being a couple, but they were laughing at something together in a way that made Liv's heart constrict and her breath catch in her throat.

In the picture, Charlie looked happier than she had seen him in years. He looked like a man in love, she thought. But who the hell was this woman? She wasn't an actress as far as Liv could remember, but there was something familiar about her. Maybe it was the fact that she looked like a young Julia Roberts, with her dark hair, dark eyes and full, sexy mouth. The caption simply described her as a 'mystery woman' and was accompanied by a gushing article suggesting that Charlie's new love meant that he was finally over his ex, Liv Mason, who had 'heartlessly dumped him for her Hollywood lover'.

Liv swallowed hard. She had indeed dumped him for Danny. But that didn't mean she no longer had feelings for him or could help the jealousy that was welling up inside her now. On the contrary, she was certain that a part of her would always love him.

They had met when they were both still very young. In Liv's case, she had been just twenty-one, straight out of university and starring in a British TV series as the beautiful daughter of an unconventional but close farming family, set in the idyllic countryside of the 1950s. The series turned out to be a surprise smash hit and was recommissioned, with Charlie Simmons cast as her love interest.

At twenty-five, Charlie was a few years older than her, and Liv could hardly conceal her delight when she was first introduced to him. He was over six feet tall with a wiry, firm body and wild, dark curls that dropped casually over his dark, brooding, long-lashed eyes. He seemed dangerous and arrogant, but his looks, she quickly discovered, were deceiving. Unlike every other actor she had ever come into contact with, Charlie was totally lacking in vanity, saying he preferred to secure roles based on his acting ability rather than his appearance.

Not that he was unaware of the benefits his looks could bring him. Charlie had already dated some of the most beautiful up-and-coming actresses of the time, and he was savvy enough to know that being described as a heart-throb and being seen with a succession of gorgeous women would certainly do his career no harm. But aside from getting his hair cut occasionally and running when he got the chance, he wasn't prepared to put much time or effort into maintaining his God-given gift.

And as for being dangerous, Liv soon discovered that he was actually surprisingly conventional. He came from a stable, middle-class family in Wales, with one younger sister and parents who were still happily married, and he made it clear that he wanted the same for himself one day.

Liv's background couldn't have been more different. Her

mother, Mariella, had been a wild-child of the Sixties, who had made sex, drugs and rock 'n' roll her mantra. As a result, she had had two daughters by two different men, neither of whom was involved in their lives, mainly because Mariella wasn't entirely sure which men they were from the long line of lovers she had enjoyed.

Liv and her older sister, Sierra, often entreated Mariella to track down and identify their fathers, confident that they would turn out to be the offspring of rock royalty. But Mariella would give a knowing smile and insist that it was sometimes better to 'imagine what you want your truth to be'. That put either of them off finding out for certain.

Mariella had never needed the security of marriage because she was part of the famous Mason acting dynasty and, as a result, was independently wealthy. Liv's upbringing had been unconventional and nomadic, as she and Sierra were trailed around the world by their mother, never quite sure who they would be living with from month to month, yet always surrounded by an array of loving but eccentric aunts, uncles, cousins and grandparents.

But Liv had grown tired of the endless upheaval and had yearned for some structure in her life, so it was a surprise to everyone except herself when she got married at the tender age of twenty-three to sensible, conventional Charlie Simmons, who also wanted nothing more than to settle down and have a family. On her wedding day Mariella had muttered darkly that Liv was a Mason and would soon tire of being a housewife, but Liv had laughed and shaken her head. She knew what she wanted.

For the first year of their marriage, Liv had been deliriously happy. Charlie was her soulmate, the love of her life. Despite both of them working in a precarious profession, they seemed to bring luck to one another and neither of them was ever out of work for a day longer than they wanted to be. They were able to pick and choose their roles and opted for those that meant they were able to spend as little time apart as possible.

Although Charlie was working with some stunning actresses, Liv never once had cause to doubt him. She trusted him implicitly, knowing that he felt fidelity went hand in hand with marriage. He simply wasn't interested in anyone but her and she felt the same about him. With hindsight, she realised that that was because she hadn't yet met anyone else that she felt as attracted to. Mariella's warning that she was a Mason and therefore incapable of settling for one man should have been ringing loudly in her ears. But it wasn't. Yet.

They hadn't planned to have children immediately, but when Liv discovered that she was pregnant with Felix, both she and Charlie had been thrilled. After the birth, Charlie was so smitten with his new son that he suggested that he take on the bulk of the childcare while Liv kept on working. Liv was equally in love with her baby boy, but she agreed on the grounds that they could swap roles if she found it too difficult being away from him during the day.

Yet to her surprise, she enjoyed being able to go to work and feeling like a person in her own right, rather than just a wife and mother. She was gaining a reputation as an actress and it was obvious to everyone that she would soon be getting the call from Hollywood. Sure enough, legendary film director

Eric Summers had seen her latest drama and had asked her to audition for his next film.

Liv had felt nervous about broaching it with Charlie, worried that he may feel upstaged or jealous, but he reacted to the news with typically generous jubilation, telling her how proud he was of her.

'Don't get too carried away,' she had laughed. 'I probably won't even get the part.'

'You will,' Charlie had replied emphatically, kissing her lips and beaming with pride. 'You definitely will.'

He was right, and a few weeks later the three of them had set off for Hollywood and a six-month adventure, full of excitement about what the future might hold for their little family.

The first thing that Liv hadn't bargained for was the incredibly long working hours in LA. Because budgets were being squeezed, as the big studios demanded more than ever for their money, film sets operated seven days a week and often involved night shoots.

Liv also quickly discovered that acting was only part of the job. In addition she was expected to do a daily workout with a personal trainer, due to several scenes in which she was either semi-naked or wearing only her underwear. She had tentatively suggested, in a very polite, British fashion, that maybe the director could employ a body double. But Eric had flashed her his beaming Hollywood smile and told her matter-of-factly that body doubles were only employed for 'the really big names'.

Another thing she hadn't reckoned on was her leading

man, Danny Nixon. She had expected him to be slightly put out that the role had gone to some relatively unknown British actress, but he had been charming to the point of flirtatious from the moment she had been introduced to him.

Danny Nixon was a heart-throb in every sense of the word. He looked as if he spent every spare moment on a surf board, with his shining, wavy blond locks, lean tanned body and piercing bright blue eyes that smiled even when he didn't. He had been linked with all of his leading ladies to date and seemed unconcerned with his reputation as a lothario.

Liv could tell that there was a connection between them from the moment they shared their first screen kiss. In the past, love scenes had been perfunctory affairs – except of course with Charlie – requiring all her acting ability to make it look as though she was quivering with passion. But she didn't need to act with Danny. As the director shouted 'Cut!', Danny slipped his tongue into her mouth and continued to kiss her deeply for a couple more seconds.

Liv didn't know why but she couldn't bring herself to pull away from him and instead found herself responding. Eventually, they pulled apart and Danny looked at her with a curious expression. 'Wow!' he mouthed.

Liv's cheeks blazed with embarrassment and shame. She glanced around the set and caught the eye of one of the make-up artists, who smiled knowingly. Liv guessed that she had seen this trick of Danny's many times before. 'Please don't do that again,' she told him curtly, before marching off to her trailer.

After that, Danny became transfixed by her. No woman

had ever turned him down before and Liv could tell he was puzzled by her reticence. But she had Charlie and Felix to think about, and a womaniser like Danny Nixon wasn't worth risking her marriage for.

But the truth was, thanks to the rigours of the filming schedule and the necessity to keep in shape, she barely saw Charlie and Felix any more. Felix would be asleep in his cot by the time she arrived home and he wouldn't have woken up by the time she left the next morning. She could already feel herself becoming distanced from him and she didn't like it.

Charlie's wide, generous smile began to grow tighter as the weeks passed. He was miserable sitting at home in their rented house, waiting for Liv to appear late at night for five minutes before slumping into bed, exhausted. He became more remote every day and Liv started to lose patience with him. 'Why don't you just bloody well go home then if you're so miserable?' she had barked during one particularly heated row.

Charlie had looked at her in disgust. 'Maybe because I want our son to have at least *some* contact with his mother?' he had snarled sarcastically.

Liv had recoiled in horror. Charlie had never been aggressive towards her before and she felt sick with guilt that he was right. 'Well, what do you expect me to do?' she had yelled, her voice quivering. 'Do you think I should walk out on the film? I'd be sued for millions and my career would be over.'

Charlie had closed his eyes and sighed. 'No, no, of course not,' he had said in a more conciliatory tone. 'It's just ... well, this is pretty miserable right now.'

Liv had softened and wrapped her arms around him. 'I know, baby, but it'll all be over in a couple of months' time and we can get back to normal. I know how hard it is for you, but I love you and appreciate what you're doing. Really I do.'

For the next week or so, things were better, but gradually Charlie retreated into himself again. 'I've been invited to the Baftas,' he said as they lay in bed one night. 'I think I'd quite like to go.'

Liv turned to look at him in alarm. The Baftas were held in London, which would mean Charlie leaving LA for at least a couple of days. 'What about Felix?' she asked.

In the semi-darkness, she could see him shrug. 'How about you take him onto the set with you? It's only for a few days. A week, max.'

Suddenly, Liv saw the solution to their problem appear like an oasis before her. 'Oh my God!' she cried in delight. 'Of course he could come on the set with me! Why didn't I think of that before?' Despite her tiredness, she was tempted to scramble out of bed and go and get her baby boy there and then.

So the next morning, while Charlie packed his bag and headed for home, Liv excitedly took Felix onto the set with her for the first time, to be greeted by nothing short of rapture from the cast, crew and most of all, Danny. And that's when she discovered that she was more like her mother than she would ever have cared to admit. That's when she fell in love with him.

Liv closed her laptop and spun on her chair thoughtfully. Felix was a lucky little boy, she mused, having two dads who adored him. No, she corrected herself quickly, not two dads. Charlie would kill her for even thinking such a thing. One dad and one *step*-dad who thought the world of him. Danny had taken to step-fatherhood with incredible gusto and he seemed to really love Felix. She just wished she could be as certain of his love for *her*. She glanced at her watch. It had just turned midday. *Perfect*, she thought, heading back towards the kitchen. *Time for a large glass of wine*.

Chapter 6

'Time for a large glass of wine!' Martha declared, slumping down at the table with a dramatic groan.

'Don't panic, it's coming!' Jamie poured red wine into two glasses for him and Martha, before settling down across the table from her and looking at her expectantly. 'So how did it go with the famous Mr Simmons then? Tell me all.'

It was one of the things Martha loved so much about Jamie. He was such a great listener and never seemed bored or disinterested in her stories.

'Oh, it was bloody awful!' Martha cried, taking a slurp of her wine. 'You do know that you burnt a huge great hole in my favourite dress this morning, don't you?'

Jamie frowned. 'Did I?' he looked upwards, as if wracking his brains to retrieve the memory.

'Yes!' Martha replied. 'You did! Haven't you wondered why I'm wearing these clothes?' She gestured down at the navy blue t-shirt and grey sweatpants she was still wearing.

Jamie raised his eyebrows as he noticed her unusual outfit

for the first time. 'Oh!' he exclaimed in surprise. 'Where did
you get those?'

Martha tutted in mock frustration. 'Honestly, Jamie! I sometimes think you wouldn't notice if I came in wearing nothing.'

'I'd definitely notice that,' Jamie cut in.

'Stop it!' she chided, secretly delighted that he still fancied
her after all these years.

She proceeded to tell Jamie the whole sorry story of her dis-
astrous first meeting with one of the biggest names in British
films.

Jamie roared appreciatively with laughter. 'Oh my God,' he
said, shaking his head, still smiling broadly. 'Was he a bit of a
twat then?'

'No!' Martha protested. 'He was great, actually. He even
offered to lend me something to wear.'

Jamie's smile narrowed slightly. 'I bet he bloody did!'

'Hey!' Martha replied with her best coquettish look. 'You
know I only have eyes for you ...'

Jamie fixed his deep blue eyes on her and blinked extra
slowly, in the way he always did when he was feeling horny.
'And you know I only have eyes for you, even if you have
come home wearing another man's clothes ...' He stood up
and came round to Martha's side of the table, then knelt
down on the floor beside her and carefully removed her gold
platforms, before gently massaging the ball of her big toe with
his thumb. Martha grinned down at him, feeling herself
beginning to melt. He knew every inch of her body inti-
mately and could bring her to orgasm by stimulating the
strangest parts, just as he was doing now with her toe.

Without taking his eyes off hers, Jamie lifted her foot to his mouth and began to suck the toe he had just been massaging. Martha wanted to protest that she needed to wash her feet after her day running around London, but she couldn't. She was enjoying the sensation too much.

After a minute, Jamie stood up, and as he did so he pulled Martha to her feet in front of him. He picked up a glass of wine from the table and took a sip, before bending to kiss her and releasing some of the wine from his mouth into hers. By now, Martha was aching for him, but she knew Jamie would take his time and bring her to boiling point before he would finally allow himself any pleasure. He was without doubt the best lover she had ever had, even after all these years.

'Let's go upstairs,' she whispered, as his fingers explored her, sending her into shudders of ecstasy.

'No,' he said, gruffly. 'Let's not.' He lifted Charlie's t-shirt over her head, before unclipping her pink lacy bra and beginning to lick her nipples.

'Oh my God!' Martha gasped. 'Jamie . . .'

'I love you so much,' he whispered into her ear, lifting her up as if she weighed nothing and laying her down on the table. Slowly, he removed her sweatpants and knickers so that she was naked before him. He gazed at her adoringly. 'You are the sexiest woman in the whole wide world,' he said, before unzipping his jeans and kicking them off, along with his boxers, and sliding into her.

Almost immediately, she yelled out. Jamie looked at her in shock and put his hand over her mouth. 'Shh,' he gasped, smiling as he began to thrust harder. 'We don't want to wake the children!' Both of them groaned as they climaxed together and Jamie slumped down on top of her, panting furiously.

'Well, that's your exercise for the day!' Martha giggled playfully, stroking his shoulder, which was damp with sweat.

Jamie raised his head and grinned at her, before kissing her on the lips. 'I love you,' he murmured. 'You know that, don't you?'

Martha frowned and began to gently push him off her so that she could sit up. The hard wood of the table didn't make a very comfortable bed and her back was aching. 'Of course I know that, silly,' she smiled, climbing off the table and looking back at it with a grin. 'God, if the kids only knew what this table gets used for sometimes,' she added.

Jamie bent down and collected his jeans and boxers from the floor. 'Funnily enough, today we had a very in-depth discussion about what the table should be called. I don't thinking "shagging table" was one of the suggestions!'

Giggling like naughty children, she and Jamie switched off all the lights and climbed the stairs. 'So what did you do today?' Martha asked, once they were lying in bed, each with a book poised and ready to read.

Jamie put down his copy of *Freedom* by Jonathan Franzen and looked up, stroking his jaw as if trying to remember. 'Well now, I put on a wash, then I went to the supermarket. By the time I came home, the washing was ready to be hung out on the line and then—'

'OK! OK!' Martha cut in, laughing. 'I get it. Your job can be mundane at times, but you'll get your reward in heaven . . .'

'It certainly feels like it'll be the death of me sometimes . . .' Jamie muttered back.

Martha put her book down and looked at him in the rosy glow of his bedside lamp. '*Do* you feel like that? I thought you liked being here with the kids?'

'I do,' he said. 'But the kids aren't here for most of the day now. It gets a bit boring sometimes. You know how it is ...'

Martha nodded. 'Well, I think you're doing a great job.' She reached over to kiss him. 'And I so appreciate what you do.'

'And I so appreciate what you do,' Jamie replied, smiling back at her. 'But don't you sometimes compare me with some of the people you interview, like that Charlie Simmons? I mean, when was the last time I wore a suit or had anyone ask for my opinion? I must seem like a right loser in comparison to him, with all his money and success.'

'Pah!' Martha spluttered. 'All his money hasn't brought him much happiness, with his wife and kid buggering off to the other side of the world. Yes, Jamie, I *do* compare you with the people I interview, and believe me, you come out on top every time. You're worth a million of any of them.'

Jamie smiled and dropped his book onto the floor beside him. 'Yes, when you put it like that, I am a bit of a catch, aren't I?' he said teasingly. 'Fancy going again?' he added, as he rolled onto his side and gazed at her.

'No!' Martha protested, pulling the duvet up over her naked breasts. 'God, you're insatiable!' she giggled. 'Now go to sleep!'

The next morning, Tom came slouching into their bedroom. Martha opened her eyes sleepily to find his cheeky little face peering at her from just a few inches away. 'Hey, handsome,' she murmured, reaching out for him and pulling him into bed so that his back curled against the contour of her stomach. She loved the smell of sleep that always clung to him first thing, and she nuzzled her face into his messy hair, inhaling deeply. Tom squirmed for a few minutes in mock protest, but she knew that it was for show. He loved these early-morning cuddles as much as she did.

Beside her, Jamie stirred and reached his arm over so that he was embracing both her and Tom. 'Morning, champ,' he said, his voice thick and croaky.

'Morning, Dad,' Tom replied, lifting his head to peer at Jamie over the top of Martha's body. 'Will you come and play on my Xbox?'

'It's a bit early ...' Jamie sighed, throwing back the duvet and rolling out of bed nevertheless. 'But go on then!'

Martha watched as Jamie threw on his t-shirt and jeans and signalled to Tom to follow him. 'Let Mum have another half-hour's sleep,' he said.

Tom squeezed himself into Martha for one more hug before climbing out of bed and following Jamie downstairs. Martha snuggled back down under the duvet and was just dozing off again when her mobile phone, which was plugged into a charger on the bedside table, beeped.

Sighing, Martha reached out and unplugged the handset. She rolled onto her back and looked at the screen. The message was from her best friend, Lindsay. *OMG!! What u doing leaving hotel with Charlie Simmons??? X*

Martha's senses tingled. *Eh? What u on abt? x* she hurriedly texted back.

A few seconds later, her phone beeped again. *Photo of u together on MailOnline! U wearing his clothes???? WTF???*

Martha sat up in shock. Immediately, she clicked on Lindsay's number to call her.

'Well, good morning!' Lindsay answered in her broad, northern accent. 'You have got some explaining to do, young lady!'

Martha laughed, despite her concern. 'I really haven't. But I have got probably the most embarrassing story ever to tell you . . .'

She regaled Lindsay with the details of her encounter with Charlie Simmons the day before, to be met with howls of laughter from her friend and former colleague. Lindsay and Martha had worked on the same newspaper together before going in different directions. Martha had focused on doing in-depth celebrity interviews, while Lindsay gave up journalism altogether and went into teaching. But her background meant that she still read all the papers online every morning, which was why she had been the first to spot the paparazzi picture of Martha and Charlie.

'Well, you could be a bit more sympathetic!' Martha spluttered indignantly, as Lindsay continued to laugh loudly at her misfortune. 'Jamie!' she called out, putting her hand over the speaker for a second, 'I'd love a cup of tea!'

'No need to shout!' came the answer, as Jamie entered the bedroom carrying a cup of tea.

'Aah, thanks, babe.' She smiled, and blew him a kiss as he put the cup down on her bedside table, before returning to her phone call. 'My lovely husband just brought me a cup of tea.'

'Tell him I want one too!' Lindsay said.

'Lindsay says she wants one too,' Martha relayed to Jamie's retreating back.

'What, me or the tea?' Jamie replied cheekily, closing the bedroom door behind him.

'I heard that!' said Lindsay. 'Tell him both.'

Martha laughed. Lindsay adored Jamie, as did all of her friends. Lindsay was divorced after her ex-husband had cheated on her, and often told Martha that whenever she got fed up with Jamie, she would happily take him off her hands.

'Anyway,' Martha said, 'I need to go and have a look at this bloody newspaper story. I can't believe they photographed us and made it look as though I'd spent the night with him!'

'Are you absolutely sure you didn't? And then came up with that cock-and-bull story to cover your tracks?' Lindsay's voice had taken on a mischievous air. 'No-one would blame you.'

'Bugger off!' Martha cried good-naturedly. 'As if! I don't have the imagination to make up a story like that anyway. And I'm far too old and far too dull for him. By the way, how do I look in the picture?'

There was a pause and she could hear the clicking of a keyboard as Lindsay looked again at the photo. 'Good,' she said at last. 'Kind of dishevelled sexy, I'd say. Not sure the gold platforms were a good idea though.'

'Well, strangely enough, his trainers would have been too big for me,' Martha protested.

'So, have you still got his clothes then?'

'Of course I have! But I've promised to return them to him when I've washed them.'

54

'I wouldn't,' Lindsay said. 'I'd keep them. They'll be worth something one day.'

'It's a good job I'm not you then, isn't it? Anyway, I need to go and see if I can find the article online. I'll call you back later.'

She hung up and jumped out of bed, her heart beating a little faster. She felt disconcerted at the idea of being photographed with Charlie. Even though there was an innocent explanation, she somehow felt guilty. She didn't want the children to see the picture either, in case it planted a seed of doubt in their minds.

She put on her bathrobe, made her way into the study and closed the door behind her. She opened up her laptop and logged onto the MailOnline site. At first she couldn't see it as she scrolled through the numerous thumbnail-sized items, and let go of the breath she hadn't realised she was holding. Perhaps it had only made the first editions and had now dropped off the listings. But just as she was about to log off, she realised that not only was it there, but it was right at the top, meaning it was one of the stories that had already been 'most read' that morning.

By now, her heart was racing. She clicked on the link. In the colour photograph, she and Charlie were leaving the hotel together, with her obviously wearing his clothes, and both laughing about something. What had they been laughing at? She thought back to the previous day. After the interview, as she was leaving, Charlie had said he was meeting someone for a late lunch, so he would walk out with her. As they reached the door of the hotel and walked out into the forecourt, Charlie had suddenly got a fit of the giggles about her travelling home on the tube in his baggy clothes and her gold platforms, which had started her giggling too. He had offered her a lift in his car, but she had mustered as much dignity as she could and said she would be fine, thank you very much.

She had waited until Charlie was out of sight before hailing a cab. There was no way she was going to travel on the tube looking the way she did, and anyway, she would be able to claim it on expenses later.

Behind her, she heard the door to the study open and she closed the screen guiltily. 'What's wrong?' Jamie asked, coming in and looking at her suspiciously. 'Why did you close your computer like that? What are you hiding? Have you been Internet shopping again?'

'Oh God,' Martha sighed, biting her lip. 'I wish I had. There's a bloody photo in the *Mail* that makes it look as if I spent the night at a hotel with Charlie Simmons! It's why Lindsay called so early.'

'No way!' cried Jamie, his mouth dropping open. 'Show me!'

Reluctantly, Martha opened up the laptop once more and sat back as Jamie peered at the article. She wasn't quite sure how he would react. He could be a little possessive sometimes, even though he knew she would never cheat on him, and she didn't want it to cause friction between them.

'You look hot, baby!' he said at last, causing her shoulders to drop with relief.

'You're not cross?' she glanced up at him tentatively.

'Well, it's a bit humiliating, I suppose,' Jamie rubbed his

stubbled chin thoughtfully. 'But I guess anyone who knows us would know the truth. At least it doesn't name you.'

'True,' Martha agreed. 'Anyway, it'll be chip paper tomorrow ...'

'Sadly that's not true,' Jamie reminded her. 'It'll actually be there for ever and ever now. The joys of the Internet.'

Martha let out a long sigh. 'Shit. How embarrassing. I'm sorry, honey.'

Jamie bent down and kissed the top of her head, before backing out of the room. 'Forget it,' he said, as he closed the door behind him.

Martha turned back to the computer screen and looked at it thoughtfully, as an idea began to take shape. She would get a photo of Jamie and transfer his head onto Charlie's body in the newspaper photo and write him a cute little message for when he next logged onto his own computer.

She closed her laptop and scooted her chair over to Jamie's, which sat on the opposite desk. She logged in using his password and the screen fired into life. First, she needed to find a really nice picture of Jamie. She scanned through his home screen, trying to suss out which icon represented his photo library. Jamie was a keen photographer, especially since she had bought him a top-of-the-range camera for Christmas, and he was also a whizz with graphics, so he had several applications that she didn't recognise.

In the end, she clicked on the icon showing a camera, and a page of photos duly appeared. Each photo represented a folder of pictures and she scrolled through, looking for one that might have something suitable. Most of the pictures were of their various holidays, but there was one that stood out and caused Martha to suddenly stop scrolling. It was of a woman Martha didn't recognise, sitting on an unfamiliar bed, smiling at the camera.

Martha clicked on the image, her throat suddenly dry with foreboding. Immediately, further photos filled the screen and Martha gasped in shock. As the series of photos unfolded, the woman gradually undressed until she was completely naked, pulling sultry faces at the camera and posing in obscene positions. Martha's hands started to shake and she moaned to herself slightly as she continued to click on pornographic picture after pornographic picture. Could there be an innocent explanation for it? She didn't recognise the woman. Perhaps they were images Jamie had downloaded from the Internet? Even happily married men sometimes looked at porn, didn't they?

She hesitated, wanting to stop, so that whatever she had stumbled upon could be unseen once more. But as the next picture rolled up, she knew that it was too late. On the screen in front of her, causing her to physically retch, she watched as the woman was joined on the bed by a naked man. There was no mistaking who he was. Jamie.

Chapter 7

The LA sunshine was really getting on Liv's nerves. She had lived here for over four years now and had never quite adapted to the place. So many things that she had loved at the start now grated on her. Like the beach, for instance.

Danny, in keeping with his surfer-boy appearance, loved to go to the beach and had bought a beautiful house in Malibu so that they could spend the summer there. In the beginning, the three of them would drive up to the beach house whenever they could. Danny had patiently taught Felix to surf, and even at six years old, Liv had to admit he was pretty good. But these days, with Danny on location so much, they went to the beach house less and less, so she only really got to go if she took Felix herself, and then it didn't seem quite so much fun for either of them.

She would sit on the sand watching Felix splashing in the crystal-clear turquoise water, wishing that Danny was there. She'd spy Felix looking longingly at other kids who did have their dads with them and her heart would ache for him.

She had once tried to surf herself, but she was afraid of water after a bad experience when she had nearly drowned as a child. Aged seven, she had been paddling on a beach in Australia when a large wave had swept her off her feet and sucked her under the water. She was so disoriented that she couldn't find her feet and was pulled further and further out to sea. She had started to lose consciousness by the time she was plucked to safety and the fear of the sea had never left her. She would often wonder how different Felix's life would have been if he had grown up in the English countryside. If she and Charlie had stayed together. Had had another baby . . .

Today had been a difficult day, which was why the sunshine was irritating her. She had realised at lunchtime that her period was late and she had begun to wonder if she might be pregnant. The thought had taken root and a tiny kernel of excitement had begun to build inside her. Her mind automatically leapt forward, as she tried to calculate what her due date might be, and she had even tipped a glass of wine down the sink. Being pregnant would be the perfect excuse to stop drinking. Not that she drank very much anyway.

But this evening, when she went to the loo, there it was. Taunting her. She had tried to take it in her stride and carry on as usual, but after an hour spent prowling around the house, she found herself crouching in her bathroom, the almost-empty vodka bottle beside her, sobbing uncontrollably.

Just as she was beginning to pull herself together, her cellphone rang. Naturally, she had it with her, even in the bathroom. She never wanted to risk missing a call from her agent, even amidst her emotional turmoil. LA did that to you. 'Hello?' She coughed slightly to clear her throat.

'It's Charlie,' he said, in that formal, stilted voice he seemed to have invented especially for her ever since their break-up. She half expected him to add, 'Charlie Simmons?' as a prompt.

'Oh, hi!' she spoke as brightly as she could, sitting down cross-legged on the tiled floor with her back against the side of the huge stone bathtub.

'What's wrong?' he asked immediately.

Liv smiled to herself. Even after all these years, and down a phone line from the other side of the world, he knew just by an inflection in her voice that something was wrong. 'Nothing. I'm, er, not feeling too good, that's all,' she replied, hoping that she wasn't slurring her words and wishing desperately that she could pour her heart out to him. But it wouldn't be appropriate. Or fair.

'Well, as long as you're OK. You sound a bit ...' Charlie said, bringing Liv back to the present with a start.

'A bit what?'

There was an awkward pause. 'Nothing,' he said at last.

'Um, Felix is out ... He had a playdate after school,' Liv cut in, when the silence had gone on long enough.

'I know.' Of course he knew. He was diligent about keeping in touch with his son and always made sure he knew where he was. 'I'm coming to LA and I wanted to surprise him, so I thought I'd wait until he was out to call and let you know the details.'

'OK, great!' Liv wasn't sure why she felt so piqued. 'Are you coming just to see Felix?' she couldn't help asking, as her curiosity got the better of her.

'No, actually,' Charlie said, and she could tell that he was reluctant to be drawn into conversation with her. 'I've got a . . . couple of meetings as well.'

Liv bit her lip. She knew from various press stories she had seen that some big-name directors were wooing Charlie. 'I see. Well, Felix will be thrilled to see you. When are you coming?'

'Next week. Tuesday.'

'Great. He breaks for the holidays then so that's perfect. And . . . are you coming alone?' she added.

'Yes . . .' Charlie said, and she could almost see him frowning down the phone line. 'Why wouldn't I be?'

'Well, it's just that I wondered if you might be bringing your new girlfriend? She looks gorgeous, by the way!' she added, much too effusively.

'My *what*?' Charlie snapped, and she recoiled slightly at the tone of his voice.

'Sorry, I didn't mean to pry—' Liv began, her throat feeling suddenly dry. She desperately wished she had some water.

'I haven't got a girlfriend,' Charlie interrupted. 'I don't know what you're talking about.'

'Oh, OK, I get it,' Liv said quickly, eager to change the subject. He was obviously telling her that it was none of her bloody business.

'You don't "get it", Liv, because there's nothing to get. I haven't got a girlfriend and I have no idea what you're on about.'

62

'But, I saw a picture on the *Mail* website ...' Liv stammered, embarrassed. 'Of you and her leaving the hotel together? I just assumed you were an item. Sorry, none of my business ... sorry,' she said again miserably.

There was a long silence at the end of the line. 'Which website did you say?'

'The *Mail*. Haven't you seen it? God, I'm sorry, I'm really putting my foot in it, aren't I?'

Charlie didn't reply and she could hear him tapping at a keyboard. 'Oh shit!' she heard him say, presumably when he had found the offending article. Finally, he came back on the line. 'Not quite how it looks,' he said wryly. 'Anyway, I'll be coming to LA alone, without my new girlfriend,' he added, amusement in his voice.

Liv felt a spike of jealousy shoot through her. Whoever the woman was, he was obviously keen on her. After agreeing the details of his arrival to collect Felix the following week, Liv hung up feeling a million times worse than she had before.

Not least because Charlie would know that she had been Googling him. She felt miserable and foolish. And lonely. She picked up her phone again and dialled Danny's number. He was filming on a Hawaiian island, starring in a movie in which he was supposed to survive alone on a desert island for years. To Liv's huge relief, there was no beautiful leading lady to worry about on this one *and* she had a feeling he would win all sorts of awards.

'Hey, baby!' he answered breathlessly after just a couple of rings. 'How you doing?'

'Am I interrupting filming?' Liv tried to keep her voice as steady as possible, but she could tell it was quavering.

'No. Finished for the day,' he said, exhaling loudly, as if to catch his breath. 'Liv? Are you OK? You're not crying, are you?'

'No!' Liv said automatically. 'Well, yes, I am, I guess.' In a faltering voice, she told Danny about her not getting the part, about her period arriving and then about Charlie's impending visit. 'I just feel really down,' she finished.

'Baby, have you been drinking? You sound a little out of it.'

'No!' Liv snapped, indignation bubbling up inside her. 'I'm fine. It's just ... I really want to see you. Could I maybe come down and visit you on set for a few days? Charlie could have Felix while he's here and you and me could have some grown-up time. What do you think?' Now that the idea had formed, her indignation was rapidly being replaced by excitement. It seemed so long since they had spent any real time together, just the two of them.

There was another pause before Danny answered. 'Uh, yeah, I guess ... Next week, you say?'

'Yes. Oh my God, it would be so fantastic!' Liv cried.

'Yeah, I guess ...'

Liv wished Danny sounded a bit more enthusiastic, but it was the evening and he was probably tired.

'Listen, I gotta go,' he continued, 'but why don't you book a flight and let me know when it's all happening?'

Liv hung up and stood up purposefully, suddenly happy and excited at having something to look forward to. She grabbed the vodka bottle and her phone, before bounding out of the room. She would call Carrie right away and get her to book her flights.

It was only later, lying awake in the small hours of the morning, that she suddenly wondered why Danny had answered the phone sounding so breathless, and why he had had to go when filming had finished for the day.

Chapter 8

Charlie sat staring at his laptop for a long time after he had hung up on Liv. The phone call had unsettled him hugely. He couldn't put his finger on what, but he knew there was something wrong with Liv. He was sure that she had been drinking, just as he had been sure that she had been drinking on other occasions when he'd called over the past few months. Although she had never actually had a breakdown, there had been times in the past when Liv had suffered from bouts of depression and panic attacks, and Charlie was becoming increasingly concerned for Felix's welfare.

He gazed at the paparazzi photo of him and Martha emerging from the hotel the previous afternoon. Laughing in the sunshine. Looking happy. Looking like a couple. Martha seemed especially beautiful and Charlie wondered if it was because in his world it was so rare for someone to have such a lovely face, untouched by cosmetic surgery, or hair that was shining and thick without the aid of extensions. Even wearing his baggy sweatpants and t-shirt, she looked effortlessly stylish.

He had been unable to stop thinking about her for the past twenty-four hours, and it was such a new sensation for Charlie to feel anything other than a passing interest in a woman that he was unnerved by it. Only Liv had ever had that effect on him before.

He had even resorted to going to the bathroom and fishing her dress out of the bin so that he could inhale her scent. Then he had called his assistant, Jess, and asked her to go and buy a new one. He would give it to her at their next meeting. He smiled to himself at the thought of how pleased she would be.

When Martha had first turned up yesterday, Charlie's heart had sank. Despite her large, dark eyes and long, lustrous hair, she looked breathless and sweaty in the way that, in his considerable experience, only cokeheads could. And when she immediately excused herself to go to the loo, he had felt sure that his instinct was correct.

But spotting the giant hole in her dress had made him immediately soften towards her. He was unsure whether to say anything, but she had darted into the loo before he'd had the chance to speak anyway.

She had finally emerged, wearing his massive t-shirt and sweatpants and looking, he thought, spectacularly sexy. Despite her embarrassment, she had met his eye with such a defiant, stoic gaze, that Charlie had felt something inside him stir that had long been dormant.

During the interview, which had felt to him more like a first date than a grilling by a journalist, he had found himself opening up to Martha more than he ever had to any other interviewer. She was disarming because she would ask him questions, but she would relate his answers to her own life, which put him at ease and led him to reveal much more than he had intended. She had a son who was a little older than Felix and her stories about him made Charlie laugh, which helped him to talk about Felix without getting choked the way he usually did.

When the subject of Liv came up, Charlie had tensed, waiting for the inevitable questions about her leaving him for her Hollywood superstar. But to his surprise, Martha wanted to focus on the early days of their relationship, on the happy times, and he found himself relaxing and enjoying the memories of the woman he had loved so much, instead of clenching with the pain of her loss.

Martha seemed non-judgemental about what Liv had done, which pleased him, although he wasn't sure why.

After a couple of hours, she had reached over to switch off her recorder and sat back on the sofa, smiling at him through white teeth which were natural rather than veneered. 'Shall we leave it there for today?' she had said.

Charlie had sagged with disappointment. He liked talking to her. Liked her presence. Liked her feet in the ridiculously high gold sandals she was wearing. He loved her deep, throaty laugh, her brown eyes and full mouth . . .

Charlie slammed the laptop shut. He needed to stop thinking about her because it wasn't going to happen. Just then his mobile rang, causing him to jump guiltily. He silenced *The Sopranos*' theme tune quickly. 'Hello?' he gulped, wishing he had stopped to look at the caller display first.

'What the hell?' said a strangled voice, before lapsing into a coughing fit that lasted several seconds.

'Hi Louisa . . .' He sighed, knowing he was in trouble.

When she had finished coughing, Louisa came back on the line. 'What did I say to you yesterday? Don't *sleep* with her! And then I open the paper to see you both leaving the hotel with her wearing your clothes. For Christ's sake, Charlie! How the hell did that happen?

Charlie took the opportunity of another coughing fit to buy himself some time. 'It's not at all what it looks like,' he said when she eventually stopped spluttering.

'You know she's married?' continued Louisa, as if he hadn't spoken at all. 'And she's got kids?'

'Yes.' Charlie tried to sound more patient than he felt. He would have quite liked to have spent the day in bed with Martha, so it was annoying that he was getting blamed for something that he hadn't done. 'I know she's married. Which is fine because nothing happened. If you must know, her husband had ironed her dress and put a bloody great hole in it, so I offered her my clothes to change into to save her the embarrassment of travelling home again showing her knickers.'

Louisa burbled with laughter. 'Seriously? Oh my God! Poor Martha. She must have been *mortified*!'

Charlie grinned to himself at the memory. 'You could say that. She locked herself in the loo and wouldn't come out until I came up with the idea of offering her my t-shirt and sweatpants.'

'Oh Charlie!' Louisa cried. 'What a sweetheart you are! I'm

sorry for doubting you. Of course you didn't sleep with her. As if!'

'Yeah, as if!' Charlie replied, feeling uncharacteristically annoyed with Louisa, who he loved and trusted.

'Well, that's a relief, I must say,' she continued, unaware of the effect her words were having on him. 'It could have got really messy if something had happened between you—'

'Well, it didn't,' Charlie cut her off sharply.

'OK, OK! So did you arrange your next meeting?'

'No, I thought you would have done that.'

'I would, but I've been laid up in bed feeling like crap, thanks for noticing. Why don't you give her a call? You can apologise for letting her get papped wearing your clothes.'

'It wasn't my fault!' Charlie protested.

'No, but you should have known they'd be there. Not that I'm complaining. As long as there's nothing going on between you, and we don't have some irate husband going to the papers, it's not bad publicity to have you linked with someone mysterious . . .'

'Makes me sound like less of a loser, you mean?' But Charlie's tone was amused rather than cross. He knew Louisa was only doing her job, which was to make him look as good as possible.

'Oh, Charlie. No-one would ever think of you as a loser.'

'Hmm,' Charlie replied, before bidding Louisa goodbye and hanging up. Louisa was probably right. No-one would think of him as a loser. Except himself. And that was probably the worst person of all.

He searched through his contacts list until he came to her

name. Butterflies began to dance in his stomach as he tried to summon up the nerve to call her. His thumb hovered over the name. It was just a call to someone who was very much taken; he had no need to be nervous. But he was.

He could feel the adrenaline pumping through his veins and his mouth suddenly felt dry. He just needed to press on the name but his hands were trembling and he wasn't sure he could. He thought back to yesterday, remembering her throaty laugh and the sexy huskiness of her voice as she talked. Finally, the urge to hear that voice again overtook him and he pressed 'Call'.

Chapter 9

The first thing Jamie heard was the sound of retching from upstairs. Mimi looked up in alarm from her bowl of cereal. 'It sounds like Mum's being sick,' she said.

Jamie cocked his head and listened. 'Oh, poor Mum.' He turned on the tap so that the water would run ice cold. He took a glass from the cupboard and filled it, before taking it up the stairs.

'Jesus, babe,' he came into the bathroom to find Martha hunched over the toilet bowl. 'What's brought this on?'

Martha continued retching. Finally, she finished and reached up feebly to flush, panting with exhaustion and gulping furiously.

'I brought you some nice cold water,' Jamie held the glass out towards her.

Before he knew what was happening, Martha had swung around and punched the glass out of his hand, causing it to smash into dozens of pieces against the wall and the water to explode like a bomb all over the bathroom. 'Take your fucking water and fuck off out of here!' she screamed at him, her eyes blazing with fury.

Jamie recoiled in horror. He had rarely seen Martha lose her temper. 'Martha!' he yelled back. 'What the hell's wrong with you?'

In response, a long, low wail emitted from somewhere deep inside her and she slumped down onto the slate floor, either unaware or unconcerned by the shards of glass that were everywhere. Jamie went cold inside as fear gripped him. Was she having some kind of breakdown?

'Why ...' she began in a quiet yet malevolent voice, '... don't you go and take a look at your filthy fucking computer screen?'

'Oh my God.' Jamie knew immediately what he would find as he ran into the study. There on the screen of his laptop was a colour photo of him having sex with Debra. 'It's not what you think,' he started to say to no-one in particular as he reached for the delete button.

'I've seen them all,' said Martha in a strange, detached voice, coming into the study behind him. 'So it's no use deleting them.'

Jamie closed his eyes to try to block out what was on the screen and continued to press the delete button furiously. How the hell had those photos stayed on the computer? He was sure he had got rid of them as soon as they were downloaded. He thought for a minute he might be sick himself. 'Oh God, oh God,' he muttered, his whole body shaking with shock. 'Martha, baby, please believe me, it's not what you think ...'

73

'Fuck off, Jamie.' Martha sat down at her own desk with her back to him.

'Martha! Listen ...'

'No,' she said, in that eerily calm voice that was scaring the hell out of him far more than if she had ranted and railed. 'I won't listen to anything you have to say any more. Let's get the children off to school. And say a proper goodbye to them because you won't be here when they get home this afternoon.'

'No!' Jamie cried in an agonised voice, dropping to his knees in front of Martha. 'Oh God, please don't let this be happening. Please, Martha, please listen to me. It was nothing. It meant nothing ... I don't know, it just ...' he clasped his hands together in a pleading gesture. 'Please, baby, listen, I ...'

'You're a cheating bastard,' she said coolly, finally turning around to face him and looking at him with eyes that said she despised him. 'You used the camera I bought you for Christmas to photograph yourself screwing your whore while I went out to work to support you and the children. Christ, your mother would be so proud,' she added, causing him to flinch more than if she had actually stabbed him. His mother had died the previous year and Jamie had been utterly devastated by her loss. Her death had been sudden and unexpected and the shock had left him reeling for months.

'Oh my God!' he whimpered, as the tears began to course down his cheeks. 'Martha, please, please believe me. I love you so very much ... I love you and the children ...'

'Yeah, course you do,' she snarled, still fixing him with a

look that chilled him to the core. 'Devoted husbands and fathers always photograph themselves screwing other women while their wives are at work and their kids are at school, don't they? You love us *so* much that you were quite happy to put our happiness, our security at risk for the sake of a fuck with some sad old whore. And while we're on the subject, I don't think much of your taste. You make me sick to my stomach,' she spat. 'Quite literally.'

Jamie leaned his head on the floor, sobbing uncontrollably. After a few moments, Martha spoke again.

'Right, I'll see the kids off to school, shall I? I don't think you're in any fit state. I don't want them seeing you like this.'

'No!' Jamie sobbed, trying desperately to recover his emotions. 'I always see them off, they'll think it's odd if I don't.'

'Well bloody well pull yourself together then!' snapped Martha, standing up and heading for the door.

'Don't go!' he cried, gripping her ankle. Her perfect, slender ankle. 'Don't leave me!'

Martha looked down at him contemptuously. 'Oh don't worry, I won't leave you,' she said, causing his heart to jump momentarily with hope. He looked up at her beseechingly but her expression was set like concrete. '*You're* the one who'll be leaving.' She shook her ankle free of his grip and walked out of the room, slamming the study door shut behind her.

For a few seconds Jamie thought he might pass out. He loved Martha and the children so much. The idea of losing them made him dizzy with fear. What the hell had he done?

With an almighty effort, he lifted himself off the floor and slumped into his desk chair, his head in his shaking hands. He tried to get his thoughts into some kind of coherent order. He had to get Martha to let him stay. He couldn't lose her. It would kill him.

When he had finally composed himself, he wiped the last vestiges of tears from his eyes and made his way out of the study. He glanced nervously towards Mimi's room, where she was getting dressed, apparently unaware of the turmoil that had erupted into the midst of her safe little world that morning.

'Hey Dad,' she grinned. 'Poor Mum's been hurling. Did you hear?'

'I did.' Jamie tried to smile but his mouth wouldn't let him. 'Anyway, gorgeous, get yourself dressed and brush your teeth, eh? And ... I, er, dropped a glass in the bathroom, so use the ensuite until I've had time to clear it up, OK?'

'Aw ... can't Tom brush his first?' Mimi whined, as she always did every morning.

'Look, just bloody well do it, OK?' Jamie snapped, causing Mimi's big blue eyes to widen in astonishment.

'Jeez, Dad, no need to get in such a strop!' she shot back. She harrumphed a couple more times but finally clomped across the landing and began to brush her teeth.

'Come on, Tommy boy,' Jamie tried to keep his emotions from spilling over as he went into Tom's bedroom, to be met with the sight of his son curled up on the bed, still in his pyjamas, reading his latest *Horrible Histories* book. How long had he been there? Had he heard any of the awful exchange between him and Martha? Tom looked unconcerned so Jamie decided to hope for the best. 'You need to get dressed and brush your teeth too,' he said, his voice catching.

'OK, Dad,' Tom closed his book and smiled up at Jamie in a way that made him want to cry for ever more.

As the children finished getting ready, Jamie made his way downstairs and into the kitchen. Martha was standing at the French doors, clutching a cup of coffee and staring out over the garden with a closed expression on her face. Jamie eyed her warily as he made his way over to the coffee pot and poured himself a cup. He took a sip and then replaced the cup on the work surface, all the time watching Martha, who seemed to be standing as still as a statue.

He moved towards her. 'Don't. Touch. Me,' she hissed, as he was about to put his hand on her shoulder. He whipped his hand away as if he had been stung and stood awkwardly behind her, unsure what to do next.

To his relief, Mimi breezed into the kitchen. Almost immediately, she stopped dead in her tracks and looked at her parents curiously. 'Everything OK?' she asked, frowning with concern.

'Er, yes,' Jamie said quickly. 'Mum's just not feeling very well . . .' He tailed off as Martha snorted derisively.

'Mum?' Mimi prompted, coming to her mother's side and looking at her in concern. 'Are you OK?'

Suddenly, Martha seemed to snap into life. 'Yes!' she said, over-brightly. 'I'm fine, darling. It's just something's upset my stomach,' she added, shooting Jamie a look of contempt that only he could see.

'Can I get you anything?' Mimi persisted, rubbing Martha's back softly.

For a second, Jamie thought Martha might lose it, as her face crumpled piteously. 'No,' she whispered, before shaking her head slightly and gathering herself. 'No, darling, honestly, I'm fine. I'll go back to bed for a couple of hours and I'll be right as rain.'

Mimi nodded, apparently satisfied. 'OK, well, bye then. Love you.' She kissed Martha on the cheek as Jamie watched her, the pain in his chest growing by the second. Then she came over to him. 'Bye, Dad,' she said softly, standing on tip-toes to kiss him too.

'Bye, gorgeous,' he replied in a strangled voice. 'I love you.'

'Love you too, Dad,' Mimi called happily as she headed for the front door.

'Wonder if she'd love you quite so much if she knew what a cheating bastard you are,' Martha hissed under her breath, turning back to face the French doors.

Jamie swallowed hard and rubbed his forehead. He literally didn't know what the hell to do. He *had* to make Martha let him stay. He couldn't leave the children. He may as well be dead without them.

He went to the bottom of the stairs and waited helplessly for Tom to come down. 'Tom!' he called out eventually. 'You need to get to school – you're going to be late!'

'No I'm not,' said Tom cheerfully, as he skipped down the stairs. He scooped up his book bag and lunchbox and opened the door. Jamie felt a sudden urge to leave the house with him, so terrified was he of what Martha might be about to do next.

'Tom!' he called, as the boy headed down the front path.

'What?' Tom stopped and looked round at Jamie, puzzled.

78

'I love you.'

Something in his voice must have got through to Tom because instead of scowling, as he usually did when Jamie yelled out to him down the street, he smiled softly back at Jamie and nodded. 'I love you too, Dad. To infinity and beyond,' he added, before heading off once more.

Jamie closed his eyes and tried to think what to do next. Reluctantly, he returned to the kitchen, where Martha was still standing like a statue, staring at the garden. It was as if there was a force-field around her, preventing him from getting anywhere near her. He picked up the cup of coffee he had poured earlier and took it to the table, where he sat down, watching her carefully.

Suddenly she turned around and came towards him with all the force of a tidal wave. Before he knew what was happening, she was raining blows down on his head, swearing and screaming abuse at the top of her voice. Jamie put his arms up to try to protect himself, but he was astonished at the power of her punches.

'Martha!' he yelled. 'Don't!' But she either didn't hear him or didn't want to stop, and the onslaught continued.

After a while, it was as if all the fight left her body, and she slumped down onto the floor, crying as if she was in agony.

Watching her, the tears began to course down Jamie's face again and he knelt on the floor beside her. 'I'm so sorry! Oh my God, I am so, so sorry,' he put his arms around Martha and held her as she cried, rocking her backwards and forwards like a baby.

It was nearly half an hour before either of them had composed themselves enough to get up off the floor and sit at the table, looking across at each other, exhausted and dazed. Jamie couldn't bear the dull pain he could now see in Martha's eyes, which normally shone with happiness and love. He shook his head, not knowing what to say or where to start.

Reading his mind, as she always did, Martha said, 'Just tell me everything. Who is she?'

Jamie swallowed but his throat was so dry it came out as a cough. 'She's ... well, she's no-one. She means absolutely nothing to me.' It was the truth, but the look on Martha's face told him that he needed to do better than that.

'OK,' he said, taking a nervous sip of his cold coffee, his hands shaking so badly that it splattered onto the wooden table, leaving miniature muddy brown puddles. 'I met her in a coffee shop in town ...'

'When?' Martha's question flew at him like a bullet.

'About six months ago.'

She half-closed her eyes. 'So how did you go from sitting in a coffee shop minding your own business, to taking pictures of yourself having sex with her?'

Jamie gasped at the horror of what he had done. When it was spelled out by Martha in such a matter of fact voice, it sounded so much worse than it had seemed when he was actually doing it. He shook his head and sighed. 'Well, to be honest, it was obvious what she was after ...'

'And obvious what you were after too, I'm sure.'

Jamie recoiled guiltily. He *had* been open to Debra's advances when she'd asked to join him at his table that day.

Martha was away on an assignment and he was feeling bored and disillusioned with his life. Another woman complimenting him and making it obvious she fancied him had instantly made him feel better about himself. The irony of it. He couldn't feel worse now if he tried.

'Go on,' said Martha curtly. 'I want to know exactly how you came to be having an affair with some old tart ...'

'It wasn't an affair!' Jamie cried. 'It was just ... sex. Not even very good sex.'

Martha snorted derisively. 'Listen, you fucking bastard, you have been having "not very good sex" with some tart for six whole months. It is an affair, I can assure you.'

Jamie put his face in his hands, unable to bear the contempt in Martha's voice. He had never thought of it as an affair, he had just thought of it as sex. And he was telling the truth about the sort of sex it was. Debra was years older than Martha, she wore clothes which left little to the imagination, smelt of cheap, cloying perfume and had absolutely nothing that made him fancy her, except the fact that she had offered herself on a plate and didn't want anything else from him but sex. They barely even talked and he would leave the second it was over. What he did with Debra bore no resemblance to the sex he had with Martha, which was incredible in every way.

'So why did you do it then?' Martha spat, when he tried to explain that to her.

Again, he shook his head helplessly. He had no answer. When Debra had said, 'I live quite near here. Would you like to come back to my house?', why the hell did he not say, 'No, thank you. I am a very happily married man and I wouldn't dream of cheating on the woman I love.'

But, as he thought back, he knew exactly why he had taken up Debra's offer so casually. He was bored and lonely and was flattered that another woman found him sexually attractive. Martha would never find out and as it was clear that Debra was only interested in a sexual relationship, he was able to compartmentalise it as something purely physical that wouldn't impact on his family life. In fact, he had justified to himself, it would improve his relationship with Martha if he was happier.

They sat in silence for several minutes, each lost in their own desperate thoughts. Finally, Jamie spoke again. 'Martha ... I know that what I've done is awful. That I deserve absolutely everything that you're saying to me right now. But please, Martha, please don't tell the children ...'

'Well they'll find out when we split up. And that's what's going to happen,' she said, wearily but firmly.

'No!' Jamie wailed, as he burst into tears again. 'Please, Martha, please ... it'll kill them. And it'll kill me,' he begged.

Martha shook her head and stood up. 'I think maybe you should have thought about that before.' She stalked past him towards the door. Just as she was about to go into the hallway, she stopped and turned around. 'You need to pack a bag,' she said coldly. 'Our marriage is over.'

Chapter 10

Martha was shaking so badly she could barely turn the taps on the bath. She leaned over and looked down into the water as it swallowed her falling tears, cascading into the violent dark purple rivers of the Molton Brown bubble bath. Despite the never-ending torrent of tears, she was calmer now after the violence of her earlier outburst, when she had wanted to hurt Jamie physically, just as he had hurt her.

And it *was* physical, the pain she was feeling. It was as though she had been kicked in the stomach by a horse and she felt faint with shock. A million thoughts were whirling through her brain and she wanted to grab hold of just one, so that she could figure out what was going on and what she should do for the best, but she was too exhausted. In a split second, her perfect life had disintegrated.

Jamie was everything to her. Her whole life revolved around him and the children. But suddenly it was all a sham. He was just a selfish, shallow bastard who didn't give a damn about his supposedly beloved family as long as he was able to indulge his own whims and desires. Where before Martha had felt secure and loved, now she felt as if she was walking on shifting sands and could fall through the huge cracks at any moment.

She stepped into the bath; it was too hot, though she liked the sensation. It told her that she could still *feel*. She sank down until her whole body was submerged beneath the bubbles and rested her head on the little white bath pillow at one end. The bath pillow that Jamie had bought her when she told him that she loved to read in the bath but it made her neck ache. He was always buying her thoughtful little presents or making her favourite dinner when she was feeling low. Now she wondered if he had only done that to salve his guilty conscience. If that was the case, he had felt guilty a hell of a lot of the time.

The realisation hit her with another jolt and she flinched. Still the tears rolled unchecked down her cheeks. They seemed to flow out of nowhere and she regarded them dispassionately, as they plopped into the bubbles and disappeared forever.

She thought back to their wedding day, as her dad had proudly walked her down the aisle towards Jamie, who had looked impossibly handsome and nervous in his morning suit, before promising to 'cherish' her and 'forsake all others'. The memory of her dad's face that day brought a fresh torrent of tears. Her mother and father's relationship had been such a strong one. Her father would *never* have cheated on her mother the way Jamie had on her.

How many more affairs had he had, and how could she have been so stupid? He must have been laughing his head off as she took on the burden of providing for the family, with all the stresses that entailed, while he spent his days having sex with anyone who came along. She had been such a bloody fool thinking that he loved her and the children, when the only person he really loved was himself.

It was the shock that was the worst thing to deal with. If she had had suspicions about him, it might have been less devastating. But he had never given her any cause for concern. She had trusted him with every fibre of her being and would have sworn on the children's lives that he would never cheat on her. Again, she shook her head at what a complete fool she had been.

As the hot water soothed her aching body, her thoughts began to gather into some kind of coherent form. Memories drifted through of evenings spent eating dinner together, a glass of wine in their hands, laughing as they chatted about their respective days. Of Jamie shrugging like the expert liar he clearly was as he told her that he had 'just mooched around town' that day. Of Jamie occasionally claiming that he was 'too tired' for sex.

As the memories began to gather pace, like a train chugging relentlessly through her brain, the anger that had abated now returned and overwhelmed her, so that she found herself roaring with rage and pain.

The bathroom door flew open and Jamie's face appeared. 'Martha! Martha!' he yelled over the noise. 'What's wrong?' Instinctively, he came over to her and tried to embrace her, as he had a million times before, but she clawed at his face like a tiger, sending water spraying everywhere as she drew three perfect trails of blood down his left cheek.

He clamped his hand to his face in shock as Martha scrambled out of the bath, still crying. 'Leave me alone!' she screamed, now totally out of control. 'Don't *ever* touch me again! Get out! Get out! Get out of this house! I *hate* you!'

She ran into her bedroom and slammed the door shut, before throwing herself on the bed. She had never felt so alone.

On the one hand, she wanted Jamie to pack his bag and get out. She couldn't bear to look at his lying, cheating face. But on the other hand, she was so scared of what would happen after he'd gone. How would she explain to the children where he was? Could she bear to tell them the truth, knowing the pain it would cause them?

They were so happy. So balanced. The trauma of this would change everything forever. How the hell could Jamie have risked jeopardising all that, she raged, as her chest tightened so much that she thought she might be having a heart attack.

In the midst of her anguish, she was dimly aware of her mobile phone ringing. She ignored it. A couple of minutes later it rang again, and this time she sat up and picked the handset up off the bedside table. She glanced at the screen: Charlie Simmons.

'Oh no!' she sighed, swallowing hard and roughly wiping the tears that continued to fall down her cheeks. Should she answer it? *Could* she answer it? Before she could make up her mind, the ringing stopped. After about thirty seconds, the alert told her that he had left a message. She clicked on to her voicemail and listened as his soothing, deep voice filled her ear.

'Hi, er, Martha, Charlie here, Charlie Simmons,' he stuttered nervously. 'So, it appears we were snapped leaving the hotel yesterday ... Really sorry about that. It happens so often that I forget about them, but I should have warned you ... I, er, I hope it hasn't proved problematic for you in any way ...'

Martha snorted as she listened. 'It's not *that* that's problematic!' she growled.

'Anyway,' Charlie continued, his cheery tone so at odds with how she was feeling right now. 'Give me a call. We need to arrange the next interview, don't we? And, er, I've got something to give you ...' He paused while he laughed. 'Something I think you might like. In fact, maybe we could do a swap and you could return my sweatpants?' He paused. 'So, listen ... call me. Bye.'

Martha stared at her phone for a long while, trying to recover her composure. She hummed slightly, to see how her voice sounded. Although it seemed as though it was coming from a long way away, the shudders that had convulsed through her body had now slowed and at least it was steady.

She went into the ensuite shower room and blew her nose. In the mirror above the sink, her eyes were small in her head, while her face was puffy. Or maybe it was because her face was puffy that her eyes looked small, she thought distractedly. Either way, she looked bloody terrible. Still, Charlie wouldn't be able to see her over the phone, and she was grateful for that as she pressed his contact number.

'Hi!' he said cheerfully as he answered.

'How did you know it was me?'

'Well, there's this really clever device on mobile phones these days, so that when someone calls you can—'

'OK! OK!' she interrupted him, smiling for the first time that morning, despite herself. She felt strange knowing that he had put her name and number into his phone. Pleased, but strange.

'So ...' he began, slightly nervously, 'sorry about the picture ... I didn't even think of how it might look. Louisa's been on, having a massive go at me already.'

Martha knew Louisa Thomas, Charlie's publicist, well. She had interviewed many of her clients over the years. 'Yes, I can just imagine. Was she cross with *me*?' she said suddenly.

'No, of course not. I think she felt more sorry for you when I told her the story of how you came to be wearing my clothes ... I hope you gave that husband of yours a telling off when you got home, letting you go out like that!'

At the mention of her husband, and taking her entirely by surprise, Martha burst into furious, uncontrollable sobs.

'Oh God!' Charlie said on the other end of the line. 'I'm so sorry. I didn't mean to upset you ... you didn't look that bad. You looked good, actually. Oh crap. Why are you crying?' His words were tumbling over each other as he spoke, while Martha's sobs grew louder and louder.

'No!' she managed to gulp. 'Nothing to do with you.'

'No. Quite,' Charlie sounded embarrassed. 'None of my business. Sorry. Look, shall I call back later?'

'No!' Martha shook her head and tried desperately to calm herself. 'Something's happened. Something really bad. I didn't mean it's none of your business, I just meant it's nothing *you've* done wrong.'

'Oh, I see,' Charlie said, before lapsing into a silence that meant he didn't see at all.

'Sorry,' Martha gulped, finally gaining control of herself. 'I've ... well, I've had a bit of a personal trauma.'

There was a long pause. 'Do you want to talk about it?' Charlie said eventually.

Martha shook her head wearily. 'It's a long and awful story,' she began. 'And it's too personal for a phone conversation. But thanks anyway.'

There was another pause. 'Why don't you come to the hotel today? You don't have to talk about it if you don't want to, but it might help to get away? I could go out and you could just sit in the apartment and read or watch TV or something?'

'I couldn't ...' Martha started to say automatically, before stopping. Getting out of the house was *exactly* what she needed to do, and talking to someone like Charlie, who didn't know her or Jamie and wouldn't make judgements might help. 'But you must have lots on?' she protested.

'Day off. I'm completely free. As I said in my message, I've got something to give you anyway. Get on a train and come.'

Something about his voice soothed Martha so much that, without giving it any more thought, she found herself agreeing to go and meet him. She bundled his t-shirt and sweatpants into a bag – she had intended to wash them but there was no time, and she figured he would have 'people' to do that sort of thing for him anyway – and threw on her own t-shirt, jeans and Converse trainers.

She splashed her face with cold water, cleaned her teeth and put on some mascara, before heading down the stairs. Jamie was in the kitchen, slumped over the table. He looked up as she came in and his eyebrows shot up in surprise when he saw that she was dressed and apparently about to go out somewhere. 'Where are you g—?' he began, standing up.

'None of your business,' she snapped, picking up the car keys and walking out of the kitchen towards the front door.

'Martha!' he begged, as he followed her. 'Please don't go like this. We need to talk.'

Martha ignored him and headed out of the house. Jamie stood on the doorstep, watching her. Just as she was about to get into the car, she looked up and met his eye. He looked so confused and anguished that for a split second she felt sorry for him. Then an image of him doing unspeakable things with that revolting woman flashed into her mind and her lip curled in disgust. She got into the car and drove off without looking back, knowing that he was still standing on the doorstep.

As she drove to the station, she started to have second thoughts, wondering what the hell she was doing. Charlie Simmons was one of the most famous actors in Britain and she was heading off to meet him so that she could pour out the story of her marriage breakdown.

She pulled over and stopped the car in a lay-by overlooking a wide green field bordered with poppies. On any other day she would have enjoyed the beauty of the view, but today she was blind to it. Should she just go home and discuss things properly with Jamie in a grown-up fashion? But, she reasoned,

Charlie Simmons, for all his fame and money, would know exactly how she was feeling today. He had been through it too, and it must have been so much worse for him because it had played out on the front pages of the tabloid newspapers. And he had asked her to come, so it wasn't as if she was turning up uninvited. She started the car again. She would go. Jamie could spend the day stewing in agony over what she might do next.

Chapter 11

Jamie stood on the doorstep long after Martha had driven off, staring with blank eyes at the space on the drive where her car had been. The look she had given him before getting into the car would stay with him forever. In one small glance, she had managed to say so much. He could cope with her contempt, even her disgust; what he couldn't cope with was the hurt and pain in her eyes.

Martha was such a sunny person. The way she had reacted that morning had scared him because it wasn't something he had ever seen before. He didn't know how to deal with it or how to help her. And knowing that he was the cause of such pain compounded his guilt a million times over.

Finally, he closed the front door and stood in the hallway, listening to the sounds of the house; normally so familiar and comforting, today they felt threatening and reproachful. He slouched into the kitchen and looked around at the usual chaos and detritus of family life. Only this morning everything had changed. What he had done might mean that family life as he knew it was over.

He didn't know if Martha was serious about wanting him to leave but he knew he should be prepared to go. As he looked around him, the thought of leaving their happy home, of never having ridiculous, meaningless debates with the children over meals, or putting them to bed, suddenly hit him and a tsunami of misery washed over him. He slumped down onto the cold tiles of the kitchen floor as the emotion overwhelmed him.

After a while, his tears subsided and he looked up, almost in surprise, as he heard a voice inside his head telling him clearly what he needed to do. He frowned, wondering if the voice was real. *Of course it wasn't real*, he told himself crossly, *there's no-one else here*. But he had heard a voice, quite clearly.

He stood up, feeling shaky and stunned. It was as if he had had an out-of-body experience. As if his mum had been with him, stroking his back like she used to when he was small. His yearning to speak to her just then was so intense, as if all his grief had been distilled into that one moment. She would have given him hell, but she would have been there for him, just as she always had been in the past.

Tears poured down his face as he moved, almost on autopilot, towards the table. He carefully collected up the cups and bowls left over from the children's breakfast and put them into the dishwasher. Then he took the dried washing that had been in the tumble dryer for two days and put it onto the worktop, ready for ironing, before he put the washing that had been in the washing machine for two days into the dryer.

For the next three hours he worked meticulously through the house, tidying and cleaning, putting away things that had needed putting away for months, ironing and clearing out cupboards that no-one had seen the back of for years. He felt as if he was cleansing himself as well as the house as he worked, vacuuming, dusting and scrubbing until the sweat was pouring off him with the effort.

As if to inflict as much pain on himself as possible, he put his headphones on while he worked and listened to the playlist of their favourite songs that Martha had made for them to take on their honeymoon. As each track started, it brought with it a fresh stab of shame at how he could have wrecked something so precious.

When the house was clean, he mended the bookshelves in the study that had been broken for two years, wishing as he did so that he could mend his marriage as easily. Then he went through the piles of paperwork that had been gathering dust on the desks for months, sorting and filing until each surface was clear.

By the time he had finished he felt slightly better. At least he had done something useful instead of lying around feeling sorry for himself. He stripped off his jeans and t-shirt and stepped into the shower where he stood for a long time, letting the jets of water pummel his skin and wash away the sweat and grime from his exertions. He lathered up some shower gel and rubbed his skin furiously, pleased when it reddened under the pressure. The welts on his cheek where Martha had scratched him were stinging like hell and, again, this pleased him. He deserved to suffer.

'Win her back,' his mum's voice had told him, and that was exactly what he intended to do. He had made the worst, most catastrophic mistake he could ever have made, but he was going to put it right. If it took him the rest of his life, he was going to prove to Martha that he loved her and that it would never happen again. He had to win her back because losing her would destroy him and everything they had built together.

As he stepped out of the shower, he caught a glimpse of his face in the mirror. He looked awful. His eyes were sunken, he badly needed a shave and the scratches on his face were vivid and angry. He peered at them closely. It was almost as if he had been branded an adulterer.

It had never even occurred to Jamie that every time he had had sex with Debra he was committing adultery and betraying his marriage vows. After the first time, when he had felt horribly guilty and dirty, it had got easier. He had put all his clothes into the wash to remove any trace of Debra's cloying scent, but when it became clear that he had got away with it, that Martha had absolutely no idea what he had done, he felt the urge to do it again. And again. And the more he did it, the less guilty he felt. It seemed so meaningless, and because he felt absolutely nothing for Debra, he convinced himself that what Martha didn't know wouldn't hurt her.

Except that now, of course, she did know. And worse, she had discovered his treachery in the most shocking and upsetting way possible. While other wives might torture themselves imagining their husband having sex with his mistress, Martha had actually seen it with her own eyes. The thought of it was nauseating to him, so he could only imagine how it felt for Martha. The images would be burned indelibly into her memory and nothing could ever erase them.

He dried himself, shaved, brushed his teeth and put on a clean t-shirt and jeans. A new feeling of determination had replaced the helplessness he had felt that morning. He went back into the study where Martha's awful discovery had taken place earlier. He swallowed hard and stared at his computer, suddenly scared to look at it again.

But he knew he had to. Had to get rid of those awful photos for good. He thought he had deleted them but something must have gone wrong. He sat down and looked at the dock along the bottom of his screen. The icon Martha had clicked on was one that kept duplicate copies of his main photographic folders and wasn't one he ever used. Why on earth hadn't he thought about that?

His hand shaking, he clicked on the icon again and immediately the screen filled with a shocking picture of him and Debra, naked on her bed, his head between her legs. Jamie closed his eyes as his head swam with the shame and horror of what he had done. Why the hell had he taken the pictures? He tried to think back to the day in question. He had told Debra that he had got a camera for Christmas and she had leeringly suggested that he use it to photograph her the next time they had sex.

'Oh God!' he moaned, putting his head in his hands and trying not to cry again. Forcing himself to look up, he began to go through the folder, systematically deleting each horrific image. Debra looked grotesque. Her body was flabby and her empty eyes were cold in her hard face. Over and over again, he shook his head, trying to understand why the hell he had been stupid enough to wreck his marriage.

When all the photos had gone, he took a deep breath and logged into the mail account he had set up especially for contacting her. He had never given her his real name or his phone number, just in case. So they had contacted each other via email instead. Sure enough, there was an email from her. He clicked on it. She had attached a link to a hard-core porn site and added the message: *this is what you will be doing to me next time!*

The bile rose from Jamie's stomach and he put his hand over his mouth, suddenly afraid he might throw up. He deleted the message and then deleted his email account. Debra wouldn't care that she would never hear from him again. He suspected she picked up men all the time.

Once he had deleted everything, Jamie closed his computer and thought about what to do next. He wondered where Martha had gone and whether she would be back that night. He had a cold fear in the pit of his stomach that she might have gone to stay with her mother in Surrey.

Jamie was terrified of Martha's mother. If Martha was to tell Jane what had happened, there was no telling how she might react. Jane had always been pleasant towards Jamie, but she had made it clear that she thought he wasn't good enough for her daughter.

Jane had also made it clear that she thought it was wrong that Jamie 'sat at home all day' while Martha took on the role of breadwinner. Her own husband had died several years previously, and until his sudden death he had been a very successful editor of a national newspaper. Jane had had her own career as a garden designer, but it was always more of a hobby than a necessity and she thought it wrong that Jamie was happy to see Martha bear the burden of supporting the family financially.

If she discovered what Jamie had been up to while Martha was working so hard, he knew for certain that Jane would tell Martha to kick him out immediately and find someone who was worthy of her.

Again, Jamie opened his laptop. He would send Martha an email. It might be easier to get through to her in writing, if she was refusing to speak to him. It took a long time before he could think of the right words. What the hell could you say when you had betrayed someone so badly?

When he had finished, Jamie re-read the words several times. She would get it on her phone, wherever she was. He hoped desperately that it would make her think twice before ending their marriage. Losing her for ever was unthinkable. He pressed 'Send'.

Chapter 12

Four thousand miles away, Liv was also lying awake, trying to figure out how to save her relationship. She looked at the clock beside her bed. It was exactly three a.m. She had come to bed at around eleven but had slept fitfully, her dreams unsettling and vivid. She felt groggy and tired, as if her hangover had already kicked in, yet her heart was racing. Something was going on with Danny. She knew she was being neurotic when she had no proof that he had done anything untoward, but her instinct was strong and she always trusted her instinct. *Plus*, said a little voice inside her head, *you cheated on Charlie, so you know the signs*.

She felt a sudden, desperate urge to talk to Charlie. Maybe he could come to LA earlier and she could fly to Hawaii and surprise Danny? She turned over in bed, pulling the duvet around her to prevent the chill that was spreading through her body. Did she *really* want to do that? Catch him red-handed, with all the humiliation that would entail? Maybe. If she was prepared for it, maybe she would be able to handle it more easily.

And what would she do if Danny *was* cheating on her? Would she leave him? She loved him so much and he was so good with Felix. Felix would take it very hard if he lost Danny as well as Charlie. The tears swam behind her closed lids. It was no good, she decided, sitting up irritably. She wouldn't be sleeping again tonight.

She leaned over and switched on the bedside lamp, looking around her palatial bedroom, now bathed in a soft pink glow, her eyes coming to rest on Danny's side of their vast bed. She felt so alone and there was no-one she could talk to who wouldn't say, 'I told you so.' Well, maybe her mother, but Mariella wasn't exactly the best example to follow, or very good at giving advice for that matter. She would probably tell Liv to ignore the infidelity and make herself feel better by taking a lover of her own.

Liv thought for a moment before picking up her phone and dialling Charlie's number. It would be around eleven a.m. in the UK, so she hoped he would be able to talk. She listened to the ringing tone nervously. She never, ever called him when she didn't have Felix with her to speak to him, so he would know something was up.

After six rings, his voicemail clicked in. '*Hi, leave me a message and I'll do my best to get back to you . . .*' he said in his deep, resonant voice. Liv stared at her phone in disappointment. Should she leave a message? No, she decided, ending the call, she would try again later.

She lay back down, feeling lonely and lost. She had been so cruel to Charlie and now she was reaping what she had sowed. It was inevitable and she deserved it. She thought back to that awful time four years previously, when Charlie had returned to Los Angeles after his trip to Britain, expecting to find his wife and son waiting for him. Instead, he had found their rented house empty, with a letter from Liv telling him that she needed some 'time out' from the marriage.

She remembered Charlie's anguished phone call as he begged her not to leave him, not to take his son away. Looking back now she couldn't believe how cruel she had been, but she had already moved on. Danny and Hollywood were her life. Charlie was history.

Charlie had returned to the UK, broken and humiliated. He had thought about staying in LA to be near to Felix but was worried he wouldn't be able get work there, whereas he knew he could get numerous roles in the UK.

And sure enough, over time, he started to rebuild his shattered life and reputation by throwing himself into acting. As far as Liv was aware, he hadn't had any other serious relationships. Charlie was loyal and a one-woman man. He wouldn't have been interested in playing the field or exploiting his fame.

And as for Liv, she seemed to have made the right choice. Everyone had warned her away from Danny. Warned her that he was a womaniser who would move on to his next leading lady when their movie finished shooting. But he hadn't. Instead, he'd moved Liv and Felix into his multi-million dollar home and lavished them both with love and affection. He told her that he had hated the emptiness of his old life and had been looking for something more meaningful when he

101

met her. 'I didn't even know what I was looking for until I found you and Felix,' he would say, making Liv sigh with happiness.

Felix was young enough not to understand his father's hurt and heartbreak and, to Charlie's credit, he had always behaved impeccably towards both Danny and Liv. As far as she knew, he had never said anything horrible about her to Felix and, as a result, the little boy was as balanced and happy as he could be, with two fathers who loved him deeply.

On the bed beside her, Liv's phone rang, the sudden noise jarring her already jangling nerves. The ringing echoed loudly around the room and she snatched it up, suddenly worried that the reverberations might wake Felix, asleep in the next room.

'Yes?' she snapped.

'It's Charlie.' His voice sounded slightly irritable. 'I just saw I had a missed call from you . . .'

'Oh, yes!' She tried to breathe slowly, to stop her heart pounding. 'Thanks for calling back. I hope I'm not calling at a bad time?'

There was a pause. 'Um, well, it's not great,' he said, and she could tell he was mouthing something to someone. 'But I can spare a minute.'

Liv wondered who he was with. 'Well, you know you said that you were coming next week?'

'Yes.' He was definitely keen to get her off the phone.

'Well, I wondered if you might think about coming a little earlier?'

'How early?'

'As soon as possible.'

There was another pause. 'I'll think about it. I'm not sure I'll be able to get everything sorted here.'

'OK,' she said, knowing that it was the best she could hope for.

'Just out of interest,' he added, taking her by surprise. 'Why do you want me to come earlier?'

Now it was her turn to hesitate. 'I just thought that maybe . . . maybe I would go and see Danny . . .' She tailed off as she finished speaking. Charlie knew her too well. He would know that wasn't the whole story.

'You want to surprise him?' he prompted.

Again, Liv hesitated. 'Something like that,' she said at last.

On the other end of the line, Charlie let out a breath. 'Well, it's none of my business but I'm not sure that's a good idea.'

'Why?' Liv snapped, her defences immediately up.

'In case you find something you don't like.' She thought she could detect a trace of bitterness in his tone. She almost expected him to add, 'Like I did.'

'Well, as you say, it's none of your business, but thank you for your concern,' she said in a clipped voice. She knew she was being unfair. She had no right to expect anything at all from Charlie, least of all compassion or sympathy.

She heard a noise on the other end of the line that sounded like a woman crying, and she sat up straighter, straining to hear. 'Is everything all right there?'

'I'd better go,' Charlie said, not answering her question. She heard the noise again. It *was* a woman crying. 'I'll see what I can do about coming over a bit earlier. Goodbye,' he said, in the usual curt tone he reserved for her.

The line went dead and Liv frowned. Why would a woman be crying in Charlie's hotel room, and who was she anyway? Was it the one from the photo in the paper?

She got out of bed and padded to her bathroom where she retrieved her silk robe and pulled it tightly around her, tucking her phone into the pocket. She felt agitated, as if she was standing on some kind of precipice.

She headed out into the hallway and crossed to Felix's room. It was a child's utopia, expensively decorated with all the paraphernalia of his favourite American football team, and big enough to house a basketball net, an air hockey table and, in a nod to his British roots, a full-size snooker table.

She made her way over to his car-shaped bed and looked down at his sleeping form. His dark curls, so like his father's, were spread out on the pillow. His duvet was bunched by his feet, leaving his pyjama-clad body exposed. He was getting so tall that he almost filled the length of his child's bed, and she wondered as she gazed at him where her baby boy had gone. His long lashes rested on the top of his cheeks and his full lips trembled slightly with each outward breath. She bent to kiss him, savouring the warm touch of his skin on her lips, soothing her aching heart and filling the empty space inside her with love for her only child.

After watching him for a while longer, she left Felix's room and headed for the vast steel and gloss-white kitchen. She stood for a moment by the glass wall, looking out onto the glimmering turquoise pool and terrace that overlooked the dusty green Hollywood hills and, further down, the bright white lights of LA.

She opened the fridge and looked in at the bottle of white wine that she had started last night. It was only around a quarter full, so she picked it up and drank greedily from the bottle, closing her eyes with pleasure at the deliciously cold, sharp tang. She deposited the bottle at the back of the cupboard under the sink, then made herself an espresso. Definitely no more sleep tonight. In her pocket, she felt the phone vibrate against her thigh, the signal that it was about to ring, and she snatched it up quickly, before it could chime through the house again. 'Yes!' she said, wondering who the hell would be calling at this time.

'It's me, Charlie. You sound a bit odd again.'

'Oh! Hi, sorry, it's just it's the middle of the night and—'

'Well you called me just a short while ago,' Charlie cut in, pre-empting any rebuke from her. 'So I thought it would be ok . . .'

'It is,' Liv said quickly. 'It is. Sorry.'

'OK,' Charlie replied, failing to mask the note of irritation. 'Well, I just called to say that I am going to be able to come over a bit earlier . . .'

'Oh that's great.' Liv took a sip of her espresso and wondered if it *was* great. It might mean she got to find out once and for all whether Danny was cheating on her.

'But there's just one thing . . .' Charlie continued, suddenly sounding slightly nervous.

'Hmmm, what's that?'

'I think I might be bringing someone with me after all.'

Chapter 13

Martha couldn't remember anything of the train journey to London. She had sat in a daze, staring blankly out of the window over the undulating countryside, as images of Jamie and that woman flashed before her eyes.

It had been just a few short hours since her whole life had fallen apart. This time yesterday, she had felt happy and content. As if things couldn't get any better. She loved her job, she loved her children and she loved her husband. But he didn't love her. He couldn't have done. Not only had he cheated on her, he had done it so casually. So easily. And he had almost got away with it. Almost.

The bile rose in Martha's throat and she put her hand over her mouth, suddenly terrified that she might be about to throw up again. She glanced towards the toilets, praying that the *engaged* sign wasn't illuminated.

She wondered why she had agreed to meet Charlie. On the worst day of her life, when she so desperately needed someone to talk to, she was heading up to London to meet with a man – a film star at that – who she didn't really know at all.

And yet it felt like the right thing to do. They had got on so well yesterday and he had been so sweet about the embarrassing hole in her dress that she already felt as though she could trust him.

She headed for the tube in a daze, barely aware of where she was going, and yet she managed to get on the right train and before she knew it she was standing in front of the hotel once more. Suddenly, she felt conspicuous in what she was wearing. Her t-shirt and jeans felt scruffy in such opulent surroundings, but just as she was thinking about turning around and leaving, her phone buzzed. She fished in her large leather bag, and as she retrieved it she could see immediately that she had a message from Charlie. *I can see you! Come on up. Room 802.*

Instinctively, she looked up and could just about make out a dark, curly head leaning out of his window. She smiled, despite herself, and headed into the hotel towards the lifts. After what seemed like ages, she arrived at the eighth floor and knocked at the door of his room, by now feeling nervous and again wondering why she was doing this. But as soon as the door swung open and Charlie greeted her with a wide, warm smile, she knew she had done the right thing.

'I brought back your clothes.' She held out the carrier bag containing his sweatpants and t-shirt.

'Thank you.' Charlie took the bag and led her into the suite. 'I've got something for you too . . .'

Martha followed him in. 'You said.'

Charlie glanced back at her with a sweet smile before disappearing into the bedroom. Martha frowned to herself and shook her head. What was he up to? A few seconds later he emerged carrying a stone-coloured dress on a hanger.

'Is that ... my dress?' Martha frowned again, her weary brain unable to compute.

'No. It's a new one that is exactly the same as your dress.'

Martha shook her head, feeling the tingling sensation behind her nose that signified fresh tears. 'I can't believe you did that,' she murmured, her voice thick. 'Thank you.'

Charlie laid the dress over a chair and waved his hand dismissively before motioning for Martha to sit down. 'So,' he said, once they were perched on the pale blue sofas facing each other. 'What can I get you? Tea, coffee or hard liquor?'

Martha bit her lip, which had started to quiver dangerously. 'I'm not sure what I want ... I don't know why I'm even here ... This is ridiculous,' she finished with a whimper. She could feel fresh tears sliding down her face and she swept them away irritably. 'Sorry,' she added, embarrassed.

Charlie looked at her with an expression that she read as sympathetic but which could also have been awkwardness. She hoped he wouldn't feel the need to move over to her sofa and comfort her. She needed space. To her relief, he stayed where he was. 'You don't have to apologise,' he said, shaking his head slightly. 'Never apologise. Why don't I get you some coffee and then maybe you can tell me all about it?'

He got up and poured coffee from the silver pot on the stone table into a fine china cup. Then he added a tiny bit of milk, just as she had asked for yesterday. He slid the cup towards her then poured his own, which he took black.

Suddenly his mobile phone rang and he looked at her apologetically.

'Sorry,' he said, leaving the phone unanswered until it went to voicemail.

'Why don't you see who it is?' Martha prompted, feeling conspicuous in her misery and keen for him to leave her alone for a minute.

'OK. Excuse me a sec?' he said, as he disappeared into the bedroom with the phone.

As soon as he had gone, Martha began to cry, glad that she could do it in private. Through her sobs, she was dimly aware of him speaking on the phone in the other room, before he returned carrying a box of tissues, which he put down beside her. Then he sat back down on the opposite sofa and looked at her expectantly.

Martha took a sip of her coffee, trying to compose herself. 'I've had . . . a bit of a shock,' she managed, looking up and meeting his eye.

He nodded. 'Do you want to talk about it? Don't worry if you don't. We can either chat or I can make myself scarce?'

'No!' Martha said, a little too quickly. 'No. I really need to talk about it. It just feels strange talking about it to *you*. We barely know each other.'

Charlie nodded. 'I think that's probably a good thing. Consider me a free therapist. You're lucky, I had to pay for mine!'

Martha felt the faint trace of a smile play on her lips. Of course, Charlie had been through all this himself. He would understand more than most. 'Well,' she began tentatively,

'I discovered this morning that my husband ...' She had to stop speaking for a second to recover her composure. 'My husband has been having an affair—'

Her voice broke and she felt the tears starting to slide down her cheeks again. She grabbed a tissue from the box beside her and dabbed as delicately as she could at her face. She stole a glance at Charlie, who was looking at her with such a pitying expression that she almost felt as though he was embracing her.

'And the way I found out,' she continued as strongly as she could, 'was by finding photos of them having sex on his computer.'

'Oh God,' Charlie murmured, looking shocked. 'I'm so sorry.'

Martha continued to cry quietly for a few moments.

'Did you have ... any suspicions?' Charlie asked after a while. 'Is that why you were looking at his computer?'

Martha blew her nose and shook her head. 'No. That's why it was such a shock. Jamie is such a devoted father and, I thought, husband. He's literally the last person in the world you'd expect to do something like that. Ironically, I was looking for a photo of him to superimpose on your head, so that he wasn't upset about those pictures of *us* leaving the hotel together. I wasn't snooping. I've never felt the need to snoop. I trusted him completely.'

'Oh God,' Charlie said again. 'I'm so sorry.'

The kindness of his tone set Martha off again and this time she didn't cry quietly, she literally howled with anguish. 'The pain ...' she gulped between sobs. '... is physical. I feel as though I've been kicked in the stomach repeatedly.'

Charlie nodded and finally got up and came to sit beside her. He reached out and took her hand, which he stroked gently. 'I know exactly what you mean,' he murmured. 'I remember it so well.'

Martha sniffed hard to try and quell the outpouring of grief and looked up at Charlie. His dark eyes looked pained, whether for her or for himself she didn't know, but she knew that they mirrored her own. 'But ... it passes, right?' she asked, her tone slightly pleading.

Charlie hesitated. 'Yes,' he said at last. 'I suppose you could say it passes.'

'How long does it take?'

He looked away and didn't answer for a long time. 'Well, I guess that depends ...' he said finally.

'On what?'

'On whether the cause of that pain remains in your life.'

Martha's stomach froze. Even though she had told Jamie their marriage was over, she wasn't sure she could really picture her life without him. She imagined the years stretching ahead, with them living separate lives. She imagined Mimi's wedding day, Jamie walking her down the aisle while Martha looked on. Would they both have new partners by then? She imagined Christmases where they had to take it in turns to have the children. College graduations. Shared custody. Separate houses. It was all too awful to contemplate and she put her head in her hands. Jamie hadn't just ruined their marriage, he had destroyed their children's future happiness too.

'Where is he now?' Charlie asked, pouring more coffee.

'At home.'

'Does he know where you are?'

'No.'

Charlie nodded. 'What about the children? You've got two, haven't you? Are they aware of what's gone on?'

At the mention of the children, Martha groaned. 'I told them I wasn't feeling well. I think they bought it. I *hope* they bought it.'

All the while, Charlie continued to stroke Martha's hand, soothing her frayed nerves.

She looked up at him apologetically. 'I'm sorry. I know you must have loads to do. I shouldn't have come ...'

'Shhhhh ...' Charlie interrupted her. 'Of course you should. I asked you to. What do you want to do now? Are you hungry?'

Martha shook her head miserably, not knowing what to do with herself.

'OK,' Charlie said, getting up. 'Why don't you go and have a long, hot bath and I'll order up some food. If you don't want it, that's fine, but at least you'll have the option.'

Even though she'd had a bath at home, the thought of a soak in Charlie's beautiful large bathtub was desperately appealing. 'Are you sure?' she asked, still not quite able to believe she was sitting in the hotel suite of one of Britain's biggest film stars, pouring out her tales of marital woe.

'I'm sure,' Charlie replied emphatically, reaching out a hand to pull her up.

Martha took it gratefully. Her legs were trembling and she realised that all she had had today was coffee, which had only added to her shakiness. 'Thank you,' she said, looking up at him to try to convey that she was thanking him for so many things.

'No problem,' he replied, flashing her a sad smile. 'Do you want me to run the bath for you?'

Martha smiled back and shook her head. 'No, I think that might be what's called "above and beyond", but thank you all the same.'

She walked stiffly towards the bathroom, where she had discovered the gaping hole in her dress yesterday. So much had happened since then. She closed the door behind her and looked at herself in the giant mirror above the double sink. In just twenty-four hours she had become a completely different person. She felt older, more haggard, and above all she felt as if Jamie had smashed every ounce of confidence out of her, as surely as if he had hit her repeatedly with a hammer.

She filled the huge bathtub and added some of the Jo Malone bath oil that was on the side. Stepping into the comfortingly hot water, she had a sudden memory of her and Jamie, staying at a spa for the weekend, getting into a similar bath together, her leaning back against his naked body while he soaped and stroked her breasts. Had he done that with *her*?

The dull pain in her chest that had been there ever since she saw those photos suddenly intensified and she cried out. Immediately, she heard Charlie's footsteps running towards the door. 'Martha!' he called out. 'Are you OK?'

'Yes!' Martha replied in a strangled voice.

'You don't sound OK,' Charlie said through the door.

'I am,' she said, trying to sound stronger than she felt.

There was a pause and she could hear Charlie sitting down on the floor. She imagined him leaning with his back against the door, his long legs stretched out in front of him. The thought that he was there, guarding her, was at once soothing and comforting and the pain in her chest began to ease.

Later, when she was out of the bath, Martha and Charlie sat on the sofas and ate the chicken soup he had ordered from room service. She had no appetite, but as soon as Charlie started eating she realised that she was absolutely starving.

'You look like you needed that,' Charlie remarked, watching as she wiped her mouth with the thick cloth napkin.

'Sorry.' Martha shook her head. 'I didn't realise how hungry I was.'

'After Liv ...' Charlie began, then stopped.

Martha looked up at him in surprise. So far, they hadn't talked about what Liv had done. They had only focused on the early years of his relationship, on the happy times. Martha had sensed that it would be hard for Charlie to talk about the split, so she had proceeded gently.

'After Liv,' he repeated, 'I fell apart, both mentally and physically. People joke about the heartbreak diet but it's nothing to laugh about. It's so important, to help you get through this, that you look after yourself. It's important for you and it's important for your kids.'

Martha nodded, recognising the truth in his words.

'Right now, you feel as though your whole life has ended and your heart will never heal. But it will. In time.'

Martha allowed herself to be soothed by his voice and his gaze to hold hers. 'Thank you,' she murmured at last.

'So,' he said, breaking the emotion of the moment as a sudden glint of mischief appeared in his eyes. 'I have an idea.'

'Oh?' Martha frowned, wondering what was coming next. The whole day had taken on a surreal quality and she felt like nothing could surprise her again.

'I think you should come with me to LA for a couple of days.'

Nothing except that, she thought, as her mouth dropped open in shock. 'I can't,' she replied automatically.

'Why not? You need something to take your mind off what's happened. Plus, we need to push on with the memoirs and I've got meetings in LA that might be relevant to the book. It's your *job* to come with me!' His grin took away any barb that may have been contained within his words.

Martha paused to formulate her thoughts. 'I can't come because I have two children who will be wondering where the hell I am. Because you are a huge movie star. Because I don't know you from Adam.'

Charlie's eyes danced. He held up three fingers. 'OK, firstly, your children will be fine with your husband.' He pushed down one of the fingers. 'Presumably you often have to go away for your job?'

Martha nodded slowly.

'Me being a movie star is irrelevant ... except that it means I can afford to take you with me,' he continued, pushing down another finger. 'And finally, I don't know who the hell Adam is, but I think you know me well enough to know that you will be quite safe with me.' He pushed down the final finger. 'So, what do you say?'

Martha smiled. 'I say you're crazy.'

Charlie considered it for a minute. 'Of course I'm crazy. But don't forget I've been where you are. I know exactly how you feel right now and I think a bit of crazy might be just what you need.'

'You're really serious?'

Charlie raised his eyebrows. 'Deadly.'

'When?'

'Tonight.'

Martha shook her head. 'No. There's no way I can get all my bits and pieces together and come to LA tonight . . .'

'You don't need anything except your passport,' Charlie persisted. 'I don't suppose you've got it on you?'

Martha hesitated. 'Well, yes, actually. I always carry it in case I need ID'.

Charlie raised his eyebrows. 'That sounds like fate to me. I'll get Jess, my assistant, to go out and buy you the essentials. Really, Martha, do it. Just get on that plane with me tonight.'

In Martha's head, she pictured Jamie at home, waiting for her return. He would be a mess. And as for the children . . . No, she couldn't do it.

But just as the thought left her head, she realised that she couldn't face going home tonight either. She didn't want to look into Jamie's lying eyes and feel any kind of sympathy for him as he pleaded with her to give him another chance. Most of all, she didn't want to have to put on an act for the children. Didn't know if she even could. What if she went home and fell apart in front of them? It would scare them and she couldn't bear to think of them being unsettled or upset. Maybe it would be better for them if she *did* just disappear for a couple of days?

And Charlie was right, she often went away for a few nights when she was on an assignment, so they wouldn't think it weird. She could call them and tell them there had been a sudden change of plan.

Martha had always been such a good girl. She had worked hard as a journalist and a mother, had always put her family first and she had never cheated on any of her lovers, least of all Jamie. Maybe now was the time to put herself first. Maybe now was the time to jump.

As the thoughts tumbled through her head and her heart started to race, she looked up and met Charlie's eye. 'OK,' she said. 'I'll come.'

Chapter 14

Jamie jumped as his mobile rang, cutting through the silence of the house. He had been sitting at the table with his head in his hands, praying that Martha would come home. That she would give him a chance to explain. Not that he could explain it, even to himself. He just wanted to talk to her.

'Hello?' he said, his heart pounding. The number was withheld.

'It's me, Martha.' Jamie shivered at the icy tone to her voice.

'Martha! Where are you? I've been worried sick—' he began.

'I'm phoning to tell you that I'm going away for a few days,' she cut in.

Jamie's stomach dropped. 'Oh God! No ... please, Martha, don't go. We need to talk.'

'*You* might need to talk, but I don't want to hear any more of your bullshit.'

Jamie felt the tears flash into his eyes. He hardly recognised Martha's voice. She sounded so different. So distant and angry. Obviously his email had had no effect whatsoever. 'What about the kids?' he managed to croak.

Martha let out a small sob. 'I'm not sure I'll be able to keep it together in front of them. I think it might be better if I get away for a couple of days until I can.'

Jamie put his hand over his eyes, as if doing so would block out the horror of what was happening. 'Martha . . . please,' he began.

'I'll call them later,' she interrupted, sounding slightly more conciliatory. 'I'll explain that I've got a last-minute assignment.'

There was a pause. 'Where will you be?' Jamie said at last.

'It's none of your business, but I'll be in LA.'

'LA?'

'Yes.'

'Who with?'

'Again, it's really none of your business,' she said, her tone even colder than before, 'but I'm going with Charlie Simmons. I'll call the children later,' she finished, hanging up abruptly.

Jamie stared at the handset in shock. This was bad, really bad. Martha would never leave the children if she didn't have to, and how the hell had she come to be going to LA with Charlie Simmons so suddenly? But the biggest and most pressing question, he thought, standing up and staring out over the back garden as Martha had done only that very morning, was how on earth was he going to hold it together himself in front of the children?

*

It was 3.15 p.m. by the time Mimi rang the doorbell. She had her own key but never used it, saying she preferred to see her dad or, on occasion, her mum, as soon as she possibly could.

Jamie opened the door and stood back as Mimi stepped through.

'Hey Dad,' she smiled brightly, immediately causing tears to well up again in Jamie's eyes. 'What's the matter?' she said, looking at him closely. 'What's happened to your face?'

'Um, nothing ...' Jamie wiped his eyes and rubbed the scratches on his cheek. 'Cut myself shaving,' he mumbled unconvincingly. He grabbed Mimi and hugged her tightly to him. 'I really love you, you know that, don't you?'

He felt Mimi nod into his chest. They stood together for a few moments as he rubbed her back, more to soothe himself than her, until finally they broke apart. Mimi walked slowly into the hallway and dropped her bag on the floor, just as she always did. 'Something's not right,' she said, looking around her slowly.

Jamie swallowed.

'The house is the tidiest it's *ever* been. What the heck is going on?'

Jamie followed her gaze. He had almost forgotten that he had spent hours cleaning. It seemed like a lifetime ago. It was as if the whole day had been suspended in time. 'I, er, I decided it was time I cleaned up my act.'

Mimi frowned, her large blue eyes narrowing as she did so. 'Well, about time too,' she said, in that voice that was so like Martha's, as she walked slowly into the kitchen, looking around her in wonderment as if seeing the house for the first time. 'Where's Mum?' she said suddenly, spinning around to look at him.

Jamie looked away, unable to meet her eye. 'She's not here,' was the best he could manage.

'I can see that. Where is she?' Mimi wasn't going to be fobbed off.

Jamie rubbed his face, playing for time. 'She's . . .' he began, just as the doorbell rang again. 'That'll be Tom,' he said, heading for the door, relieved to have been saved from an explanation, for the moment at least.

Tom was pressing his smiling face to one of the small glass squares in the front door, his white blond hair visible in the square above. Jamie tried to smile back as he opened the door. Tom trudged past and dumped his bags beside Mimi's on the hall floor.

'Don't I get a hug?' Jamie said, his heart aching at the sight of Tom's trusting, open face, so secure in his happy little life. The happy little life that was about to be blown apart.

Tom gave Jamie a perfunctory hug before following Mimi into the kitchen. 'Wow, everything looks different,' he said, looking around. 'Tidy,' he added, as he helped himself to a chocolate Hobnob from the biscuit tin and got himself a drink of orange squash.

Jamie leaned against the doorframe, watching his children as they settled at the table, ready to talk about their day, just as they always did before they would go off to do homework, play on their computers or listen to music.

He hesitated, then poured himself a coffee and joined

them. Mimi looked up at him expectantly. 'So, what's going on?' she said, as direct and no-nonsense as her mother.

Tom looked at Mimi in surprise, before turning to Jamie. Jamie felt his face burn under the scrutiny of the two pairs of eyes boring into him. 'Well …' he began, before shrugging helplessly, at a loss to know what to say.

Tom frowned. 'Where's Mum?'

Jamie took a deep breath. 'She's … well, she's gone away for a few days.'

'But she wasn't well this morning,' Mimi said quickly, and Jamie could almost see the cogs of her brain whirring as she spoke. 'And she didn't mention any assignments.'

'No,' Tom agreed solemnly. 'She was throwing up this morning. So how could she go anywhere? I always have to stay in bed with a bowl beside me when I throw—'

'Yes, we know!' Mimi snapped. 'So, what's going on, Dad? Something's not right.'

'Oh God,' Jamie mumbled to himself, rubbing his face again. 'Look, your mum has had to go away for a few days unexpectedly …'

Mimi frowned. 'Where's she gone?'

'LA. She had to do an interview for the book she's doing … um, with that guy,' he continued, deciding that keeping his explanation as honest as possible was the best idea. 'You know, Charlie Simmons, the actor? He's gone to LA and Mum has to follow him to see how he gets on.'

Mimi's face crumpled slightly. 'He's the one she was photographed with in the paper …'

Jamie clasped Mimi's hand. 'How do you know about that?'

'Some of the girls at school had seen it. They said Mum spent the night at his hotel with him ...' A fat tear slid down her smooth, pale cheek.

'Oh darling,' Jamie reached over to hug her awkwardly across the table. 'That's not true at all. I burnt a hole in her dress, so he lent her some of his clothes to wear. It was completely innocent!'

Mimi looked at him suspiciously. 'You're just saying that to protect her,' she began, shaking her head. 'Otherwise, why has she gone off to LA with him?' She burst into noisy sobs as she finished speaking, and Tom, who never cried, followed suit.

Jamie watched both his children helplessly, unable to reassure them. The only way he could convince them that Martha was innocent was by confessing to what he had done himself and he wasn't ready to do that just yet. He couldn't even begin to find the words.

'Come here,' he said in a choked voice, standing up so that he could hug them both. 'I promise you, your mum has done nothing wrong. She has just had to go on assignment for a couple of days. I spoke to her earlier and she is going to call you later to explain. So, dry your eyes and let's do something fun.'

After a few moments, both children had calmed down. Mimi got up and took a tissue from the box on the window sill, with which she dabbed at her eyes. Tom wiped his eyes and nose on the back of his sleeve.

'OK,' Mimi fixed Jamie with her wide blue stare. 'Do you promise, I mean absolutely promise, that nothing is going on between Mum and that guy?'

Jamie blinked as he thought quickly. It was strange that Martha had gone off to LA with Charlie Simmons, but it was only because of what he had done. She couldn't be blamed in any way. 'I promise you, your mum has done nothing wrong,' he said, wishing so badly that he could say the same for himself.

Chapter 15

Martha gazed unseeingly out of the window of the limousine that was taking her and Charlie to the airport. It was early evening and the pubs and cafés of London were alive with throngs of after-work drinkers, laughing and chatting in the late sunshine. She felt strangely numb. Only this morning she had woken up feeling so happy and content with her life. Nothing could have prepared her for the way she was feeling now, just fifteen hours later, as if she had had a terrible crash and was in some sort of suspended coma.

The day had passed by in a fog. Charlie had listened patiently while she tried to make sense of what had happened. From the moment she arrived at the hotel, she had forgotten that he was a celebrity and had seen him as just another human being who had been through the same sort of trauma as her, albeit in a much more public and humiliating way. He had an amazing way of looking at her that made her feel as if he was embracing her, while giving her enough space to think and breathe.

Although he didn't offer any opinions about what Jamie

had actually done, he did attempt to give a male perspective on what the reasons behind it could be; that maybe Jamie had felt emasculated being a house-husband and having to rely on Martha for money.

Martha had shaken her head. 'No, he did feel like that when he was first at home. But we found a way round it and he loved being at home. He loved being with the children.'

'But I remember being at home with Felix, when he was small . . .' Charlie tailed off as he wrestled with the memory, before continuing. 'I loved it, but I think it's human nature for men to feel as if they aren't quite fulfilling their genetic potential if they have to rely on a woman for money.'

'But you didn't repay Liv by going out and sleeping with someone else, did you?' Martha spat, desperately trying not to sound too bitter.

'I didn't,' Charlie said quietly. 'But she did, unfortunately.'

'Would you . . .' Martha began, before hesitating, not sure if she should risk intruding too much so soon after meeting him. But then, he already knew far more intimate details about her than he could ever reveal about himself. 'Would you have forgiven Liv?'

Charlie held her gaze for a while before replying. 'Yes, I would have forgiven her. I think I did forgive her ... but would I have taken her back? I don't know. I think that's another issue.'

'So would you?' Martha's breath caught in her chest as she waited for his answer.

'Yes. Probably. But our relationship would have been so damaged ... who knows whether it would have worked.'

Martha chewed the inside of her lip. There was no doubt that whatever happened, her relationship with Jamie would be badly damaged by what he had done. Could there ever be a way back for them?

'How are you holding up, Martha?' Charlie asked now, interrupting her gloomy thoughts.

'I'm not sure I should be doing this.' She turned to look at him. 'I should really be at home with the kids.'

'Why don't you give them a call? Make the decision once you've spoken to them. It's not too late to go home if that's what you want.'

Martha smiled at Charlie gratefully. She couldn't believe how understanding, kind and patient he had been. She reached into her bag and pulled out her phone. She hadn't looked at it since she had left home that morning and had used the hotel phone to call Jamie. There were several missed calls and emails, which made her heart quicken in alarm.

She scanned through the missed call list first. There were several blocked calls, which would probably have been from Louisa, Charlie's PR, plus two calls from Lindsay. She thought back to the morning, when she had last spoken to Lindsay, just before making her horrific discovery. It was as if her life was suddenly divided into two parts: before the affair and after. Then she had felt so bad for Jamie, seeing her picture in the paper with another man. 'Pah!' she snorted aloud, drawing a quizzical look from Charlie.

'Nothing,' she said, shaking her head. She clicked onto her inbox to find that, among several others, there was an email from Jamie. The bile rose in her throat as she tried to pluck up the nerve to open it. She had a pretty good idea what it would say, but she didn't know if she could stand to read his hollow words. Taking a deep breath, she clicked on it.

My beautiful, darling Martha,
she read, and the tears flashed into her eyes before she could stop them.

I love you so much and I am so, so sorry about what I did. I hate myself for causing you such pain and I would do anything to take it back.

There are no excuses for what I did. It was madness. I never considered it an affair because I felt nothing for her, but I can see now that it was. Please believe me, though, Martha, that it is the only affair I have ever had, I promise you. And I am going to spend the rest of my life proving to you that I regret it more than anything.

I can't believe I have been such a fool to risk the relationship I have with you for something so sordid and horrible. You are my life. I can't live without you. Please give me a chance to make it right again.

I love you with all my heart.
Jamie
xxx

Martha swallowed a lump in her throat as the tears began to plop onto her jeans.

'Martha!' Charlie said, sitting up in his seat and reaching out to put his arm around her.

Martha felt too distraught to resist him and fell against his chest. 'I'm sorry,' she managed to gulp, unable to stop the onslaught of grief.

'No, no,' Charlie hushed her, stroking her hair. 'Nothing to be sorry for. You've had a terrible shock.'

After a while, Martha's tears seemed to slow and she sat up again. 'I need a tissue,' she half-smiled.

Charlie reached out and plucked three tissues from the box provided in the back of the limo. He handed them to her and waited while she blew her nose and wiped her face.

'He sent me an email,' she said, when she had composed herself enough to speak. 'That's what set me off again.'

'I gathered as much. Do you want to talk about what it said?'

Martha loved the fact that Charlie seemed to be able to judge her perfectly. He didn't pry when she didn't want him to, but he seemed to know when she needed to talk about something.

'He's so apologetic, says it's the only time it's ever happened and that he's going to spend the rest of his life making it up to me, if I'll let him.'

Charlie looked away.

'What?' Martha said. 'Why are you looking like that?'

He met her eye again. 'Nothing, really. It's just ... well, words are cheap, aren't they?'

Martha nodded slowly. He was right. Words were cheap when your actions had said something entirely different. And Jamie was a writer. He could use words so effectively. Even in the short space of time since she had last seen him, Martha felt as though Jamie was a stranger now, with a whole life that she knew nothing about. She had always assumed that he was spending his days at home working on his book or preparing meals for the children or thinking of ways to entertain them when they got in from school. Never, even in her wildest imaginings, had she thought that he might be having sex with other women behind her back. Now she had to consider that she didn't really know this person at all. Had never known him.

'I'll try calling the children,' she said, sitting back against the soft beige leather seat.

Her heart was hammering as the phone rang. She pictured it on the table in their messy hallway, with Tom and Mimi both racing to answer it first. 'Hello?' said Mimi, who had clearly won the race and sounded slightly out of breath.

'Hi sweetheart, it's me, Mum.' A wave of emotion surged upwards through Martha's body.

'Oh, hi,' said Mimi, her voice flat.

'What's the matter?' Martha sat up straighter, alarmed by Mimi's tone.

There was a long pause and for a moment Martha wondered if she had hung up. 'Where are you?' Mimi asked at last, her tone hard and accusatory.

A trickle of coldness filled Martha's belly. 'I'm on my way to the airport. How are you, darling? Are you OK?'

'No,' squeaked Mimi, before dissolving into tears.

Martha's nose tingled as her own tears threatened again. 'Sweetheart!' she cried. 'What's wrong? Why are you crying?'

'Because you're going off to LA with that bloody ... that

man! The one you were photographed leaving the hotel with,'
Mimi snarled through her hiccuping sobs.

'Oh my God!' Martha cried, leaning forward and running
her hand through her hair in a panic. Beside her, Charlie mirrored her actions and leaned forward too, looking at her with
concern.

'Well?' Mimi shouted. 'Are you going to LA with him or
not?'

'I . . . Look, Mimi, this is not anything to be worried about.'
Martha took a deep breath so that she sounded as reassuring
as possible. 'I am going to LA with him because I'm writing a
book with him and he's got a couple of really big meetings
that might be crucial. I'm following him, that's all.'

'So how come you were wearing his clothes then? The girls
at school were teasing me, saying he was your new boyfriend!'
Again, she dissolved into tears on the other end of the line.

Martha closed her eyes and tried to collect her thoughts.
'Look, darling, it was just because Dad had ironed a hole in my
dress and I had to borrow something from Charlie – didn't you
talk to Dad about it? Didn't he explain that?'

There was another long pause. 'Yes,' Mimi said at last. 'He
said the same thing.'

'Well, then, silly! I'm sorry you got teased but I promise you
that it was all perfectly innocent. There's nothing to worry
about. OK?'

'Will you get me a photo of the Hollywood sign?' Mimi
sniffed, making Martha smile. Mimi adored all things
Hollywood and often said she wanted to be an actress when
she grew up.

"Course I will. And I'll get a pic of some of the stars on the Walk of Fame.'

'Really?' Mimi cried, her tears already forgotten. 'Cool! Do you want to speak to Dad?'

Martha hesitated. Jamie was absolutely the last person she wanted to speak to but she didn't want to upset Mimi any further.

'Er, yes, OK then. Put him on. And listen, darling, I love you. You know that, don't you?'

'I know. I love you too, Mum.'

Martha heard the phone being handed over to Jamie. 'Hi,' he said, sounding sheepish.

Martha suddenly felt a surge of anger towards this man who had made such a good job of destroying her happiness. 'So, my children apparently think *I'm* the one who's doing the dirty, while their cheating bastard of a father gets off scot-free! How did that happen, do you think?'

'Martha, I swear I told them it was innocent!'

'Really?' Martha shot back sarcastically. 'Except that you also swore that you loved me and that you would never cheat on me, so we all know how much your *word* counts for! You were probably thrilled to find a way of shifting the blame for our break-up onto me.'

Martha could hear Jamie closing a door. 'Break-up?' he hissed. 'Is that what this is? Are you leaving us, Martha?'

The agony in his voice was unmistakable but it only added to Martha's fury. 'No, Jamie, I am not leaving the kids, I am leaving *you*!'

'Look, Martha ...' Jamie began, and she could hear that he

was struggling desperately to keep his emotions in check. 'Please come home. We need to talk.'

'I can't,' Martha's voice cracked as she started to cry again. 'I can't do it just yet. I can't look at you without seeing . . . It's just too raw.'

'Baby, I know,' Jamie replied, and he was crying too. 'But I have to be able to show you how sorry I am.'

'You're only sorry because you've been caught,' Martha shook her head wearily. 'Before being caught you were having a great time. You weren't sorry at all.'

Jamie didn't answer. She knew it was because she was right. She sniffed and cleared her throat. 'I need to talk to Tom. Can you put him on?'

There was a long pause. 'OK,' he said at last. 'Martha, when will you be home?'

'I don't know,' she replied truthfully. 'I don't know. When I can face the kids without losing it, I suppose.'

'What shall I tell them?'

'Just tell them I love them and I'll be home as soon as I can.'

After a few moments, Tom came on the line. 'Hi Mum,' he said brightly.

The contrast in his voice to those of Jamie and Mimi was so marked that it caught Martha by surprise and she had to swallow hard before she could speak. 'Hi, darling! How are you?'

'Fine,' Tom said cheerfully, giving the stock answer he always gave.

'How was school?' She glanced at Charlie, who was still watching her. He smiled reassuringly.

'Fine,' Tom replied again. Martha had had the same conversation with him many times in the past and it comforted her to have it now. It made her feel as though at least some things were still normal.

'That's good. Well look, darling, I've got to go away for a few days but I'll bring you something nice back, OK?'

'Cool. I'd really love the new Pokemon game for my DS . . .?'

Martha laughed. 'I'll see what I can do. Love you, darling.'

'Love you too, Mum. Bye.' Tom hung up and Martha looked up at Charlie.

'Well?' he said. 'Do you feel a bit better?'

'A bit,' she agreed.

'Are you coming with me to LA?'

Martha took a deep breath, still finding it hard to believe that she was actually doing this. 'I'm coming,' she said, hoping desperately that it was the right decision.

Chapter 16

Jamie pulled the door to Tom's room until it was open about six inches ajar, allowing a strip of light from the landing to seep in. 'Night Tom, love you,' he whispered into the darkness behind him. There was no reply. Tom was legendary for dropping off to sleep almost the moment his head hit the pillow.

Jamie made his way along the landing towards Mimi's room. The music she was listening to filtered out under the door jamb and Jamie listened for a little while before knocking.

'Come in!' she called cheerily. Jamie entered to find her sitting cross-legged on her bed reading some kind of vampire book. She was already wearing her blue and yellow pyjamas and her long blonde hair was loose, with crinkles where her plait had been during the day.

'How's the book?' he said, sitting down wearily beside her.

She closed it and looked up at him. 'It's good.'

Jamie nodded and they sat in silence for a while, listening as some American teenager belted out a song that sounded to Jamie exactly the same as all the other American teenager songs that Mimi loved so much. 'Time to turn it off and brush your teeth, I think,' he said, clapping his hand on her leg.

'Are you OK, Dad?' Mimi uncrossed her legs and shuffled forward on the bed. 'Only, you seem a bit ... I don't know, sad, I suppose.'

Tears flashed into Jamie's eyes and he blinked them away in horror. 'Me?' he said, over-brightly. 'Nah, I'm fine. Just a bit tired maybe.'

'Something's not right,' Mimi continued, causing his heart to trip with fear.

When Jamie didn't reply, she got up and switched off her iPod dock. 'I'm not stupid, you know, Dad. I know there's something wrong. Why won't you tell me what it is?'

Jamie opened his mouth to speak, then closed it again. Mimi was just eleven. Although she was a clever girl and mature for her age, she was still too young to be told what had happened. She wouldn't understand. He didn't understand it himself, so how could she? In the end, he decided to tell her a half-truth.

'Mum and I did have a bit of a row this morning, but it's honestly nothing to worry about ...'

'What was the row about?'

Jamie closed his eyes for a moment, thinking. 'Well, Mum is a bit fed up at the moment. You know ... the house is a mess, she's fed up with having to work when she'd rather be at home with you guys ... just general things that lots of couples argue about. It'll be fine, sweetheart. Honestly.' Jamie mentally crossed his fingers as he spoke, praying that what he was saying was true.

Mimi's big blue eyes bored into him as she tried to decide whether to believe him. 'Hmmm. Well, I hope you sort it out soon. I miss Mum . . .' she started to say, then stopped as her voice caught in her throat. 'I'll brush my teeth,' she added, leaving Jamie sitting on her bed.

He leaned forward and rubbed his face for what seemed like the millionth time that day. He had no idea how long Martha was going to be away, and he didn't know if he could keep up the pretence that everything was OK in front of the children. He gave himself a shake and stood up. He had to keep it together. He had no choice.

After kissing Mimi goodnight, Jamie came downstairs. Normally, at this time of night, he would be bustling about getting dinner ready for himself and Martha, but tonight there was no Martha and he had no appetite. He sat at the kitchen table and stared out into the encroaching darkness, wondering what the hell he was going to do.

He felt like he needed to talk to someone. But who? It was so hard finding male friends when you were at home all day looking after the kids. All of his old friends lived in London and they had gradually lost touch over the years anyway. As a result, he tended to gravitate towards the mothers, whose conversation he found limited if he was honest. There were a couple of other dads at the school who were in the same situation as him, but he knew that if he confided in any of them, it was only a matter of time before their wives got wind and he would inevitably become the latest piece of gossip on the school grapevine.

In the past, he would have talked to his mum. He could just

imagine the sorts of things she would be saying to him right now, but he would give anything to hear her voice and feel her presence, even if it was an angry one. He had been devastated by her death, but now, a year later, her loss seemed to hit him again with the same force as if it had been yesterday.

His relationship with his mum had been a close one; his dad had died of cancer when Jamie was just twelve, leaving his mum with three young boys to bring up alone. His brothers, Matt and Sam, had been nine and seven at the time, so, as the eldest, Jamie had been forced to take on the role of supporting his mum, and being as much of a father figure to the younger boys as he could.

Clare had never remarried, and even when Martha came on the scene, she and Jamie remained as close as ever. Clare had often said that she was grateful to Jamie for choosing Martha, who embraced and welcomed Clare's relationship with her son instead of being threatened by it.

Clare's sudden death from a brain haemorrhage had hit Martha almost as hard as it had Jamie, and she had been so understanding of his grief. Martha had loved her mother-in-law unconditionally, just as she had loved Jamie unconditionally. And he had betrayed that love in the most callous way possible.

Jamie must have nodded off, because when he awoke the sky outside had darkened to a deep navy-blue and the kitchen was in complete darkness. He stood up groggily and switched on the light, his eyes flinching at the sudden brightness. He picked up his mobile phone and looked hopefully at the screen. He had a message. He clicked on it with trepidation. It was from Martha's best friend Lindsay.

Hey babe, Martha hasn't replied to my texts today. Everything ok? X

Jamie sat down and stared at the screen, wondering what to reply. Or whether to reply. He looked at the clock on the kitchen wall. 10.15 p.m. His thumb hovered above the screen while his mind whirred. He loved Lindsay. She was a good friend to both him and Martha. Could he risk telling her what had happened? She would be livid with him but she might also be able to give him some advice.

Things not OK. Martha gone to LA. Can you come round tomorrow?

He pressed 'Send' and put his phone back down. Almost immediately it beeped again.

Working tomorrow. Shall I come now?

Jamie was about to text back to say that it was too late, but he was desperate to talk to someone and she only lived about five minutes away.

OK. I'll put the kettle on.

He pressed 'Send', before getting up and switching the lights on in the downstairs rooms. The house felt cold, despite the fact that it was summer, and he climbed the stairs two at a time to get a jumper. He had only just put it on when the doorbell rang. Lindsay must have driven like a lunatic to arrive so quickly.

'What the hell's going on, Jamie?' she said, as soon as he opened the door.

Jamie stood back to let Lindsay into the house. She was a

tall woman and quite large with it, so she had a very forceful stride which seemed to brook no argument. Much like her personality, Jamie thought, as he watched her head straight for the kitchen where she immediately filled the kettle and flicked it on. 'I knew you wouldn't have done it,' she explained when he raised his eyebrows at her.

Jamie sat down at the table, suddenly unsure how he would even begin to explain to Lindsay what had happened.

'So?' she said, getting two cups out of the cupboard and putting teabags into them while she waited for the kettle to boil. 'What's happened then?'

Jamie swallowed hard and tried to speak but he couldn't get the words out.

'Jamie?' Lindsay came over and sat opposite him, her pretty face scrunched up in confusion. Impatiently, she pulled her thick, highlighted hair back from her face and deftly tied it into a knot. 'Is it to do with the photos?'

Jamie's head shot up and he looked at Lindsay in panic. 'You know about them?'

'Yes!' she snapped. 'Of course I know. I was the one who rang Martha this morning to tell her they were in the paper. Don't you remember?'

'Oh God,' Jamie exhaled as he spoke. 'No, it's not about those photos.'

Lindsay frowned heavily, her pale blue eyes hooded with suspicion. 'Well, if it's not about those photos, what photos *is* it about?'

'Martha found some photos ... on my computer,' Jamie began. His throat was so dry he could barely speak. He got up and took a glass from the cupboard before filling it with tap water.

'Porn?' Relief crossed Lindsay's features. 'Is that all? I'll talk to Martha. Lots of blokes—'

'No,' Jamie cut her off, having gulped down the whole glass. 'Not porn. Well, not exactly . . .'

Lindsay's frown returned and she shook her head, causing the knot to unravel and her hair to fall loose around her shoulders again. 'I don't know what you mean, Jamie. Were they porn photos or not?'

Jamie refilled the glass and took several more gulps before replying. 'Yes, they were . . . but unfortunately they weren't photos of strangers.'

Realisation seemed to dawn and Lindsay stood up so that she was facing him. 'Then who was in the photos?'

Her voice had the same eerie coldness as Martha's that morning, and once again Jamie felt a shiver of fear shoot through him. 'Me,' he said in a small voice.

'You and Martha, I hope?' Lindsay's face was set in a hard grimace and her voice was flinty.

Jamie took a deep breath and tried to meet her eye, but it was impossible and he looked down again. 'No. Me and someone else.'

'Oh my God,' Lindsay gasped, sinking back down into her chair. 'Oh my God, Jamie, what the hell have you done?'

'It meant nothing . . .' Jamie started to say, but Lindsay was on her feet before he finished speaking, crossing the kitchen and slapping him hard across the face. He clamped his hand to his cheek, where the scratches Martha had inflicted

141

earlier were now zinging with pain, along with the sting of the slap.

'That poor, poor girl,' Lindsay hissed, her face contorted in fury.

'I know.' Jamie put his hands over his eyes to try to hide his shame. 'I've fucked up, Linds, I've really fucked up and I don't know what the hell to do.' He was shaking so much he had to crouch down in case he fell.

Lindsay watched him coldly for several minutes until, eventually, she stomped over to the window sill and grabbed a handful of tissues, which she thrust at him. He hadn't even realised he was crying. 'Get up,' she said, her voice full of disgust. 'Stop feeling sorry for yourself and tell me exactly what happened.'

Jamie slumped into a chair. He blew his nose and wiped his face while Lindsay finished making the cups of tea. She banged a cup down in front of him, so hard that several splashes of tea slopped over the rim. She sat down opposite him and glared at him so furiously that he could feel the white-hot anger coming off her in waves, and it was several minutes before he could find the courage to look up and meet her eye.

'Well?' she demanded. 'Who is she?'

'No-one,' he replied. 'She's no-one. Oh God, Linds, I don't know what to do ...'

'When you say "she's no-one", what exactly do you mean by that? If you were having an affair with her then it—'

'It wasn't like that!' he interrupted her, shaking his head. 'It was just sex.'

'Oh please!' spat Lindsay. 'That old chestnut! Presumably you told her your wife didn't understand you as well?'

Jamie shook his head again. 'No. I didn't tell her anything. We didn't really talk. We just used to meet and have sex.'

Lindsay's mouth dropped open as if she was going to say something but she closed it just as quickly. The ticking of the clock on the kitchen wall sounded heavy in the thick silence. Jamie realised that he had never noticed it before.

'How long?' Lindsay said, after sipping her tea. She couldn't meet Jamie's eye.

'About six months ...' He said, closed his eyes at the memory. 'God, what have I done?'

'Yes, what *have* you done, you arsehole! Poor Martha. I just keep thinking about how she must have felt, seeing those pictures ...'

'Don't,' Jamie cut her off. 'Please don't.'

'She *trusted* you, Jamie! She never, ever doubted you and neither did I. Why did you do it?'

Jamie threw his hands open helplessly. 'I've been trying to answer that question myself ...'

'Too much money and too much time on your hands!' Lindsay snapped. 'That's what I think the trouble was. If you'd had to go out to work every day and support your family like most men do, you wouldn't have had the time to be looking for other women to have sex with.'

Jamie's face burned. He knew he deserved the verbal onslaught but it was so humiliating.

'How did Martha react?'

Jamie bit his lip and shook his head again. 'It was awful ...'

he said, recoiling at the memory. 'She was ... destroyed. I think it might have done less damage if I'd taken a baseball bat to her.'

'I just want to see her,' Lindsay said, wiping away a tear. 'To give her a hug and be there for her. She must be in despair for her to have run off to LA like that. It's so unlike her.'

'She's gone with Charlie Simmons ...' Jamie hated the little spark of pleasure that he could see ignite in Lindsay's eyes. 'She said she didn't feel able to come home yet in case she fell apart in front of the kids. And she couldn't face looking at me.'

'I don't blame her. I feel the same way and it's not even me you cheated on.'

'Please, Lindsay,' Jamie beseeched her. He stood up and walked over to the French doors. The garden was in darkness now. 'I'm desperate here,' he added, folding his arms across himself, suddenly feeling cold. 'I know I deserve to be given a hard time but I also need to know what to do. I need your advice on how to get her back. At least so that she'll talk to me and I can try and prove to her that I know I've done wrong and it will never, ever happen again. I love her so much ...' He said, dissolved into tears of despair again. 'I can't lose her. I just can't.'

Lindsay didn't reply but he could sense that her expression had softened slightly. He turned to look at her again. 'Tell me what to do.'

She shook her head and shrugged. 'I don't know, Jamie. She's probably in shock and isn't thinking straight. Maybe you need to go after her?'

'I can't! What about the children?'

'Oh God, the children!' cried Lindsay, putting her hand over her mouth as her eyes widened in horror. 'Do they know what's happened?'

'No. Mimi knows something's wrong but she doesn't know what it is. Ironically, she thinks there's something going on between Martha and Charlie Simmons, because of the photo in the paper.'

'I hope you put her straight!' snapped Lindsay, snatching up a napkin and distractedly tearing it into tiny pieces.

'Yes, Lindsay, I put her straight,' Jamie sighed. 'But the girls at school were talking about it and it's made her suspicious.'

'How very convenient for you,' Lindsay sneered, standing up and rubbing her back. 'Look, Jamie, I'm going to go home. I'll have a think, and I'll keep trying Martha. I really want to speak to her and make sure she's OK.'

Jamie nodded slowly. He felt faint with tiredness and grief, but he also felt relieved that he had been able to talk to someone, even if that someone now hated his guts.

'Please let me know if you hear from her,' he pleaded, as he followed her to the front door. 'And please let me know if you can think of any way at all that I can try to get us through this.'

'I will,' Lindsay said, without turning round. 'Not that you deserve it.'

After he had let Lindsay out, Jamie climbed the stairs and walked wearily into the bedroom, where he pulled up sharply. A feeling of emptiness enveloped him as he looked at the bed.

The bed where he and Martha had laughed, kissed, had sex and made their two perfect babies.

Suddenly he couldn't bear the thought of getting into the bed without her. He grabbed the duvet and a pillow and threw them onto the hard wooden floor. He wanted some way of punishing himself and he decided that this was as good a way as any to start.

He plugged his phone into the charger and put it beside him, just in case Martha should call or text him during the night. Then he lay down and prepared for what he already knew would be the worst night of his life.

Chapter 17

'There's someone at the door, Felix!' Liv shouted from the kitchen.

Felix came into the kitchen looking bemused. 'Why don't you answer it then? Or Juanita?' he said, frowning up at Liv, who was sitting at the steel and granite island, reading a magazine and drinking tea.

'Because I think *you* should,' she grinned.

Felix's dark eyes widened. 'Is it a delivery for me?' he said, a gappy smile splitting his face in half.

'Might be!' Liv replied in a sing-song, teasing voice.

Felix didn't need telling twice and spun on his heel. Liv grinned to herself and climbed off her stool, following Felix towards the front door. She felt a tingle of excitement and curiosity herself; excitement at seeing Charlie, and curiosity as to whether he had brought his new girlfriend with him.

Felix swung the huge, heavy wooden door open and screamed as he saw Charlie standing on the step, a large wrapped parcel at his feet.

'Dad!' he cried, leaping over the parcel and straight into Charlie's outstretched arms.

Liv felt her eyes watering at the reminder of how much love there was between her son and his father. Over Felix's head, Charlie met her eye and smiled. It was the first time since their break-up that he had looked at her properly, and certainly the first time he had smiled at her. She nodded by way of reply.

'Hey, Charlie,' she said, as cheerfully as she could. 'Why don't you come on in?' She stood back as if to usher him through the door.

Charlie hesitated and placed Felix on the floor again. 'You sure? We could just wait in the car while you get Felix's things ready?'

'We?' Liv raised a quizzical eyebrow.

Charlie smiled again. 'My, er, friend, Martha, is with me.'

'Well, go and get her!' Liv cried, over-enthusiastically. 'Bring her in for tea.'

Charlie hesitated again as he looked back at the car. 'OK then.' He rubbed Felix's hair. 'You go on in with your mum, buddy. I'll be right back.'

Liv loved the way Charlie's British accent immediately became more Americanised as soon as he was with Felix, helping his son to reconnect with him the minute he saw him.

Felix bent down and scooped up the parcel, before heading back inside with Liv. 'Who's he got with him?' he whispered, as they headed for the day room that opened out from the kitchen.

Liv glanced back to make sure she wasn't being overheard. 'His new friend.'

'Is it a girl?'

'Woman, yes.'

'Then it's his new girlfriend, isn't it?'

Liv shrugged. 'I'm not quite sure, honey. Oh, look, here they come now.' She ran back towards the door as Charlie and a woman hovered on the doorstep. 'Come in! Come in!' she said, trying to sound as welcoming as possible. They stepped through the door and headed warily down the long, wide, double-height hallway.

Liv closed the door behind them and followed, looking curiously at the woman. She had obviously just stepped off an eleven-hour flight, but even so, she looked terrible. In the photo her hair had been thick and glossy. Now it hung in gnarled tangles. She didn't appear to be wearing any make-up and her jeans and Converse sneakers didn't even look particularly clean. She looked generally grubby and dish-evelled.

As they reached the day room the woman turned. 'I'm really sorry.' She looked at Liv with a slightly pleading expression. 'I haven't introduced myself. I'm Martha. Martha Lamont.'

Liv took Martha's hand and shook it, still reeling at how terrible she looked. She hoped for her sake that she and Charlie hadn't been papped as they landed at LAX. 'Lovely to meet you,' she said, glancing at Charlie as she spoke.

Charlie was watching Martha with a concerned expression. He seemed protective of her in a way that reminded Liv of how he had been with her. Before she threw it back in his face and broke his heart.

149

'Dad!' Felix yelled, breaking the tension. 'You got me an Arsenal kit!'

All three adults whirled around to look at the little boy, who was delightedly holding up a red football strip, boots and a leather football. Liv looked at Charlie and grinned, shaking her head. 'You boys and your football!'

'Not football, Mum, *soccer*!' Felix corrected her, drawing a laugh from both Charlie and Martha.

Martha walked over to Felix and knelt down beside him. 'I've got a little boy who's just a bit older than you. He loves football . . . I mean, *soccer*, too.'

Felix looked up at her curiously. 'Who does he support? Does he support Arsenal like me and my dad?'

Martha smiled and Liv marvelled at how much it changed her whole face in an instant. 'No,' she said. 'He supports Manchester United. Most of the time.'

Liv looked at Charlie and motioned for him to follow her towards the kitchen area of the big open-plan space. 'She seems nice,' she said carefully.

'Yes,' Charlie agreed, leaning against the island while Liv put the kettle on. She waited for him to continue but he didn't. He seemed lost in thought.

'Would you like to stay and have something to eat? I could get Juanita to make something or we could get a take-out?'

'Thanks, but no. I think we'll get off to the hotel. Martha's exhausted. She didn't sleep on the plane.'

Liv busied herself making tea, her mind whirring. She couldn't work out what was going on here. Martha didn't seem very happy, considering she had just been flown to LA first class by her new film-star boyfriend. And she had mentioned a son, which confused Liv even more.

'You know,' she began, handing Charlie a mug of tea, 'this might sound like a weird suggestion but you guys could always stay here. It might be less unsettling for Felix and we've got plenty of room.' She motioned around her, as if to convey the size of the place.

Charlie didn't answer at first and Liv wondered if he had even heard her. Finally, he spoke. 'When are you planning to leave?' he asked, fixing her with those dark eyes that she had loved so much. Still loved.

'Tomorrow. So it shouldn't be too awkward.' She half-laughed as she spoke.

Charlie looked back towards Martha and Felix, who were still sitting on the floor, chatting like old friends.

'I'm not sure. How do you think Danny would feel about your ex-husband camping out at his house?'

Liv hesitated. She wanted to say that it was the least Danny could do to make up for stealing Charlie's wife, but instead she shrugged. 'I'm sure he wouldn't mind.'

'And you're still sure you're going to surprise him like that? What if you catch him out?'

Liv looked sharply at Felix, who had stopped talking for a moment and was watching her and Charlie curiously. 'I'm still going,' she replied, trying to hide her annoyance. 'What do you think about staying here then?' she added, keen to change the subject.

'I'll talk to Martha,' Charlie said, taking another mug of tea from Liv and heading over to Martha, who took the mug gratefully. 'Thanks. I really need this,' she said, taking a sip.

'So … Liv has suggested we stay here while we're in LA and she's in Hawaii …' Charlie began, sitting down on the floor beside Martha. 'What do you think?'

'Oh yeah!' Felix shouted. 'That'd be so cool! Please stay here, Dad!'

Charlie smiled. 'Well, let's see what Martha thinks first, shall we?'

Martha turned towards Liv, who had come over from the kitchen. 'I think it seems a bit … of an imposition. Maybe you could stay here, Charlie, and I could go to the hotel?'

'No!' Liv cried. 'I wouldn't hear of it. You can't stay in two different places.'

Martha's eyes flashed in alarm. 'No, really, it would be fine. Wouldn't it, Charlie?'

'It would be fine …' he began. 'But it sort of defeats the object of you coming with me to work on my memoirs, don't you think?'

'Oh,' said Martha, as if she hadn't thought of it before. 'Yes, maybe you're right. I had totally forgotten why I was here.'

Liv frowned to herself. This was getting weirder and weirder.

Chapter 18

Martha walked out of the French doors into the surprisingly chilly darkness of the LA night. The wide stone terrace opened onto an illuminated turquoise infinity pool that looked as if it was dangling over the Hollywood hills, ready to drench the parched scrubland at any moment.

She wandered towards the pool and sat on the edge, dipping her toes into the deliciously warm water. All around her, the sound of insects filled the still night air, a cacophony of noise against the backdrop of suspended silence.

She felt better now that she had taken a shower and changed into some clean shorts, a t-shirt and sweater that Charlie's assistant, Jess, had gone out and bought for her before they left. Goodness knows what Charlie had told her, but somehow she had managed to buy Martha exactly what she would have chosen for herself: a selection of shorts, t-shirts, jeans, dresses and skirts, all in exactly the right sizes and styles that Martha liked.

Under normal circumstances, Martha would never have dreamt of accepting anything from Charlie, let alone a first-class

153

plane ticket and a suitcase full of brand-new clothes and make-up. But these weren't normal circumstances and Martha was no longer the person she had been; the person who would have protested furiously that she could buy her own things, thank you very much. Now she felt unable to object about anything and was being carried along on a wave of unreality.

She looked up as she heard a noise from the house behind her. Liv was emerging through the doors clutching two glasses. She made her way towards Martha and handed her one. 'Gin and tonic,' she explained, smiling. 'It's another of my little traditions that helps me to feel less homesick.' She sat down beside Martha and dipped her toes into the water so that their feet were side by side.

'Where's Charlie?' Martha asked, taking a sip of her drink and gasping at the strength of it. It was almost half gin.

Liv took a long sip, seemingly unaware that it was so strong. 'With Felix. They're both so happy to be together again.'

Martha looked down through the blurred water at Liv's feet in distracted fascination. They were the feet of someone who was used to pedicures. They were the feet of a film star.

'Are you OK?' Liv asked, after a while, as Martha continued to gaze at her feet.

Martha shrugged. 'I don't know.'

Liv nodded but didn't say any more, and the two women sat side by side in comfortable silence, sipping their gin and tonics, each of them deep in thought.

Liv had ordered pizza for them all earlier in the evening, but Martha had had no appetite and had only nibbled a slice before almost falling asleep at the table. Liv had shown her to a bedroom then, saying, 'I'll put you and Charlie in here, if that's ok ...' Despite her desperate tiredness, Martha had gasped in horror and was just about to explain to Liv that she had got the wrong end of the stick when Charlie appeared.

'Thanks, Liv, but we need a room each, if that's ok,' he said easily. 'I might have a nap myself actually,' he added.

Liv had flushed with embarrassment but had quickly recovered, showing him to a bedroom further down the hall.

Martha didn't even remember lying down, but when she awoke two hours later, she did feel slightly better. Until she remembered where she was and what had happened.

'Has Charlie told you?' she asked Liv, breaking the long silence and looking up at this woman who was so famous, yet somehow so very familiar. 'I mean, has he told you what happened before we came?'

Liv shook her head. 'No. We're not ... well, we're not really on such good terms any more. You know, ever since ...' she tailed off.

Martha held her gaze and waited for her to continue.

'So I don't think he would confide in me, is what I'm saying,' Liv concluded.

Martha sighed and looked back into the pool. It didn't matter if you were a VIP or plain old Martha Lamont, the pain and the hurt were exactly the same. Charlie had felt the desperation that she was feeling now when this woman had decided that she didn't want him any more.

'You're so lucky,' Liv said suddenly, causing Martha to look up in surprise.

'How so?'

Liv smiled ruefully. 'Oh, I don't know ... having the freedom to do what you want without the press dogging your every move, describing you as fat if you put on three ounces, calling you a bitch because of who you fall in love with – that sort of thing. If you're going to be with Charlie, make damn sure you protect your privacy. Once it's gone, it's gone for good.'

For a moment Martha couldn't think what to say. The idea that Liv Mason, with her famous boyfriend, her successful career and her multi-million dollar home, could be jealous of her was breathtaking.

'I don't think it's ever likely to be a problem,' she said at last, frowning slightly.

'Are you ...?' Liv began, and Martha could see a tiny pulse throbbing in her neck. 'Are you and Charlie not together?'

Martha half-smiled. 'God, no!' she said, then immediately felt disloyal to Charlie. 'I mean, I only met him for the first time the day before yesterday,' she added. As she spoke, Martha thought back to just two short days ago, when her life was so simple and so happy. Before her whole world had fallen in on itself and left her wrung out and empty.

'I'm ghosting his memoirs,' she continued by way of explanation. 'So I've got to hang out with him for a bit. I'm researching him, that's all.'

Liv frowned, unsure why she felt relieved by the news. 'Oh, I thought there was more to it than that! I don't mean to sound rude, but you don't seem very fired up by the project. And Charlie is ...'

'What?' Martha prompted, when Liv had hesitated for too long.

'*Different*,' Liv said carefully. 'He's sort of protective of you. Reminds me of how he used to be with me.' She paused again and Martha again detected that note of envy in her voice. 'Are you *sure* there's nothing going on between you? Not even a spark?'

Martha swallowed. 'Something happened after we met that has made it very difficult with my husband . . .' she began.

Liv nodded knowingly. 'The photos.'

Martha didn't have the energy to correct her. 'Let's just say the photos didn't help. So . . . you're off to Hawaii tomorrow?' she said, desperately wanting to change the subject.

Liv nodded. 'Yup.'

'Sounds exciting.'

Liv looked at Martha and smiled. 'I hope so.'

Martha thought Liv's eyes were like deep pools of sorrow. There was angst and disquiet behind her stare. She also noticed that Liv had drained her drink in seconds, while she had managed only a couple of sips.

'What's he like – Danny, I mean?' she asked, wondering if he was the source of her troubles.

Liv's face lit up. 'He's . . . well, he's great, actually. Very cool and not at all how you think he'd be. He's—' She stopped speaking suddenly. 'Oh my God,' she said, her expression dropping once more. 'What am I thinking? You're a journalist!' She shook her head as if furious at her own stupidity.

Martha reached across and grabbed Liv's hand. 'Believe me,' she said, fixing Liv with an intense gaze. 'I am more grateful than you can imagine for you welcoming me into your home the way you have, when I am at possibly the lowest point in my own life. I won't betray you, I promise. Believe it or not, journalists are the most discreet people ever when they have to be.'

Liv picked up her glass and gave it a disappointed stare, as if she had only just realised it was empty. 'OK, fair enough.' She stood up and brushed herself down. Her bare feet left perfect wet footprints on the stone terrace surrounding the pool, as she began to walk slightly unsteadily back towards the house, leaving behind a trail of Hermès scent. 'Oh, and Martha?' she said, turning back. 'While you're feeling in a benign mood towards me . . .'

Martha looked up. 'Yes?'

'Don't be too hard on me in his memoirs, will you?'

Chapter 19

Jamie opened his eyes and looked around in surprise, momentarily forgetting where he was and why he was lying on the floor of the bedroom. His back was stiff where the wide wooden floorboards had refused to yield to his spine during the long night.

A stark strip of light was slicing the gloom over the top of the blackout blind. Despite the early hour, he could already tell that it was going to be a beautiful day. The sort of day he usually loved, especially if Martha was around to share it with him. Often they would see the kids off to school and then pick up a couple of coffees and go and lay on the beach, reading. One of the advantages of a freelance life.

He picked up his phone and rolled onto his back to check whether he had any messages from Martha. There was just one message, from Lindsay, sent at 5.04 a.m.

Can't sleep for worrying about Martha. Think you should go to LA and get her. She must be in pieces. PS, you are such a f**kwit!

Jamie closed his eyes and laid the phone back on the floor.

That was being kind. There weren't the words to describe what he was. Eventually, he picked his phone up again.

What about the kids? he texted.

Lindsay was right. He needed to go to LA to try to get Martha back. He needed to prove to her that he was serious. But he couldn't just walk out and leave the kids home alone. And he had to be careful not to alarm them or alert them that something was seriously wrong between their parents. His phone rumbled on the floorboards beside him and he snatched it up hopefully.

'It's me,' Lindsay said in her brusque, northern twang.

Jamie's heart plummeted. He had been hoping it was Martha. Even though he was terrified of what she might say to him, he was more terrified of her not calling at all. 'Oh, hi,' he managed.

'What about Martha's mum? Couldn't she come down and look after them for a few days?'

'But she'll want to know why,' Jamie's insides churned at the thought of Jane's wrath if she were to discover what he had done to her only daughter.

'Then grow some balls and bloody well tell her!' Lindsay snapped. 'If she gives you a hard time, tough. You deserve it.'

'Christ, Lindsay,' Jamie sighed. 'I'm not trying to wheedle out of anything here. I know what I've done is terrible ...'

'The worst,' Lindsay hissed.

Jamie continued, trying to ignore her. 'If I tell Jane the truth, she might refuse to have the kids. She might think Martha's better off without me and not want me to go chasing across the world after her.'

'She won't. Jane's a grown-up. She'll give you a hard time,

sure, but she won't refuse to have the kids. You know she won't.'

Jamie thought about it. He was absolutely petrified at the idea of confessing all to Jane, who scared him even when she was feeling benevolent towards him. 'I'll think about it,' he sighed.

'Well don't think too long – you need to go and get her.' She hung up without saying goodbye.

Jamie rolled onto all fours and stood up stiffly. He went out onto the landing, where he met Tom coming back from his regular early-morning visit to the bathroom. 'Hey champ,' he smiled, ruffling Tom's already dishevelled hair.

'Hey,' Tom replied, raising a lazy hand by way of salute as he headed for the stairs.

'Listen, Tom,' Jamie began. 'What would you think about Granny coming to look after you for a few days?'

Tom looked back at Jamie and shrugged nonchalantly. 'Fine,' he said, before continuing down the stairs.

'Why, where are you going?' said Mimi, coming out of her room and startling Jamie.

'Um, well, I thought I might go to LA to meet Mum for a few days.' Jamie was aware that he couldn't meet Mimi's suspicious gaze.

'Why? You don't usually go.'

Jamie sighed. Mimi's radar was so finely tuned that it was nigh on impossible to get anything past her. Unable to answer her straightaway, he reached out and pulled her into his embrace, resting his chin on the top of her silky blonde hair, which smelt of sleep and shampoo. 'Well, you know that I mentioned we

161

had a bit of a row yesterday? I just thought I would surprise her by going out there, to show that things are cool between us.'

'But *are* things cool between you?' Mimi murmured into his chest. 'Because I don't think they are. I think,' she said, pulling away from Jamie and looking up at him, 'that she has run off with Charlie bloody buggery Simmons and that you want to go out there and have a fight with him to get her back'

Jamie almost smiled but his mouth wouldn't let him. 'She hasn't run off with Charlie bloody buggery Simmons and I'm not going to have a fight with *anyone*. I just want to see her and show her how much I love her.'

Mimi's eyes narrowed but she shrugged. 'You're obviously not going to tell me what's really going on ... but I would be fine for Granny to come down for a few days to look after us. In fact, I'd like to see her.'

'Thanks, darling.' Jamie stroked her face tenderly and cursed himself for the millionth time that he could have put the happiness of the three people he loved most in the world in such jeopardy.

He went downstairs and prepared breakfast for the children, then set to work on their packed lunches, all the while trying to pluck up the courage to call Jane. On autopilot, he printed out some puzzles from the Internet and put them in each of their lunchboxes, grimacing with shame as he realised that because of what had happened yesterday, he had completely forgotten to put anything in. He knew he had to try to restore normality as quickly as possible. Mimi was already suspicious, but if he could just get through the next day or so, he might get away with it. At least as far as the children were concerned.

162

He picked up the landline phone and scrolled through the pre-set numbers until he came to Jane's. With a shaking hand, he pressed 'Dial'.

'Hello?' Jane answered as curtly as she always did, her voice a combination of suspicion and worry.

'Jane, it's Jamie,' he began.

'What's wrong? What's happened?' she said immediately, sounding panicked.

'No! Nothing's happened. Well, nothing terrible. I mean, nothing that I can really go into over the phone . . .' Jamie was rambling and could feel the sweat starting to bead on his forehead. 'I just need your help with something . . .'

'OK,' Jane replied carefully. It was rare for Jamie to call her, let alone ask for her help, and he could tell that she didn't trust him.

'Martha's had to go to LA for a few days, and I was thinking of going out there to surprise her.'

There was a pause. 'Are you sure that's a good idea?' Jane said. 'Presumably she's working, so she might not want to be distracted?'

'I think she would quite like me to come,' Jamie lied. 'She's feeling a bit homesick and she's not working twenty-four hours a day, so we'd have some time to be together.' He hoped he sounded convincing.

'Um, well, I suppose I could,' Jane said after another interminable pause. 'I'll need to rearrange a few things. When were you thinking of going?'

'As soon as possible,' Jamie replied, trying not to feel

frustrated at his mother-in-law's lack of enthusiasm. She didn't get to see the children that often. Surely she should be delighted by the opportunity to spend some time with them? 'Could you come now?' he prompted.

'*Now?*' Jane repeated, sounding aghast. 'Couldn't you have given me a bit more notice?'

'I only just thought of it!' Jamie cried through gritted teeth. Now that he had decided to go, he wanted to get on a plane as quickly as possible.

Jane sighed heavily, as if the weight of the world was now resting on her shoulders. 'Oh, OK then. I suppose you'll want me to drive myself down?'

'That would be great,' Jamie admitted. He had so much to do and such a short space of time in which to do it that taking a couple of hours out to drive to Surrey would be an almighty nuisance.

'Fine,' Jane said, with a large sigh that suggested it wasn't really fine but that she would put up with it.

Jamie hung up, then logged onto the computer to see about getting a flight. His heart had started beating faster and he felt the first spark of optimism since Martha had made her awful discovery. He felt as though he was doing something positive. Something to show her how serious he was about winning her back.

Having booked his flight, he texted Lindsay.

Leaving for LA today. Jane coming to look after the kids.

Normally, he would have signed off with a kiss, but he felt that Lindsay probably wouldn't appreciate it under the circumstances.

Just as he was waiting for a reply, Mimi came into the kitchen, dressed and ready for school.

'I've booked my flight and Granny's coming,' he told her, smiling reassuringly.

'OK,' Mimi said with a disconsolate sigh.

'Hey,' Jamie looked at her closely. 'Everything's going to be OK, you know?'

Mimi nodded without returning his gaze. 'I'd better go,' she added, picking up her lunchbox and heading for the door.

Jamie watched her go guiltily. 'Love you,' he said.

'Whatever,' she replied, closing the door behind her without a backward glance.

Just then, his phone beeped.

What do you want? A bloody medal?

Jamie shook his head at Lindsay's text. Every single one of the women in his life hated him.

By the time Jane arrived, Jamie was packed and raring to go. He watched out of the window as his mother-in-law pulled onto the drive and climbed out of her Ford Fiesta, looking around her with a slightly disdainful air.

'Hi Jane!' Jamie called, as he opened the front door and walked over to greet her with a stilted kiss on each cheek. Jane was a very attractive woman in her early sixties with shoulder-length brown hair that was only just beginning to be flecked with grey, and a slim, toned figure that any woman would envy.

But even though she had only ever been pleasant to him, Jamie was terrified of her. Her grey-green eyes seemed to bore

165

into him in a way that always made him feel as if she could see right through him. And sure enough, as she walked into the kitchen and sat down at the table, once again he felt himself floundering in the spotlight of her incisive gaze.

'So what's going on then, James?' she said matter-of-factly.

Jamie's mouth dropped open, then closed again.

'And don't say "nothing" because I won't believe you,' Jane added.

'Phew ...' Jamie exhaled as he sat down and faced her. 'Well, I don't know why you would think something was wrong ...' he stammered, playing for time.

'You've been married to my daughter for all these years and never once have you felt the need to race across the world to see her at a moment's notice when she's on an assignment. There's obviously something wrong. You don't have to tell me what it is but I suspect I can guess.'

Jamie swallowed. There was never any possibility of pulling the wool over Jane's eyes. She was like a sniffer dog for the truth.

'OK,' he shrugged, resigned to having to confess. 'OK, I'll tell you. Before she left ... Martha found out that I had ...' he tailed off again, unable to find the words.

'That you had had an affair,' Jane finished the sentence for him. Her face remained impassive.

'It was nothing,' Jamie insisted, shaking his head. 'It meant nothing.'

'I hope you didn't tell Martha that!' Jane snapped.

Jamie frowned in confusion. 'Yes, I did,' he said, chewing his lip nervously. 'Why?'

'Because it's pathetic, that's why!' Jane snapped. 'Did you or did you not have sex more than once with someone other than Martha?'

'Oh God,' Jamie groaned.

'Well?' Jane pushed. 'Did you?'

Miserably, Jamie nodded his head. 'Yes,' he mumbled.

'Then it was a bloody affair!' Jane hissed. 'You claiming that "it meant nothing"', she made speechmarks with her fingers while simultaneously shooting Jamie a look of pure disgust, 'only makes it worse. You need to man up and admit that you're a cheating little shit and do whatever you can to make it up to Martha. And after everything she's done for you too!'

Jamie had always known that Jane was feisty but he had never seen her so fierce.

'Well, that's what I'm trying to do . . .' he mumbled, when he found the ability to speak again.

'And what about the woman?' Jane spat.

'What woman?'

'The one you've been having an affair with!' Jane's eyes blazed with exasperation as she spoke.

'What about her?' Jamie shook his head, unsure what Jane was getting at.

'Have you told her it's over?'

'Yes! No! Well, not exactly . . . I mean,' he added, as Jane made as if she was going to leap across the table and hit him, 'I mean that I didn't need to "end it" because it wasn't a relationship.'

'How long did it last?'

'Six months,' Jamie admitted sheepishly.

'Well then it was a bloody relationship! Just like it was a bloody affair! God, you're pathetic ...' she glared at him malevolently.

Jamie took a deep breath. 'Look, Jane,' he began, trying to meet her eye. 'I know that what I've done is bad. I'm not trying to wriggle out of anything. All I'm saying is that apart from ... well, apart from the sex, I had no kind of relationship with this woman. I don't know her at all, really. She won't care that it's over because there was nothing else there.'

Jane blinked slowly and deliberately, as if she was weighing up whether or not to believe him. She must have decided to give him the benefit of the doubt because eventually she nodded. 'OK, well you should probably get going,' she said, standing up stiffly.

Jamie stood up on wobbly legs. 'Yes,' he agreed. 'Are you sure you'll be OK with the kids? I've left all the instructions about their after-school clubs and lunches and—'

'I'll be fine,' Jane cut him off firmly, her normal composure now apparently restored. 'Take as long as you need,' she added awkwardly.

Jamie hesitated, unsure whether or not to embrace her, but decided that Jane wasn't normally one for hugs, let alone when she had just discovered that he had cheated on her daughter.

'Well, I guess I'll be off then.' He headed gratefully for the front door, where his bag was packed and waiting. He snatched it up and closed the door behind him, suddenly desperate to get started on the most important journey of his life.

Chapter 20

Charlie knew as soon as he woke up that it was still ridiculously early, but he couldn't sleep any longer and his body clock was all over the place. He glanced around the room he was sleeping in. It was white and minimalist, very LA. He felt as though he should have been more ill at ease, staying in the home his ex-wife shared with her boyfriend, but he had been too tired last night to argue and was actually quite grateful to Liv for her suggestion that he and Martha stay here while she was away. But this morning he was filled with a renewed sense of unreality about the situation.

He was worried about Martha. He had encouraged her to come with him because he recognised in her all the same feelings he had experienced four years ago and he felt sorry for her; now he wasn't so sure it was the right thing to have done. She looked so worn out, so stressed and devastated that he was scared she might have some sort of breakdown and he would feel entirely responsible.

Martha hadn't slept at all on the plane, despite being in the first-class compartment with free-flowing champagne, the best food and wine on tap and a cosy bed-pod to snuggle up in. But every time he woke up and looked over at her, she was wrapped tightly in her duvet and staring glassily into space. She didn't watch any movies or read a book. She didn't even eat or drink anything other than water. She just stared.

With a shudder, Charlie thought back to his own journey home to the UK after Liv had left him, and he knew that he had behaved in exactly the same way. It was impossible to think about anything else, let alone read or eat or talk. Heartbreak was an utterly debilitating illness, impacting on both your physical and mental health.

Charlie rubbed his face in an effort to erase the hideous memories and rolled out of bed. The sandstone tiles felt deliciously cool beneath his bare feet as he padded to the vast bathroom, listening out for any signs of life in the rest of the house, but all he could hear was the whirring of the air conditioning.

He peered at himself in the mirror above the sink. Despite his lack of sleep, he was surprised to see that he looked less tired and anxious than usual and that his skin appeared to be glowing with good health. He knew why. It was the only medicine that ever worked for him and it was the only one he couldn't get on prescription. It was Felix. Being with his son was like a drug that nourished and revitalised him in a way that nothing else could. As soon as he held the boy in his arms and kissed his smooth cheek, it was as if his internal battery was instantly recharged and he felt as though he could take on anyone or anything.

He had spent four long, draining years aching for the

day-to-day contact that he had been able to have in Felix's early years and now he wanted to have that again; he deserved it and he needed it. It had never occurred to him to go for custody at the beginning. The shock and the stress of the break-up meant that he couldn't think clearly about anything but trying to get through the next day.

He tensed as he thought about Liv. She would fight him, he knew that. But he had been Felix's main carer and had turned down several acting jobs to look after his son, whereas Liv had put her career first and then run off with her leading man without a second thought about what was best for her child's wellbeing. And, more importantly, he wasn't entirely sure how stable Liv was right now. She seemed to be drinking too much and, having suffered from depression in the past, Charlie suspected that she might be on the verge of succumbing to its grip once again. And with all the rumours of Danny's infidelity, he was fairly certain that he and Liv wouldn't be together much longer, which only strengthened his resolve. It would mean Felix was in an unstable environment with an unstable mother. Surely no judge in the world would decide that he was better off with her than with his devoted father?

A little voice at the back of his mind whispered that Liv was a good mother to Felix, but he pushed it aside. He had let her have things her way for too long because he was still in love with her. Well, not any more. He would probably always love her but he wasn't *in love* with her now. The hurt and pain she had inflicted was beginning to fade at last and he felt as though he was finally starting to get over her, to move on with his life.

He padded out into the hallway and blinked at the light, which even through the customary smog that hung over LA in the early mornings was still somehow searing. The light always caught him unawares when he came here, even though he had been so many times now.

The house was spectacular, Charlie had to concede, as he made his way into the kitchen, which, like everything else, had been designed on a grand scale. He grinned to himself as he thought back to the little cottage in Surrey where he and Liv had begun their lives together and which had been Felix's first home. It seemed like a doll's house in comparison to this place. Charlie hadn't counted but he already knew the house must have at least six bedrooms and bathrooms. But then, Danny Nixon was one of Hollywood's biggest names. It would be strange if he didn't own some massive pile in the Hills.

Charlie put the kettle on to boil and rummaged around for some English teabags, which he knew Liv would have. She couldn't start the day without it. He opened the cupboard nearest to him but it contained only cleaning products, and he was just about to close it again when something caught his eye.

He bent down and peered in beyond the various cleaning sprays and bleaches, noticing that there were several empty wine bottles, two empty gin bottles and an empty bottle of vodka at the back. He hesitated for a second before closing the cupboard again. It wasn't that unusual to have empty bottles in the house. If anyone checked his 'empties' count for a month, it would probably amount to much the same. But why were they hidden in the cleaning cupboard?

He opened another cupboard and found the teabags and cups. He took one cup out, before taking out another two. He had always made Liv a cup of tea in the mornings when they were together and she used to say that no-one could make it like him. Maybe he would make her one now.

Just as he had finished preparing the tea, Martha came into the kitchen wearing a white vest top and a pair of denim shorts. She looked fresh and pretty but there was a pain in her eyes that Charlie recognised all too well. When he had first met her those eyes had sparkled with life and humour; now it was as if the brightness control had been turned down.

'Morning,' he smiled, suddenly feeling shy. He barely knew this woman and yet he had dragged her halfway across the world with him. 'Couldn't sleep either?'

Martha looked around distractedly and shook her head, making her hair sway in dark brown rivulets over her shoulders and causing a stirring in the pit of Charlie's stomach. 'I made you some tea,' he said, handing her a cup.

'Oh. Thank you.' Martha took the cup gratefully and sank down into one of the chairs around the huge table, where she drank it greedily.

Charlie watched her, amused. 'You needed that!'

'I did,' she agreed, smiling, although the smile didn't reach her eyes.

'I, um . . .' Charlie began haltingly. 'I made Liv a cup too but I'm not sure if she'll be awake yet . . .' He looked anxiously towards the hallway leading to Liv's bedroom.

Martha stood up immediately. 'Would you like me to go?'

'Thanks,' he nodded.

173

Charlie watched, transfixed, as she picked up the cup and headed out of the room. He couldn't take his eyes off her. Her husband was an idiot, he decided.

'Actually,' he said, snapping out of his trance and stopping her just before she reached Liv's door. 'Don't worry. I'll take it.'

Martha's blank eyes didn't flinch. 'OK.' She handed him the cup and retreated back into the kitchen.

Charlie hesitated outside the door before knocking gently.

After a few seconds, the door opened and Liv gazed up at him with a look of delighted surprise. 'Oh, hey, Charlie!'

'I brought you some tea,' he said unnecessarily, handing her the cup. Liv ran her hand through her hair self-consciously before taking it. Charlie had always loved Liv fresh-faced and without make-up first thing in the morning. She had stunning bone structure and huge, almost violet-coloured eyes that reminded him a little of a young Liz Taylor. But he noticed that her skin, which had always been flawless, now looked puffy and slightly spotty. Her hands shook too as she took the cup and Charlie felt a little stab of guilt. Liv would be devastated if she lost Felix. He knew it could destroy her. But then, he reasoned, trying to harden himself against her, she would know how he had felt over the past four years.

'Thanks, Charlie,' she said, with a tiny nod. Her hands were definitely shaking.

He gave a curt nod back and headed into the kitchen again. Through the glass doors, he could see Martha down by the pool, staring into space. He made his way out onto the terrace. The sun was only just starting to burn through but already he could feel the heat from its rays. He stared out over the dusty scrubland below towards LA. He still didn't know if he could really make a life here. He so loved the changing seasons and the lush green beauty of home, particularly the part of Wales where he had grown up, that it would be a wrench to leave it. LA was spectacular in some ways and yet spectacularly disappointing in others. There was so little culture and so little real beauty to be found here that it depressed him.

And yet, if he was going to have Felix full-time, he would need to be based here, in the city that his son now viewed as home. He couldn't do to Liv what she had done to him, by taking Felix to live 4,000 miles away from her.

He watched Martha as he moved towards her. She had her hands tucked into the pockets of her shorts, and her shoulders and head were dropped. She looked a world away from the confident, funny woman he had met just a couple of days ago, but, Charlie thought as he watched her, no less beautiful.

He smiled down at her as he came to a halt beside her, her bare feet making her seem tiny. 'No gold platforms today then?' he said, grinning at the memory of Martha in sweatpants and high heels.

A sudden machine-gun burst of laughter emitted from Martha's belly and was quickly silenced, as she said, 'No, I left them at home ... along with my husband and children.'

Charlie looked away, feeling uncomfortable.

'Jesus, what am I doing?' Martha added, looking up imploringly at Charlie. 'Why am I here?'

'You needed to get away. That's why. You needed time to think and to decide what to do. I'm glad you came.' He nodded encouragingly at her.

'Are you?' Martha looked puzzled. 'I can't imagine why. I'm not exactly great company.'

'It's been good for me having you here. There's no way I'd be staying at Liv's house if I was on my own. It's broken down some of the barriers that have been there for years.'

'I haven't even asked you,' Martha shook her hair out of her eyes. 'How are *you* feeling about things? About Liv?'

Charlie smiled and looked at Martha with a twinkle in his eye. 'Ever the journalist, eh?'

'Don't forget that's supposed to be why I'm here,' she shot back, tilting her chin up defiantly.

'No, it's not,' he replied good-naturedly. 'But I think it's good that you have another focus. I feel ...' he paused and looked up at the sky, as if searching for the answer to her question up there. 'I feel ... lighter somehow. As if things are finally starting to slot into place.'

'You mean you've finally accepted the way things have worked out?'

Charlie laughed ruefully and shook his head slowly. 'Oh no, quite the opposite. It's just that I've finally decided to do something about it.'

Martha frowned. 'I don't understand.'

'I've realised ...' Charlie began, '... that the greatest source of pain for me has been losing Felix. Losing Liv was bad but losing Felix was much, much worse.'

'You didn't lose Felix, though,' Martha countered, touching Charlie's arm and sending a little jolt through him. 'He loves you desperately and you have an amazing relationship.'

Charlie smiled, a warm swell of pride filling his body. 'We

do. But it's a long-distance relationship. And that's not what I want any more, so I'm going to do something about it.'

Martha nodded to herself. 'You're moving to LA to be nearer to him.'

Charlie hesitated. Should he confide in Martha? He barely knew her and, worse, she was a journalist.

'Yes,' he said, deciding to tell her only part of the story, 'but I've also been wondering if maybe I should try to get a more formal arrangement regarding Felix.'

'Liv's pretty good though, isn't she? She never stops you seeing him?'

Charlie nodded slowly. 'But what if she suddenly decided to be less agreeable? She's not the most stable person …' His words hung in the humid air between them. He didn't want to mention Liv's drinking, but he was fairly sure Martha would know what he was talking about. 'I just think it might be a good idea to protect myself for the future with a more formal arrangement.'

Martha put the flat of her hand to her chest, as if she was struggling for breath.

'Are you OK?'

'Sorry,' she muttered, closing her eyes for a few seconds. 'I just suddenly imagined me and Jamie having to agree access. Who has them on what weekends. Who gets custody. It's such a horrible thought.' Her large dark eyes overflowed with fat tears that spilled down her cheeks.

Instinctively, Charlie reached for her and pulled her tightly to his chest.

'And it's only just occurred to me,' Martha sobbed, pulling

away and looking up at him, 'that if I was to leave Jamie, he's the main carer, so he would get the kids. Oh my God!' she cried, putting her hands to her face.

'No!' Charlie tried to sound soothing. 'That's not necessarily true—'

'But it is!' Martha interrupted him. 'Jamie's been the most constant presence in their lives since they were babies.'

'I'm sorry,' Charlie sighed, shaking his head and feeling like a heel. 'I should never have said anything.'

'No,' Martha gulped, wiping her face furiously. 'It's fine. I'm fine. I'll be fine,' she repeated.

'Look,' Charlie said, desperately trying to think of a way to distract her, 'why don't we go out for some breakfast? You've barely eaten a thing for two days now and I'm starving. Felix won't be up for ages and we should probably take advantage of our jet-lag.'

Martha nodded quickly. 'Yes. Yes that would be good. Let's do that.' She was already turning and heading for the house again.

Charlie watched her go, wondering how she could possibly be having such a powerful effect on him in such a short time. He had only ever felt this way about a woman once before in his life and it had almost broken him. If he had any sense he would buy Martha a one-way ticket out of his life before things got any more complicated. But, he decided, as he turned to follow her, admiring her strong, toned brown legs in her denim shorts, sense had never been his strong point.

Chapter 21

'Where's Dad gone?' asked Felix, coming into Liv's room and throwing himself on the bed beside the suitcase she had just finished packing.

Liv shrugged. 'I'm not sure, sweetie. Maybe he and Martha have gone out to get some breakfast?'

'But they could have had breakfast here!' Felix frowned as he rolled onto his back and glared up at the ceiling.

She zipped up the suitcase and heaved it off the bed onto the floor. 'They'll be back soon,' she soothed. 'At least, I hope they will. I need to leave for the airport within the next hour.'

'Oh, Danny said not to bother coming,' Felix said chirpily, as Liv began to roll the case out of the bedroom.

Liv did a double-take and looked back at her son. 'What did you say?'

'I said, "Danny said not to bother coming",' Felix repeated more hesitantly, sitting up and looking at Liv with a puzzled gaze. 'What's wrong? Why do you look all cross?'

Liv ran a hand through her hair distractedly. 'Felix, when did Danny tell you that?'

'I spoke to him,' he said. 'About half an hour ago, while you were in the shower.'

'Oh shit!' Liv snapped, then clapped her hand over her mouth. 'Sorry, honey. What did you tell him?'

'I said you were coming to Hawaii to surprise him and that daddy and his new girlfriend were staying here to look after me while you were gone.'

Liv closed her eyes as an icy feeling filled her belly. 'Oh God,' she muttered to herself. 'Did you say anything else?'

'No.' Felix's eyes shot to the left, as they always did when he was fibbing.

'Felix ...' Liv began. 'I won't be cross ... just tell me everything that was said.'

'Well,' he said, looking guilty, 'I also said I heard Daddy saying that you thought you might catch Danny out.'

'Oh God,' Liv repeated, heading towards her bed and sinking down on it.

'Did I do something wrong?' Felix asked, his eyes widening in alarm.

'No!' She reached over and gave him a reassuring hug, despite the fact that her whole body was shaking. 'It's just ...'

'Just what?' Felix looked up at her and her heart turned over at the innocence in his dark eyes.

'It's just that I really wanted to surprise Danny,' she said, rubbing his silky curls. 'Did he sound ... cross?' she ventured. 'When you spoke to him?'

Felix considered the matter carefully. 'Yes, he sounded pretty cross,' he agreed. 'But why? It's nice that you wanted to surprise him, isn't it?'

Liv swallowed the lump that had formed in her throat. 'Yes, but maybe Danny doesn't like surprises,' she managed.

Felix shook his head solemnly. 'Who wouldn't like surprises? That's totally *crazy*!'

'I guess I should probably call him.' Liv stood up and reached for her cellphone, which, as ever, was close by. 'Felix, why don't you go and see if Daddy and Martha are back yet?'

'Sure!' he cried, scrambling off the bed and running out.

She closed the door behind him and pressed Danny's number, her heart thumping all the while. He answered immediately. 'Hey,' she said in her most confident voice, 'it's me.'

'I know it's you,' Danny's usually soft, husky voice sounded cold. 'So, I hear you were about to fly out here and surprise me?'

'I was!' Liv laughed nervously. 'But I hear a certain six-year-old boy scuppered my plans!'

There was a pause that lasted far too long. 'Why were you going to do that, Liv?'

'To surprise you!' she replied, aware that her voice had gone up several octaves.

'No,' Danny said. 'I think you thought you would catch me out.'

She opened her mouth to reply but nothing coherent would form in her brain. She felt as if she had been caught red-handed and could feel herself blushing, even though no-one could see her. 'Danny . . . I really, really want to see you. Don't be like this.'

There was another achingly long pause during which Liv could hear her own heartbeat.

'You know what?' he said at last. 'I don't want to see you.'

'Oh God!' she whimpered. 'No, Danny. Please don't say that. I love you ...'

'But you don't *trust* me,' Danny said, his tone more conciliatory, which only made her feel worse. 'And without trust there's no point.'

Liv's head swam with shock. 'What are you saying, Danny? Are you saying that I shouldn't come and visit you?'

Danny sighed heavily on the other end of the line. 'I'm saying I think we're through, baby.'

Liv sank down onto the bed and put her head in her hands. 'Look, Danny,' she said, desperate to rescue the situation. 'I was coming to surprise you, that's all. You can't throw away four amazing years over a simple misunderstanding. I do trust you. I do,' she repeated, wondering even as she spoke if it was entirely true.

'No. I don't think you do.' Danny's voice sounded resigned now rather than harsh.

'Please, Danny ...' she begged. 'Please don't say it's over. I love you. I can't live without you. And what about Felix?' she added desperately.

There was a strange sound from the other end of the line and Liv realised with a start that it was a sob.

'Don't do it, Danny!' she cried, grasping at his emotion in an effort to dissuade him. 'Felix and I love you too much ...' Her heart was racing as she prayed that she could make him reconsider.

'No,' Danny gulped eventually. 'I'm sorry, Liv. I'll make sure you and Felix are taken care of ... but it's over, baby.'

The line went dead and Liv stared at the handset in shock.

As she stood up her head swam and her legs buckled. Her ears filled with the sound of rushing air and suddenly everything went black.

'Liv! Liv! Wake up!' said a voice above her.

'Danny?' she murmured, blinking rapidly as the light hit her eyes.

'No, it's me . . . Charlie,' said the voice.

The memory of what had just happened began to swim through Liv's consciousness. 'Danny!' she wailed, as the tears began to slide down her face.

Voices murmured words that she couldn't make out as someone sat her up and pressed a glass of cold water to her lips. She took a couple of grateful sips and then opened her eyes again. Charlie's face came into focus just a few inches in front of her, watching her with concern. 'What happened?' he asked gently.

Liv closed her eyes again, unable to bear the sympathy in his expression. 'I got what I deserved. That's what happened,' she managed to say, although the effort of speaking was almost too much.

'Mummy?' Felix knelt down beside her and wrapped his arms around her neck, pushing his cheek towards her so that it was touching hers.

She could feel wetness and looked at Felix in alarm. His long lashes were glistening with tears and his little forehead was crinkled with worry. 'Oh, it's OK, honey,' she said, immediately starting to gather herself. 'I just had a bit of a funny turn – I'm fine! See?' She removed his arms from around her neck and attemped to stand up.

Her head was pounding but she managed to get to her feet. Felix looked up at her warily. She put her hand out to him and he took it, getting to his feet and burying his face into her stomach. Over his head, Liv met Charlie's eye. 'Sorry,' she said, her voice sounding croaky. 'I'm not sure what happened ...'

'Hey, Felix,' said a woman's soft voice behind Liv. It took Liv several seconds to remember who Martha was and why she was here. 'Why don't we go and lay out the breakfast we brought back for you and your mum?'

Felix looked up at Liv questioningly. 'That's a good idea,' she nodded encouragingly. 'I'll just freshen up and then I'll join you.'

As Felix and Martha headed off to the kitchen, Liv slumped down onto the bed and looked up at Charlie. 'What happened?' she asked.

Charlie shook his head uncomprehendingly. 'We just came back from getting breakfast and found you ... lying there.' He stopped for a second and swallowed. 'I don't think you had been out long, but it gave us all a bit of a shock. Are you OK?'

Liv nodded shakily. Then she looked up and met his eye again. 'No!' she cried, 'I'm not OK! Danny just ended it ...' She leaned forward and put her face in her hands. 'I just can't believe it!' she added, shaking her head in bewilderment.

Charlie sat down beside her. 'Why?'

'I don't know ... apparently Felix said something to him on the phone about me wanting to catch him out and he went mad. Said I didn't trust him ...' She stopped speaking and dissolved into tears. 'What the hell am I going to do, Charlie?' she wailed piteously.

Hesitantly, Charlie put an arm around her shoulders. She leaned into his embrace gratefully. Charlie had always been able to soothe her when she was stressed. His arms felt familiar and comforting.

'You'll be fine,' he said quietly. 'It feels like the end of the world now, but it's not.'

Liv looked up at him gratefully. The irony of Charlie trying to comfort her didn't escape either of them. Now she knew how Charlie had felt when she did it to him. Although it must have been ten times worse, because of Felix. 'At least we didn't have kids,' she muttered.

Charlie took his arm away awkwardly. 'No, but he was good to Felix, wasn't he?'

Liv nodded and wiped her face with the back of her hand. 'Yes, he was. Oh, God, Felix will be devastated!'

Charlie pursed his lips but didn't say anything. He didn't need to. Liv suspected she knew what he was thinking – that he wasn't Felix's dad and therefore Felix might be upset but he certainly wouldn't be devastated.

'So,' she said at last, 'I guess I won't be going to Hawaii after all . . .'

'Would you like us to leave?' Charlie asked. 'It's no problem. We're booked into the Four Seasons anyway. We could take Felix for a few days . . . give you some space?'

'No!' Liv said quickly. 'I really don't want you to leave. And I can't bear the thought of being parted from Felix right now, though I'm not much fun for him on my own. It would help to have company in the house. It's a bit big with just the two of us here.'

'OK.' Charlie stood up. 'Well, let me know if you change your mind. Come on, how about trying to tackle some of the breakfast we brought back?'

Chapter 22

Before he set off for the airport, Jamie called into a garage to get petrol and pick up a few of the tabloids. He could read them on the way. His stomach began to churn with uncertainty. He rarely travelled without Martha and he suddenly felt scared about flying alone to LA, without any real idea of where to find her when he got there. He scrolled through his contacts until he found Lindsay's number, then pressed 'Dial'.

A few seconds later, Lindsay answered. 'I'm at school,' she said, 'so I can't really talk. Have you heard any more from Martha?'

'No. She called the kids but made an excuse so she didn't have to speak to me. I was hoping that maybe you had.'

'No . . .' Lindsay sighed. 'But there's another photo in the paper again today. Of them together at LAX. She looks awful.'

The hair on the back of Jamie's neck prickled. 'Which one?' He glanced down at the innocuous pile of papers on the seat beside him.

'*Mirror* and *Sun*.'

He snatched up the *Mirror* and flicked through it until he came to the picture. Charlie and Martha were making their way out of LAX and Lindsay was right, Martha did look truly terrible, as if she was in some sort of trance. Charlie, on the other hand, looked fresh-faced, tall and handsome as he strode beside her, carrying both their bags. He slammed the paper shut. 'Great,' he said in a flat voice.

'Make sure the kids know the truth, Jamie ...' There was an ominous inflection to her voice.

'Well, we don't exactly know what the truth is, do we?' Jamie snapped back, feeling cross with Lindsay, cross with Martha and, most of all, cross with himself.

'Yes, unfortunately we *do* know the truth, Jamie, which is that Martha is in no way to blame for any of this and you have got to make sure the kids know that.'

He didn't reply, too confused to know what to say.

'Are you on your way then?' Lindsay prompted, when the silence had gone on for too long.

'Just setting off now, that's why I was calling,' Jamie sighed. 'Can you keep trying her? I've just realised that I'm going to turn up with no clue where to find her. She's probably more likely to tell you than me.'

'OK,' Lindsay said, before hanging up without saying good-bye.

Jamie pulled out of the garage and drove for a few more minutes. Then he reached out and pressed the voice dial again. 'Martha Lamont,' he said, his voice cracking as he said her name out loud. After a couple of seconds it dialled Martha's number and he held his breath as it began to ring with the long, slightly high-pitched dial tone that signified she was abroad.

'Hello?' Her voice filled the car and Jamie's insides tightened at the sound of her voice.

'It's me,' he said simply.

There was a pause. 'I know.' She sounded tired.

'Babe, I am so desperate to see you!' he blurted, before he could think too much about it. 'Where are you?'

Martha sighed. 'I'm in LA. You know that.'

'I know. But where in LA? Where are you staying?'

'Why do you want to know?' Martha replied wearily. 'What does it matter?'

'I just . . . I just want to know that you're OK. That you're safe.'

'I'm fine. Well, maybe not fine, but I'm safe.' Martha's voice was hardening again. 'How are the kids?'

'They're OK. Mimi knows something's going on, but—'

'But she doesn't know that her bastard father has been cheating on her mother?' Martha cut in.

'No,' Jamie said, clenching his fists around the steering wheel. 'Martha, your mum's here.'

'My mum! But why?'

Jamie hesitated. 'I called her. I asked her to come. I was worried about the kids. I'm not coping too well . . .'

There was a long, ominous pause. 'What did you tell her?' When she finally spoke, her voice was little more than a hoarse whisper.

'I told her the truth.'

'Oh my God!' Martha wailed. 'As if I haven't been

humiliated enough! You shouldn't have done that, Jamie, without talking to me first.'

'Well, you wouldn't talk to me so I had no choice,' Jamie replied, trying to remain as calm as possible.

There was another long silence before Martha spoke again. 'What did she say?'

Jamie took a deep breath. 'What do you think she said? She read me the riot act and told me I wasn't fit to be your husband. But she just wants you to come home, sweetheart. We all do.'

'I can't!' Martha's words burst out in a giant gasp. 'I came here because I needed to get my head together . . . to get away from you.'

'I know,' Jamie agreed. 'But it's not the answer. You know how we are. We don't function well apart . . .'

'We didn't function well together either, seeing as you were screwing other women behind my back!' Martha was trying to sound hard again but Jamie could hear the pain in her voice.

'But we need to talk this through. I am going out of my mind here and I need to be able to put right what's happened.'

'You can't ever put it right,' Martha said, the weariness returning to her voice.

'Don't say that,' Jamie told her, shaking his head at the thought. '*Please* don't say that.'

'But it's true.'

'No!' Jamie said, with renewed determination. 'I'm not giving up without a fight. I love you so much, Martha. I need you. Come home. I can't bear to think of you on the other side of the world in some hotel room . . .'

There was a pause. 'I'm not in a hotel. I'm staying at someone's house.'

Jamie's spirits slumped. His chances of finding her if she was in a house rather than a hotel were zero. 'Whose house?' he prompted, trying not to sound too desperate. He didn't want to alert her to his plan, but he needed to know where she was.

'Liv Mason's.'

It took a few moments for Jamie to realise who she meant. 'Liv Mason, as in the film star, Liv Mason?'

'Yes. She's Charlie's ex, so we're staying here to look after his son while she goes away for a few days. Or at least we were. It's got a bit complicated . . .'

Stinging jealousy prickled its way through Jamie. 'You and Charlie?' he said. 'On your own?'

'Oh, no you don't!' Martha growled. 'I think you'll find you have absolutely no right to be possessive of me any more. No right at all!'

'I'm not!' Jamie protested quickly, but he had to admit to feeling jealous as hell. He knew all too well the tricks men used to get women into bed, having employed them himself when he was younger. There was no doubt in his mind that Charlie Simmons would be exploiting Martha's vulnerability for all he was worth right now. The thought of Martha being with someone else absolutely killed him, even though he knew he was the one to blame. If it wasn't for him and what he'd done, Martha would never have run off to LA with Charlie in the first place.

He cleared his throat and took a deep breath, trying to regain some composure. 'How long are you going to be there?'

Martha didn't answer at first and Jamie wondered for a moment if the connection had been lost. Finally, she spoke. 'For as long as it takes,' she said, before hanging up.

Chapter 23

Martha awoke with a start the next morning. She could have sworn that she hadn't slept at all, but she must have dropped off at some point, exhaustion and jet-lag finally catching up with her. Jamie's phone call had shaken her. He was right. They didn't function well apart, but the longer she was away from him, the easier it was for her to think straight.

Running away to LA had been such an uncharacteristic thing for her to do. She had always put Jamie and the children first. But even though it was painful to be without the children, she had no doubt that it had been the right thing to do. She'd had to put some space between her and Jamie, so that she could decide for herself what to do without him watching her with terrified eyes and begging her to forgive him.

And being with Charlie had been strangely comforting, considering they didn't really know each other and that he was such a star and she was just a jobbing journalist. It was as if the shared experience of heartbreak had given them the sort of connection that other couples take a lifetime to find.

Other couples? Martha pulled the plump white duvet up to

193

her neck to keep out the chill from the air conditioning and rolled onto her side, shocked that she should even be thinking about her and Charlie in such terms.

Not that she didn't find him attractive. Charlie was a gorgeous man inside and out, and she couldn't understand how Liv had ever thought that she would be better off with the womanising Danny Nixon than the devoted father of her only child.

Martha's musings were interrupted by the sound of Felix laughing as he ran past her door with Charlie, clearly having just roused his dad and demanding that he get up and play with him. 'I'm gonna thrash you!' he squealed, to which Charlie calmly replied, 'Oh yeah? Well we'll see about that, my little buddy!'

Martha smiled to herself. Charlie seemed like a wonderful dad and she could see how deeply it had affected him to be parted from his beloved son.

Like so many people, Martha had followed the lives of Liv and Charlie through the countless articles and gossip columns she had read over the years and felt as if she knew them. But the truth was, while they might seem to be perfect people living perfect lives, they were really no different to anyone else, with all the same problems and traumas.

Liv, in particular, seemed to be just as lonely and vulnerable as Martha at that moment. She had drunk heavily again last night, but worryingly, she didn't seem to get drunk. Despite her petite frame, she had managed to polish off several large glasses of wine and a couple of gin and tonics without any apparent ill-effects.

To Martha's surprise, not only did she relate to Liv, she also felt desperately sorry for her. Despite everything Liv had done, Martha wondered if she now regretted the turns her life had taken. Should she have ignored her feelings for Danny and made it work with Charlie? *Could* she have ignored how she felt about Danny? Maybe not. Maybe it was just too strong.

As for herself, Martha was proud that she seemed to be just about holding up, despite the constant, gnawing pain in her stomach and the squeezing sensation in her chest. Her heart literally felt as if it had broken in two, but she had managed to continue to function, albeit in a robotic fashion. Her senses were dulled, the way that she imagined you felt when you were on anti-depressants. Maybe that was yet another of the physical symptoms of heartbreak.

Being in LA with a famous film star, having been flown there first class and taken to some lovely places, as Charlie had done yesterday when he took her and Felix out for the day, ought to have felt glamorous and exciting, but Martha could just as easily have been in Clacton. She'd felt numb to the whole experience and wasn't able to embrace it with her usual enthusiasm, thanks to the huge rucksack of misery it seemed as if she was carrying around on her back.

She had brought her notepad and recorder with her so that she could use the time with Charlie to push on with her research for the book, but Charlie had seemed surprised, even slightly offended, when she had first pulled them out of her bag. She had told him, not realising until she said it how true it was, that work was 'distraction therapy' for her.

Reluctantly, Martha threw off the duvet and climbed out of bed. Her eyes felt as if she had rubbed sandpaper over them during the night and, as she looked at herself in the bathroom mirror, she saw that the circles beneath them had darkened.

She stepped into the shower and let the stinging jets of hot water pummel her skin for several minutes, enjoying the sensation as the warmth seeped into her chilled body. Once she had finished, she stepped out and wrapped the fluffy white robe that was hanging on the door tightly around her body. She picked up her phone and noticed with alarm that she had several missed calls, but as she scanned her 'recent calls' list, she could see that they were all from Lindsay.

She hadn't been able to face calling Lindsay yet. Although she loved her friend and knew that she would always be there for her, she didn't want to disillusion her about Jamie. Since her own marriage had collapsed, Lindsay had held Jamie and Martha up as role models for the perfect relationship. Many times she had said that she would never settle down again, unless she believed that there was a real chance her relationship could be like theirs. If she didn't see that potential within the first three dates, she ended any burgeoning new romances.

Martha looked again at the calls list and bit her lip guiltily, as she realised that Lindsay had tried ringing her almost fifty times. She would be going out of her mind with worry; Martha had to return her call.

Lindsay picked up immediately. 'Jesus, I was imagining for a while there that you must be dead!'

'Sorry,' Martha said, feeling sheepish. 'It's just that it's been a bit of a hectic few days and—' she started to gabble her excuses.

'I know,' Lindsay interrupted her.

'Yes, so I had to come to LA because obviously I'm doing the book and I'm on a deadline and if I don't get on—'

'I *know*,' Lindsay interrupted her again, this time more forcefully. 'I know about Jamie. About what he did.'

'Oh God,' Martha sank down onto the unmade bed, her insides immediately churning again, as the horror of what had happened washed over her anew. 'H . . . how?' she stuttered.

'Jamie told me.' The gentleness of Lindsay's voice made Martha feel a million times worse. 'Babes, I am so sorry you have had to go through that. I can't bear to think how you must have felt . . .'

'Don't,' Martha cried, putting her hand over her face. 'I can't bear it myself.'

'You sound awful,' Lindsay said after a pause. 'How are you feeling?'

Martha tried to speak but her throat felt as if it had closed up. She wanted more than anything to be with Lindsay right now, to pour out everything that she was going through.

'Oh God, what a stupid bloody question!' Lindsay said, when Martha didn't reply.

'No! It's OK,' Martha croaked. 'I feel really bad. I still can't believe it.'

'Neither can I. Oh, Martha, I nearly battered him but . . .'

'. . . but I got there first?' Martha finished the sentence for her.

Lindsay laughed a dry, humourless laugh. 'Something like that,' she agreed. 'Martha, I just feel so helpless. Please tell me what I can do to help.'

'You can keep an eye on the children for me,' Martha said in a small voice. 'I'm really worried that they'll be thinking that *I'm* the one that's in the wrong. Especially Mimi. You know how smart she is.'

'I know,' Lindsay agreed. 'Did you see that you were papped again at LAX?'

'Oh God, no!' Martha cried. 'The kids . . .'

'I'll make sure the kids know it means nothing,' Lindsay said quickly, reading Martha's mind.

'Thank you,' Martha breathed, relieved. 'My mum's there – apparently Jamie couldn't cope on his own – but I'm not sure they'd take much notice of anything she says, whereas they'll listen to you.'

'Of course,' Lindsay said. 'I'll nip round now.'

Martha felt a surge of gratitude towards her friend. The children idolised Lindsay because although she was a teacher, she was also great fun and just a little bit naughty. She smoked, drank more than she should and watched all the teen American shows that Mimi in particular loved.

'So . . . where are you staying?' Lindsay asked. 'And are you still with Charlie Simmons?'

Martha sighed. 'Well, it's all a bit of a long story but, yes, I'm here with Charlie. We're staying at Liv's house.'

There was silence for a moment while Lindsay digested what Martha had just said. 'Liv *Mason's* house?' she spluttered at last. 'His ex-wife?'

I know,' Martha agreed, shaking her head. 'I can't quite believe it myself. It's all so surreal.'

'What's it like? Tell me everything!'

Martha laughed. She could just picture Lindsay, smoking furiously, her eyes agog, as she waited for her to impart the juicy details. 'Well, it's certainly an eye-opener ...'

'Describe the house in every detail,' Lindsay ordered, exhaling loudly.

'A-mazing. Huge, double-height ceilings, lots of glass and steel. Everything's white so it looks even bigger. Fabulous infinity pool overlooking the Hollywood Hills, and when you're in it you can see the sea in the distance once the smog clears ...'

'Of course! Danny Nixon's bachelor pad – I saw it featured in a magazine just after he bought it.'

Martha grinned to herself. Lindsay had every celebrity magazine, filed in date order, from the past five years, and she had a photographic memory when it came to the lives of the rich and famous. She was momentarily sorry that her friend wasn't there to see it for herself.

'And what's she like? The ex?'

Martha sighed. 'She's lovely but a bit of a mess, to be honest. So we have a lot in common right now ...'

'A mess in what way?'

Martha lowered her voice to a whisper, even though it would have been impossible for anyone to hear her from outside the room. 'I'm pretty sure she's got a drink problem. I've never seen anyone put away quite so much. And, please don't tell anyone this ...'

'Who am I going to tell?' Lindsay cut in indignantly. 'My headmaster?'

Martha laughed. 'Well, it looks like Danny's dumped her.'

'Shit!' Lindsay gasped.

'I know. So, as I say, me and Liv Mason have rather a lot in common right now. It's all so weird . . .' Martha suddenly felt all the energy draining out of her and she lay back on the bed. 'I'll tell you all about it when I get home.'

'So you *are* coming back then?' Lindsay said, a mischievous note to her voice. 'You're not staying there and shacking up with Charlie Simmons?'

Martha laughed nervously. 'No! Of course I'm not. I've still got two children to think about, remember? Even if my supposedly devoted husband is a cheating shit.'

'Oh Martha!' Lindsay cried. 'I really hope you work it out with Jamie. He does seem absolutely devastated . . .'

'So he should!' Martha snapped. 'And he's only devastated because he's been caught. He certainly wasn't devastated before, when he was shagging his mistress behind my back.'

Martha could hear Lindsay gulp. 'I still can't believe it,' she said. 'Not Jamie . . .'

'Me neither,' agreed Martha ruefully. 'Listen, Linds, I'd better go. Thanks for . . . well, you know . . .'

'I know,' Lindsay said. 'Love you and take care. Come back soon. I miss you.'

Tears flashed into Martha's eyes as she hung up. She had always known that Lindsay was fiercely loyal to her, but she could actually hear the pain in her voice and it touched her deeply. She stood up and went to the dressing room. She suddenly felt as if she needed to get out of the house and go for a run. Her head felt so crowded and muddled. She wanted to do something physical that didn't require any thinking; something that would block out the pain.

Although she hadn't unpacked, her new case full of stuff that Charlie's assistant had bought for her had been removed and all the new items either hung up or folded and put away. That was one of the stranger things about staying here, Martha thought. She had yet to actually see any of the house-keeping staff, but they were obviously there, as things were miraculously put away or tidied up as soon as they had been used. It was as if there was a houseful of helpful ghosts on duty.

Somewhat different to home, thought Martha ruefully, picturing her chaotic hallway, over-spilling with odd shoes and out-of-season coats, as she picked out a t-shirt and a pair of shorts and quickly pulled them on. She ran her hands through her hair and went into the bathroom, where she peered at herself in the large mirror. She hadn't put any make-up on for more than three days now and instead of looking fresh, she thought she looked more like an old flannel that had been repeatedly wrung out.

She had always been fairly happy with her appearance and rarely gave it much thought. But now that her husband had so effectively demonstrated that she wasn't attractive enough for him, she found herself scrutinising her face and body with something approaching contempt. Overnight, it seemed as if all the confidence had drained out of her, leaving her feeling like an old, empty, ugly shell.

There was a knock at the bedroom door. 'Martha?' said Charlie's voice. 'I've brought you some tea.'

Martha walked to the door and opened it. 'Come in,' she gestured with her arm. 'I was just thinking that I might go for a run ...'

'You sure that's a good idea?'

Martha took the cup of tea he was holding. 'I think I need to get out for a bit, clear my head, you know?'

Charlie nodded. 'How you doing?'

Martha sat down on the bed, while Charlie sat on the chaise longue opposite. She took a long, grateful sip of her tea before she spoke. 'Jamie called last night ...'

Charlie's eyes flickered and she thought that they darkened slightly. 'And?' he said, pursing his lips.

'It's just ... hard. I hate to admit it but I miss him.'

Charlie didn't reply and she watched his Adam's apple rise and fall as he swallowed hard.

Martha frowned, wondering why she suddenly felt guilty. She felt as if she was betraying Charlie somehow by talking about Jamie.

'Anyway, do you fancy joining me on my run?' she tried to lighten the mood, which had inexplicably darkened.

Charlie smiled, his eyes shining again. 'Sure,' he said, standing up. 'Can't have you heading out there all by yourself. Give me five minutes.'

'Charlie!' she called, as he was about to leave the room.

He stopped and looked back over his shoulder at her.

Martha hesitated. She wanted to say so much but didn't know where to begin. 'Thank you,' she said at last.

Charlie nodded and left the room, closing the door behind him. Martha shook her head, trying to identify the confused emotions that were tumbling over themselves. Just then her mobile rang and she snatched it up.

'It's me,' said Jamie, sounding as exhausted as she felt. 'I'm here. In LA.'

Chapter 24

Half an hour later, Charlie made his way into the kitchen where Liv was sitting at the huge island in the middle of the room, staring into space. 'Hey,' he said, putting his hands on his hips and looking around distractedly, suddenly unsure what to do with himself. He felt irritated and upset at the news of Jamie's impending arrival. And inexplicably cross with Martha, although he knew that was unfair.

Liv looked up wearily. She looked dreadful: the whites of her eyes were yellow and bloodshot and her complexion was grey and dry-looking. 'Hey,' she replied in a monotone voice. 'You OK?' she added after a few moments when Charlie didn't say anything but continued to look around in bewilderment.

'Hmm,' he replied, finally coming over to join her. He pulled out a stool and perched opposite her. 'It's just ... well, I think I may have made a mistake bringing Martha here.'

'Why?' Liv's dull, lifeless eyes suddenly flickered with interest.

Charlie looked up at the ceiling while he thought of the

right answer. He couldn't explain it himself. 'Because I really like her,' he said. 'And it's complicated . . .'

Liv rolled her eyes and smiled a dead smile. 'Isn't it always?'

Charlie nodded his acknowledgement. 'I know. Why do we always want what we can't have?'

Liv's eyes brimmed and Charlie immediately regretted his choice of words. 'Sorry,' he quickly tried to correct himself. 'I mean . . . well, you know what I mean,' he tailed off feebly.

'I don't think you made a mistake bringing her,' Liv said, brushing her hand over her eyes as she spoke.

'Really?' Charlie looked up in surprise.

'Really,' Liv nodded. 'I mean, things haven't exactly been brilliant between you and me up till now, have they? You bringing Martha has helped us to . . . reconnect. And I like her – even if she is a journalist!'

Charlie smiled ruefully. 'She *is* great, isn't she?' he said, before he could stop himself.

Liv raised her eyebrows. 'Wow,' she mouthed. 'You've got it *bad*.'

Charlie could feel himself blushing. 'It's pointless,' he said, shaking his head. 'She's about to go and meet her husband from the airport. He's just flown in to see her.'

'Oh . . .' Liv replied, her forehead creasing. 'So there really isn't anything going on between you two then?'

'I wish!' Charlie cut her off, again feeling the heat in his cheeks as he realised he had said more than he should.

'So what's the story then? With her husband?' Liv picked up a napkin and began twisting it around her finger.

'The oldest story in the world,' Charlie replied, feeling the annoyance and jealousy prickle up inside him again. 'He cheated on her. He's a bastard who doesn't deserve her. But she'll probably forgive him and then he'll do it all over again.'

'Poor Martha,' Liv said, looking down. 'And they've got kids, haven't they?'

'Two. Christ, I don't know why women put up with it,' he burst out bitterly, standing up again and throwing his hands in the air.

Now it was Liv's turn to redden. 'No. Or men,' she said, dropping the napkin onto the work surface before getting to her feet. She poured Charlie a coffee and brought it over to him. His face relaxed as he took it and smiled at her.

'What?' The mischievous glint in her eye had returned momentarily.

Charlie shook his head. 'Nothing. Just a bit of déjà vu. Remembering something.'

Liv grinned back. She knew exactly what he was talking about. The day they had moved into their cottage in Surrey, they had arrived well before the removal van and had immediately taken advantage of the fact by making love on the bare wooden floor. Afterwards, as they lay naked in each other's arms, Liv suddenly shrieked and leapt to her feet. 'Shit, they're here!' she'd cried, scrabbling for her clothes and flinging Charlie's at him, just as four burly removal men appeared, peering through the window. Giggling like schoolchildren, they had managed to get dressed just in time to open the door to find the main removal man presenting them with their kettle and telling them to get the tea on. The knowing look Liv had given Charlie as she handed him his cup still tickled him all these years later.

'That was a good day,' she murmured, as if lost in her own memories.

'It was,' Charlie agreed, before the sound of Martha's footsteps coming down the hall brought him back to the present with a jolt.

Liv heard them too and the moment was broken. 'How's she getting to the airport?' she asked briskly.

'I don't know,' Charlie replied, shaking his head. 'I didn't think to ask.'

'Well, she'll need a lift, won't she?' A look of exasperation skittered across Liv's brow.

'I suppose . . .'

'So, are you going to take her or shall I get a driver? It's not as if she can go out in the street here and hail a cab.'

Charlie hesitated. He wanted to spend as much time as he possibly could with Martha, but he wasn't sure he could bear to see her with her husband. What the hell was happening to him? 'I'll take her,' he said at last.

'OK. Then I guess you'd better let her know.'

'Let me know what?' said Martha, coming into the kitchen, her sandals making a clacking sound on the tiled floor.

'That I'll give you a lift . . . to the airport. Sorry, I should have thought of it before.'

'No, no, I'll be fine,' Martha insisted, picking up her bag. 'I'll just get a cab or something.'

Both Liv and Charlie laughed. 'I don't think so,' Charlie said, smiling. 'Strangely enough, there aren't many cabs riding up and down this road, looking for fares.'

Martha laughed too. It was the first time Charlie had seen

her properly smile since that very first day, when she had arrived at his hotel room with a giant hole in her dress and immediately captivated him. He watched her now, thinking that she looked stunning, standing in the middle of the huge white room in a pretty blue dress.

It wasn't lost on Charlie that for the few short days she had spent with him, Martha had made no effort with her appearance at all. It was only now that she was going to meet her husband that she had put any thought into how she looked. He knew when he was beaten.

Martha wasn't the type of woman who would be impressed by fame or money and he knew that however hurt and broken she was feeling, she wouldn't throw in the towel on her marriage without a fight. She was too devoted to her children not to try to make it work. But, glutton for punishment that he was, there was still something about her that was pulling him towards her.

'Let's go,' he said.

Chapter 25

Jamie walked out of the wide glass doors of the Tom Bradley terminal at LAX and squinted down the parking lot, unsure what sort of car he was looking for. He felt dehydrated, sick with exhaustion, but all of those feelings were over-shadowed by the panic he felt at seeing Martha again. It had only been five days since he had last seen her but it felt like an eternity. And the look she had given him before she drove away would stay with him forever.

His phone beeped. He pulled it out of his jeans pocket and glanced at the screen. *Call me when you're here and we'll drive round to the front. Martha.*

No kisses to end the text, Jamie noted, an ominous feeling taking root in his stomach. And who was 'we'? Charlie Simmons? Jamie hoped not. He knew he had absolutely no right to feel anything approaching jealousy but he couldn't help it. Charlie Simmons was richer, better looking and more successful than him. If there was now some kind of competition between them, Jamie was certain Charlie would win. Except for one thing. Jamie's trump card was the children.

He dialled Martha's number and she answered immediately. 'OK, we'll be round in a few minutes,' she said, without giving him a chance to say anything. 'Wait there,' she added, before hanging up.

Jamie clutched his sports bag closer to him, suddenly feeling unsettled and inadequate, and distractedly watching the succession of cars and shuttle buses arriving and leaving the undercover arrivals area, trailing behind them a fug of diesel fumes in the heat.

He had never been to LA before but already he could tell that everything was on a much grander scale than at home. Looking out of the window from his cramped economy-class seat just before landing, he could see the network of roads stretching for miles in a neatly ordered, giant grid formation. He had expected the houses to be dotted about but they were spread thickly over the landscape like a carpet.

After a few minutes, a sleek black Range Rover pulled up to the kerb beside him. Martha lowered the tinted window and locked eyes with him for a second. His heart began to hammer. 'Hi,' he murmured, unable to look away from this woman who had shared his life for so long and given birth to his two children, yet now seemed like a stranger he was meeting for the first time.

Martha's dark eyes flickered. 'Are you getting in then?'

Jamie reached for the back door and pulled it open. He swung his bag onto the tan leather seat and climbed in behind it. Sure enough, Charlie Simmons was in the driving seat, causing Jamie's heart to sink with disappointment. He didn't look round or acknowledge Jamie's presence at all, and the tension began to fizz almost immediately.

Jamie caught his eye in the rear-view mirror. 'Thanks for picking me up.' He was unable to keep the grudging tone out of his voice. He felt like a child in the company of two adults.

'It's fine,' Charlie said in a pissed-off voice.

During the awkward, heavy silence that followed, Jamie took a surreptitious look at Charlie, as he negotiated his way out of the chaos of the airport and onto the main road into central LA. Even from behind he could see that he was a breathtakingly good-looking man, with dark, glossy hair and a strong, square jaw. His perfectly manicured nails and beautifully cut white shirt made Jamie feel cheap and scruffy in comparison.

As if he could sense what Jamie was thinking, Charlie caught his eye again and Jamie quickly looked away, reddening as he did so. He hated this man already, with his money and his success and his ridiculous good looks. But most of all he hated him for being here with his wife. Jamie wanted to be alone with Martha, not with some bloody celebrity making him feel even more crap about himself. He wanted to talk to Martha, but there seemed to be an invisible wall around her and she certainly didn't seem to want to break the deadlock. In the tense silence, he stared out of the blacked-out window as the car sped along, marvelling at the number of cars and wondering how Charlie seemed to be such an expert driver when he didn't even live here.

'Where are we going?' Jamie asked at last, when he could stand it no longer.

Martha glanced towards Charlie and raised her eyebrows. 'I'm not sure, actually. Charlie, where are we going?'

From his position in the back seat, Jamie could see Charlie's expression soften as he looked at Martha. 'I thought I'd take you to the Four Seasons. We were booked in there anyway, so they'll presumably still have availability . . .' He tailed off and deliberately caught Jamie's eye in the mirror again. Jamie couldn't be sure but he thought he detected a glint of triumph in Charlie's gaze this time.

So, Jamie thought jealously, Charlie Simmons had booked himself and Martha into one of LA's swankiest hotels. It didn't take a genius to work out that he was obviously trying to get her into bed – assuming he hadn't already. Immediately, he wondered if Charlie had booked one room or two. He couldn't imagine how he would feel if they arrived to find it was one.

'OK, this is it,' Charlie said, after about thirty-five minutes, as he pulled onto the paved driveway of the Four Seasons hotel, which towered above them in pink-gold splendour. Jamie suddenly felt scared about getting out of the car. The hotel looked grander than anywhere he had ever been before, with a wall of bell-hops ready to open the doors of the cars pulling in and help their well-heeled inhabitants with their expensive luggage.

But he didn't have time to worry, as both his and Martha's doors were swung open simultaneously and he was invited to get out of the car by one of the bell-hops, who was dressed smartly in a black suit and white shirt.

'It's OK.' Charlie leaned over Martha to speak to the bell-hop. 'I'm just dropping someone off.'

The man nodded. 'No problem, Mr Simmons, sir.'

Jamie's feeling of inadequacy grew as he grabbed his shabby bag and clambered out of the car, looking back at Martha, who was talking to Charlie.

'Call me if you need anything.' Charlie was looking at her in a way that made Jamie's insides curdle. Martha nodded and leaned over to kiss Charlie on the cheek. 'I will,' she said. 'Thank you so much.' She swung her legs to the right to get out of the car and Jamie put his hand out to help her down. She pointedly ignored it and climbed out herself, giving Charlie one last lingering look and a quick wave before she turned and made her way into the palatial lobby of the hotel, escorted by a bell-hop who pulled her suitcase. Jamie trailed nervously several steps behind her, struck by how well suited she already seemed to this kind of lifestyle – unlike him, who felt awkward and out of place.

To his relief, when they checked in, he discovered that Charlie had booked two rooms. 'We'll be needing both after all,' Martha told the smiling receptionist, putting an end to Jamie's short-lived jubilation.

As they walked towards the lifts, Jamie threw Martha a sideways glance, to try to gauge her expression, but her face was impassive. The bell-hop pressed the button and the lift doors swished together. Jamie suddenly felt terrified at being in such close proximity to Martha. 'This is *ridiculous*,' he muttered, trying to lighten the mood with a slight laugh. 'I feel so nervous.'

Martha's lip curled slightly and she looked away.

'You look amazing, by the way,' Jamie added, wondering

where she had got the blue dress. He was fairly sure he'd never seen it before.

'Shame you didn't think so earlier . . .' Martha muttered.

Jamie's eyes shot towards the bell-hop, whose face remained neutral. He must have seen it all before, he thought. Especially in LA.

They arrived at the room and the bell-hop let them in. 'Wow!' gasped Jamie, looking around him and again feeling a stab of discomfort as he realised that this was the sort of luxury that someone like Charlie Simmons would be used to. 'It's fantastic!'

'I suppose so,' Martha replied, looking pointedly at the man who had just deposited her bag on the luggage rack.

Jamie followed her gaze for a few seconds before realisation dawned. He fumbled in his pocket and pulled out a bundle of dollars, tearing off first a five, then adding a ten.

'Thank you, sir,' the bell-hop smiled, discreetly pocketing the money and leaving.

Jamie and Martha stood awkwardly for a few seconds, before Jamie spoke: 'Great room,' he croaked.

Martha looked around dispassionately, before putting her handbag on the floor and kicking off the wedge sandals she was wearing. She padded over to the mini bar area of the suite and poured herself a glass from the bottle of still water provided. 'Do you want one?' She finally looked at Jamie, who was still clutching his holdall as he stood in the middle of the vast room looking lost.

'Don't suppose they've got anything stronger?' he tried to joke, before seeing from Martha's face that she was in no mood. 'Er, yes, water would be great.' He dumped his bag down and slumped onto one of the plump beige sofas.

Martha brought the glasses over to the coffee table and put them down carefully. Then she sat on the other sofa and curled her feet underneath her. 'So,' she began, fixing him with a cold stare, 'what do we do now?'

Jamie picked up a glass and took a long, thirsty gulp. 'I know what I want to do,' he said, when he felt that his throat was no longer too parched to speak.

'Let me guess. You want me to forgive you and forget that it ever happened. Forget that you slept with some whore behind my back while our children were at school and I was working hard to provide a roof over our heads. Am I right?'

Jamie shook his head, unable to bear her cold assessment. 'Don't . . .' he pleaded.

'How would you rather I put it? Because I'm right, aren't I, Jamie? That's what you've come here for, haven't you?'

Jamie took a deep breath. 'I've come here because I couldn't handle another second of being apart from you. I couldn't cope with you being on the other side of the world hating me. I don't blame you for one minute. But Martha, I promise you one thing. However much you hate me right now, it's only a fraction of how much I hate myself. I will never, ever forgive myself for what I did, but equally, I will never, ever stop trying to prove to you that I love you . . . and I . . .' He stopped for a second as the tears threatened to overwhelm him. When he felt that they had subsided enough, he continued, 'And I love our two gorgeous kids so much. It will never happen again.' He finished speaking and leaned forward, beseeching her with his eyes to understand how much he meant what he was saying. 'Please, baby ...'

Martha put her hand up to stop him talking. 'Shut up!' she cried. 'The only reason you're in such a state is because you've been caught. If you hadn't been caught, you would have carried on the minute my back was turned. If you really loved any of us, you wouldn't have dreamt of cheating on us.'

'It just wasn't like that!' Jamie protested, shaking his head.

A giant shudder passed through Martha's body and she hugged herself as she started to shake.

'You're cold!' Jamie leapt up and pulled one of the sumptuous cashmere throws off the bed. He draped it around Martha's heaving shoulders and sat down beside her, leaving one arm across her back. When she didn't shake him off, he ventured further and pulled her towards him in an embrace.

They sat for almost half an hour, both lost in their own desperate thoughts, each of them crying sporadically, before Jamie spoke again. 'I am so, so sorry, Martha,' he said.

Martha nodded sadly. 'I know. But I'm not sure I'll ever be able to forgive you, Jamie.'

Jamie's spirits, which had risen slightly when she had allowed him to hug her, now dropped again. 'I know I'll never be able to forgive myself. But if there's *anything*, anything at all that I can do to put this right, please tell me. Because I am going out of my mind and I just don't know what to do.'

'The only thing you could do to put it right is to not have done it in the first place,' Martha replied. She looked up at Jamie and her expression hardened with contempt. 'I bet you and her were laughing your heads off at stupid old me, weren't you? I bet you were—'

'No!' Jamie gasped, squeezing her shoulder. 'It wasn't like that at all.' But this time Martha shook his arm off angrily and moved away from him, pulling the throw around herself protectively.

'I feel like such a fool! I've read all the stories in the magazines I write for, about husbands who spend their days shagging anything that moves behind their wives' backs, and yet never once ... never once,' she repeated, 'did I think it might apply to you. Oh no ... not wonderful Jamie who's so helpful down at the school. Christ, I bet you've even slept with half the mums on the PTA!'

Jamie jumped up, alarmed at the way she was working herself into a frenzy again. 'No!' he shouted, loud enough to make Martha stop talking mid-sentence. 'There have been no other affairs! I'm not trying to dodge what I have done, Martha, but I'm not going to take the blame for things I haven't done either.'

'Think about it, Jamie. What you've done has shattered my confidence far more effectively than if you'd beaten the shit out of me. I can't look at my face and body now without thinking about how it wasn't enough for you. About how you weren't satisfied with our sex life, so you chose to go out and find someone else to have sex with ...'

'But you *were* enough for me!' Jamie cried, desperate for her to believe him. 'I think you're the sexiest woman alive. I love what we do together ...'

'Well here's the thing,' Martha said in a cold voice. 'Men

217

who think their wives are the sexiest women on earth don't sleep with other women behind their backs. Men who are happily married and satisfied with their sex life, don't sleep with other women behind their wives' backs. Men who—'

'OK!' Jamie cut her off, too weary to fight any more. 'I can't explain it. I am more ashamed than you will ever know, but you have got to believe me that it had nothing to do with you.'

Martha snorted. 'Nothing to do with me? I think it had something to do with me, Jamie, that I caught you red-handed having an affair.'

'I meant that it was nothing to do with the way you look or how I feel about you. It was separate. It was as if I was able to disconnect from reality. But the truth is, I am as crazy about you as the day we first met. I think you're beautiful, funny, sexy and clever. I am a shit for ever putting what we have in jeopardy, but it will never, ever happen again and I am going to spend the rest of my life proving that to you.'

Martha reached over and pulled his hands away from where he'd placed them over his eyes, so that he had to look at her. 'Aren't you just sorry that you've been caught?' she said, blinking away the last vestiges of tears.

Jamie looked into the dark pools of his wife's eyes and tried to find some kind of solace or hope there, but all he could see was despair. 'I'm not sorry I was caught,' he said, meaning it. 'I'm glad.'

As he spoke, a giant wave of grief seemed to pass through Martha's body and escape from her mouth in a strangled moan. She curled into a foetal position as dry, painful-sounding sobs racked her whole body. Jamie moved towards her again and wrapped his arms around her. She was too distraught to shake him off and he gently rubbed her back as he rocked her. Gradually, her crying became less violent until she was just sniffing quietly.

'I'm not glad,' she said in a small voice, 'because I thought we were the real thing and now I know for certain that we're not. We never were.'

Jamie desperately wanted to lie down on the floor and cry himself, but he knew it was important that he held it together. 'We *are* the real thing,' he whispered urgently. 'We've been so happy together, Martha. We love each other . . .'

As he felt her stiffen, he continued quickly, 'Since the day I met you, I have never loved anyone else and that hasn't changed.'

'But I don't believe any of it any more. I feel as if our whole life together's been a sham.'

'Believe it,' Jamie said urgently, giving her a squeeze. 'Remember all the good things. Please don't dismiss all those happy years as if they didn't happen.'

Martha pushed him off gently and sat back as she looked up at him, her dark eyes still swimming. 'I do remember the good things, Jamie, and it only makes it worse. I was so sure that we would grow old together, look after our grandchildren together, travel the world . . . We had so many dreams and now they've all just . . . gone.' She clicked her fingers together as she spoke. 'Just like that.'

'They haven't gone!' Jamie cried, kneeling in front of her and grabbing both her hands, as he looked up at her beseechingly. 'We'll still do all those things we dreamed about. We'll still grow old together, Martha. I want to be with you for the rest of my life. Please, we're too good to let it all go.'

Martha shook her head sadly. 'How can we, Jamie? How could we ever pick up where we left off? Everything we had, every memory, is tainted now.'

'Don't say that! Nothing can destroy our beautiful memories. We'll always have those.'

Again, Martha shook her head and sighed. 'No, we won't. It's like a photograph that been torn in two. We can mend it but the tear will always be there.'

Exhaustion and misery overwhelmed Jamie and he slumped down onto the floor, resting his forehead on the thick, soft carpet. She was right. Whatever happened from now on, the scars would always be there to remind them. But he had to find a way to make her give him another chance. He might as well be dead if she didn't. He got up and sat beside her, prepared to talk all day and all night if necessary. Sleep could wait. His marriage couldn't.

Chapter 26

Liv was in her office speaking to her mother when she heard Charlie calling out to her. 'I'd better go, Charlie's here.'

'Charlie?' her mother, Mariella, spluttered. '*Your* Charlie?'

'He hasn't been *my* Charlie for a long time,' Liv replied wearily.

'Well, what's he doing there? Has he come to collect Felix?' Mariella persisted.

'No, he's staying here. Oh, it's such a long story that I haven't got the time or the energy to go into it right now. I'll call you later, OK?' Liv said, before hanging up, feeling shaky and a bit sick. It had been a draining and upsetting conversation, breaking it to Mariella that Danny had ended their relationship.

Her mother would never have admitted it, but Liv knew that she was ridiculously impressed by Danny's connections, even though her own family were already famous themselves. She had secretly been over the moon when Liv had dumped Charlie, who Mariella thought would never make it big, in favour of a Hollywood A-lister, as it had

221

automatically propelled her up the fame ladder by association.

No, Liv thought, as she made her way through to see Charlie, Mariella had never tried hard to disguise the fact that she was as shallow as a paddling pool; her disappointment at Liv's wrecked relationship was definitely more for herself than for her heartbroken daughter. As the thought entered Liv's head, it was immediately followed by the realisation that maybe she herself wasn't as heartbroken as she had always imagined she would be. In some ways, now that the worst had happened, it felt like a relief. She had spent so long twisting herself in knots, worrying that Danny might be cheating on her, or would grow bored with her, that she couldn't have carried on for much longer as she was.

'Hi. I was just on the phone to my mother,' she explained, as she came into the day room to meet Charlie.

Charlie rolled his eyes. 'And how is the lovely Mariella?'

'Exactly the same as she ever was,' Liv replied, thinking how strange it was to have her ex-husband, who knew so much about her and her family, sharing her house again, and for them to be getting on so well after so many years of clipped conversations and recriminations. 'I told her about . . . me and Danny,' she said quietly. She glanced towards the kitchen. She needed a drink but suspected that Charlie might disapprove.

Charlie nodded. 'And let me guess. I bet she wasn't happy? Or at least not as happy as she was when you left me?'

Liv sighed. 'No,' she admitted. 'I hate that she didn't treat you as well as you deserved, Charlie. None of us did.'

'Forget about it,' Charlie said. 'I managed just fine without Mariella's dubious support, thanks very much,' he added, dropping down onto one of the over-sized white sofas that were dotted around the giant space and smiling up at Liv, taking the sting out of his words.

'Anyway, forget about my mother.' Liv waved her hand dismissively. God, she really did need a drink. 'How did you get on?'

'Fine,' Charlie nodded. 'I've left them to it. Dropped them at the Four Seasons ... We were booked in there anyway.'

Liv sat down on the floor, her legs crossed and her back against one of the easy chairs. 'That was very nice of you, Charlie, especially considering ...' she tailed off. 'Well, you know.'

'Yes,' Charlie stretched his long legs out in front of him and crossed them at the ankles. He frowned slightly. 'I must have "mug" tattooed on my forehead.'

'No!' Liv protested. 'You're not a mug at all. You've done really well for yourself. You're flavour of the month at the moment – everyone's tripping over themselves to offer you stuff.' She hoped she didn't sound as bitter as she felt. What would her career hold now she'd been relegated to 'Danny's ex'?

'Yes, I guess so. I've got a couple of meetings tomorrow, actually. I'd almost forgotten about them,' he replied, looking down and meeting Liv's eye.

'I remember that feeling of being fêted by every director and having to turn stuff down ...' Liv pushed out her bottom lip glumly.

'Any new roles lined up?'

'A couple,' Liv lied, before admitting, 'Actually, Charlie, the truth is, things haven't been so good lately. I've missed out on a couple of parts that I really wanted and I don't know why. Everything seems to be going wrong at the moment,' she said, her eyes filling with tears and her head swimming.

Charlie looked at her appraisingly. 'Everyone goes through lean patches, Liv,' he said. 'It'll come good, you'll see. You'll get a call tomorrow from your agent with something amazing and wonder what you were worried about.'

Liv smiled gratefully, remembering how good Charlie had been for her confidence. He had always believed in her. Believed that she would make it all the way to the top. And he had been right. For a very brief period, after she and Danny got together, she had been the toast of Hollywood, turning down endless parts because she didn't have the time to fit them all in. But then, as Danny moved on to new projects with new leading ladies and she starred in a couple of movies that were universally panned, she noticed that she was starting to lose out to other actresses for parts that she would have thought were a dead cert.

'It's amazing that you can be so generous, after what happened between us,' Liv chewed her lip nervously. She and Charlie had never actually discussed what had happened, after the initial phone calls in which he had begged her to reconsider and she had coldly told him that she had made up her mind and that she wouldn't be getting back with him.

Charlie looked up as he considered what she had said. 'I don't *feel* generous,' he said. 'But I do feel as if something has changed in me recently. Maybe I'm hardening,' he added, with a glint in his eye.

'I'm the opposite,' Liv could feel the cloud that had been hovering ominously over her shoulder start to descend just a little bit further. 'I feel a bit ... overwhelmed by everything. As if I can't cope.'

Charlie thought for a moment before he spoke. 'I felt like that for a long while after you left me,' he said, his tone matter-of-fact rather than accusatory.

Liv closed her eyes and shrank back against the chair she was leaning on, her stomach churning. It might be easier if he was a bit more aggressive and nasty, but his kindness only made her guilt a million times worse. 'I'm sorry ...' she muttered.

'I wasn't expecting you to apologise,' Charlie said quickly. 'I just meant that it's not surprising you feel like this so soon after your relationship breaking up. But it passes.'

Something inside Liv seemed to crack as he spoke and she started to shake violently, then her chest tightened and she started to struggle for breath.

Charlie jumped up in alarm. 'Liv! Are you ok?' he cried, kneeling in front of her and lifting her chin. 'Take a deep, slow breath. Come on, breathe with me, Liv! Jesus, you've gone grey. Where's your phone?'

Liv tried to focus on what he was saying but it was as if all the muscles in her neck had disappeared and she couldn't hold her head up, let alone breathe.

Charlie cast around wildly, looking for the phone as Liv slid down onto the floor so that she was lying on her back.

Suddenly, it was as if she was floating above herself, watching as her body continued to shake violently and her eyes began to bulge as she clutched her chest.

Charlie finally located a phone and dialled 911. 'Ambulance, emergency,' he said, before giving the address. 'It's Liv Mason. She seems to be having some sort of attack.'

Chapter 27

Martha leaned against the balcony rail and looked out at the view over the pool. It reminded her of an all-inclusive holiday they'd once taken with the children, the way the sunbeds were all lined up in neat rows.

Unlike the all-inclusive, however, where there was an unseemly scramble for the sunbeds each morning, many of the beds were available. Those that weren't were mainly occupied by extremely attractive young women, clearly hoping to be 'discovered' either by a passing movie director or, failing that, a very rich man who would provide a passport into a life of Hollywood luxury.

Every fifteen minutes or so, a handsome young man in an emerald green polo shirt and stone-coloured shorts would approach the sunbathers and top up their water jugs or refill their glasses.

At any other time, Martha would have lapped up this whole experience. She was in one of the best hotels in Beverly Hills, surrounded by beautiful people, celebrities and God knows how many potential stories, but she just couldn't get excited about it.

She and Jamie had talked for hours, with Jamie desperately trying to get her to focus on the good times they had had together. They had reminisced about the early days of their relationship and all the things they had achieved together; they remembered the days their babies were born and how scared they had felt bringing them home for the first time. But underlying everything was both of them trying to make sense of what had happened and why he had done it. Eventually, Jamie had succumbed to exhaustion and jet-lag, and was still fast asleep.

Martha stepped back into the room – she hadn't used the other room they had booked yet – and pulled the doors closed behind her, blocking out the sunshine and the smoggy heat of the city. She sat down on the sofa and watched Jamie as he slept, thinking how troubled he looked, with the deep frown lines across his tanned forehead that moved up and down as if they were having a conversation all of their own, his square jaw clenching every now and again as he ground his teeth together. There were still traces of the three scratches she had left on his cheek when she had clawed at him that first morning, which gave Martha a strange sense of satisfaction. She decided that it was because she had inflicted pain on him the way he had inflicted it on her. Was it really less than a week since all that had happened?

Jamie jolted violently in the bed and groaned. Clearly his dreams were as bad as hers. She had loved this man so, so much and yet, watching him, she realised how close love was to hate, because hate was definitely her over-riding emotion now. How could he have done it to her? But worse, how could he have done it to their children?

She wondered what Charlie was doing right now and why she was missing him. Probably because he had been so kind to her, she told herself. She could picture his long-lashed, dark eyes, watching her with sympathy and understanding as she talked. It was the sympathy of someone who knew exactly how she felt.

Martha shook her head, trying to clear all thoughts of Charlie from her mind, but it was hopeless. She needed to see him. Casting another glance at Jamie, she picked up her phone and left the room. She made her way along the plushly carpeted corridor to the lift and pressed the button for the pool area.

As she walked out into the sunshine, she was immediately hit by a gush of dry heat and she instinctively dropped her sunglasses against the glare. Her eyes felt sore enough without exposing them to the sun's rays. Now she understood why so many Hollywood stars were never seen without their shades. It would have been impossible to function without them here.

She headed for one of the sunbeds and was just about to lay down when one of the attendants darted in front of her and placed a thick cream towel on the sumptuous padding and another one rolled up for her head. Martha smiled her thanks and sank down onto it, suddenly grateful that she was wearing a sundress rather than a bikini, judging by the model-like beauties draped over some of the other beds.

She dialled Charlie's number and felt a stab of disappointment when he didn't pick up. She knew that he had her number in his phone; was he deliberately screening her calls because he was pissed off that she had agreed to meet Jamie? Surely not. Jamie was her husband and the father of her children. She couldn't let him come all the way to LA and ignore him.

As instructed by an automated voice, she left a message. 'Hi Charlie, it's me. Martha, that is,' she added, laughing nervously. 'I just wanted to ... um, speak to you, I suppose.' She was trying not to sound too desperate. 'Anyway, please give me a call if you get this message. Uh, thanks. Bye.'

She hung up and laid her head back on the rolled-up towel at the top of the sunbed, feeling strangely upset. 'Hi there!' said a ridiculously good-looking blond-haired man in his twenties, looming over her and making her jump. 'Can I get you a drink from the bar?'

'Oh!' Martha stuttered, sitting up quickly and automatically pulling down the hem of her dress. 'No, er, I'm fine, thank you. I'm with someone ... he's just upstairs!' she trilled over-brightly. She knew she had started to blush. It was a long time since a man had hit on her and she didn't know how to deal with it.

The man managed to smile and frown at the same time. 'No problem, just give me a shout when you're ready to order!'

'Will do,' Martha muttered, feeling idiotic and lying back down as flat as she could, in the hope that she could disappear altogether. Of course he hadn't been hitting on her. He *worked* here.

After a few moments Martha must have dozed off because she was awoken by a voice accompanied by a hand on her arm. 'No!' She opened her eyes in alarm. 'I'm still fine for a drink, thank you!'

'Martha, it's me, Charlie,' said the voice, as Charlie stepped slightly to one side so that the sun wasn't behind him and she could make out his face.

'Oh, hi!' she said, aware that she was grinning now. 'I just called you.'

'Actually, you called me a while ago but I was at the hospital.'

'Hospital?' Martha echoed, sitting up in alarm. 'Why? What's happened?'

Charlie sighed as he sat down on the sunbed nearest to her, upon which the ever-present attendant had already placed two towels.

Around the pool, Martha could see a couple of people glancing surreptitiously over the top of their sunglasses at him, and she realised with a start that it was because he was easily the most famous person here. Already it seemed as if Martha had forgotten that Charlie was a VIP – she just thought of him as the same as everyone else.

'It was Liv. She had some sort of funny turn—'

'Like the other day?' Martha cut in, turning sideways so that she was facing him, planting her bare feet on the ground.

'I guess so. Looked like she was having a heart attack but I doubt it's that – she's too young and fit.'

Martha shook her head as she absorbed the news. 'I did

231

notice that she seems to be drinking a lot. Do you think it might have something to do with that?'

Charlie shrugged. 'Who knows? I guess we all go through those sort of phases ...'

'Poor Liv. So, is she still at the hospital?'

'Yes, they're running lots of tests so there wasn't really anything I could do. I thought I'd go and get Felix from school later and take him back to get her. Then I saw that you'd called, so I decided to call in ... to see how you were getting on.'

'I'm glad you did,' Martha said, then clamped her mouth shut, wondering if she had said too much.

Charlie looked at her curiously. 'So, where is he then? He hasn't gone home already?' he added, almost hopefully.

'No. He's sleeping. The jet-lag finally caught up with him, so I left him to it.'

Charlie nodded and smiled at her. Martha had never noticed before but he had a slight dimple in his cheek that became more pronounced when he smiled.

'So, what are you going to do then, Martha?'

She shook her head slowly. 'I just don't know, Charlie. I feel a bit ...' She tailed off and shrugged helplessly.

'A bit what?' he prompted gently.

'A bit trapped,' she admitted. 'I mean, I don't really have a choice, do I? I don't want my children to grow up in a broken home. To have their lives blow up in front of them. Jamie swears it was just some kind of terrible aberration and I'm not sure I have any other option than to believe him. This woman picked him up and offered it on a plate. He says he was bored and lonely at home on his own all day and, although it was a terrible thing to do, he will regret it for the rest of his life.'

Charlie looked at her without speaking and she tried to read his expression but couldn't. 'What?' she said at last.

'We all have choices,' he said quietly. 'But I know what you mean about feeling trapped. It must be very tough for you. I think . . .' he paused as if trying to formulate his thoughts. 'I think that if you *do* decide to give him another chance, you should definitely have counselling.'

'But I've got you,' she smiled. 'You're my counsellor!'

Charlie laughed, but she noticed that a nerve in the side of his cheek had begun to pulse. 'I'm not a counsellor, Martha. I don't know why he did this. If I was your . . . Anyway,' he changed tack quickly, 'you need to get to the bottom of why he did this. You need to be one hundred per cent sure that he's never going to do it again, and you won't be able to do that unless you know why it happened.'

Martha gulped. She had always hated the thought of counselling, convinced that it could make things worse by opening up all sorts of issues that were best left buried. And what was it that Charlie had been going to say?

'I think we'd better get home as soon as possible. We can't stay here indefinitely . . .' she motioned around her as she spoke. 'And by the way, I insist that we pay you for our stay here.'

Charlie waved away her words with his hand. 'Forget it.'

'Well, anyway, we also need to get back to the children. They must be feeling so confused by what's going on.'

Charlie nodded slowly and looked around him. 'I'll miss you,' he said quietly, as he looked back at her and held her gaze.

Martha felt a shiver of excitement pass through her. She tried to look away but it was impossible. 'This can't happen,' she whispered.

'I know,' Charlie whispered back, a look of intense sadness crossing his features.

As he spoke he leaned forward until his face was just a couple of inches from Martha's. Without realising quite what she was doing, she leaned forward too and their lips brushed. For a second they looked at each other in surprise, then Charlie reached out and cupped the back of her head with his hand as he pulled her forward again and kissed her.

When they broke apart, their eyes still locked, Charlie held out his hand and pulled Martha to her feet. Without speaking, they walked hand-in-hand towards the lifts.

Chapter 28

Jamie woke with a start. The light in the room was dim. He blinked several times to try to clear his vision, which was blurred through tiredness. He glanced around the room looking for Martha, but he could already sense that he was alone. He sat up and tried to shake the residual jet-lag out of his head.

Reaching over to the bedside table, he turned the clock to check the time and was shocked to see that it was nearly eight. He had slept for hours. Immediately, he began to calculate what time it was in the UK, concluding that it would be almost four in the afternoon. He didn't know if the kids would be at home or at school because he couldn't even remember if it was a Friday or a Saturday, but he desperately wanted to speak to them.

Feeling groggy, his head thick with confusion, he fumbled for his phone and scrolled through his contacts list until he found the number for home. He pressed 'Call', while saying a mental prayer that he wouldn't get Jane.

To his huge relief, Mimi answered. 'Hi darling, it's Dad,' he said.

'Oh, hi!' she cried, sounding pleased. 'Where are you?'

'I'm in LA.'

'I know that, silly,' she said impatiently. 'I meant, where are you right now? Tell me exactly what you can see all around you. Can you see the Hollywood sign? Have you been to the Walk of Fame yet?'

Jamie laughed and felt a surge of love for her, suddenly wishing she was there with him. 'Well, actually I've just woken up. I'm just sitting in a hotel room. It's a very nice hotel room, granted,' he continued, looking around him and taking in for the first time just how plush his surroundings were. 'But it's still just a hotel room.'

'Oh.' Mimi sounded deflated. 'Is Mum there?' she added, her tone hardening.

'Actually, no,' Jamie said, wondering where Martha had gone. 'I think she must be out running . . .'

There was a short pause. 'I saw the other pictures of her and pig-face in the paper, by the way.'

Jamie smiled. He felt exactly the same way about Charlie, but he couldn't let Martha be blamed for what had happened. 'There's nothing to worry about at all,' he said soothingly. 'She's following him for work. Nothing more to it than that.'

After a little while longer chatting about what else was going on at home and narrowly avoiding having to talk to Jane, Jamie hung up and opened the curtains and doors out onto the balcony. Dawn was still hanging over LA like a dusty blue muslin, not quite blocking out the vivid colours of the Californian sky, but certainly muting them.

He leaned over the balcony rail, wishing that he still

smoked. He had given up when Martha was pregnant with Mimi, but now the craving for a nicotine hit had returned with an unexpected vengeance. He listened to the sounds of the early morning, noticing with surprise the lack of birdsong that was so loud at this time of day back home. He decided that, even though he was staying in the most luxurious surroundings he had ever seen, he didn't like LA much. It seemed too loud, too hot, too fake. Then again, he concluded, it could just be that he wasn't in the right frame of mind to enjoy it.

He was about to turn away and retreat to the coolness of the room when something caught his eye. A flash of blue. The colour of Martha's sundress. He frowned and leaned over the balcony again, as Martha and Charlie emerged from the hotel and walked out onto the driveway, where cars were being brought up from the valet parking. Although they weren't holding hands, their fingers were definitely brushing and they were walking very close to one another. Too close for Jamie's liking. He stepped back slightly, in case Martha should look up and see him, but she was deeply engrossed in a conversation with Charlie and seemed oblivious to everything around her.

Jamie strained to hear what they were saying, but even though the early morning air was still, the noise from the car engines meant he could only make out faint murmurings. As he watched, they stopped walking and turned to face each other. Jamie's stomach churned with jealousy as he caught the look on Martha's face. It was a look she had given him so often in the past.

Eventually, Charlie reached out and touched Martha's face, making Jamie want to vault over the balcony and punch his lights out there and then. Instead he had to watch as they bid each other goodbye and Charlie headed for his car, glancing back longingly several times at Martha, who had stayed exactly where she was, gazing after him.

Once Charlie had driven off, Martha turned and began to make her way back into the hotel, looking lost in thought. As she did so, she glanced up at the balcony and jumped with shock as she caught Jamie's eye.

Jamie took a deep breath to steady his nerves and went back into the cool, dark room, pulling the doors closed behind him. He switched on the lamps dotted around the room and sat on the bed, awaiting Martha's return. A million thoughts were running around in his head, but the one that kept pushing itself to the front was a hopeful one. Had he caught Martha out? And if so, did that make them even? Would it cancel out the horror and shame of what he had done? Part of him hoped that it would.

There was a whirring sound followed by a click as the door unlocked and Martha came in looking, Jamie thought, slightly guilty.

She came over to the bed and perched beside him. Neither of them spoke for several minutes and the silence grew heavier until Jamie couldn't stand it any more. 'Where did you go?' he asked, trying to keep his voice as neutral as possible.

Martha looked up at the ceiling, as if trying to weigh up what to say. 'I went to the other room,' she said at last, swallowing hard as she looked at Jamie.

Jamie frowned. 'Other room? What other room?'

'Charlie booked two rooms, remember? I went to the other one.'

Another heavy silence ensued. 'Alone?' Jamie managed to croak, when he had plucked up enough courage to ask the question.

'No,' Martha said, almost defiantly.

'Oh God,' Jamie put his hands over his face and wondered if he felt relieved or devastated. 'Well, I guess I deserved that,' he said.

Martha nodded. 'Yes, you did.'

Jamie shook his head. She had basically just admitted to committing adultery and yet she didn't even seem bothered. It occurred to him that she had changed so much in the past few days that he already felt as if she was a stranger. The old Martha would never have contemplated sleeping with some-one else. Even the thought of it would have horrified her. Yet here she was, casually admitting to it.

'I know exactly what's running through your mind,' Martha said, making Jamie look up sharply. 'But all of it is wrong.'

'I'm not thinking anything ...' Jamie started to protest, then stopped, realising how ridiculous he sounded. Martha knew him better than anyone. 'Well, maybe I am,' he admit-ted.

'I didn't sleep with him,' Martha said quietly, making Jamie feel as if all the air had been squeezed out of his lungs. 'Because then I'd be no better than you, would I?'

Jamie groaned and put his head back in his hands. 'Oh God, Martha!' he cried in a muffled voice. 'I hoped that ...'

'... You hoped that I would have done the same as you and then we'd be even,' Martha finished with terrifying accuracy. 'But that's not how it works, is it? Because I would only have done it to get back at you. So you would still be to blame. Only this time you'd be to blame for both of us.'

'Don't!' Jamie put a hand up to stop her speaking. He couldn't stand to have any more blame or shame heaped upon him.

Once again, they lapsed into silence, each of them locked in their own private hell. After a while, Jamie reached out tentatively to take Martha's hand and was gratified when she didn't shake him off. 'I think you have feelings for Charlie, though,' he said, hoping that she might at least attempt a denial.

Martha didn't reply, but when she looked up her large brown eyes were brimming with tears.

'It's OK,' Jamie said. 'I get it. And more to the point, I deserve it. But Martha, I love you so much. You have got to believe me. We have two gorgeous children and a great life together. We can't throw that away without a fight, can we?'

Martha brushed her eyes with the back of her hand and shook her head. 'No,' she said. 'We can't. But I feel so hurt, so bruised ...' she stopped speaking for a minute as her voice broke. 'I don't know if I'm strong enough to fight!' she finished.

Jamie reached over and pulled her to him, rubbing the silky skin of her arms and inhaling the smell of her perfume. 'You don't have to fight,' he said, kissing her hair. 'Just give me the chance and I'll fight hard enough for both of us.'

Chapter 29

'Where are we going?' Martha asked, looking out of the car window, as Beverly Hills disappeared into the distance behind them.

Jamie smiled through his crinkled blue eyes. 'I told you, just wait and see.'

Martha shook her head wearily. Jamie had persuaded her to let him take her out, even though they were both exhausted after the hours they had spent talking.

The taxi sped through the busy streets and Martha thought with a pang how much the children would enjoy being in LA, especially Mimi. It made her understand just how hard it must have been for Charlie to be separated from Felix for such long periods of time.

'The kids would love this, wouldn't they?' said Jamie, echoing her thoughts perfectly.

'That's just what I was thinking.'

'They miss you,' he added. 'They want you to come home.'

Martha met his eye. 'I miss them too.'

Jamie reached across the gulf between them and took her

hand. Instinctively, Martha made to pull away but he held onto it tightly. 'And I want you to come home too. I'm no good without you.'

Martha swallowed hard and bit her lip. She couldn't reply. She ached to see the children and desperately wanted to return home, but she was scared of the emotional tsunami she knew awaited her.

After about half an hour, the car drew to a halt. Martha allowed Jamie to open the door for her and take her hand as she stepped out. She recognised it immediately as the court-yard of a hotel called Shutters on the Beach in Santa Monica. Martha had been there before, when she had interviewed Robert de Niro, and had returned home to Jamie gushing about both the actor and the hotel. He'd remembered. Somewhere deep down she was touched.

The hotel itself was very pretty with its whitewashed New England clapboard exterior and its simple, nautical-inspired interior, but it was the dramatic beach-side setting that was really breathtaking.

Jamie took her hand and led her down the side of the hotel towards the beach. Martha smiled to herself as the wide, golden stretch of sand and the dusky indigo ocean came into view. The sun had almost set but there was still enough of an orange glow to bathe the water in a spectacular, fiery light. There was something about the sea that always calmed her and helped her feel a sense of perspective, however stressed she was. At home she went for a run along the beach most mornings to give herself a kick-start. Jamie knew it. That was probably why he'd brought her here. She breathed in the fresh, clean air blowing in off the Pacific and tried to feel some kind of peace amid the churning and crashing of her emotions.

Jamie led her onto the sand. They both kicked off their shoes and walked in silence in the direction of Santa Monica pier, which was flashing and twinkling in the encroaching darkness. 'This is so weird,' she said, more to herself than to him.

'I know.'

They walked on in silence for a while, as the sound of the waves crashing onto the shore mingled with the cacophony of noise from the pier. It was surprisingly loud.

'I can't go home without you,' Jamie said, and his words were carried on the air and away out to sea.

Martha stopped walking and sat down on the sand. Jamie hesitated for a second before joining her. They stared at the waves, now glinting under the pale moon. 'What happens when we get home, though?'

Jamie shook his head and brought his knees up to his chest. 'That has to be your decision. I'm in your hands.'

Martha's head suddenly swam with images of Jamie's hands holding another woman's naked body and she instinctively clamped a hand to her mouth.

Jamie, as always sensing what she was thinking, knelt in front of her, his eyes pleading and desperate. 'Don't let it enter your head. God knows, I would do anything to erase those images from your brain. But sweetheart, I love you so, so much. I will never, ever hurt you again. You're my life, Martha. My whole life. Without you I have nothing. I have no meaning and no reason to live. Please, please give me another chance. I will never let you down again.' Martha closed her eyes. She felt Jamie's hand stroke her face tenderly. 'I know you're scared. I am too. But I'm far more scared of trying to live without you. We can get through this, Martha. Just come home with me and I will do everything, literally everything, to get us through it.'

Martha listened, knowing that he meant every word he was saying, but his entreaties were being drowned out by another voice in her head. Charlie's. Charlie, who had been there when she needed him most. Charlie, who had pulled her through her darkest hour and shown her nothing but generosity and understanding. He wouldn't have treated her with such casual contempt.

'Martha?'

Martha opened her eyes and looked into Jamie's. So pale compared to Charlie's deep, dark pools.

'It's him, isn't it? That's what's keeping you here?'

Martha opened her mouth to protest but no words would come. If she and Jamie were to have any chance of making a go of their marriage, they needed to be honest with each other.

Jamie flinched with pain when she didn't answer and Martha felt a stab of something approaching pleasure. But the feeling quickly subsided. Was this how it would be from now on? Trying to score points and hurt him as much as he had hurt her?

Whatever she felt for Charlie, and it was still far too soon to say exactly what she did feel for him, she had to go home and try to make her marriage work for the sake of the children. Maybe Jamie would be able to convince her, maybe he wouldn't. But she had to give him the chance to try.

'I'm not staying here,' she said slowly, watching relief flood Jamie's features. 'I'm coming home.'

'Oh, that's great!' he breathed.

'But . . .' she interrupted him, standing up and dusting the sand off her dress. 'There's someone I need to say goodbye to first.'

Chapter 30

'So it looks like it was a panic attack then?' Charlie said, as he manoeuvred the car away from the hospital and onto the road leading up towards Liv's house.

Beside him, Liv was slumped in the passenger seat, her skin still slightly grey in colour. From the back seat, Felix met his eye in the rear-view mirror and frowned. Charlie's heart constricted, thinking of how confused the little boy must be feeling after all that had been going on.

'That's what they say ...' Liv said in a flat voice, as she stared unseeingly out of the window.

'But you're not sure?' Charlie prompted.

Liv shrugged but didn't reply.

'I'm really surprised,' Charlie admitted. 'It looked like something physical rather than something mental.'

Liv looked at him sharply.

'Sorry,' Charlie mouthed, glancing again at his son in the rear-view mirror, but by now Felix was engrossed in his DS game and didn't appear to have heard.

They drove the rest of the journey in silence, up the winding, pot-holed roads, until they reached the house. Liv pressed the remote control for the automatic gates, which slid open noise-lessly, and Charlie drove up the sparkling white driveway, which was illuminated by lights embedded in the ground. He stopped the car and looked at Liv, suddenly unsure what to do. The whole situation had changed now that Martha was no longer there to ease the atmosphere between them.

'So what do we do now?' he said.

Liv, who was still staring glassily out of the window, seemed to snap into life. 'Sorry! What did you say?'

Charlie sighed. 'Well, maybe it would be better if I went and checked into a hotel? I mean, with Martha gone . . .'

Realisation dawned in Liv's eyes. 'Martha? Oh God, I didn't even ask . . . Where's she gone?'

'She's at the hotel. With *him*,' Charlie almost spat as he spoke.

'Don't go to a hotel!' Felix cried suddenly, surprising them both. 'Stay here. With us. Please?'

Charlie locked onto his son's pleading stare and then looked questioningly at Liv. 'I think that's probably up to your mum.'

Liv nodded and smiled vacantly, before opening the car door and climbing out. 'Fine by me,' she said, as she swung the door shut behind her.

Charlie closed his eyes for a few seconds. He felt churned up and sad about Martha, and he wasn't sure that being with Liv in her fragile state was the best place for him because he felt so irritable with her. But he didn't want to desert Felix either, so he exhaled loudly and opened the car door.

Once inside, he put Felix to bed and then told Liv that he was tired and was going to bed himself, although it wasn't yet nine o'clock. Liv didn't seem concerned and had already opened a bottle of wine and poured herself a glass. He suddenly felt like he couldn't bear to be around her. He knew she was struggling and seemed as if she was on the brink of some kind of meltdown, but he couldn't cope with being her support at that minute either. Worse, he resented her for what he saw as her wallowing in self-pity. If he had given in to his own desperation when she left him four years ago, he probably wouldn't be here now, but he had fought his way through it. He hadn't started drinking heavily or collapsing all over the place and frightening Felix with his dramatics.

He took a quick shower and climbed into bed, already knowing that he wouldn't be able to sleep. He couldn't stop thinking about Martha. It seemed ridiculous after such a short time but she had got right under his skin.

He thought back to the previous night when they had gone to Martha's room in the hotel. He had known that she wouldn't sleep with him but Christ, he had wanted to. It was torture just kissing her when he was desperate to do so much more. But in a world where women threw themselves at him all the time, the fact that she had resisted only made him want her all the more.

He picked up his phone and stared at it, willing it to ring and for it to be Martha. He wanted to talk to her. To hear her voice. He thought about calling her but stopped. What if she was with *him*? Charlie felt a bubble of hatred for Jamie welling up inside. The man had an amazing wife and he had treated her like crap. He didn't deserve her forgiveness, but because of their kids, Charlie had a horrible feeling he was going to get it.

Still, Charlie reasoned, at least he would be able to continue to see her because of the book. He smiled to himself with satisfaction, knowing how hard it would be for Jamie every time Martha came to meet him. Good, he thought. Serves him right.

As if on cue, his phone beeped and his eyes darted back to the screen.

What are you up to? Need to see you.

Charlie found himself beaming at the phone, as if it was actually her.

He looked at his watch. It was only nine, but people didn't tend to stay out late in LA. They were all in bed by 10.30, due to early starts on location and early-morning yoga or Pilates classes.

Let's have dinner at a place I know. Shall I come and pick you up now? he texted back, his excitement mounting.

OK x

Charlie leapt out of bed and threw on a white shirt and a pair of jeans, before heading towards the front door.

'Where are you going?' asked Liv, making him jump in surprise. He had assumed she was in bed because the house was almost dark, but she was sitting on an easy chair in the day room, with a glass of wine in her hand, which was tilting dangerously to one side.

Charlie hesitated. 'Er, I'm going out to meet Martha. I

thought I'd take her out for dinner as she's going home tomorrow.'

Liv nodded wearily. 'How nice,' she slurred and her eyes drooped shut.

Charlie watched her for a minute, weighing up whether he should go or not. Was she in a fit state to be left alone with Felix? But then, he reasoned, Felix was asleep and wouldn't wake up until the morning. It was highly unlikely he'd need anything before then, and anyway, Charlie wouldn't be too long.

'Maybe you should get yourself to bed?' he suggested, eyeing the wine glass warily.

Liv's eyes blinked open again, as if she'd been taken by surprise. 'Hmm? Oh yes, you're probably right,' she agreed, getting up and staggering over to the breakfast bar, where she deposited the glass beside the almost-empty bottle of white wine.

Charlie nodded to himself. 'I'll see you later?' He scooped up the house keys Liv had given him on his first day there.

'Have fun!' she trilled in a falsetto voice.

Charlie closed the door behind him and waited for a few moments for the feeling of unease to subside. Then he opened the car and climbed in.

Chapter 31

Jamie could hear a phone ringing somewhere in the distance. He was shouting for Martha to answer it but still it kept ringing. He sat up with a start. It wasn't a dream. It was the phone beside the bed in the hotel room. He snatched it up and spoke gruffly into the handset. 'Yes?'

'Hello, this is reception here. We have Liv Mason on the phone, trying to contact Charlie Simmons. Do you know where Mr Simmons is?'

Jamie frowned in confusion. 'Er, no, I don't. But my wife might know. She's in room 604, along from me ...' For a brief moment, Jamie wondered if he might, in fact, still be dreaming.

'Yes, we have tried her room but she's not there ...' The receptionist hesitated and Jamie instantly knew why.

'Ah, you think she's out somewhere with Charlie Simmons?'

There was another fraction of a second's hesitation. 'Er, yes, I believe they have left the hotel together. I was wondering if you might know where they are?'

Jamie swallowed back the jealousy that was rising in his throat. Martha had told him she needed to say goodbye to Charlie, but he hadn't realised she meant she was going to meet him. When they got back to the hotel earlier, Jamie had gone to bed and immediately fallen into a deep sleep. Clearly, she hadn't done the same. 'Uh, no, I don't know where they've gone,' he replied wearily. 'Do you know what she wants?'

'No, but she sounds quite, er, distressed.'

'Put her through to me,' Jamie said, before he'd had a chance to think. In the split second before the receptionist transferred the call, Jamie remembered that Liv Mason was a famous film star who didn't know him at all, and there was absolutely no reason why she would want to speak to him. 'Hello?' he said tentatively.

'Charlie?' Liv yelled, and Jamie could hear immediately that she was drunk.

'No, er, this is Jamie, Martha's husband. I don't know where Charlie and Martha have gone, but can I help?'

There was a loud groan at the other end of the line and it sounded like the phone had been dropped. He could hear Liv repeating, 'Oh God, Oh God,' over and over again.

'Liv!' called Jamie, trying not to shout but aware that he needed to make her hear. When there was no response, he swung his legs over the side of the bed and, with his heart pounding, yelled as loudly as he could, 'Liv!'

After a brief pause, during which he could hear her scrabbling for the phone, she came back on the line. 'Oh God,' she groaned again, and he could hear that she was starting to hyperventilate.

'OK, Liv,' Jamie said, trying to keep his voice as calm as possible. He had a horrible feeling that something terrible had either happened or was about to. 'Take a deep breath. Breathe with me, Liv. Can you do that? Breathe in deeply through your nose, see, like I'm doing? Then slowly out through your mouth.' He started to take exaggerated deep breaths, to try and encourage her to follow suit, all the time speaking to her in the soothing voice he used for the children when they were upset. Gradually, Liv started to follow him until she had calmed down slightly.

'Right, that's really good, Liv,' Jamie said when he felt that she could listen to him. 'Now, can you tell me what's wrong?'

Liv shrieked and Jamie cut in again. 'Listen to me very carefully, Liv. I am going to help you. Whatever's wrong, we'll sort it out, but I need to know what's happened for me to be able to help. Do you understand?'

'Yes,' Liv whimpered. 'Felix . . . he's . . .' she managed to say, before she had to take another series of deep breaths to calm herself again.

Jamie listened to her breathing with a rising sense of panic. What had happened to Felix? 'Take your time, Liv,' he said, belying the incredible sense of impatience that he was feeling. If the child was sick or injured, they needed to get to him as quickly as possible. They didn't have time for his mother's histrionics.

'Felix . . .' she croaked again in a small voice. '. . . he's gone.'

Jamie's eyes widened in alarm. He didn't know that much about Liv Mason's private life, but he knew the child wasn't very old.

'Gone where?' He was glad that his voice sounded less panicky than he felt.

'To find Charlie. He got up and saw that Charlie had gone and that I was ... oh God,' she groaned again, sounding as if she was in agony.

'I'll call the police,' Jamie said, now desperate to get her off the phone and enlist some proper help.

'No!' Liv screamed, suddenly panicky again. 'Please don't call the police! They'll take him away from me ...'

'But we need to *find* him!' Jamie shouted back.

'I know, but please will you come and help me look? He won't have got far ... I've been calling Charlie non-stop but he's not answering his phone!'

Jamie stared at the handset in shock. He didn't know LA. He didn't know Liv Mason and he didn't know the kid. How the hell was he supposed to find him? 'Give me your address,' he groaned, groping for the pen and pad beside the bed. He scribbled it down. 'Check every room in the house and check the garden,' he said, panting slightly. 'I'll be there as quickly as I can.' He hung up and called the front desk. 'I need a taxi, really urgently,' he said, before gabbling out the address.

Where the hell was Charlie and, more to the point, where was Martha? He called her number and listened as it went to voicemail. 'Call me!' he said, when prompted to leave a message, before he hung up and scrambled out of bed, throwing on a pair of jeans and a t-shirt. He felt dazed and slightly stunned, as if he might still be dreaming. He splashed his face with cold water, grabbed his wallet, phone, the piece of paper with the address on and his keycard, then raced to the lifts. At the entrance to the hotel, one of the besuited bell-hops approached him. 'Mr Smith? The house car is coming for you now.'

'What?' Jamie gaped in confusion, as a sleek black Rolls Royce glided up and pulled to a halt in front of him. The bell-hop opened the back passenger door and motioned for Jamie to get in. 'But . . .' he stuttered, before deciding that he didn't have time to argue. He climbed in and waited while the door was closed with an expensive thunk before he spoke to the driver. 'I need to go to—' he began, squinting at the piece of paper with the address written on it.

'I have the address, sir,' the driver said smoothly and politely. 'And I will get you there just as quickly as I can.'

'Thank you,' Jamie breathed. 'But can you go as slowly as you can when we get a bit closer, as I believe there's a little boy out wandering around in the dark and we need to find him.'

If the driver felt any kind of alarm at Jamie's words, he certainly didn't show it. 'No problem, sir,' he replied calmly.

The Phantom slid through the surprisingly quiet streets until they turned off the main drag and began to climb up into the Hollywood Hills. 'You might want to start keeping an eye out about now, sir,' said the driver, again with exquisite politeness. 'May I suggest that you look out of the right-hand side and I will watch the left-hand side. What age is the child we are looking for, sir?'

'Uh, I don't exactly know, but I think he's around six or seven,' Jamie replied, shaking his head at the surreal nature of the whole evening. He peered out of the window, straining to make out anything as the car continued to climb the dark, winding roads. There was very little in the way of street lighting and Jamie thought how scared any child would be out here on his own. He thought about his own son and his heart went out to the little boy who had decided to run out into the night looking for his dad.

After about ten minutes, Jamie's shoulders were sagging. There was no sign at all of Felix. A feeling of dread started to take root in his stomach, as he began to worry about what he would find when he got to Liv's house. He wished he had ignored her pleas and called the police like he'd wanted to.

'I think this might be him, sir!' said the driver suddenly, his voice finally betraying some excitement in place of his usual stilted politeness.

The car slid to a standstill and Jamie leapt out. Up ahead of him on the dark pavement he could make out a small figure walking quickly down the hill towards him. As he got closer, Jamie could see that he was still wearing his Toy Story pyjamas.

'Felix!' Jamie shouted.

The boy looked up in alarm and hesitated, glancing around nervously as Jamie approached. Suddenly, he turned around and headed back up the hill, running.

'Felix!' Jamie repeated, jogging after him. 'There's nothing to worry about. I'm a friend of your mum and dad. They asked me to come and find you.'

The boy hesitated and looked back at Jamie over his shoulder, before he resumed running again. 'I've never seen you before!' he cried.

'I'm Martha's husband, Jamie ...' he called, struggling for breath as he shouted and ran at the same time. He was gaining on the boy easily, though, and within a few strides he had pulled level with him.

'Martha, daddy's girlfriend?' Felix glanced suspiciously up at Jamie as they ran along side by side.

'Can we stop running for a second, please?' Jamie pulled up and put his hands on his knees to get his breath back. 'I can't run and talk at the same time.'

Felix slowed to a halt slightly further up the hill and looked back at Jamie. 'Isn't Martha daddy's girlfriend?' he repeated.

Jamie felt his jaw tighten. 'Well, she's a friend of your dad's and she's a girl, so I guess that might make her his girlfriend,' he said, finally understanding the expression 'the words stuck in my craw'. 'But I'm her husband. Listen, Felix, you have nothing to be scared of. I'm just going to take you home to your mum because she called me and she's worried sick about you.'

'What if you're lying?' Felix looked around as if searching for back-up.

Sharp kid, Jamie thought. Of course, with high-profile parents like Liv and Charlie, kidnapping must be a constant threat. He considered what to do for a minute. 'OK, well, how about you call your mum before you get in the car? Ask her if it's OK if Jamie gives you a lift home.' Jamie fumbled in his back pocket for his phone and held it out towards Felix. 'Here, take it.'

Warily, Felix inched his way down the hill until he was within reaching distance and stretched out his hand to take the phone. Keeping his eye on Jamie the whole time, he edged a few feet back up the hill.

Jamie wanted to laugh; the whole situation was so ridiculous, especially now that he knew the child was safe.

'Do you know your mum's number?' he prompted.

Felix nodded and, finally taking his eyes off Jamie, began to tap out Liv's number. After a few seconds, he spoke. 'Mom? It's me. Is it OK for me to get into a car with this English guy?'

Chapter 32

'Wow, this is gorgeous!' sighed Martha, as Charlie led her into the restaurant. It certainly lived up to its name – *Little Door* – as the only indication it was there was literally a small door in the middle of a wall on a nondescript street. But inside it was like stepping into a twinkling, Italianate wonderland. Fairy lights winked from the lush canopy of dark green foliage and a pink glow hung over each of the candlelit tables, giving the whole room a slightly mystical and romantic atmosphere.

'I knew you'd love it,' Charlie smiled back at her as a female maître d' guided them to a discreet table in the corner.

Martha followed, feeling several curious pairs of eyes on her. She kept forgetting that Charlie was recognised wherever he went. The thought made her feel strangely territorial and possessive of him, and she realised with a jolt that she already thought of him as *her* Charlie.

Once they were seated, Martha picked up her menu and tried to focus on what to order, but after a couple of minutes she put it back down. 'I can't concentrate. We need to talk.'

Charlie looked up at her. 'That sounds ominous,' he said, trying to smile.

Martha exhaled. 'I'm going home. Tomorrow.'

Charlie nodded but didn't speak. After a second he reached out and took her hand in his. Martha glanced around nervously but no-one seemed to be paying them any attention.

'I'm sorry,' she said, wanting to fill the silence between them.

'No, don't be sorry.' Charlie gave her hand a squeeze. 'I knew you would.'

Martha's throat constricted and her eyes swam. 'It's … complicated, isn't it?'

Charlie pursed his lips slightly. 'The thing is, Martha,' he began, fixing her with his dark-eyed stare, 'I have feelings for you that have kind of taken me by surprise …'

Martha smiled sadly in recognition. 'Me too.'

'But whatever I feel for you, I also understand that you have to do the right thing by your children.'

'And my marriage,' Martha added, looking down.

Charlie shrugged. The meaning of the gesture was clear – he didn't think Jamie deserved to have her do the right thing by him.

At that moment the waiter appeared, breaking the tension. 'You order for me,' Martha said, revelling in the old-fashioned ambiance and smiling at Charlie. 'Let's make the most of tonight.'

Charlie smiled back, before ordering quickly and decisively.

As the waiter departed, Martha continued, 'I know what Jamie did is unforgivable and I'm not sure we can find our way through it. But for the sake of the children, I can't give up on my marriage without at least trying to make it work.'

'I know. And even though he doesn't deserve you, I wouldn't wish it on Jamie to be parted from his kids. I know how hard that is. I would have given anything to be a part of Felix's daily life, for him as much as me.' He paused and looked into the distance for a few seconds, as if remembering the pain of being parted from his child. 'I suppose what I'm trying to say, Martha, is that I understand. I don't want you to go but I also know that you have to.'

'Thank you,' Martha whispered, suddenly overtaken by sadness for what might have been. She and Charlie just clicked. They had from the start and she had no doubts that if she was to choose him over Jamie, it would work. She could so easily picture them pottering about at home together, going on holiday with all three children, and, most of all, she could imagine herself falling asleep in his arms every night.

They sat in silence for a few moments while the waiter brought the drinks and poured a glass of red wine for each of them.

'I do believe that he's really sorry for what he did,' Martha said, as the waiter left them once again.

'Are you trying to convince me or yourself?' Charlie replied.

Martha smiled. 'Maybe both.'

Charlie took a deep breath and picked up his glass of wine. 'Well then, let's drink to new beginnings with old partners . . .'

Martha picked up her glass and chinked it against his. 'Do

you think you and Liv might make another go of it?' She felt slightly sick as she said the words.

'No. I mean that it's a new beginning for me with Liv because I've realised that I don't love her any more. And I've only realised that since I met you.'

Their eyes locked and Martha felt her insides swim. 'Don't,' she said quietly.

'Sorry.' Charlie held her gaze. 'I know you have to go home. And although it kills me to admit it, I can't help noticing the change in you since he arrived here . . .'

'In what way?'

'In your appearance, in your demeanour. Everything, really. It tells me all I need to know.'

'I'm sorry.'

'I'm sorry too. Let's just enjoy tonight and make the most of our last few hours together.'

'Oh, don't say that, Charlie!' Martha cried. 'It makes me feel awful. And anyway, we'll still see each other back in the UK, won't we?'

'I don't know if that's such a good idea . . .' Charlie finally looked away uncomfortably.

Martha thought she might cry. 'You don't want me to do your memoirs?'

'It's not that I don't want you to,' he said, and she could tell that he was choosing his words carefully. 'It's just that I'm not sure it's such a good idea.'

Martha picked up her wine and took a long sip. Much as she hated the idea of not seeing him again, she also wondered if it might be fairer all round. Fairer on Charlie, fairer on her, and fairer on Jamie, not that he deserved it. But she had to give him a chance to make things right. She wasn't sure if their marriage would ever recover, but she did know they didn't stand a chance with Charlie hovering in the background. Once again, her eyes brimmed. 'Maybe you're right.'

Charlie reached out and took her hand again, stroking her skin softly with his thumb. He didn't speak but his eyes spoke volumes, reflecting her own sadness in their depths.

'So this is goodbye?'

He nodded slowly. 'I wish it wasn't. But I think we both know it's the only way.'

She felt suddenly choked. The thought of going back home scared her. While she was in LA, everything seemed so far removed from her everyday life that she could pretend none of the terribleness had happened. But she knew that running away wasn't the answer. It was time to go home, back to reality. She took another sip of her wine and blinked hard. 'Life is hard, isn't it?'

Charlie nodded. 'Love is harder.'

Chapter 33

Liv was waiting by the gates as the car slid up the driveway.

'Thanks so much!' Jamie said to the driver, handing him a bundle of notes by way of a tip before he flung the door open and lifted Felix out.

'Thank you, sir. No problem, sir,' replied the driver, now firmly back in polite mode, as Jamie climbed out after Felix and closed the door of the Rolls Royce behind him. He watched the car silently, as it turned and glided back through the remote-control gates.

Liv looked at Jamie and Felix for a second, before running towards them and scooping Felix up in her arms. 'Oh my God!' she cried, burying her face in his neck. 'I was so, so scared! Don't ever do that to me again!'

Jamie watched them awkwardly, suddenly realising that he should have gone back to the hotel in the car. Now he was stuck up here with no way of getting back.

As if reading his mind, Liv looked up at him. 'Thank you so much. I can't tell you how grateful I am. Let me get you a drink or something. Then we can call a cab to take you back.

Come in,' she added, already heading through the giant doorway into the hall.

Jamie followed, aware that he could smell alcohol fumes on Liv and that she was walking unsteadily, although he thought charitably that maybe that was down to her carrying Felix. He gazed around him as he walked, distracted by the size and scale of the house. It was vast, yet tasteful and pristine. No broken shelves or endless pairs of shoes, trainers and flip-flops kicked off in this hallway. It was stunning. But it wasn't homely.

Liv put Felix down in a large squashy armchair and kissed the top of his head. The boy curled up and put his thumb into his mouth, his eyelids already drooping shut. Liv watched him for a minute, then sighed deeply and shook her head before turning towards Jamie.

'I have never been more frightened in my life,' she said, her huge violet eyes brimming dangerously. 'Thank you so much for bringing him home safely.' She stopped speaking abruptly and put the palm of her hand against her chest, as if to steady her racing heart.

'I was happy to help,' Jamie noticed that she was swaying quite alarmingly. Probably down to a mixture of alcohol and shock, he decided.

'So,' she said, putting her hands on her hips and flushing with embarrassment. 'Listen, I'm really sorry, but I didn't get your name . . .'

'Jamie.'

'Jamie,' she nodded to herself, still looking embarrassed. 'Well, Jamie, I'm sorry to have put you in that position . . .'

'It's fine,' he said, waving his hand dismissively. 'Would you mind calling me a cab?' He was suddenly anxious to get away. 'I should have gone back in the house car. I'm an idiot!'

'Of course!' Liv picked up her phone and scrolled through her contacts list before pressing a number.

'It'll be about twenty minutes,' she said apologetically, after she hung up. 'Let me get you a drink while you wait. Would you like a glass of wine?'

'Um, sure,' Jamie followed Liv into the open-plan kitchen and taking a seat at the island in the middle, where there were two empty wine bottles and another that was half empty. He wasn't sure she needed any more booze.

She took a glass out of a cupboard and sloshed some wine into it, before refilling her own and perching opposite him. 'So, you're Martha's husband,' she said, her eyes glittering slightly.

Jamie took a sip of wine, enjoying the cold, dry sensation as it hit his throat. 'Yup,' he said, thinking how surreal it was to be sitting opposite a woman he had watched on the big screen at the cinema, sharing a drink with her. He wondered how much Liv knew about the situation.

'You've been a naughty boy, I gather,' she added, answering his unasked question.

Jamie took another gulp of wine and met her eye. 'I'm not proud of that.' He was annoyed that this stranger knew his intimate business.

Liv looked away, as if she sensed that she had said something she shouldn't.

'I love my wife,' Jamie added, not sure why he felt the need to justify himself.

Liv shook her head, causing her golden hair to pool around her shoulders. 'Don't worry, I'm not in a position to judge,' she slurred. She had drunk her whole glass of wine in just a couple of minutes. 'I did exactly the same as you.'

Jamie could feel his hackles rising. 'No, it wasn't the same. I felt nothing for . . . for her. There's no way I would have left Martha for her.'

'Some might say that's worse,' Liv shot back. 'I fell in love with Danny. What's your excuse if you felt nothing for the other woman?'

Jamie closed his eyes and let his shoulders drop. 'I don't have an excuse,' he said, in a voice that was almost a whisper. 'There is no excuse for what I did.' He opened his eyes to find Liv watching him in silence. 'I love my wife,' he repeated.

Liv blinked slowly. 'I think you might have some competition,' she said, and Jamie wondered if he detected a note of pique.

'They're just friends,' he shrugged.

She pursed her lips and Jamie felt a spike of anger that she seemed to know more than him about his own marital situation. 'Why are you looking at me like that? Do you know something I don't?'

She sighed. 'I know that I haven't seen Charlie this way with anyone. Since me. Maybe not even with me.'

A shiver of fear passed over Jamie. 'Well I'm not prepared to let her go so easily,' he said, feeling suddenly defiant.

Liv bit her lip and stared into the distance with a forlorn expression on her face. 'She's a lucky woman, having two men fighting over her.'

Jamie took another swig of wine and realised that he had almost demolished the whole glass too.

Liv slid off her stool and moved unsteadily to the fridge, where she retrieved a fresh bottle of wine and deftly twisted the lid open.

'No, I'm fine ...' Jamie started to say as Liv began to pour it into both their glasses, but he had quickly realised that where Liv and booze were concerned, resistance was futile.

'She's a very beautiful woman, your wife,' Liv said, and again Jamie wondered if he detected a note of bitterness in her voice. Liv herself was stunning, with large lilac-blue eyes, long golden hair and a very sexy, full mouth, but she wasn't as unusual or as exotic-looking as Martha. He also thought that maybe her flawless, unlined complexion wasn't entirely natural and that her pout had had a bit of assistance.

'Yes, she's beautiful,' he agreed. 'I'm a very lucky man.'

She nodded. 'I really hope you guys can work it out. It's obvious how much you love her but it's the guilt that's the real killer. It never leaves you.'

Jamie suddenly wanted to cry. He had such a mountain to climb that it seemed impossible. Hopeless.

Liv reached across and took his hand, causing him to look up in surprise. 'I think you'll make it,' she said, with a smile so sad that it only made Jamie feel worse.

He drained his glass and stood up. 'My cab will be here any minute. I'd better go out and wait for it.'

Liv's eyes widened in alarm. 'Listen, Jamie,' she said, as her voice dropped to a whisper. 'You won't . . . mention any of this to Charlie, will you?'

Jamie looked down at her pleading expression and the desperation in her eyes. 'I think Charlie Simmons is the last person I'd be mentioning anything to.'

'Thank you so much!' she said, following him down the hallway.

He opened the front door and stepped out. 'But listen,' he turned around to face her. 'You need to sort yourself out, you know that, don't you? Getting so drunk that you pass out when you're looking after a small child is no good.'

Liv physically shrank back at his words and Jamie immediately felt sorry for her. She seemed so lost and not much more than a child herself. 'I know.' She bit her lip and looked contrite. She pulled her cardigan more tightly around herself and stared at her bare feet. 'It won't happen again.'

'I promise not to mention anything to Charlie if you promise to get some help.'

Liv frowned. 'Help?'

'I think you know what sort of help I mean.'

'I'm not that bad!' she said, trying to shrug and laugh at the same time.

'You're not that good, either,' Jamie said. 'Promise you'll get help?'

Liv's eyes darted from side to side as she tried to weigh up her options. Then, realising she didn't have much choice, she nodded. 'I promise.'

'Good,' Jamie said. 'I can hear a car,' he added, indicating towards the road beyond the gates. 'That must be my cab.'

Just as he finished speaking, the gates swished open and both Liv and Jamie looked up in surprise as Charlie's Range Rover pulled in.

'Oh shit,' muttered Liv.

'Oh shit,' echoed Jamie.

Charlie got out of the car and walked towards them, frowning. 'What the hell are you doing here?' He eyed Jamie coldly.

'Charlie!' Liv yelped. 'I asked him to come. I, uh, I thought I heard an intruder and you weren't answering your phone.'

Charlie immediately felt for his phone and pulled it out of the inside pocket of his jacket. 'Ah,' he said, as he peered at the screen, which Jamie knew would show dozens of missed calls from Liv. 'Sorry, we were in a restaurant and they don't like you using mobiles . . .'

Liv waved away his protestations. 'It's fine!' She glanced for a split second at Jamie, as if to confirm that he would back up her story. 'Like I said, Jamie came and had a good look around. If there was anyone here, they've gone now.'

Charlie's eyes narrowed and for a moment Jamie thought he had clocked that she was lying, but eventually he smiled stiffly. 'Well, thanks for that. But I'm home now, so you can go.'

'I will,' Jamie said, enjoying Charlie's discomfort. He was always so composed and full of himself, with the sort of confidence that only fame and money can bring. Jamie enjoyed seeing him out of his comfort zone for once. 'Just as soon as my cab gets here.'

Charlie tutted and rubbed his forehead. 'I'll run you back. Liv, cancel the cab.' As he spoke, he turned back towards his car and climbed in without waiting for Jamie to answer.

Jamie looked at Liv but she nodded towards the car. 'Take the lift. The cab could be ages anyway.'

'OK,' Jamie agreed, still reluctant to be alone in a car with his arch rival. 'Well, goodbye then . . .'

Liv smiled and reached up to kiss him on the cheek. 'Thank you,' she whispered.

Jamie smiled back and turned towards the car, which Charlie was revving impatiently. He climbed into the passenger seat and was just about to do up his seatbelt when the car shot backwards, throwing him forward violently.

'Oh, sorry.' Charlie's voice was dripping with sarcasm.

Jamie surreptitiously rubbed his neck and clicked his seatbelt into place. Neither of them spoke for several minutes as Charlie manoeuvred the car around the twisting, dark roads.

'So, do you want to tell me what you were really doing there?' Charlie said finally, glancing slyly towards Jamie.

Jamie's skin prickled with indignation. Charlie was acting as if he had been up to no good, when little did Charlie know it but Jamie had just done him the biggest favour of his life. 'Do you want to tell me what you were doing with my wife?' he shot back.

In the dim light of the car, he saw Charlie's Adam's apple rise and fall as he swallowed. 'We were having a meal. That's all.'

'Glad to hear it,' Jamie said. 'Because if you were doing anything else I—'

'If we were doing anything else it would damn well serve you right!' Charlie spat, interrupting Jamie.

271

Jamie had no answer because Charlie was right. 'Look,' he said, trying to sound more conciliatory. 'I love Martha ...'

Charlie opened his mouth with a retort but Jamie put his hand up before he could speak. 'I know what you're going to say. I fucked up. But I won't make the same mistake again. I want to make it up to her – and to our kids.' He glanced sideways at Charlie to see if he had picked up on his mention of the children and was irritated to see a slight smirk of satisfaction on his face. 'So I guess what I'm saying is ... leave her alone.'

Charlie didn't answer for a long time, and Jamie thought he might be going to stay silent for the rest of the journey. But as they stopped at the intersection just up from the hotel, he finally spoke. 'I'll leave her alone for now. We had already decided that that would be best and anyway, I'm going to be spending a lot of time here over the next few months. But I swear to God, if you let her down again, all bets are off and, next time, I promise you, she'll choose me.'

Charlie pulled onto the paved driveway of the hotel and stopped the car slightly away from the arched entrance, so that the bell-hops didn't immediately open the door. Jamie stared ahead at the expensive waltz being danced by the succession of top-of-the-range cars coming and going, fighting a desperate urge to punch Charlie hard in his handsome face.

'Well, you don't need to worry,' he said at last, opening the car door. 'There won't be a next time.'

Charlie watched Jamie's retreating back as he made his way towards the entrance of the hotel. Here he was with the world at his feet and yet he had never felt such jealousy and loathing as he did now for this house-husband from the suburbs. Yes, Charlie could have anything and everything his heart desired, but this guy had the one thing Charlie couldn't have. He had Martha.

Chapter 34

Once they had taken off, Martha just wanted to get home. She leaned her forehead against the window as the plane climbed through the Californian sky and looked down on the sprawling white urban landscape, glinting in the incessant sun. She reached out and touched the window with her index finger, saying a mental goodbye to Charlie and the place that had been her sanctuary for the past week.

Beside her, Jamie picked up her other hand and squeezed it. Instinctively, she pulled it away, but immediately she reached out and allowed him to take it again, letting their entwined hands settle on the armrest between them. Jamie had a lot of work to do to convince her that their marriage was worth saving.

She looked away from the window and up at Jamie, who was watching her nervously. 'What are you thinking?' he asked, his bright blue eyes creasing as if he already knew the answer.

'Nothing really,' she replied, running her thumb over the back of his hand. She had always loved his hands, with their long, tanned fingers and light smattering of pale golden hair. Now she could only think about what those hands had touched and they made her shudder with renewed revulsion. 'I was thinking how good it will be to see the kids again,' she said, folding her hands together in her lap while trying not to make it seem like a hostile gesture. 'I just want this flight to be over.' She rested her head against the seat back as the plane began to level out and twisted round so that she was looking at Jamie.

He closed his eyes for a second. 'I feel the opposite,' he said, shaking his head. 'It's almost as though while we're away . . .'

'. . . we can pretend it didn't happen. I know.' Martha finished the thought for him. 'But we can't hide forever. And we need to get back to the kids.'

Martha had a physical ache to hold Mimi and Tom in her arms. She had been apart from them for longer periods in the past, but it was rare, and then Jamie would have been there for them. Along with all the other desperate emotions coursing through her body, she now felt consumed with guilt that she had deserted them by running off, and could only imagine how confused and upset they must both be feeling.

'You should have gone in first class,' Jamie said, stretching his long legs as far as they would go in the cramped economy-class seat. 'I bet it was incredible on the way out, wasn't it?'

'Strangely enough, I wasn't in any mood to enjoy it.' Martha thought back to that surreal day and remembering with a horrible clarity how awful she had felt. 'Anyway, I couldn't let Charlie pay for my flight,' she added, shaking her head. 'He's done so much for me already . . .'

She felt Jamie stiffen beside her as she mentioned Charlie's name, and it occurred to her that it was more than a little ironic, given the circumstances, that it was Jamie who was feeling jealous. 'Anyway,' she added, keen to change the subject, 'we need to talk about what happens next. With us.'

Jamie reached out and gripped her hand again and Martha had to quell her desire to recoil. 'I know what I want to happen,' he murmured. 'But I'm in your hands now. I will literally do whatever you want me to do to put this right.'

Martha looked into his sincere blue eyes that used to laugh even when he didn't, and thought how much they had both changed over the past week. They both looked older, sadder, and there was a shadow in Jamie's expression that she knew was mirrored in her own.

The aeroplane levelled out and the captain switched off the seatbelt signs. Ahead, she could already see the cabin crew making their way down the aisles with a trolley serving drinks. She felt a sudden urge to get blind drunk but knew that she wouldn't. She wanted to keep her head clear to try to make some sense of why and how her life had fallen apart so badly. 'First, I want us to go to counselling,' she said, trying to read Jamie's reaction. He didn't flinch.

'Consider it done.' He nodded emphatically as he spoke, as if he was making a mental list of things he had to do.

The truth was, she didn't really want to go to counselling because she was scared of what it might bring out. But she had promised Charlie that she would go and she wanted to keep her promise. 'And secondly,' she continued, 'you need to go and get ...' Martha hesitated, as the words threatened to choke her. 'You need to go and get checked out.'

Jamie frowned. 'In what respect?'

'In whatever respect you think that men who've been sleeping around behind their wives backs need to get checked out,' Martha growled back.

'Oh Jesus,' Jamie shook his head. 'Listen, I always used—'

'I don't want to know,' Martha interrupted him, as the bile rose in her throat. 'But it's non-negotiable.'

Jamie paused, then nodded. 'I understand. And it's fine. I'm serious about this, Martha. I will do anything to show you how sorry I am.'

By now the trolley was pulling level with them and Martha stopped to order an orange juice before replying. 'If it happens again, things will be a lot more straightforward,' she said, knowing that she sounded so much harder than she felt. 'There'll be no second chance.'

Jamie put his hand over his face. 'I know,' he whispered. 'I won't need any more chances, Martha. I have come so close to losing you that I will never, ever give you cause to doubt me again. You can trust me with your life.'

A ghost of a smile crossed Martha's face. 'That's what I thought last time.'

By the time they landed, both of them were too tired to talk any more. They had slept sporadically and uncomfortably during the ten-hour flight, both of them tortured by unsettling dreams every time they managed to doze off.

Jamie drove as if on autopilot towards home, while Martha stared out of the window at the poppy-smattered fields that seemed to be every conceivable colour imaginable, and which seemed to be taunting her with their lush beauty. The contrast with the dusty scrubland and parched hills of LA was stark, and although the weather was almost exactly the same, the cloudless blue sky seemed somehow smaller and the sun less invasive than it had back there. It had been just a week since she had last travelled these roads but it felt like an eternity. The world had turned on its axis and nothing would ever be the same again. She wondered idly how she would feel in another week, another year, another decade.

They pulled into their driveway and Martha's eyes immediately filled with tears as the door flew open and Tom came running out to greet them. He yanked open Martha's door and flung himself into her arms.

Martha buried her face in his messy thatch of white-blond hair and hugged him to her so tightly that he yelped. 'Oh my goodness, I have missed you soooooo much!' she gasped, holding up his face and kissing his cheek.

'You too, Mum,' he said in a muffled voice.

Martha gently extricated herself from him and climbed out of the car, her legs and back feeling stiff and sore. She took Tom's hand and guided him into the house, which smelt of coffee and fresh baking. She made her way through to the kitchen, marvelling to herself at the tidiness of the house and mentally thanking her mother, who she found bending over in front of the oven, removing a tray of scones. 'Ah, so that explains the smell!' she said, smiling fondly at Jane. 'Hello, Mum.'

Jane placed the hot tray down on the hob and took off her oven gloves. 'Hello, darling,' she said and reached out to embrace Martha.

Martha gratefully allowed her mother to hug her, wondering when she had last given her a cuddle. Jane wasn't a particularly affectionate woman, but Martha had never doubted how much she loved her.

'I made them in honour of you coming home,' her mum said proudly. 'I know how much you love them.'

Martha swallowed hard. This was Jane's way of showing affection, baking scones just like she used to when Martha was young, and it was even more touching than her hug. 'Where's Mimi?' she said, noticing for the first time that her daughter was nowhere to be seen.

Jane's eyes clouded slightly. 'She's upstairs.'

'I'll go and find her,' Martha said, already on her way out of the kitchen.

'Martha . . .' Jane called after her.

Something about her voice made Martha stop and turn around again. 'Yes?'

Jane came out into the hallway and faced her. Distractedly, Martha wondered when Jane had become shorter than her. 'She's very upset,' Jane said, sighing as she spoke. 'You might want to tread a bit carefully.'

Martha blinked twice. 'She doesn't know the truth, does she?' She cast around in her mind for who may have blabbed to Mimi and could only think of either Jane or Lindsay. Surely it wasn't possible.

'No,' Jane shook her head. 'She's very upset about you . . .'

She tailed off, looking uncomfortable, as if she couldn't bring herself to say anything disparaging about her own daughter.

'Me?' Martha gasped. 'But I haven't done anything!'

A look of relief swept over Jane's face before she composed herself again. 'No! No of course you haven't. It's just, well, the photos in the paper made it look as if . . .'

'But I explained those photos to her.' Martha was perplexed as to why Mimi would still be upset or angry with her.

'You explained the first ones,' Jane said, and Martha could tell that Jane herself had been nursing some kind of suspicion about her. 'But there have been quite a few others. Of you in LA. With him,' she finished.

'With Charlie?' Martha's mouth gaped as she tried to think where they might have been papped.

'Yes. I'm sure there's a perfectly innocent explanation,' Jane said, but Martha could see in her eyes that she wasn't entirely sure.

'The innocent explanation is the only explanation, because it's the truth,' she sighed, suddenly feeling overwhelmed by weariness and misery as she headed towards the stairs.

At that moment, Jamie staggered through the door carrying both of their bags. 'Everything OK?' he asked, as if he sensed that there was already a problem.

'I don't know,' Martha said in a flat voice as she trudged up the stairs to Mimi's room, feeling as though she was about to meet her executioner.

Mimi's door was closed and Martha could almost feel the waves of animosity floating through the pale painted wood.

She knocked sharply. Mimi's music, which as always was blaring out, stopped abruptly and the door swung open.

Martha almost gasped at the sight of Mimi, who seemed to have grown from a child into a young woman in the short week she had been away. Her blonde hair hung in rivers of golden silk over her shoulders, and her father's blue eyes seemed larger in her once-chubby face, which was now more defined with high cheekbones and a perfect rosebud mouth, which was at that precise moment pouting sullenly at Martha.

'Hi, darling!' Martha tried to smile but the look in Mimi's eyes caused it to die on her lips. 'Aren't you going to welcome me home?' she said, feeling uncharacteristically angry with her daughter.

Mimi stared at Martha with such an accusing expression that Martha could feel herself quail. 'I'm surprised you even bothered to come home,' she said, her chin lifting defiantly as she spoke.

'Mimi!' Martha snapped. 'What the hell is that supposed to mean?'

Mimi's face crumpled instantly as she dissolved into tears. 'I mean that you left us and Dad to bugger off to America with Charlie bloody Simmons!' she wailed, heading back into her room and sitting down on her bed, where she leaned forward and put her head in her hands.

Martha stood rooted to the spot for several seconds before she could move, her emotions crippling her temporarily. 'Mimi . . .' she said. Finally, she followed Mimi into the room, where she sat down on the bed beside her, not knowing where

281

to begin. Tentatively, she put an arm around her daughter's heaving shoulders but Mimi shook her off with a violence that shocked her.

'How do you think it made me feel ...' Mimi cried, though her voice was muffled by her hands and the sheet of golden hair that was covering her face, '... when all the kids at school kept talking about the photos of you ...' she stopped to take a gulp of air, '... with him!' she snarled, looking up at Martha with blazing eyes that she could see were more full of sorrow than anger.

'Oh sweetheart,' Martha said, still feeling paralysed by fear. 'There is nothing going on between me and Charlie. Didn't Lindsay come round to see you to explain that?'

Mimi rolled her eyes and shook her head at the same time. 'Yeah, because *you* sent her! And I didn't believe her any more than I believe you!'

'But I don't understand why you wouldn't believe either of us.' Martha shook her head. 'I've never lied to you, Mimi, and I'm not lying to you now.'

'Really?' Mimi sneered sarcastically, before reaching out and grabbing her school bag, which had been unceremoniously dumped on the floor earlier. She rifled through it aggressively until she found what she was looking for and snatched out a page from a newspaper. 'Because this doesn't look to me like there's *nothing going on*!'

She thrust the cutting towards Martha, who took it, despite feeling a desperate urge to tear it into tiny pieces. She smoothed it out on her lap and gasped. The picture had been taken in LA and showed her and Charlie coming out of the restaurant he had taken her to. He had his arm around her shoulder and was kissing the top of her head. For a second, she felt a flash of anger with Charlie. He had assured her that the paps didn't generally hang around that restaurant, but she knew it was unfair to blame him as anyone could have taken the photo. Even members of the public would snatch photos of him on their mobile phones.

Martha screwed up the cutting and threw it onto the floor. She looked at Mimi, whose expression was both hostile and vulnerable at the same time. She opened her mouth to speak, as she tried to think of a way to counter her daughter's fury, but no words would come and she was helpless against the invisible wall of hostility in front of her.

Mimi raised her eyebrows expectantly. 'See?' she said, her little pink rosebud mouth forming into a sneer. 'You've got no answer, have you? Because you're a bloody liar!'

'No!' shouted Jamie, stepping into the bedroom just as Mimi was pressing her face towards Martha's, who was experiencing an almost overwhelming urge to slap her. 'Your mum is *not* a bloody liar! *I* am!'

'Shut up!' Martha stood up shakily and walked across the room towards Jamie, so that she could face her daughter from a safe distance. Mimi glanced up in surprise but then dropped her head into her hands again.

Martha looked at Jamie, whose eyes were almost bulging at what was unfolding. 'Go,' she said quietly. 'I want to deal with this by myself.'

Jamie's eyes moved from her to Mimi but he finally nodded and left the room, closing the door behind him.

'Right,' Martha said, aware that her voice was quavering. Aside from general nagging, she had never really fought with Mimi before and the experience was both a new and shocking one. She took a deep breath. 'I'm going to tell you something that I think you need to know ...'

Slowly, Mimi moved her hands away from her face and looked up. Her huge blue eyes were still wet with tears, giving them an almost turquoise hue. Her cheeks were flushed pink and, for a moment, Martha had a flashback to her daughter at ten months old, looking piteously up at her from her cot, while her apple-shaped cheeks flamed red with the pain of the teeth that were beginning to push through her tiny gums.

'What?' Mimi said, a flicker of uncertainty making her blink quickly, causing any as-yet unshed tears to spill onto her long, sweeping lashes.

Martha hesitated. Mimi might seem like she was growing up fast, but really she was still just a little girl inside. Telling her the truth might absolve Martha from any wrongdoing in Mimi's eyes, but it would wreck her opinion of her dad forever. Mimi and Jamie had such a strong bond, borne out of spending years together at home when it was just the two of them, before Tom came along and barged his adorable way into their little family unit. With just a few short sentences, she could destroy that.

'Well, it's just that sometimes, couples need a little time out from each other ...'

Mimi's eyes filled again instantly. 'Oh my God!' she whispered, almost to herself. 'You and dad are splitting up!'

'No!' Martha said, more forcefully than she had intended, and she put her hand up as if to soften the impact. 'No,' she repeated, more gently. 'We're not splitting up. That's my point. Sometimes, having a little time out can help you remember that you love each other and that you belong together. But Mimi, all couples have arguments . . .'

'But you and dad don't argue!' Martha was gratified to see that Mimi's tears had dried and the hostility was ebbing away, her young face softening again.

'Of course we argue, Mimi. I'm glad that you don't think we argue much, but I can tell you for certain that we absolutely do. And when we argued this time—'

'About you and Charlie Simmons?' Mimi cut in, almost hopefully.

'No!' Martha snapped, feeling a spring of indignation and frustration welling up inside her. 'Charlie is a friend. That's all. I went to LA, partly to have a little time out from Dad while we both calmed down a bit and partly because I'm doing Charlie's memoirs, so I was shadowing him.'

Mimi pulled a face as if she was still trying to decide whether or not to believe Martha.

'Look, darling,' Martha continued, crossing the room to sit beside Mimi again. 'I am really sorry you got teased about those photos but I promise you I am not about to run off with Charlie Simmons. I'm staying here, with you, Dad and Tom. OK?' She reached over to pull Mimi towards her, and this time Mimi didn't resist.

'OK,' she murmured, allowing herself to be pulled into Martha's embrace.

After a while, Martha kissed the top of Mimi's silky head. 'I'd better go downstairs and see Granny,' she said. 'To thank her for looking after you while we were away.'

'OK,' Mimi murmured again, looking up at Martha with a wan smile.

Martha got up and flicked Mimi's music back on. She opened the door as Mimi called out to her. 'Mum?'

'Yes?'

'I'm glad you're home.'

Chapter 35

Charlie dived into the pool and surged forward through the cool, clear water until he reached the other side and rose up into the hot, thick air to take a breath.

'Come on, Felix!' he shouted, as his son's miniature blurry outline hove into view at the other end of the pool. Charlie rubbed his eyes and Felix became clearer, standing tentatively with his small toes gripping the edge of the pool, as he tried to decide whether to dive in or not.

'You know it makes it easier if you just plunge straight in!' Charlie said, grinning as Felix repeatedly bent at the knees, still undecided about whether to dive. Finally, he drew himself up to his full height of not much over four feet and stretched his skinny arms above his head, revealing his ribcage as he did so. After a glancing moment of hesitation, he dived neatly and deftly into the pool.

'Good work!' cried Charlie admiringly, as Felix emerged from the water and swam a few short strokes until he was at Charlie's side.

Felix beamed proudly and Charlie reached out to ruffle his

soaking wet curls. He was surprised how good the little boy had become at swimming. The last time he had been in a pool with him, he'd been nervous and lacked finesse. 'You've really come on, haven't you?'

Felix nodded. 'Danny's been teaching me. He said it will help my surfing.'

Charlie flinched slightly, as he always did at the mention of Danny's name. He didn't want another man to have taught his son to swim, even though a part of him acknowledged that it was better for Felix to have had a step-father who cared enough to teach him, than one who couldn't care less.

He wondered if Liv had told Felix yet that she and Danny had split up. He suspected not, by the carefree way Felix had mentioned his name. 'Danny's a good teacher ...' Charlie said.

Felix nodded happily. 'Yeah. Can we race?' he shouted, already gearing himself up to start ahead of Charlie.

Charlie smiled, pleased that what had happened over the last few days hadn't affected Felix adversely. 'There and back!' he yelled. 'Ready, steady, go!' Once again, Charlie was stunned by Felix's speed in the water. He would, of course, have let him win, but he actually didn't have any choice, as the little boy streaked ahead of him effortlessly.

'Gee, Dad, you're *slow!*' Felix teased, as Charlie limped in several strokes behind him.

'Tell me about it!' Charlie puffed, splashing his face with cold water. 'So ...' he said, as they floated lazily on the surface of the water, getting their breath back. 'Do you want to tell me what really happened last night?'

Felix righted himself in the water and looked at Charlie nervously. 'Mum said not to tell you.' He wrinkled up his face. 'In case you got cross.'

A bolt of annoyance shot through Charlie. Liv had no right to tell Felix to keep secrets from his dad. 'I won't get cross,' he said, glad that his voice sounded even and calm. 'Promise,' he added, when he could see that the boy was still hesitating.

Felix plopped the water distractedly with his hand. 'I came to find you.'

'What?'

Felix shrugged slightly. 'I got up and you weren't there.'

'No,' Charlie said. 'I was taking Martha out to dinner. To say goodbye,' he added, 'because she's gone home today.'

Felix squinted against the glare of the sun reflecting in the dancing silvery white stars on the surface of the turquoise water. 'Mum was asleep, but I couldn't wake her up.'

An alarm bell rang somewhere in Charlie's brain. 'Like before?' he prompted.

Felix shrugged again. 'I don't know. Anyway, I came to find you.'

'How did you come to find me?' Charlie's heart had started to hammer alarmingly and it had nothing to do with the swimming race.

'I let myself out of the gate and walked.'

The simplicity of Felix's description somehow made the horror of what he was saying a million times worse. 'By yourself?' Charlie gasped, already knowing the answer. The thought of Felix's tiny figure wandering those pitch black, winding, potholed streets all by himself was so utterly terrifying that for a second Charlie felt as if he might be sick. Every single awful scenario of what might have happened ran through his brain at lightning speed.

Felix looked down and began to make swirling movements with his hands. 'Then that guy came to get me in a really cool car.'

'Jamie?' Charlie could feel his lip curl at the mention of his name.

Felix shrugged. 'Can't remember his name. Martha's husband.'

Charlie nodded. 'Oh, well,' he said, his casual tone belying the volcano of fury that was threatening to erupt from within him at any minute. 'At least you got home safe, eh?'

Felix's face split into a wide smile of relief. 'You're not cross?'

'No!' Charlie scoffed, moving over and lifting him up. He was a light child anyway, but with the water holding most of his weight, it was like lifting a feather. Felix wrapped his arms around Charlie's neck and Charlie squeezed him tightly. 'I'm not cross at all,' he soothed, using every ounce of his acting ability.

By the time Liv arrived home, Felix and Charlie were curled up on the giant sofa in the TV room watching *Toy Story 3*, which was Felix's current all-time favourite film.

'Hi!' she chirruped brightly, as she passed by the door on her way to the kitchen.

Charlie gave Felix a quick squeeze. 'I just need to have a chat with your mum, I'll be back in a minute.' He said, ruffled his son's curls as he got up.

'Good massage?' he said, eyeing her carefully. He leaned his back against the cool white wall and folded his arms.

'Hmm,' Liv replied, either ignoring or unaware of Charlie's tone as she poured herself a coffee. She took a sip and pulled out a stool, before whirling around to face Charlie and smiling broadly. As their eyes connected, it was almost comical the way her smile shrank back until it looked more like a grimace. 'What's wrong?'

Charlie glanced towards the TV room to make sure that Felix was not within listening distance. 'I found out why Jamie was really here last night. That's what's wrong.' Charlie had to speak as precisely as possible to stop his pent-up fury from bubbling over.

'Oh.' Liv dropped her eyes as a red rash began to spread from her chest to her neck.

Charlie watched its progress in fascination. 'Is that all you've got to say?' he hissed eventually when he decided that Liv had been silent for long enough.

'I didn't tell you,' she said, gripping her coffee cup in front of her, as if in self-defence, 'because I knew that this was how you would react.'

'Bullshit!' Charlie hissed back, making Liv jump visibly. 'I have never, ever lost it with you, even though you damn well deserved it!'

'Please, Charlie ...' Liv begged, her face beginning to crumple.

'Oh no you don't,' Charlie growled, unfolding his arms and pointing at her. 'Don't you dare turn on the waterworks now. You told our son to lie to me!'

'I didn't!' Liv protested, her eyes widening as if to emphasise her innocence. 'I just told him not to tell you,' she added in a smaller voice.

'It's the same bloody thing,' Charlie snarled. 'And now I'm indebted to that . . . that arsehole! Arrrgh!' He flung his arms out in frustration.

'Charlie, I'm sorry, OK?' Liv said, putting her coffee down and standing in front of him, as if she was ready to do battle.

Charlie looked down at the face that had tortured him for years now and wondered why he felt absolutely nothing for her. The glossy blonde hair, the smooth, peaches and cream complexion and that full mouth had haunted his days and his nights for as long as he could remember. Yet in an instant everything he had felt for her had just evaporated.

'You were drunk,' he said, looking at her dispassionately. 'And I can smell alcohol on you now. You've been drinking again today, haven't you?'

Liv closed her eyes for a second. She took a moment to compose herself before she spoke. 'Yes, I was drunk,' she admitted. 'But I've had a very stressful few days, Charlie. Come on, cut me some slack!'

Charlie shook his head, still stunned by the epiphany he had just experienced; the realisation that she no longer had any power over him. 'No,' he said, aware that his voice sounded harsh, 'I've cut you too much slack in the past. I should never have let you have custody of Felix . . .'

Liv's eyes widened in terror as he continued.

'But it's not too late to put it right. I'm going to file for custody. I should have done it years ago. You're not fit to look after him …'

Liv gasped and shook her head furiously. 'No! No, Charlie, please! Don't take Felix! It was a one-off … I'll stop drinking altogether,' she gabbled. She shuffled towards him and grabbed both his hands. Charlie tried to pull away but her grip was vice-like. 'Listen to me, Charlie. I love Felix. I would never, ever do anything to harm him or put him at risk.' As she spoke, she fixed Charlie with a wild stare that scared him.

He shook his head. 'Well, that's not true because you already did. No, it's no good, Liv,' he said, keeping his voice firm. 'You need help. The panic attacks, the passing out … it's not normal. You've got a problem and you need help to fix it.'

'I don't!' she cried, dropping to her knees in front of him. 'I can do it on my own! Please, Charlie, I'm begging you, please don't take Felix. It would kill me.' She slumped down so that her forehead was inches from the stone floor and lifted her head slightly.

'No!' cried Charlie, bending to grab her. But it was too late. Liv brought her head down onto the hard surface and Charlie winced as it made contact with a sickening crack. She looked up at him as a trickle of blood began to snake a path down the centre of her smooth, white forehead. Then, with an expression that almost looked like a smile, Liv's eyes rolled and she slumped backwards, unconscious.

Chapter 36

Jane was in the kitchen making tea by the time Martha came downstairs. Her mum glanced at her and motioned towards the table, where Martha obediently sat. 'Thank you,' she said, as Jane placed a steaming cup of green tea in front of her and sat down opposite with her own cup.

Jamie was upstairs putting Tom to bed and Martha could just about make out his melodic voice as he read aloud to him. She took a sip of her tea and finally looked up to meet her mum's eye. Jane was watching her with an appraising gaze.

'So,' Martha began, knowing that she had to have this conversation but at the same time wishing desperately that she didn't. The creeping blanket of humiliation, that had become so achingly familiar over the past week or so, now crawled back into place and settled around Martha's shoulders, making them droop with the weight.

'So,' Jane echoed. 'What now, my love?'

Martha swallowed. She wasn't going to cry any more. It didn't help. It just made her feel a thousand times worse. 'I honestly don't know,' she said, when at last she was able to speak.

'It's very tough on you.' Jane nodded slightly and sighed heavily. 'But I take it the fact that you came home with him means you're going to try to make a go of it?'

Martha didn't answer. She stared out over her mum's shoulder into the garden, thinking how unfamiliar it looked after just a short time away. Dusk was falling and the colours were tinged with a faint orange glow that made it look warmer than it was. After the searing heat of LA, the coolness of an English evening seemed comforting and reviving. She wondered what Charlie was doing right now and who he was with. Already she missed him. Missed those eyes and that mouth, the smell and the touch of him. Wondered if he was missing her too.

'Oh, God,' Jane whispered, breaking into Martha's thoughts. 'You're going to leave him, aren't you?'

Martha glanced back at her in surprise, as if she'd forgotten she was there. 'I don't know,' she repeated.

'Look, Martha, I know how hard this is for you but, darling, you mustn't give up everything you've got over one indiscretion.'

Martha looked at her mum curiously. Jane's cheeks were flushed and she was blinking quickly, making her appear nervous. 'It wasn't just one indiscretion,' she said, tilting her head and raising her eyebrows.

'You know what I mean ...' Jane frowned as she spoke, causing two deep vertical lines to appear between her eyebrows.

'You mean that it was just the one whore he was sleeping with repeatedly behind my back?'

Jane blanched as she spoke and Martha almost wanted to laugh at the expression on her mum's face. She had always been such a good girl; her mother had probably never even heard her swear before. Martha decided it was a good job Jane hadn't been in the house the morning she discovered the pictures, remembering some of the language she had used then and feeling a glint of renewed anger with Jamie as she did so. That was his fault, too.

'It didn't mean anything. It's not worth wrecking your marriage over,' Jane continued, her tone brisk and business-like.

Now it was Martha's turn to frown. She took a sip of green tea to calm the jitters that were causing her hands to shake slightly. 'I think you'll find that it's not *me* who's wrecking the marriage.'

'Well it would be you if you decided you didn't want it to continue.'

Martha's mouth dropped open in indignation. 'Jesus, I can't believe what I'm hearing! Why are you taking his side?'

'I'm not!' Jane snapped, quickly and emphatically. 'I could quite happily strangle him with my bare hands ...' She paused for a moment as if she was enjoying the fantasy of murdering Jamie. 'But I do think that apart from this ... *fling*,' she spat the word out with distaste. 'Apart from that ... you have a good marriage. And it would be awful for the children ...' Jane bit her lip and closed her eyes. When she opened them again, Martha could see that she had been on the verge of tears. 'Mimi has been so upset while you were away, thinking that you had run off with some film star.' She rolled her eyes. 'The irony of it,' she tutted.

'I know,' Martha agreed. 'How do you think I felt, getting the blame when I've done nothing wrong?'

'I mean,' Jane continued, as if Martha hadn't spoken. 'As if!'

Martha felt herself bridle and knew she shouldn't rise to it but she couldn't help herself. Why was it so unlikely that Charlie would be attracted to her? 'Well,' she said, wishing she could keep her mouth shut, 'as a matter of fact, Charlie *was* interested in me.' She paused for a moment to enjoy the look of utter astonishment on Jane's face. 'But unlike my husband, I wasn't prepared to put myself before my marriage and my children. I love them too much for that.'

Jane opened her mouth to speak but no words came out. Martha could see her brain trying to compute the information and make sense of it.

'Oh God,' Martha sighed. 'What a bloody mess.'

'Please don't give up on your marriage, Martha. I know that what Jamie's done is desperately hurtful for you, but I promise you that it's not worth sacrificing all those happy years over.'

Martha frowned again at the realisation that Jane was trying to tell her something. 'And you know this because . . .?'

The pale pink tinge of colour that had flushed into Jane's cheeks intensified to a deeper shade of red. 'I know because . . .' Jane swallowed, '. . . because I've been in your position.'

Martha shook her head furiously. 'No!' she cried. 'That's not true!'

Jane took a deep breath and looked at her with such an honest stare that Martha knew for certain that she was telling the truth.

'Dad?' she said, her voice trembling. 'Dad cheated on you?' She continued to shake her head, as if it would somehow make what her mum had said untrue.

Jane shrugged. 'It doesn't have to mean the end of the marriage,' she said, sounding pained, as if recalling the memory had hurt her anew.

Martha got up and turned her back on Jane, suddenly unable to bear the sight of her face. Her legs wobbled under her and she leaned over and clutched the worktop for support. First Jamie, now her father. Were there any men on the planet who could be faithful? '*Charlie*,' whispered a little voice in her ear. Charlie could be faithful.

'It's almost as much of a shock as finding out about Jamie,' she murmured.

'I'm sorry, darling.' Jane got up and came to Martha. She put her arms around her daughter's shoulders and squeezed gently. 'I never wanted you to know but I hope that it might make you think differently about what's happened to you.'

Martha didn't reply and continued to lean over, clutching the worktop, still unable to meet her mother's eye.

'Your father and I . . .' Jane continued with a slightly more desperate tone. 'We were very happy together. Our marriage was strong, maybe even stronger after . . . it.' She stopped speaking for a second and Martha knew that she was watching her with a pleading expression, wanting Martha to give her some sign that she had done the right thing by telling her.

'Who was it?' Martha whispered, finally looking up. 'Was it somebody you knew?'

Jane's eyes clouded. 'It was Michelle.'

'Michelle, as in his secretary Michelle?' Martha gasped, remembering the frumpy, intense girl who had been her father's secretary for a while when she was a teenager. They had teased him about her being in love with him and he had scoffed at the idea. 'Jesus, what a cliché!'

Jane swallowed and looked away uncomfortably.

'How did you find out about it?'

Jane sighed and met Martha's eye again. 'She told me. She was probably hoping I would throw him out and he would go to her.'

Martha gasped. 'Could she have been lying?'

Jane shook her head. 'No. I confronted your father about it and he admitted it. I think he was relieved to have been found out.'

'And you *forgave* him?' Martha couldn't keep the incredulity out of her voice.

Jane hesitated. 'Not immediately, no. It was such a shock. I didn't know what to do. But he regretted it so much and made it clear how sorry he was. I think it was almost as much of a shock for him as it was for me . . .'

Martha nodded, recognising exactly the same emotions in her own situation. She looked at her mother with new-found respect. Not only had she coped with such an awful discovery on her own, but she had never given Martha the slightest hint that there was anything wrong in her parents' marriage. She had grown up convinced that they were the happiest couple on earth.

'I never forgot it but I did forgive it and we were able to recover,' Jane continued, giving Martha's shoulders another squeeze, before pulling her gently upright. 'And you will be able to recover too. You are so strong, Martha ...' she said, tilting Martha's chin so that she had no choice but to look at her. '... I know you can survive this.'

Martha put her hands over her face to hide the tears that threatened to fall in torrents. 'I don't know what to do now. I don't know where to begin.'

Jane gently peeled Martha's hands away from her face and held them in her own. 'Let him figure that out,' she said. 'You have worked so hard over the past few years. Being a mum, being the breadwinner, being a wife,' she added. 'Now it's his turn.'

Chapter 37

With Liv in rehab, Charlie was struggling to look after Felix on his own. He had had to cancel several high-level meetings with producers and directors at short notice, much to his agent's fury. He hoped that he had built up enough of a reputation from his Oscar nomination to persuade those in question that he would be worth waiting for. Right now, his priority was Felix.

He had expected Felix to adapt to Liv being away, as long as Charlie was there with him full-time, but he could see that the little boy was clearly pining for his mum. Normally so cheerful and lively, he had become quiet and withdrawn, only speaking to Charlie when he had no choice and sometimes being openly hostile towards him.

The long school holidays had started and Charlie was finding it increasingly difficult to think of things to do to entertain him. When they did do things together, like going to the park or the movies or the beach, Felix would invariably make it clear that Charlie was no match for Liv in the parenting stakes.

'Mom would have brought a picnic for us,' he told Charlie coldly, when it got to lunchtime at the beach and there was nowhere for miles around to get something to eat.

'Mom knows that this park is too babyish for me now,' Felix sneered when Charlie took him to the park he had always used in the past. Charlie had looked around and realised with a start that most of the kids there were toddlers and that Felix was indeed too old for it.

But it was when he was poorly that Charlie really felt inferior. 'Mom always makes my special drink if I'm sick,' Felix had murmured weakly from his bed after he had spent the night throwing up.

'Well I can get it ... what's in your special drink?' Charlie had replied, taking Felix's hand and giving it a squeeze.

Felix pulled his hand away and turned his back on Charlie. 'I don't know,' he said, his voice wobbling dangerously. 'It's Mom's special recipe ...' he added, before descending into pitiful tears.

In the end, feeling increasingly desperate, Charlie suggested that maybe Felix could go to summer camp, but his son looked at him through narrowed brown eyes and said coolly: 'Why did you make Mummy go away if you don't want to look after me?'

They were sitting at the table, having eaten a dinner that Juanita had prepared in total silence. Or at least Charlie had eaten; Felix had played with his food a bit and then left most of it. Charlie looked at Felix in shock. 'I didn't make Mummy go away!' he retorted.

Felix's mouth formed into the shape of a sneer and he looked away sulkily.

'Look, Felix, Mummy isn't well, that's why she had to go away. Not because I sent her ...'

'You did! You sent her away!' Felix cried, drawing his small frame up to its full height. 'And it's all my fault because I told you that I came to find you that night and you promised you wouldn't get cross, but you lied because you did get cross and then you sent Mummy away!' The tears that had been brimming for days now tumbled over Felix's black lashes and splashed onto the plate in front of him. He pushed back his chair and stood up. Instinctively, Charlie reached out to grab his wrist to stop him running off.

'Ouch!' yelled Felix, now openly sobbing. 'You hurt my arm! I hate you!' he screamed, before running at full-pelt towards his bedroom.

Charlie watched him go, temporarily paralysed with shock. It had never occurred to him that Felix might blame him for Liv going away. His heart was hammering with panic as he tried to think what to do. There was no doubt that Liv had had a breakdown and that going into rehab was the only option for her, but sitting here now, it occurred to him that maybe he could have handled it differently. Felix saw him as an enemy, which made Charlie feel desperately hurt and yet also ashamed that he hadn't dealt with the whole situation more sensitively.

For the first time, he started to think about how hard things must have been for Liv. Yes, she had done an awful thing when she'd dumped him for Danny. But she had been trying to make things right ever since. She had never stopped him from having access to Felix whenever he wanted and she had clearly never bad-mouthed him to their son. And in many ways she had paid a heavy price for her betrayal. Her career had really started to go wrong once Charlie became a big-name in Hollywood himself, and the public turned against Liv for being so heartless towards him. And if he was honest, he had enjoyed seeing her get her comeuppance.

And then there was her relationship with Danny. Only now did it occur to Charlie how lonely Liv must have felt, with her career taking a nosedive and her boyfriend being linked to endless other women while he was away on constant shoots. Charlie had never felt any kind of sympathy for her drinking before, but now, sitting at her table with Felix crying loudly for his mum from his bedroom, he finally understood.

Swallowing hard in his dry throat, he stood up and walked uncertainly towards Felix's room. He found him lying on top of his duvet, crying and shouting, 'I want my mom! I want my mom!' over and over again.

Charlie stood at the door watching him and felt a sudden urge to lie down on the floor and cry himself, but he knew he had to be strong for his son. He walked over to the red-painted car-shaped bed and knelt down beside it. Tentatively, he put a hand on the small of Felix's back, which was rising and falling as each sob convulsed through his small body.

'It's going to be OK,' he said, when he couldn't think of anything else.

Felix sat up and glared at him, his eyes blazing with rage. 'No it's not!' he cried. 'It's not going to be OK at all because I want my mummy and she's not here!'

Charlie held out his hands in a gesture of helplessness. 'Listen, Felix, Mum is going to be home really soon.'

Felix's sobs calmed momentarily and he looked up at Charlie suspiciously. 'How soon?' he said in a croaky voice, followed by a loud sniff.

'Well . . .' Charlie began, thinking furiously. He actually didn't know for certain how long Liv would be away. 'I think she'll be home in just a few weeks.' He remembered as he spoke that her course of treatment was supposed to last eight weeks. Even to him, that sounded like a very long time right now. To a six-year-old boy, he knew it must sound like an eternity.

'A few weeks!' Felix cried in anguish and burst into a fresh bout of tears.

Charlie reached out and lifted him off the bed and into his lap. Felix stiffened his back and lashed out but Charlie made sure his grip was firm enough to hold him tight. Gradually, the fight went out of his little body and he sagged in Charlie's arms. Charlie kissed the top of his head tenderly. 'I promise you,' he whispered, 'that it wasn't your fault that Mummy had to go into . . .' he stopped, unable to say the word 'rehab'. It didn't sound like the right sort of thing to say to an already confused little boy. '. . . hospital,' he said instead.

Felix wiped the remnants of his tears with the backs of his hands and looked up at Charlie. 'Hospital?' he said, and Charlie could see the cogs of his brain starting to whir. 'I didn't know she was in hospital.'

Charlie nodded emphatically, frustrated with himself that he hadn't thought of saying it sooner. It would have made so much more sense to Felix if he had been told that his mum had had to go into hospital because she was sick. All he knew was that she had 'gone away'. It was no wonder he was so distressed.

'Your mum is a bit poorly at the moment but she is definitely going to get better and before you know it she'll be home again,' he said, managing what he hoped was an encouraging smile. 'So you see?' he continued. 'It's nobody's fault when someone gets sick. It's not your fault, it's not my fault, and most of all, it's not Mummy's fault.'

A tiny glint of light appeared in Felix's eyes as he digested Charlie's words. 'OK,' he said, and gave a tentative gap-toothed smile that almost broke Charlie's composure. 'But I'm still really sad without her.' His eyes widened earnestly, as if he was trying to apologise for his earlier outburst.

'Of course you are!' Charlie soothed, hugging him tightly. 'It's completely normal to feel that way. You love your mum and she loves you.'

Felix nodded slowly, his lip drooping dangerously again.

'But hey!' Charlie said, keen to distract him. 'We just have to think of the best thing we can do to make the time go as quickly as possible until she's back home again. And I have had an idea ...'

Felix's brow crinkled as he gave Charlie a puzzled look. 'Really? What's your idea?'

Charlie smiled as relief flooded through him. The thought had flashed into his head as he was speaking – just in the nick of time. 'Well,' he began, 'how would you feel about a trip to Britain? We could go and visit Granny and Grandpa in Wales and I could take you to where we used to live and show you where you were born?'

As he was talking, Charlie began to feel more and more excited by the idea. His parents hardly ever saw Felix and they would be thrilled if he were to visit. And Charlie had never taken Felix away on his own for any long period of time. It would give them the chance to bond the way they had when he was little. 'What do you think?' he finished, biting his lip to try to curtail his obvious eagerness. It was a big deal for a small child and Felix might not want to go, he reminded himself, while giving his son his most beseeching look.

Felix raised one eyebrow in a way that made him look older than his six years. 'When would we go?' he asked.

Charlie shrugged. 'We can go anytime you want. How about tomorrow?' he said, winking.

Felix's face split into a wide grin and he reached up and wrapped his arms around Charlie's neck in a hug. 'That would be cool,' he said.

Charlie held him at arm's length. 'Seriously?'

Felix smiled again and nodded. 'Yeah, sure. It'll be fun!'

'It really will!' Charlie agreed, as the excitement bubbled up inside him. He felt energised and happy at the thought of taking his son back to where he was born and to see Charlie's parents. 'Come on then!' he beamed, lifting Felix off his lap and standing up. 'What are we waiting for? We've got a trip to plan!'

Chapter 38

Four thousand miles away and three weeks after returning from LA, Martha and Jamie were sitting opposite a counsellor, waiting expectantly for her to tell them how to salvage their broken marriage.

They sat beside each other on low wooden chairs in a small, purpose-built summer-house in the therapist's garden. Through the open windows summer sweltered on, but inside it was cool and shaded from the heat. Between them sat a small table with a jug of water, two glasses and, rather ominously, thought Jamie, a box of tissues.

He was nervous about this session because he had found the relationship therapist himself, after Martha told him that she wanted to go to counselling but didn't want to have anything to do with organising it. She had also insisted that he go through the utter humiliation of a visit to a sexual health clinic, which Jamie decided was something that all men thinking of having an affair should do, because it would put them off straying for life. All of it he agreed to willingly, hopeful that it would help prove to Martha that he would do anything to win her back.

The counsellor was a slim woman in her fifties called Karen, with a friendly face and a gentle way of speaking that seemed to put them both at ease. She sat opposite them on a slightly higher chair, with her back straight and her legs crossed in a position that suggested that she did a lot of yoga. Jamie threw Martha an anxious sideways glance to gauge her reaction. Normally by now they would be communicating with knowing smirks at each other, but today Martha kept her eyes firmly forward.

He knew this would be difficult for Martha. Although it was essentially what she did for a living, ironically she wasn't comfortable talking about her personal problems with a stranger.

Jamie started to breathe a little more easily, though, as he saw Martha visibly start to relax as Karen talked. Her face, which had been taut with strain since that first, dreadful morning, looked softer and more alive and her shoulders seemed to have dropped from their permanently hunched position.

He looked back towards Karen, hoping his desperation didn't show too much. He wondered if this was what people meant when they talked about the 'last chance saloon'. That was certainly how it felt to him.

'So,' Karen began, after she had written down all their details. 'Can you each start by telling me what you think the other wants to get out of this? It will help to determine if this is the right path for you to be taking.'

Jamie and Martha looked at each other in surprise. They had discussed what they thought the therapist might ask, but neither of them had anticipated that particular question.

'You go first, Martha,' Karen prompted, nodding encouragingly.

Martha thought for a few moments before speaking. 'I think,' she began, glancing at Jamie again, 'that he wants you to tell me how to deal with this, so that I'll forgive him and forget about it and we can all move on.'

Jamie's eyes widened. That was exactly what he was hoping the therapy would achieve.

Karen wrote something down in her book but maintained a neutral expression. 'Jamie?' she said, turning her gaze on him.

'Well,' Jamie stuttered, completely at a loss for what to say. What *did* Martha want to get out of counselling? He thought hard. 'I think she wants to be one hundred per cent sure that it'll never happen again . . .' he said finally, not entirely certain if what he was saying was true. 'And to know that she can trust me.'

Karen nodded as she again wrote something down. Then she looked up and smiled at them one after the other. 'OK,' she said. 'Well I can tell you now that neither of those things is going to happen.'

The wideness of her smile contrasted so starkly with the bluntness of her words that Jamie and Martha were momentarily baffled. Was Karen saying she couldn't help them? They looked at each other with mirroring frowns.

'*But* . . .' Karen continued, 'if you're prepared to work at this and be completely honest with me and with yourselves, then hopefully we'll be able to find a way through it. But I have to warn you that it's not going to be easy and you will probably find some of the things we discuss upsetting. So, the decision is yours. Do you want to continue?'

Jamie took a deep breath and looked shyly at Martha. He was banking on this counselling to save their relationship, and if she refused to carry on he had absolutely no idea where to go next. 'I do,' he said, raising his eyebrows at Martha questioningly. *Please*, he begged her silently. *Please don't give up now.*

Martha held his gaze for a few moments, as if she was weighing up what to say. As he watched her he could see in her eyes the history of their relationship playing out as clearly as if it was on a big screen in front of him.

He saw the day she finally agreed to go out with him, when he thought he must be the happiest man on earth. Then he discovered what the happiest man on earth really feels like when she gave birth to Mimi, her dark eyes shining up at him as she held their precious first-born baby. He saw his own loss reflected in her eyes the day they got the news that his mum had died, and finally he saw the bleak devastation of her discovering that he wasn't the man she had always thought he was.

When Martha opened her mouth to speak, Jamie felt as if he had been holding his breath for hours as her lips moved in slow motion to form the words he was so desperate to hear.

'I do,' she said.

Chapter 39

The summer that year seemed never-ending, though not in a good way. Martha felt as if the blue skies, the warmth and the sunshine were taunting her somehow, as she dragged herself through the weeks, yearning to put as much time as possible between her and the worst day of her life.

Jamie was trying so hard. He was loving and attentive towards her in a way that he had never been before, as if the shock of almost losing her had opened his eyes for the first time. He applied for and got a job on a trade magazine that he could do from home, and in his free time he was working furiously to finally finish the children's book he had started many years ago.

A part of Martha could understand why some couples claimed that an affair actually helped their marriage, because on the surface it had definitely given theirs a shot in the arm.

But lying awake in the middle of the night, staring wide-eyed at the ceiling because every time she closed her eyes she saw the images of Jamie having sex with a stranger, Martha wondered if she would ever feel the same way about him again. Too often, she would find herself staring at him, consumed by a venom and hatred that was almost overwhelming.

She had insisted that they sleep in the same bed when they got back from LA because she didn't want to give the children any cause for alarm, but it had been several weeks before she felt able to have sex with him again. When it happened, it was surprisingly fine. Good, even. But it wasn't the same. She couldn't enjoy the moment without thinking about him doing those things with *her*. Worse, because she had seen it with her own eyes, she could actually picture it and it left her feeling sick and miserable afterwards, instead of basking in a post-coital glow the way she used to.

'Isn't the counselling helping?' Lindsay asked, when they were out one evening walking along the beach together.

Martha pushed her hands deep into the pockets of her long cardigan. The sun was just beginning to set and the sky was already turning pink, promising another scorching hot day tomorrow, but for now there was a slight chill coming off the teal-coloured sea. 'Yes, it's helping. But the trouble is, those pictures are indelibly etched on my brain, Linds, and even the best counsellor in the world can't change that.'

Lindsay glanced at her with a look of concern and exhaled loudly. 'No, I guess not. It's still so shocking, even now, to think that Jamie of all people could have done that.'

Martha shrugged. She found it less shocking now that they had spent several sessions discussing why it had happened. The counsellor seemed to think that his mum's death had hit Jamie much harder than anyone realised, causing him to behave in a way that he wouldn't normally. She also suggested that because Jamie was feeling increasingly bored and lonely at home all day, while Martha was going from strength to strength in her career, his affair was a subconscious way for him to hit back at her. Jamie had furiously denied this, insisting that he was pleased and proud of Martha's success, but Martha suspected that the counsellor was right.

'Anyway,' she said to Lindsay, looking out towards the horizon and thinking, as she seemed to do every time she looked at the sea, of Charlie, 'I'm sure it'll sort itself out. It's not surprising that things are still a bit difficult. It was only a matter of weeks ago that it happened.'

They walked along in silence for a while, listening to the sand and shells crunching beneath their feet, before Lindsay spoke. 'What went on with Charlie, Martha? You've never really talked about it.'

Martha's heart skipped at the mention of Charlie's name. 'Nothing.' She glanced sideways at Lindsay with a sheepish expression.

Lindsay smiled slightly. 'OK, I get it. You're not going to tell me . . .'

'No!' Martha insisted quickly. 'It's not that at all. It's just that there's nothing really to tell.'

'So why do your eyes light up at the mere mention of his name and you get this funny look on your face when you're talking about him?'

Martha flushed furiously. 'I don't!'

Lindsay didn't reply but raised her eyebrows knowingly instead.

Martha wanted to tell Lindsay what she was feeling, but she

couldn't put it into words because she was frightened of revealing too much. She wanted to tell her that she thought about Charlie almost every minute of every day. That she felt an ache and a longing to see him that was so strong it caused a physical pain in her chest. She wanted to tell her that whenever Jamie kissed her now, all she could think about were Charlie's lips on hers, and how the lightest of his touches had made her almost melt with desire.

But there was no point in saying any of it because she had made the decision to try to forgive Jamie and make a go of her marriage and she couldn't go back on it. If she were to leave Jamie now, he would get custody and the children would be devastated. They wouldn't understand, and worse, they would blame her. One thing Martha was proud of was the way she had protected the children from the fallout from Jamie's affair. They were as happy and balanced as they had ever been and seemed blissfully unaware of any undercurrents in their parents' relationship.

'That's because of you,' Jamie had told her earnestly as they discussed the children over dinner one night. 'If you'd reacted differently ... if you'd thrown me out,' he said, closing his eyes and shaking his head at the thought, 'they would have been so damaged. You've been amazing,' he had added, reaching across and taking her hand in his.

'Have you heard from him at all?' Lindsay interrupted Martha's thoughts and pulling her back to the present.

Martha sighed. 'No. We agreed that it would be best if we didn't contact each other, for a while at least, to give me a chance to sort things out with Jamie.'

'That's probably for the best.'

'I guess so,' Martha agreed. 'But I've been keeping up with Charlie's movements through the papers and Twitter ...'

'So have I!' Lindsay blurted, before having the good grace to look ashamed. 'Sorry.' She wrinkled her nose slightly. 'It's just that it's so easy to be a stalker these days!'

Martha laughed. 'Tell me about it!' She had become slightly obsessive about Googling Charlie and had started following him on Twitter without being logged as a follower, so that he didn't know she was keeping tabs on him. 'He's been in this country for a couple of weeks now. With Felix, his little boy.' Learning that Charlie was in the UK had only added to Martha's disquiet. Now that he was no longer thousands of miles away, it made her feel closer to him. As if he was somehow within touching distance.

Lindsay nodded. 'Yeah, and what about the ex-wife going into rehab? That was a bit of a shock, wasn't it?'

Martha shrugged. 'I wasn't that shocked, actually. Not after seeing her in LA. I think she just went to pieces when Danny Nixon dumped her. Poor girl. I feel really sorry for her. Despite what she did to Charlie, I liked her. She was a nice person.'

'Well it hasn't done her career any harm, that's for sure,' Lindsay cut in with a cynical smile.

'No,' Martha agreed. Liv's stint in rehab had been well publicised and it seemed likely that when she came out, she would be in demand again. 'But I got the impression that Liv wasn't very happy in LA and was only there because of Danny. I wouldn't be surprised if she decided to come back here, now that there's nothing worth staying for.'

'Charlie would be pleased about that, wouldn't he?'

Martha nodded hesitantly. 'Yes and no. Ironically, he's just been signed up for two big new movies, so he's going to be LA-based for a while.'

She thought back to Charlie confiding in her that he was thinking of applying for more formal access to Felix. Now that Liv had gone into rehab, it would surely strengthen his case. Maybe he would even get custody. It made her feel even more sorry for Liv.

She shook her head, as if to clear all thoughts of Charlie from her brain. 'I just need to focus on Jamie and the children,' she said, as much to herself as to Lindsay as they walked towards her car. The sun had set and the sea looked almost black under the inky sky.

Lindsay climbed into the passenger seat and did up her seatbelt. 'Definitely. And Jamie's doing everything he can to put things right, isn't he?'

Martha nodded dully.

'I mean, when I discovered Pete was having an affair, he treated me like crap,' Lindsay sighed. 'He made out it was all my fault and didn't do anything to try to convince me that it wouldn't happen again. At least Jamie is doing everything he can to show you how much he loves you. And you're good together, Martha,' she added. 'Your marriage is strong and it's worth fighting for.'

Martha smiled gratefully. 'I know, I know. I love Jamie, I really do. But sometimes I hate him too, do you understand what I mean?'

Lindsay rolled her large blue eyes dramatically. ''Course I

bloody do! What he did was awful. But I don't think it'll ever happen again.'

'No,' Martha agreed. 'Neither do I.'

Lindsay reached over and took her hand. 'So you *do* feel like you can trust him, then?' she said, looking at her closely. 'Because that's huge, Martha. I knew I couldn't trust Pete again after what he did, and a relationship without trust isn't worth having. But if you're already saying that you trust Jamie again, so soon after . . . well, after *it*, then I think you're going to make it.'

Martha nodded slowly and started the engine, her heart feeling a little lighter suddenly. Maybe Lindsay was right. Maybe everything was going to be alright. Maybe in time, all thoughts of Charlie would fade, along with the memories of Jamie's awful betrayal, and she and Jamie would return to normal. Maybe they would grow old together after all, just as she had always thought they would. She smiled to herself and pulled away, suddenly desperate to get home.

Chapter 40

Jamie scanned the history on Martha's computer. As usual, she had started the day by Googling Charlie Simmons and reading all of the resulting articles, as well as his Twitter feed. Then she had logged in several more times throughout the day to repeat the exercise. He felt the familiar weight of jealousy in the pit of his stomach and tried to ignore it, while at the same time cursing his bad luck that his love rival was so famous that the press seemed to track his every move.

Jamie knew that he had no right to check up on Martha or be possessive of her after all he'd done, but he couldn't help it. He was terrified that she might try to get back at him by having a revenge affair, or worse, that she might be so disillusioned by his infidelity that she fell out of love with him.

And Charlie Simmons was tough competition. The toughest. He was rich, famous and very handsome. Jamie knew Martha well enough to know that none of those things on their own would be enough to attract her, but he also realised that Charlie now had another trump card. He wasn't a cheat.

He sighed heavily and closed Martha's laptop. She was so hopeless with technology that it wouldn't even occur to her to cover her tracks by deleting the history on her computer. Not that she would do it, even if she knew how. Martha was an open book. She wasn't a cheat either, meaning her and Charlie were probably very well suited.

Jamie got up feeling irritable and unsettled and went out onto the landing. He went to Tom's door and peered in at him. Already he had turned himself upside down in the bed and his feet were sprawled across his pillow as he slept. Jamie walked over to the end of the bed and bent down to kiss Tom's cheek. The little boy stirred slightly as Jamie pushed his hair back from his forehead and rubbed his thumb over it.

Next, he headed for Mimi's room. Mimi was also fast asleep, a book propped open on her chest. Jamie smiled and gently removed the book, before bending down to kiss her cheek. As he did so, her eyes blinked open in shock. 'Dad?' she croaked in a sleep-drenched voice.

'Go back to sleep, baby,' he whispered, thinking how much like a fairytale princess she looked, with her perfect hair spread out on the pillow. Instantly, her eyes drooped shut once more and she was asleep before he left the room. Jamie paused at the top of the stairs, wondering how to shake off the heavy feeling of gloom that seemed to stalk him at the moment.

Downstairs, the house was in darkness. Martha had gone for a walk with Lindsay earlier and Jamie had spent the evening upstairs in the office, working on his book and checking up on Martha's search history.

He shivered slightly as he switched on the lights in the kitchen and sitting room, before making himself a cup of black coffee. He sat at the table to drink it, deep in thought. Things were gradually getting better between him and Martha. The counselling seemed to be helping and they had started sleeping together again, which was a monumental leap for both of them. They were able to have conversations about things other than his affair and they had managed to keep all the turmoil and upheaval in their relationship completely hidden from the children.

And yet, every time he started to feel hopeful that their relationship was gradually repairing itself, she would give him a look that told him in no uncertain terms that something was missing. It was a mixture of pain and contempt, both of which killed him. He could cope with anger and disgust, but seeing her so broken was something he couldn't deal with. For the millionth time, he cursed his utter stupidity. He wished desperately that he could do something physical to show her how sorry he was, like rip off his own arm. Pleading with her and repeatedly telling her just seemed so futile and ineffectual.

He was doing absolutely everything he could think of to make it up to her and his greatest desire was to make her proud of him again. Over the past couple of months, he had got a job and had finally knuckled down to finish his book, yet he somehow knew that it wasn't enough. He had a horrible feeling that he was living on borrowed time.

He was sure that she wouldn't leave him now, while the children were still young, but he wasn't so sure about what the future held and wondered if she was just biding her time until she felt the children could cope with them splitting up. The prospect of losing her made him feel hollowed out with grief.

He took a sip of his coffee, enjoying the bitter kick it gave him. Anything to feel less weak. Less helpless.

From where he was sitting, he could see right through to the front door, and as he watched, it opened and Martha came through. She breezed into the kitchen, bringing with her a gust of fresh air.

'You smell like the sea,' he murmured.

She came over to the table and sat down opposite him. They locked eyes for a few seconds. 'Why so sad?' she said, her big, dark eyes almost black as the pupils dilated.

Jamie tried to smile but instead he felt his own eyes fill with tears. 'Because I love you. But I'm not sure you love me any more. And I don't blame you.'

Martha reached across the table and took his hands in hers. 'I do still love you,' she said, before hesitating. 'But it's hard, Jamie. It's just really hard.' As she spoke, she looked up at him and he felt as if he could melt into those lovely eyes that he knew so well.

'I know.' He shook his head. 'Believe me, I know what you mean. You've been so incredible. I just want to make you proud of me again. I want you to look at me the way you used to . . . instead of the way you look at me now.'

Martha blinked twice quickly. 'How do I look at you now?'

Jamie half-smiled. 'You look at me now like you hate me.'

Martha smiled back. 'Well, a lot of the time I do hate you,' she said bluntly, the gentleness of her voice softening her words. 'But not *all* the time. And it's getting better every day.'

'Yes, but I worry that you're going to wake up one morning and think, "I don't need to feel this bad," and go.'

Martha pressed her lips together. 'There's just as much chance of you waking up one morning and feeling the same thing.'

'Ah, but that's where you're wrong.' Jamie could feel a veil of sadness wrapping itself around his shoulders. 'I will spend the rest of my life proving to you that I made a terrible mistake but that I love you and I will never, ever let you down again.'

Martha nodded slowly. 'Well I've got no intention of leaving either, so it looks like we're in it for the long haul, doesn't it?'

'I hate the thought that you view it like that. Like a long haul.'

'I'm afraid it's the best I can do right now,' she said, giving his hands a gentle squeeze. 'And given the circumstances, I don't think it's so bad.'

Jamie tried to shake himself out of his malaise. If Martha could be so positive, then it was the least he could do to try and be positive too. 'No,' he agreed. 'I guess we're doing OK, aren't we?'

Martha nodded. 'We are. There'll be good days and bad days, but hopefully when we look back at this period we'll think of it as a blip. And Jamie, this was the perfect opportunity for me to leave. No-one would have blamed me if I'd told them the real reason, so the fact that I'm still here has got to be a good sign, hasn't it?'

Jamie exhaled. 'I can't believe how amazing you're being. How amazing you've been.'

Martha pondered his words for a moment. 'Yes, I am pretty fantastic, aren't I?' she said with a grin.

Jamie smiled too. He opened his mouth to speak, then closed it again, unsure whether to risk upsetting her upbeat mood.

'What?' she asked. 'What is it?'

Jamie decided to take the risk. 'It's just that there is still an elephant in the room, isn't there?'

'Er, yes!' Martha cried. 'The elephant being that you had an affair, you mean?'

'No, that's not what I'm talking about.'

Martha frowned, then grimaced as the light dawned. 'Ah . . . Charlie, I presume?'

'You presume right.'

Martha tutted irritably. 'Well, what about him? I haven't seen him or spoken to him since LA . . .'

'Maybe not. But you've certainly been keeping up to date with his movements, haven't you?'

'And how would you know that, I wonder?'

Jamie sighed, regretting that he had brought the subject up. He could almost see the hostile vibes now swimming in the air around Martha.

'Wow. Ironic, isn't it, that you're the one checking up on me?'

'I know,' Jamie muttered, looking down. 'But still, it doesn't change the fact that you've been following his every move.'

There was silence for a while before Martha finally spoke. 'He was very kind to me, Jamie, when I desperately needed that. And if I'm really honest, I do miss him.'

Jamie felt himself bristling. Charlie had really worked a

number on Martha when she was at her most vulnerable. And yet, though he felt jealous, he knew in his heart that it was all his fault. Martha would never have opened herself up to Charlie if she hadn't discovered what Jamie had done.

'And it feels like things are still unresolved where he's concerned . . .'

Jamie looked up, feeling a little jolt of alarm.

'Doing his memoirs was such a great opportunity for me,' Martha continued, with a nervous bite of her lower lip. 'And his agent called me yesterday, saying they hadn't been able to find anyone else at such short notice. She asked if I would still like to do it . . . and the fact is, I would.'

Jamie swallowed hard. It would mean her having regular contact with Charlie again. Yet what right had he to stop her?

'I know that it would be very hard on you,' Martha interrupted his thoughts, 'so if you really don't want me to, I won't.' She gazed up at him with a pleading look in her eyes.

Jamie pursed his lips together, thinking. He desperately didn't want her to see that slimy bastard ever again, but if he stopped her she would resent him forever and their relationship wouldn't stand a chance anyway. 'No.' He tried to sound more upbeat than he felt. 'If it's what you want, you should do it. I won't stop you.'

Martha's eyes lit up in a way that made Jamie's stomach churn. 'Really?' She leapt up and planted a kiss on the top of his head. 'Thank you!' she said, before skipping out of the kitchen and upstairs to the office, no doubt to email Charlie.

Jamie watched her go. He had a bad feeling about this. A very bad feeling.

Chapter 41

Charlie's phone made an off-key sound, which signified that he had a new email. He picked up the phone and waved it at his mum, Jo. 'OK if I go and take this call?' He didn't bother explaining that it was an email as his mum wouldn't know the difference and wouldn't much care either. Jo was an artist who didn't have time for modern technology.

She pushed back a strand of her shoulder-length, wavy grey hair and beamed at him from the kitchen table where she was showing Felix how to paint some famous cartoon characters. 'Ay, go ahead,' she motioned with her hand, speaking in her lilting Welsh accent.

Charlie smiled his thanks, enjoying watching his son and his mother deep in concentration for a few more moments before heading out of the room into the bright, airy hallway. They had been staying at his parents' modest house for nearly three weeks now and Charlie marvelled at how easily his mum and dad had adapted their lives to accommodate their only grandson. They had seen him just a handful of times in his short life, but over these last few weeks they had developed such a strong connection that it seemed as though they had spent every waking minute of his six years together.

They would take Felix to play pooh sticks in the stream that ran under the pretty little bridge in the dappled woods that backed onto their house; they would roll down the steep sand dunes at the beach, making them all dizzy with laughter; and they would sit for hours playing Scrabble, with Charlie's parents squealing with delight at the American words Felix conjured up, while teaching him some new Welsh ones in return.

They would have to leave to go home that weekend, as Charlie started shooting his next movie in LA shortly, and he was dreading the wrench of saying goodbye. Liv would be out of rehab within a few days and it wasn't fair on Felix to tear him away from everything he knew for too long. But it had been an idyllic summer for both of them and he already felt that it was one they would never forget. More than once he had said a mental prayer of thanks to Liv for unwittingly giving him the opportunity to spend so much time with his son.

In the past, his mum had been extremely frosty about Liv, ever since she had dumped Charlie so publicly, but these days she seemed to have softened her opinion of her. 'She's done such a good job with Felix, and she's obviously got her own demons to fight. I can't go on being angry with her. It's time we all forgave and forgot,' was all she would say when Charlie asked her about it.

And Charlie could feel that he was starting to forgive Liv too. He had to admit that although spending time with Felix was wonderful, it was also tough going at times, even with so much help from his parents. Liv had done it more or less alone for four years. Yes, her own mother visited, but Mariella was as much of a handful as Felix sometimes and Charlie knew that she wouldn't have given her daughter much help or guidance. Liv's breakdown had shown him that although she had always tried to keep it hidden from him, she had clearly been finding life a struggle. Her guilt over leaving Charlie had tarnished everything for her, meaning that she had never really been able to kick back and properly enjoy her supposedly charmed life.

Charlie climbed the stairs to the bedroom he had had when he was a child and which his parents had kept more or less untouched since he had left home. On his wall were still the oh-so-cool film posters he used to collect, along with the Arsenal paraphernalia that his father, an ardent Swansea City supporter, had been so disgusted by. Charlie smiled as he sat down on his old single bed, waiting for the shocked twang of the spring that had been broken since he was seventeen, which duly came as it absorbed his weight. Despite the fact that he was now a wealthy man, Charlie found comfort in the familiarity of his old home and was grateful that his parents had politely but firmly refused his offer to buy them somewhere bigger and more glamorous.

He scrolled through his email folder. He had several from his personal assistant, Jess, who was busy organising the itinerary for his up-and-coming film shoot, plus two from Louisa, his trusty, long-suffering publicist. He opened Louisa's first email.

Hey Charlie
    Just had an email from Martha Lamont saying she
would be happy to finish your memoirs if we still couldn't
find anyone. What do you think?
    Lx

Charlie felt a spike of excitement at the sight of Martha's
name in print. Why had she emailed Louisa? Her next message contained the answer:

OK, so I called her anyway when you couldn't be
bothered to answer my email . . . It turns out she would
agree to finish your memoirs but was nervous about how
you might feel (anything I should know btw!???). I told
her that I would speak to you and get back to her.
    So . . . What are your thoughts?
    Lx

Charlie re-read her emails twice to make sure that she was
saying what he hoped she was saying. He had missed Martha
desperately since she had left LA and had thought about her
constantly. He had promised Jamie not to get in touch with
her and although he wasn't bothered about keeping that
promise, he had also promised Martha that he would leave her
alone to give her enough time to get her head together.

He stared out of the window as his mind whirred with possibilities. He couldn't work out if this meant that she had split
from her husband and was letting him know via Louisa, or
whether she had managed to work it out with Jamie so that

329

it wasn't an issue if she saw Charlie. Suddenly, he was desperate to hear her voice and see her face again. He needed to know if he had imagined what he thought they had between them.

With a dry throat, he scrolled through his contacts list until he came to her name. He could feel himself grinning stupidly as he looked at it, remembering her dark eyes and wide smile; her full, sensual mouth as he kissed her. His thumb hovered over the number, making him feel about fifteen again. It was just a friendly call. No big deal. So why was he trembling with nerves as his thumb made contact with the screen?

'Charlie!' she cried, answering almost immediately. 'Oh, how lovely. I was hoping you would call. Did Louisa get in touch?'

Her voice seemed to ooze like melted chocolate down the phone line, causing Charlie's stomach to turn somersaults. He could tell she was gabbling, that she sounded nervous, and it made him feel even more tense.

'Yes, she emailed me.' He tried to picture Martha as she sat talking to him. 'So ... I hear you're thinking that you might still finish my memoirs after all?'

'Um, yes.' Martha sounded embarrassed. 'But I would understand if you don't think it's a good idea ...' Her words hung in the ether for a few seconds before she spoke again. 'So, how *would* you feel about it?'

'Well now ...' Charlie leaned back against the wooden headboard of his childhood and instantly remembering how ineffective and uncomfortable it had always been, 'I think maybe a more pertinent question would be, how does your husband feel about it?' He held his breath as he waited for her answer. When it came, it felt as though the air had been knocked out of his lungs momentarily.

'We've talked a lot and he's fine about it.'

'Oh.' Charlie tried not to sound too deflated. If Jamie didn't see him as a threat any more, it must mean that he was fairly confident that Martha didn't have feelings for Charlie.

There was an awkward silence. Charlie wanted to see her so badly, but at the same time he knew that he had to protect himself from getting hurt. If she had worked things out with Jamie, it must mean that he didn't stand a chance. Maybe he needed to cut his losses and move on before it was too late.

'Charlie?' Martha prompted.

He coughed. 'I don't really know, Martha. Maybe it's not such a good idea . . .'

Now it was Martha's turn to sound deflated. 'Oh,' she said, as if he had somehow wounded her with his words, before lapsing into a hurt silence. 'I understand,' she added, after several seconds.

'Do you?' Charlie shot back quickly.

'Yes,' Martha replied, with a slight break in her voice that suggested she didn't understand at all.

Charlie sighed deeply. 'Look, Martha, I would love to see you again. But I can't risk—'

'No, it's OK,' she interrupted him, and he could hear that she was trying to sound stoical. 'I get it.'

'I'm not sure you do . . .' Charlie began.

But Martha was clearly desperate to get off the phone. 'It's fine, really!' she trilled. 'Look, I shouldn't have bothered you.

I'm … well, I'm sorry about everything, Charlie. But maybe you're right and it's best to leave things be.'

Charlie could feel a lump forming in his throat. The last thing he wanted to do was to say goodbye to her for good. But at the same time, she had made her decision and chosen her marriage and children over him. As he had always known she would. The realisation only made him want her even more. 'I'm going back anyway,' he managed to croak, trying to salvage some pride. 'This weekend.'

There was a pause before Martha replied, 'To LA? Are you moving there permanently?'

'I think so, yes.'

'Well, I guess that's that, then,' she said, with another catch in her voice.

'I guess so.'

'Well, thank you, Charlie,' she said quietly. 'For everything. You were there for me when I needed you. I don't know how I would have coped without you.'

'Glad to have been of service,' he replied, wishing he didn't sound so bitter but unable to help it. Why was it that he was the one who was always so loyal and faithful, and yet it was cheats like Jamie and Danny Nixon who ended up getting the girl? It seemed so unfair. Maybe he needed to rethink the way he treated women. Maybe if he was a bit more of a bastard himself, he wouldn't keep finding himself in this situation.

'Charlie?' Martha jolted him out of his reverie.

'Hmmm,' he replied in a gruff voice.

'If things had been different …' she began.

'No, don't,' he cut her off. He couldn't bear to listen to her platitudes. Whatever she was about to say, she would only be saying it to try to make herself feel better. Well, he wasn't going to give her the satisfaction. 'I'm fine, really,' he lied. 'And I wish you all the best. I hope you're happy.' He wanted to add a warning that if Jamie had done it once, he was more than likely to do it again, but he couldn't bring himself to say anything that would hurt her feelings. She had decided to take a leap of faith and trust him, so he needed to back off and let her find out for herself if she had made the right decision.

'Goodbye, Charlie,' she said, with a longing in her voice that was unmistakable.

The urge to relent and to ask her to meet him was almost overwhelming, but Charlie swallowed back the words. 'Goodbye, Martha,' he said, before quickly pressing the 'End Call' button.

He leaned his head forward onto his chest, feeling drained. He allowed himself to dwell on his misery for a while before telling himself crossly that he needed to get a grip and stop being so negative. He had so much that was good in his life. He was rich, famous, and he had a wonderful son who brought him more joy than he ever thought possible. In time, he would meet another woman and he would be happy again. He swung his legs over the edge of the bed and stood up, feeling like a giant as his frame dwarfed the small room.

He walked over to the window and pulled back the curtain to look out at the pretty garden, now bursting with all the colours of the summer flowers his parents had lovingly planted. A small fence separated it from the moss-green woods beyond, which nestled under a low blue sky scuffed with puffy white clouds. It was so different from the vast haziness of LA, which looked as if someone had taken an eraser to a watercolour and rubbed out some of the intensity.

He had loved being back here. It was good for his soul. He loved spending time with his family, he loved the lilting accent of the locals in the village and he loved the slower pace of life. But it wasn't his home any more and he knew that he didn't belong. LA had its faults but it was where his future lay.

He took a deep, soothing breath and smiled to himself. For the first time ever, he felt something approaching a thrill of exhilaration at the prospect of going back. It felt as though he was being given the chance to build a new life. He would throw himself into his work and focus on Felix and, with a bit of luck, he would meet someone else and forget about Martha Lamont altogether.

Chapter 42

To Liv's delight, Charlie brought Felix with him to collect her. She ran towards them and scooped the little boy up in her arms, savouring the smell of his hair and his skin – a smell she had dreamt of for the past eight weeks – whilst smothering his face in kisses. Felix giggled and squirmed with delight and hugged her tightly, wrapping his skinny legs around her waist to get a better grip.

Over the top of his head, Liv locked eyes with Charlie, who was watching them with a sad expression that made Liv tremble with fear.

It felt like such a long time since she had first come here, railing at Charlie's cruelty and desperate to escape. She could see now that he had been right, that she *had* had a problem. But now that she was finally free to leave, the outside world suddenly seemed like a big, scary place and she didn't know if she would be able to cope out there, especially if Charlie went through with his threat to go for custody of Felix. One thing she knew for absolute certain after her enforced separation from him was that she couldn't live without him.

'Come on,' Charlie said, reaching down to pick up Liv's case. 'Let's go home.'

'Are you . . .?' Liv began, wanting to ask if they would all be going home together. But she stopped mid-question, as she realised that she was too scared of what his answer might be. It occurred to her in a horrified flash that maybe Charlie had found himself somewhere else to live and had already taken Felix with him.

'Am I what?' Charlie looked back at her curiously. Liv thought distractedly how handsome he looked, with his crisp white shirt emphasising his tanned skin.

'Are we going home together?' she asked, as she pressed her face against Felix's curls.

Understanding dawned in Charlie's eyes and he nodded. 'For the time being.'

'Thank you,' Liv mouthed over the top of Felix's head.

Charlie half smiled and gave a curt nod. 'Come on, Felix, you can walk to the car, buddy,' he said, as he turned and headed out onto the gravel courtyard where he had parked.

'No!' Liv cried, tightening her grasp on her son's body. 'It's fine. I'll carry him.' She had no intention of letting him go for as long as possible.

Charlie smiled and rolled his eyes good-naturedly.

Liv sat in the back seat with Felix for the hour-long journey home as the boy talked non-stop about his trip to Wales to see his grandparents. Liv tried to smile but felt her stomach knotting with concern. Was this part of Charlie's grand plan to have Felix living with him permanently? Could he be thinking of taking him back to Wales? Even the thought of it made her feel nauseous. She caught Charlie's eye in the rear-view mirror but couldn't read his expression.

As they pulled up outside her home, Charlie pressed the remote control for the gate and it swished open. Liv's heart began to pound as she remembered with horrible clarity the last moment she had been in this house, and instinctively she put her hand to her head. The wound had healed but the scar still remained in a faint rubbery line. Charlie leapt out of the car and took her bag from the boot, before opening her car door. 'You coming then?' he asked, holding out his hand for her to take.

Liv reached out a shaking hand and put it in his. It felt smooth and cool and reassuring.

'It'll be fine.' Charlie gave her hand a squeeze. 'Everything's going to be OK.'

Her legs felt like jelly and she had to concentrate to make them move as she shuffled behind Charlie towards the front door. Just as he was about to put the key in the lock, she stumbled.

Charlie reached out a hand to steady her. His forehead creased into a look of concern. 'It's fine,' he murmured gently, reading her fear. 'You can do it.'

'Come on, Mum!' Felix yelled, scampering through the huge door as soon as it swung open. He beamed up at her expectantly.

Suddenly, Liv's shoulders seemed to drop. Of course she could go back into the house. It was Felix's home. It was all he knew. Whatever Charlie was planning to do, she had a trump card. Felix loved her and he loved his home. To him, the two were inextricably linked.

She stepped into the huge white hallway and was immediately flooded with a sense of calm. Everything looked so different and yet so much the same. 'Wow,' she breathed, following Felix into the kitchen. 'It's good to be home.'

Charlie put her bag down and looked at her, as if seeing her for the first time. 'It's good to have you home,' he said. 'We've missed you.'

Later, Charlie came into the day room where Liv was lying on a sofa cuddled up with Felix. He was watching *Toy Story* for the millionth time while Liv was just watching him, revelling in his presence.

She looked up at Charlie. 'What have you got there?' she asked, nodding towards his right hand.

Charlie uncurled his hand. 'It's your phone.' He held it out towards her and smiling encouragingly.

Liv's heart skipped slightly. Before rehab, she had never let her phone out of her sight. Now, having been without it for eight whole weeks, she was wary of it, as if it might possess some kind of evil power that would suck her into its grasp once more.

'I think it might have some good news for you . . .' Charlie said, when she hesitated.

Liv frowned and stood up, edging Felix carefully to one side. She reached out and took the phone, surprised that it felt so familiar in her hand.

'You look like you're carrying a bomb!' Charlie said, as Liv headed for the kitchen, holding the phone out in front of her.

She headed for the island in the middle of the kitchen and perched on her favourite stool. She put the phone down in front of her and peered at the screen. 'What good news?' she asked, wondering if he was going to tell her that he'd changed his mind about filing for custody, which was the only news she wanted to hear.

Charlie reached over her shoulder and tapped the email icon. Immediately dozens of new emails began to scroll down the screen.

Liv frowned, overwhelmed by the sheer number. 'Can't you just tell me what they say?' she asked, looking up at Charlie, fear gripping her anew.

He shrugged. 'Well, let's just say that your agent has been very busy since you went into rehab . . .'

'Why?' Liv frowned, followed by, 'Oh my God!' as she realised what he was saying. 'Does everybody know?'

'Well, it's always hard to keep something like that secret, Liv. You know that.'

Liv closed her eyes to try to block out the sense of shame that was enveloping her.

'It's OK,' Charlie said, putting a hand on her shoulder.

She shrugged him off. 'OK that the whole world knows I'm a drunk?' she cried. 'That certainly plays into your hands, doesn't it?'

Charlie sighed and shook his head. 'That's not what anyone thinks, Liv,' he protested. 'And look, you've got so many offers of work that Jonathan can't cope.'

'I don't *care* how many job offers I've got!' she shouted. 'I'm a failure as a mother, a failure as a wife, and I'm such a drunk that you think I can't look after my own child and are going to take him off me!' She looked at Charlie, with his sweet dark eyes and gentle expression, and felt a sudden urge to punch him, to make him feel just a tiny fraction of the pain she was feeling right now.

Charlie looked away.

'Well?' Liv prompted. 'I'm right, aren't I?'

Charlie shook his head and exhaled in a long, slow breath. 'Let's not talk about this now, Liv. You've just got home and you need to concentrate on getting completely well.'

'I am well!' she snapped, furious at his insinuation that she still needed help.

'I know, I know . . .' Charlie put his hands up in a gesture of surrender. 'Liv, you've done incredibly well to come through this past eight weeks and I'm sure you'll be fine from now on. But let's just see how things go, shall we?'

Liv could feel the tears of frustration threatening so she snatched up her phone and took it to her bedroom. She had just gone through eight weeks of hell thanks to Charlie and she suddenly felt like she wanted to get away from him.

She walked into her bedroom and had to stop for a minute to take in the sheer size and scale of it. Her room in rehab had been pretty but small and very simply furnished. The opulence and vastness of her bed alone was breathtaking. She lay down on top of the silk throw that she had bought from a souk on a visit to Morocco with Danny and stared up at the ceiling. She wondered if Danny knew about her stint in rehab and, if so, whether he had been in touch with Felix. She suspected not. Danny had been a wonderful step-father to him, but now that he had moved on she imagined he would probably think it was best to cut all ties. Anything else was too painful and complicated.

She missed Danny, but to her surprise she felt as though she had accepted their break-up with remarkable calmness. She had had a lot of time to think while in rehab and had decided that it was probably because she had felt all along that she only ever had him on loan. Danny had loved her, she was in no doubt about that, but he was also a womaniser. It was something that was in his blood and it was almost as if he couldn't help himself. It was just another character trait, like having a good sense of humour or a bad temper.

And now that Liv had been punished for what she had done to Charlie by being dumped herself, she felt cleansed. It had taken away a lot of the guilt she had been carrying, as if she had been absolved from her sins, and it was only now that she was clean of alcohol that she could allow herself to be for-given.

She lifted her phone and began to read through her mes-sages and emails. Most were from her agent, Jonathan, or her personal assistant, Carrie, outlining various roles she was being offered and asking her to get in touch as soon as she felt ready. But in amongst them was a short email from Danny, telling her that he was glad she was getting the right help and that she didn't need to worry about the house – he had already instructed his lawyers and would be signing it over to her as soon as possible. He ended by telling her that a part of him would always love her and that he had no regrets about the past four years, which had been the happiest of his life. He asked her to send his love to Felix but said he thought it was best for everyone if he didn't see him again and wished them both happiness in the future.

Liv felt a familiar tingle at the back of her eyes and blinked furiously. She refused to cry over Danny any more. It was what she had expected and it was what she deserved. At least she didn't need to fret about being homeless, on top of everything else. Now all she needed to do was persuade Charlie that she was well enough to look after her own son. And do it she would. She put her phone down and sat up straight. She was ready for the fight.

Chapter 43

'So ... Charlie Simmons seems to be doing rather well for himself in Hollywood, doesn't he?' Martha said, trying to keep her voice light.

She was having lunch with Louisa Thomas, Charlie's PR, at The Wolseley, a beautiful art deco restaurant in London, where most of the city's media contingent gravitated to do business.

Louisa's eyes narrowed slightly. 'Yes, he's doing brilliantly. I spoke to him yesterday. He's on location in New York at the moment, lucky thing. Actually, Liv's doing really well too. I've just started doing her PR and it's a gift – her stint in rehab did wonders for her career.'

Martha smiled and nodded. 'I'm glad for her,' she said, meaning it. 'She's a good person. I liked her a lot.' She speared a slice of tomato from her salad and ate it, thinking back to her strange time in LA.

'Oh, yes, of course. You went with Charlie to LA, didn't you?' Louisa eyed Martha closely. 'What happened back then, Martha? I could never really get an answer out of Charlie.'

Martha pushed out her bottom lip and shook her head.

343

'Nothing happened,' she said, trying to keep her answer clipped so that Louisa wouldn't be tempted to ask any more.

'Oh, you know me better than that, Martha!' Louisa laughed. 'That's nowhere near good enough! Something went on. I just can't figure out exactly what.'

Martha took another mouthful of her salad, followed by a sip of her wine, trying to stall for time. 'Charlie was very kind to me,' she said carefully. 'At a very difficult time of my life.'

Louisa frowned. 'So why did you back out of doing his memoirs, then? It doesn't make sense if he was so kind to you.'

'Actually it was Charlie who decided that I shouldn't do them,' she said, immediately feeling disloyal.

'Hmmm,' Louisa murmured, her eyes narrowing slightly. 'I still feel as if something happened in LA, and I have obviously jumped to certain conclusions . . . but I would really love to know if I'm right.'

Martha sighed. She desperately didn't want to talk about what had happened, but she did owe Louisa some kind of explanation. She had given her an incredible opportunity and she deserved to know why Martha hadn't taken it.

'We just became very close,' she said, before stopping for a few seconds, lost in thought. 'And then,' she continued, 'perhaps not surprisingly, my husband felt a bit threatened by Charlie. To do his memoirs would have meant us spending an awful lot of time together, and in the end I decided to put my marriage first.' As she finished speaking, the tears flashed into Martha's eyes and she blinked them away, embarrassed.

'You don't seem too happy about that decision,' Louisa prodded, frowning slightly.

'I am!' Martha brushed away a stray tear that had refused to stay put with an irritable flick of her napkin. 'It's just that . . . well, things are never black and white, are they?'

Louisa nodded, apparently satisfied. 'Well I've got Kevin Porter doing them now and I don't think Charlie finds him quite as appealing as he did you!'

Her words lightened the mood and Martha grinned, her stomach flipping over at the idea that Charlie was missing her. If he felt anything like her, that would mean he was thinking about her all day, every day.

Jamie had been delighted when Martha had told him that she wouldn't be seeing Charlie again, but Martha herself still hadn't managed to shake off her sense of loss. She couldn't get him out of head and she couldn't stop dwelling on what might have been.

Jamie was proving himself to be a model husband at home and she couldn't fault him. But she also couldn't fully forgive him either, no matter how hard she tried. So many things reminded her of what he had done. Even the children's birthdays had made her think with fury of what he had put in jeopardy. Every time someone told her how lucky she was to be married to such a wonderful man, she wanted to scream that he was a cheating fraud. And all the time she was with him, she felt as though there was a massive gulf between what they said and what they actually meant.

To the outside world, they appeared to have the perfect marriage and to be as happy as ever. But in reality, she increasingly felt that she was putting on an act and it was draining her. She felt tired and miserable most of the time and her work was suffering. The last couple of profiles she had done were fine, but she knew that they weren't up to her usual high standard. If she wasn't careful, PRs would stop asking for her, which is why she had contacted Louisa to ask if she could take her out for lunch.

'So,' she said, as the waiter brought them both coffee. 'What's on the horizon work-wise at the moment? Anything I could help you with?'

Louisa took a sip of her black coffee and tilted her head to one side as she looked at Martha. 'Well it's funny you should ask . . .' she said with a sly smile.

'Really?' Martha replied, her heart beginning to flutter with anticipation. 'Tell me more.' She could sense from Louisa's expression that it had something to do with Charlie.

'Based on what you've said today, I think it might be something you'd like.'

'Is it . . .' Martha began, aware that her voice had risen an octave. 'Is it to do with Charlie?'

'Yes and no,' Louisa replied, again tilting her head.

Martha felt like she might explode. 'Oh stop being so cryptic!' she cried. 'Tell me!'

Louisa laughed. 'Sorry. It's a profile interview with Liv. It'll be the first one she's done since getting out of rehab, so her agent wants to make sure it's someone good whom she can trust.'

Martha almost squealed with excitement. 'Wow! That would be amazing.' She tried to sound measured but failed. Instantly, she felt a little of her old enthusiasm and fire returning. She already knew that she could make an amazing job of this profile and she couldn't wait to see Liv again. She had thought about her so much over the past months and had wanted to get in touch but could never really think of a good enough reason. She didn't know her well enough to just phone out of the blue for a chat, even if she had her number. This was perfect.

'So you'd be interested then?'

'Yes, definitely!' Martha shot back eagerly, before hesitating, already thinking about how she might feel returning to LA, and about how Jamie might react when she told him she was going.

'Charlie's moved out of Liv's house,' Louisa said, interrupting her thoughts. 'So I don't think you have to worry about bumping into him.'

Martha nodded distractedly. 'That's probably for the best.' Bumping into Charlie wasn't something that worried her – far from it – but she knew that it would worry Jamie and cause problems when it came to her going. Jamie would definitely ask if he'd be there and she wouldn't have been able to lie.

Then again, she thought mutinously, what right did Jamie have to dictate what she did? She had already turned down the opportunity to do Charlie's memoirs to appease him. No, she decided, this time she was taking the assignment. If Jamie didn't like it, that was his problem.

Chapter 44

Jamie watched Martha drive off with a sense of foreboding. He closed the front door and trudged listlessly into the kitchen where Mimi and Tom were sitting at the table eating their breakfast.

'Dad?' Mimi said, through a mouthful of Cheerios. 'How do you think different types of fruit got their name?'

Jamie made himself a coffee and sat at the head of the table, in between them. 'Clarify what you mean,' he said, trying to focus but feeling distracted.

Mimi put her elbows on the table and steepled her fingers together, like an eminent professor. 'Well, an orange is called an orange for fairly obvious reasons. But then why isn't a lemon called "a yellow"? Or an apple called "a green"?'

'Well you couldn't call an apple "a green" because there are lots of fruits that are green. How would you distinguish between them?' Jamie countered with a sigh.

Tom put his spoon down and clapped his hands together as he had an idea. 'You could call an apple "green number one"!

And grapes could be "green number two" and a melon "green number three" and a—'

'Yes, we get the idea, thank you!' Mimi interrupted her younger brother briskly. 'But frankly, who's going to want to eat a fruit that's called a "green number two",' she said, wrinkling her nose in an exaggerated fashion and sniggering to herself as she did so.

Tom looked puzzled for a few seconds as his brain caught up, then he too started to giggle. 'Ha ha! "Green number two"!' he laughed. 'Do you get it, Dad?'

Jamie nodded and took a sip of his coffee. 'Yes, I get it,' he said without enthusiasm. 'Anyway, you guys, it's about time you were getting ready for school. Come on, finish up and then go and brush your teeth.'

Both children looked at him in surprise. It wasn't like Jamie not to throw himself into their morning discussions, but he just didn't have the heart this morning. Not when Martha was heading off to LA.

He was still reeling from the terrible row they had had last night, when Jamie had asked her if she would be seeing Charlie while she was there. Martha had reacted with the fury of a snarling animal, screaming that he had no right to question her since *he* was the only one who had screwed around in this relationship. That it was no longer any of his business.

Jamie had been shocked by the fresh venom that she had thrown at him, as forceful as the day she had discovered his betrayal. He had never really appreciated how resentful she was about the fact that she had missed out on doing Charlie's memoirs because of him, but it was clear that she wasn't prepared to put him before her career any more.

He was trying so hard to make things right between them but whatever he did, it just wasn't enough. He could see for himself that Martha's spark had been extinguished, and the raw guilt he felt, knowing that he was the cause, gnawed at him from the inside, making him feel like he was mentally and physically half the man he used to be.

Forever more, he would be the weaker half of the couple, prepared to do whatever it took to prove to Martha how sorry he was. He felt a bit like her slave and it made him feel even more inadequate than he had before he had embarked on his stupid affair. He could never again win an argument because each time it would end with Martha playing her trump card: everything that was wrong was his fault and could be traced back to what he had done.

Before, Jamie had had such a lust for life and had always been an outgoing, sociable person, but he certainly wasn't that person now. He felt weak and useless and instead of looking forward to the future, he dreaded what it might hold instead. He knew that Martha would never leave him while the children were young, which bought him a certain amount of time. But he also knew that the rest of his life was going to be spent on tenterhooks, in case she woke up one morning many years from now and decided that she was going to leave anyway. The prospect made him feel bleak.

He still loved her so much and every single day he wished he could turn back the clock and change what he had done. But he no longer felt as if he knew what was going on inside her head the way he used to. They had been so in tune with one another, each knowing exactly what the other one was thinking. Now it seemed as though they circled each other warily, both scared of saying how they really felt.

And although they had resumed having sex again, Jamie could sense that Martha no longer gave herself up to the experience completely. That she was holding something back. He understood why – it was her way of protecting herself in case he did it again – but it saddened him that yet another part of their relationship had been tarnished.

Martha had leapt at the chance to go to LA again, and although it was Liv she was interviewing, not Charlie, he still felt threatened. Jamie was desperate to forget about that awful time but Martha seemed intent on revisiting it.

He was worried that she would arrive in LA and it would bring all the memories of that terrible week flooding back. That she would return home to him with a renewed sense of injustice. But he had no choice. He just had to sit tight and wait.

'Dad,' said a gentle voice, as Jamie sat with his head in his hands at the kitchen table. He looked up into Mimi's large blue eyes, which at that moment were flooded with concern. 'Are you OK?'

He nodded, unable to find his voice.

Mimi sat back down in the chair she had been using earlier. 'OK, I'll rephrase that,' she said in a clear, strong voice that reminded him of how Martha used to be. Before he had reduced her to a shell of her former self. 'I know you're not OK,' Mimi continued. 'So, what's wrong?'

Still Jamie couldn't speak and he shook his head.

'Is it to do with Mum going off to LA again?' Mimi persisted. 'Are you worried about her seeing that guy again? The film star.'

Jamie gazed back at her in admiration. She was so perceptive for such a young girl. Finally, he felt able to answer. 'No, it's not that I'm worried about Mum seeing him again. It's just that . . . I wish she hadn't gone, that's all. I miss her,' he finished feebly.

Mimi reached out and took his hand. 'Are you and Mum splitting up?' she asked in a small voice that instantly reminded Jamie of just how young she still was.

'I hope not.'

Mimi's eyes flashed with tears but she fought to hold them back, swallowing hard. 'I think you are,' she croaked.

He squeezed her hand in what he hoped was a reassuring way, while a mounting sense of panic swept over him. 'What makes you think that, darling?' he said in as even a voice as he could manage.

She shrugged, still fighting against the threat of tears. 'You don't seem very happy any more.' She looked down at her lap as she finished speaking.

Jamie's stomach dropped. Both he and Martha had congratulated themselves on protecting the children from the fallout from their problems. Neither of them had even considered that they might have picked up on the atmosphere in the house.

'Everything's fine!' Jamie lied, sounding unconvincing to his own ears, let alone Mimi's.

She took a deep breath, as if she was steeling herself to say something. 'OK. The truth is, I heard you arguing last night,' she said, the tears finally spilling over her long black lashes and splattering onto her cheeks like little fat raindrops. 'I got up this morning and pretended that it must have been a bad dream because I didn't want it to be true. But it wasn't a dream, was it? It was real.'

'Oh God,' Jamie groaned, reaching over to hug her awkwardly across the corner of the table. He stroked her hair while she cried, frantically wracking his brains about what might have been said during their row. What did she hear? Gradually, with a dawning sense of horror, he remembered Martha yelling about his affair. 'Oh God,' he said again, this time with a resigned acceptance that he had been well and truly found out.

'I heard every word,' Mimi sobbed, as if to hammer home the point.

Jamie had no answer. Instead, he clung to her as a feeling of loss washed over him.

Mimi pulled back from him and pushed his chest, so as to completely extricate herself from his embrace. She wiped her eyes with the sleeve of her school jumper, then pulled herself up to her full height and met his eye defiantly. 'Poor Mum,' she murmured, giving Jamie the full benefit of her steely expression of pure disgust.

Mimi had never, ever looked at Jamie like that. He was her friend. Her hero. The first man she had ever loved. Now she despised him, just like her mother. Jamie shook his head helplessly. What could he possibly say that would make this right? 'Look,' he said at last, 'I made a terrible, terrible mistake, Mimi . . .'

'You had an affair!' Mimi snapped back, attempting to look defiant, but Jamie could see that her chin was still wobbling. 'How could you do that?'

'But, darling, this all happened a long time ago and Mum and I ... well, we're working our way through it. She's forgiven me,' he added, hoping that she would believe him.

'She didn't sound like she'd forgiven you,' Mimi said, shaking her head as her mouth formed into a sneer. 'And I don't blame her.'

'Oh, Mimi ...' Jamie felt desperate. He adored this child too much to cope with her despising him. 'Please don't say that. I love your mum and I'm doing everything I can to show her how sorry I am.' He reached out to try to take Mimi's hand but she snatched it away as if she had been burnt.

'I hope she never forgives you!' she cried, pushing back her chair so that it scraped angrily against the slate floor and standing up. 'Because I know I never will!' She burst into noisy sobs again and ran from the room. Jamie got up and watched her helplessly, as she grabbed her school bag and flung open the front door. 'I hate you!' she screamed, shooting him a look of pure, cold venom before slamming the door shut behind her.

Jamie could feel his whole body start to shake uncontrollably and he put his hand to his mouth in shock. He had always thought that Martha finding out was the worst thing that could possibly have happened. Now he knew that your child discovering that you were a cheat and a fraud was much, much worse.

Chapter 45

Travelling to LA economy class made Martha wish she had been in the right frame of mind to enjoy first class when she had had the chance. She was sat beside an American whose fat spilled over not just the top of his jeans but also his seat, meaning Martha had to lean to one side for almost eleven hours to avoid accidentally resting her arm on his flab.

Last time, she vaguely remembered that travelling with Charlie meant they were chaperoned through security and immigration by a special VIP greeter, who deftly propelled them to the front of the queues. Now she found herself waiting in a seemingly endless line to be rudely interrogated by one of the expertly miserable immigration officers.

Not that she was in any mood to enjoy anything after the terrible row she had had with Jamie. She really had begun to feel that she was getting better. That she had started to move forward. But the emotions that had swept over her like an unstoppable wave last night didn't feel very much different to how she had felt when she first found out, except that perhaps they were less raw.

The worst thing of all, she thought, as she inched her way along the queue at an agonisingly slow speed, was that she couldn't shake the sense that she was trapped. She still loved Jamie but the fissure in their marriage had turned into a huge, permanent crack that no amount of counselling or talking could mend. Yet she had made her decision and she couldn't go back on it. She couldn't risk losing the children and she owed it to them to stay. And although it pained her to acknowledge it, she owed it to Jamie too.

Through their counselling sessions, Martha had had to accept that although it wasn't her fault that Jamie had had the affair, she had to shoulder some of the responsibility for not noticing how emasculated and unfulfilled he was feeling, or what an impact his mother's death had had on him.

But every time she tried to open herself up to him emotionally, the hurt would come seeping through her veins again and she would retreat back into herself. And then she would think that she deserved better than a husband who cheated on her so casually. That she deserved a man who could stay faithful. A man like Charlie.

The irony of the situation she had found herself in was that it wasn't Jamie's tart who was the third person in their marriage, it was Charlie. Martha believed Jamie when he said that he never gave Debra a thought, except to think that he wished he had never clapped eyes on her. But they both knew that Martha couldn't honestly make the same claim about Charlie. She thought about him endlessly, and because Jamie knew her so well, he could always tell.

In many ways she was relieved that Charlie had made the

decision for her not to do his memoirs, thus ensuring that it was highly unlikely that they would ever see each other again. But on the other hand, Martha couldn't get over her sense of loss at the prospect of losing him for good, and many times found herself fantasising over what might have been.

Finally, she reached the immigration desk and after a sullen interrogation, she was free to go. She hailed a taxi and ordered it to go to the Four Seasons, where she would be spending two nights before returning home. Peering out of the window from the back seat, as the cab raced towards Beverly Hills, she was struck by how many memories of Charlie there were here. Everywhere she looked, there seemed to be reminders of him and their short time together.

Almost immediately, the sun began to lift her spirits and cheer her mood, which had been further dampened at home by autumn creeping in with a smoky, grey chill. And as the warmth seeped into her bones, she began to look forward to the meeting she had lined up with Liv.

Although she knew that it must have been painful for her, Martha was relieved that Liv had got help for her drinking. It had been clear when they last met that she was on a dangerous path and she could understand why Charlie had been thinking of going for custody of Felix. But at the same time, Liv's devotion to her son was evident and Martha hoped that Charlie would have a change of heart. She couldn't imagine anything worse than the pain of losing your child, even if you still had access. Martha knew for certain that it would absolutely kill her to lose Mimi and Tom and she felt sure that Liv would be the same.

The taxi dropped her in the familiar courtyard in front of the hotel and Martha looked up at the towering building, feeling a swirl of affection for its golden pink walls. After checking in, she made her way down to the pool, where an attendant immediately made up a sunbed for her. Martha slipped off her boots, which she had needed back in the UK as protection from the incessant rain, and lay down with her bare feet and legs exposed to the sun, enjoying the delicious warmth that immediately spread from her feet through her whole body.

She lay with her eyes closed for a little while, before a voice caused her to open them in shock.

'Is this bed taken?'

'What the hell are you doing here?' Martha gasped, sitting up and shielding her eyes with her hand to make sure she wasn't seeing things.

Charlie sat down on the bed beside hers and stretched his long legs out in front of him, then he turned to look at her with a wide, mischievous smile. 'Louisa,' he said, rolling his eyes.

'But Louisa said you were away filming.'

'Filming, yes. Away, no. I'm filming here in LA.'

'Then why did Louisa . . .?' Martha shook her head, feeling baffled.

'She seemed to think you wouldn't come if you thought you might bump into me,' Charlie interrupted. 'Or more to the point, if your husband thought you might bump into me, which is pretty ironic, isn't it? So she was a bit economical with the truth. She said you seemed pretty unhappy and she thought it might have something to do with me. She seemed to think we might have some unfinished business.'

Martha could feel the heat in her cheeks that was nothing to do with the sun beating down. Had her unhappiness been that obvious, even to a relative stranger? Her mouth felt dry and her heart was suddenly pounding. 'Do we?' she managed to say, her voice sounding higher than usual.

'I think we do, yes,' Charlie said. The fact that he didn't move from his position on his lounger and didn't look at her somehow made her feel even more exposed to his proximity.

'Why are you even bothering with me, Charlie?' she murmured. 'You could have any woman you want.'

'But I don't want any woman ...' He smiled at the sky before turning his dark brown eyes towards her and saying the words that made her whole body turn to liquid: 'I want you.'

'I want you too,' she replied, before her brain had time to censure her words. And as she spoke she realised that it was the truth. 'But it's all much too complicated ...' she added, feeling a sense of sadness wash over her, slowing her heart and drenching the swell of excitement that had started to build inside her.

Charlie didn't speak for a while and her words hung in the still air between them. 'You see,' he said at last, 'I've had a lot of time to think while Liv's been in rehab and me and Felix were off travelling. And I've decided that things are only as complicated as you allow them to be.'

'Sorry, Charlie,' Martha sighed, shaking her head sadly. 'I

don't agree. If we didn't have kids, then yes, it would be straightforward. I would have gone by now. But when you have kids . . .' she tailed off as the thought of Tom and Mimi caused her to choke up. 'Well, it changes everything,' she finished.

'But look at Felix,' Charlie said, swinging his legs over the side of the sunbed and sitting up so that he was facing her, instantly reminding her of the time they were here before, when he first kissed her. 'His mum left me for someone else and yet both of us still have such a close relationship with him and he's a very happy, balanced kid.'

'But they'd blame me!' Martha cried, also swinging her legs round and putting them on the ground, so that they were sitting with their knees almost touching. 'That's the bit I couldn't bear!' She looked up at Charlie, silently pleading with him to understand.

'Then maybe you should tell them the truth.'

'No,' Martha said, shaking her head emphatically. 'No, I could never do that. It would destroy all of us.'

'Instead of just destroying you, you mean?'

She took a deep, shuddery breath as her mind whirled. 'But what if we're not compatible?' She reached out and took Charlie's hand in hers. 'What if I leave him for you, only to find that we didn't really know each other after all and it doesn't work out?'

Charlie's eyes bored into her. 'Then don't leave him for me,' he said. 'Leave him for yourself.'

Martha's heart plummeted. 'But I thought . . . I mean . . . you said you wanted me . . .?'

'I do.' Charlie gave her hand a firm, reassuring squeeze. 'But don't leave him for me. Leave him because you're not happy to stay. If things were to work out with us – and I really hope they do – then great.'

It felt to Martha as if a rollercoaster was running through her head, as her emotions rose and fell with each breath.

'I don't know, Charlie,' she said, her voice sounding as tiny as she herself felt.

'I think you do know,' he murmured, leaning forward and touching his lips against hers, causing her head to swim. She closed her eyes as his tongue began to explore her mouth and she could feel herself sinking into him.

Charlie pulled away from her and looked into her eyes, as if he was searching her soul for something. Without speaking, they stood up together, their hands still clasped, and Martha nodded, almost imperceptibly.

Chapter 46

Liv opened the huge front door. 'Hi, again!' she smiled, reaching out to kiss Martha on both cheeks.

Martha appeared to do a double-take. 'Wow,' she said, following Liv through the hallway into the kitchen at the back of the house. 'You look amazing!'

'Thanks!' Liv smiled shyly, as she headed for the kettle and flicked it on. She was pleased at the compliment, but equally she felt embarrassed and ashamed to think about how bad she must have been before. 'You look great too,' she added quickly, taking in Martha's shining eyes and glossy hair, so different to how she'd looked when she arrived at the house with Charlie all those months ago. 'Actually, you look ... glowing. You're not pregnant, are you?'

'No!' Martha gulped, immediately flushing bright red and looking down, making sure that her hair fell in front of her face and covered her blushes.

Instantly, Liv's radar was up and she was itching to ask more, but instead she made herself and Martha some earl grey tea and led her out through the French doors towards the table and chairs by the infinity pool. 'It's such a gorgeous day,' she said. 'I thought maybe we could do the interview out here?'

'Great!' Martha followed her down the path. 'Wow, I'd forgotten how amazing this view is,' she added, as they reached the table and sat down.

'It is, isn't it?' Liv agreed, looking out over the Hollywood hills towards LA and the sea beyond, which was usually blanketed by the smog but today glittered cobalt blue in the shimmering sunlight.

Martha took her mini recorder out of her bag and placed it on the table between them. 'You don't mind, do you?' she asked, raising her eyebrows questioningly at Liv.

Liv swallowed and shook her head quickly. Even though she felt as if she knew Martha and could trust her, she still had an innate mistrust of journalists. So much horrible stuff had been written about her, Charlie and Danny in the past that she had come to expect it.

As if reading her thoughts, Martha spoke: 'I'm not here to stitch you up, Liv. You can trust me.'

Liv smiled. 'I know. It's just that they all say that, don't they?'

'Yes,' agreed Martha with a good-natured grin. 'But I'm better than all the others!' She leaned forward and switched the recorder on, then pulled a notepad and pen out of her bag and wrote something on the pad.

Liv watched her intently. She really did look radiant in a way that was not attributable to just diet and exercise. In Liv's experience, only being in love could make you look so good ... or make you look so bad when it went wrong. 'So, how are things?' she said, her curiosity getting the better of her. 'You know, personally?'

Martha looked up in surprise. 'Um, good,' she replied, her eyes darting from side to side as if she was an animal trapped within range of a hunter's rifle.

'I'm glad,' Liv said, smiling. 'He's a lovely man, Martha.'

Once again, the blood raced to Martha's cheeks as she flushed deep red. 'He is,' she agreed, picking up her cup of Earl Grey and taking a long sip.

'I really appreciate what he did for me,' Liv continued. 'I don't know what I'd have done if it wasn't for him that night ...'

Martha frowned. 'The night you went into rehab?' Her eyes took on a sympathetic look and her voice softened as she spoke, making Liv want to curl up with shame.

'No. That was the next day, after Charlie found out what had happened.'

Martha's frown deepened. 'But I thought you were talking about Charlie?'

Liv's radar, which had already been on high alert, suddenly felt as if it had started whirling around with a klaxon sounding. 'No. I was talking about Jamie.'

'Jamie?' Martha's mouth dropped open in shock. 'My Jamie?'

Now it was Liv's turn to frown. 'Yes, Martha, *your* Jamie! Didn't you know what happened that night?'

Martha shook her head mutely.

'I can't believe he didn't tell you!' Liv shook her head in disbelief. 'He was such a hero.'

'Sorry,' Martha stammered. 'I have got absolutely no idea what you're talking about!'

'Wow,' Liv mouthed. 'A modest hero too. He went out and found Felix for me, after he'd run away . . .'

'Felix ran away? Why? Where were you?' Martha interjected with a battery of questions, still frowning in confusion.

Liv swallowed hard and could feel her cheeks burning just like Martha's. 'I was here.' She hoped that her quiet tone would convey just how ashamed she felt. 'But I was sleeping. Well, that's not strictly true. I was drunk,' she admitted. 'So I passed out and Felix went off looking for Charlie . . .'

Martha clapped her hand over her mouth. 'On his own?' she gasped, her eyes widening in horror. 'Around these roads?'

Liv nodded meekly as the memory forced its way to the front of her brain. 'It was horrific. Anything could have happened to him . . .' the tears flashed into her eyes. 'But Jamie found him and brought him back. And he didn't tell Charlie because I asked him not to . . . and he obviously didn't tell you either. He's a really special guy.'

Martha bit her lip and looked away.

'Martha?' Liv prompted. 'Please tell me you guys have worked through your problems?'

'You mean him cheating on me?' Martha spat back, and Liv reeled at the sudden hostility in her expression.

'Well, yes,' she said. 'I did know about that but he seemed genuinely sorry, Martha. And he really seemed to love you very much.'

Martha closed her eyes, as if to compose herself. 'And I loved him . . .' she murmured.

'Past tense?'

Martha opened her eyes and considered. 'No, not really. I still do love him. But . . .'

'But you also love Charlie?' Liv finished the sentence for her.

Martha shrugged. 'I think maybe I do, yes.'

Liv nodded to herself. She had known all along that there was something between them. There was an energy and tension that you could almost see whenever they were together.

'Have you seen him again?'

Martha didn't answer at first and Liv wondered if perhaps she was prying too much. But then Martha gave a tiny nod. 'Yes,' she murmured. 'Yesterday. He came and found me.'

The tone of Martha's voice was wistful, making Liv feel as if she was intruding on a deeply personal memory. She wasn't surprised that Charlie and Martha had got together, but it made her feel sad for Jamie. Like him, she had been the guilty party and she knew how hard that was to cope with. Although she had only met him once and even then she was far from sober, she had felt that he was essentially a good guy who had made a bad mistake.

'What are you going to do?'

Martha's eyes swam with tears which began to run down her cheeks. 'I'm going to stay with Jamie!' she wailed, leaning forward and fishing in her bag for a tissue. 'What else can I do? I have no choice because of the kids . . .'

Liv could feel her own throat tightening and the tears welling up behind her eyes. She felt so sorry for them both. And a small part of her felt sorry for Charlie. 'It'll be OK,' she said, knowing that it sounded pathetic and also that it wasn't necessarily true.

Martha blew her nose and wiped her face briskly. She looked up at Liv with damp eyes and forced a smile onto her face. 'I know. It'll be fine. Anyway, this interview isn't supposed to be about me! We need to talk about you ...'

Liv took a deep breath and nodded. 'OK,' she said, sounding much stronger than she felt. 'Where do you want to start?'

By the time she waved Martha off, Liv felt wrung out and emotional, but she also felt cleansed, as if she had just spent several hours confessing her sins. She still found talking about herself a surreal experience, even though she had done it many times in the past when promoting some film or TV series. But this time was different because there was nothing to promote except herself. On Martha's advice, she had found it easier to imagine that she was talking about someone else. That way she could take a step back and cast a more dispassionate eye over her train-wreck of a life.

Martha was a skilled and brilliant interviewer and Liv could see why she was so renowned in her profession. Despite everything that was going on in her own life, she was able to focus on Liv's story and give her room to speak, while prompting her gently when she faltered. She had a natural 'bedside manner' that Liv had never encountered before. All the journalists who had interviewed her in the past had a hard, ruthless streak that was impossible to conceal as they grappled for sensational headlines or tried to get a rise out of her if they felt the interview was in danger of becoming too boring.

Martha had a way of making her interviewees feel safe and Liv knew that the piece would be very strong.

After she had finished and the recorder switched off, Liv had asked Martha to speak to Charlie, to get him to reconsider going for custody of Felix. It was the only area of her life that was causing her stress now and she couldn't feel completely well until it was resolved. Martha had agreed to speak to him but had said she couldn't make any promises about what he might do. Liv knew that this was the best she could hope for.

She inhaled deeply, before making her way back into the house. On autopilot, she headed for the office, feeling the usual urge to log onto her laptop, when something made her hesitate. She had become as addicted to surfing the Internet for stories about her, Charlie or Danny as she had to alcohol and it needed to stop. It wasn't healthy and, worse, it was a waste of precious time. She had already lost so many days, weeks and months and she wasn't going to lose any more. From now on, she was going to make the most of every single moment.

She glanced up at the clock. It was a quarter to three. Felix didn't need to be picked up for another couple of hours. If she hurried, she could make a Pilates class at three. Her diary for the next couple of months was packed and once she started, there wouldn't be many free days for her to do her own thing. She grabbed her gym gear and stuffed it into a kit bag, as a tiny kernel of happiness began to take root. She headed to the garage where her beloved Fiat 500 was parked. She couldn't remember the last time she had driven it. She unlocked the door and climbed in, smiling at the distinctive smell of the ancient beige leather seats that she loved so much. Gingerly, she tried the engine and felt a thrill of pleasure when it started first time.

She clicked the remote control and the garage door slid up with a purring sound. Liv inched the car down the gleaming white driveway and waited for the gates to swish open. As she drove through them, she smiled to herself. For the first time in years, she finally felt as though she was on the right road.

Chapter 47

Charlie let himself into the hotel bedroom and shut the door behind him. The blinds were closed and there was a triangle-shaped beacon of light splashing over the huge bed from one of the bedside lights, giving the room a faintly pink glow.

From the bathroom he could hear the sound of running water, which stopped abruptly as he listened. He imagined her emerging wet and naked from the shower and he could feel himself hardening instantly. Any concerns either of them may have felt about whether they were compatible had been well and truly laid to rest last night. She was without doubt the sexiest woman he had ever made love to. Or rather, she was the sexiest woman who had ever made love to him.

He pressed down the gold-plated handle on the bathroom door and opened it. There was a tiny yelp of surprise from Martha as he stepped into the room and gazed at her. She was naked, except for a white towel that she was attempting to wrap around herself but through which Charlie could still see her full breasts and her flat, tanned stomach. Her long, dark hair was slicked back from her high forehead in soaking rivulets that dripped onto the marble floor with indelicate splatters.

She smiled shyly up at Charlie as he moved towards her and pulled the towel away, discarding it behind him in a careless heap. He lifted her, so that she could wrap her strong, toned legs around his waist and kissed her, exploring her warm, sensual mouth with his tongue.

With a balletic grace, she unwrapped her legs and stood in front of him, her eyes never leaving his as she unzipped his jeans and pulled them down. She knelt on the floor and slid his erection into her mouth, still holding his eyes with hers. Charlie groaned and pulled her back to her feet. He cupped her face in his hands and kissed her again, before lifting his t-shirt over his head so that he was naked too.

Martha turned and stepped back into the shower, pulling Charlie by the hand to make him follow her. She turned to face him and switched the shower on behind her back. Immediately, a monsoon of water gushed from the dinner-plate-sized shower-head, drenching them both and making them laugh out loud. Charlie picked her up as if she weighed barely anything and slid her onto his erection. Martha arched her back and moaned as he entered her, giving Charlie the full benefit of her perfect, full breasts with every thrust and making him slow his movements in case he came there and then.

Martha gasped as she climaxed for the first time and Charlie covered her mouth with his, filling it with his tongue and wanting to devour every part of her. He reached behind her and turned the shower off. Then, gently, he lay her down on the floor and entered her again. This time he moved rhythmically and more slowly, his eyes holding hers as she orgasmed over and over with a series of animalistic groans.

She pushed him off her and knelt up so that she was facing him, before bending to take him in her mouth again, her tongue dancing from side to side. Charlie cried out with a mixture of pleasure and pain. It was like nothing he had ever known before. 'No,' he gasped, pushing her head back. Martha smiled, before straddling him and riding him to a huge, shuddering climax.

'Wow,' Charlie panted, laying back and looking up at her, still sitting astride him. Her hair and body were soaked with a combination of sweat and water, making her skin glisten and giving her an other-worldly appearance. She smiled at him but there was something about the look in her eye that made Charlie's insides freeze. 'What? What is it?'

She didn't say anything as she lay down beside him with her head on his chest. Charlie wrapped his arm around her smooth brown back and squeezed her to him. 'I can tell there's something you want to say.'

'I don't *want* to say it.'

Charlie's heart, which had started to slow after his exertions, suddenly started to pound again. He could hear their breathing, perfectly in sync, meaning her heart must be pounding too. 'It's OK,' he whispered into her ear, inhaling the clean, citrusy smell of her wet hair and closing his eyes as he tried to commit it to memory. 'Whatever it is, you can say it.'

Still Martha didn't reply and Charlie began to hope that

maybe he was mistaken. Maybe she wasn't going to say what he had thought. He stroked her damp skin with his thumb, waiting.

Eventually she lifted her head and rolled over so that she was looking at him with those huge, dark eyes. 'I don't *want* to say it but I have to.'

'Say what, Martha?' Charlie tried to hold her gaze but felt as though he might cry, so he looked up at the ceiling instead.

He heard Martha swallow and felt her drawing an outline of something on his chest with her nail. 'I have to say goodbye,' she whispered through her tears.

The next morning, Charlie woke early. Martha lay sleeping beside him, curled up with her back to him. He rolled onto his side and put his arm over her stomach, so that he was cradling her.

Immediately, she awoke with a start and he felt her suck her stomach in with an automatic reflex. 'Sorry,' he whispered, kissing the back of her neck. Martha didn't reply but pushed herself back into him. They lay entwined for several minutes, only the sound of their breathing breaking the silence.

'Why don't I drive you to the airport?' Charlie said, glancing at the clock on the bedside. It was just gone seven and he had to be on set by nine.

Martha sighed and rolled reluctantly away from him, turning so that she was facing him. Charlie smiled.

'What?' she demanded, frowning and smiling at the same time.

'You've got mascara all down your face.' He reached out and tenderly rubbed away the black smudges with his thumb.

Martha bit her lip and pulled the sheet around her, covering her exposed breasts. 'Well taking my make-up off wasn't exactly a priority last night.'

Charlie loved the way her cheeks flushed as she spoke, embarrassment making her suddenly coy. 'You look so beautiful,' he murmured, feeling the sadness wash over him again. He just wanted to stay there, in bed with her, forever. But their time was almost up and he felt numb with loss and longing.

Martha leaned forward and kissed him. 'Don't look so sad,' she said, stroking his face.

Charlie leaned his face into her palm. 'I can't help it. I don't want you to go.'

'I know.'

'Is this the end? Could we maybe see each other once in a while . . .?'

'No. You know we can't. It's not fair on you and it's not fair on—'

'Him!' Charlie interrupted with a snarl. 'But he doesn't deserve to be treated fairly.' He knew there was a pleading tone to his voice and it infuriated him. He didn't want to beg. He just wanted her to want him.

Martha sighed. 'Maybe. Maybe not. I don't really feel that I have the choice.' The light that was shining in her eyes just a few seconds previously was extinguished in an instant as she contemplated going home to her cheating husband, and Charlie felt a bolt of red hot fury shoot through him. If he had a woman like her he would never betray her. But being loyal and faithful had brought him nothing but heartbreak either, so who was the fool?

Martha sat up and looked back at him. 'There's something I want to tell you, though, before I go.' She hesitated and seemed to question herself.

'Go on . . .' Charlie prompted, sitting up too.

Martha took a deep, slow breath. 'I love you,' she said. 'I think I'll always love you.' Quickly, she jumped off the bed, her cheeks blazing and her eyes watering, as she headed for the shelter of the bathroom and slammed the door shut behind her.

Charlie watched her go, temporarily stunned. He got out of bed and walked to the closed bathroom door. Through it, he could hear Martha quietly crying.

'Martha,' he said, his voice sounding hoarse and raw. 'Martha, listen to me. I love you too. And I understand. It's OK.'

After a few minutes, the crying stopped and he could hear her blowing her nose. He leaned against the door and waited. He could feel that she was standing close to the other side. Could almost feel her breath on his face.

'Charlie? Do you remember that first day, in your hotel room, talking to each other through the bathroom door?'

He smiled at the memory. 'I do. And I remember you looking ridiculously beautiful in my t-shirt and sweats with your ridiculously high gold sandals. I think I fell in love with you that day.'

There was a pause and Charlie knew that she was leaning

her head against the door, millimetres from his. 'I'll never regret you, Charlie.'

Charlie closed his eyes. 'And I'll never regret you, Martha,' he managed to say. But as he gathered up his clothes and prepared to leave her for good, the pain in his heart told him that he regretted her already.

Chapter 48

Jamie was watching out of the window, waiting for Martha to return. He needed to get to her before Mimi did, to warn her that she knew. Martha had called home a couple of times but Jamie hadn't wanted to tell her over the phone. He decided that it would only upset her and there was nothing she could do about it anyway, so far away.

Mimi was upstairs, with her door closed and her music blaring, just as she had been for the past two days. She refused to eat and wouldn't talk to Jamie, although he had tried several times. He felt gripped by the fear that she may never speak to him again and the thought crucified him. Mimi and Tom were everything to him, but especially Mimi. They had had three years of it being just the two of them, before Tom was born, and he had thought their bond was unbreakable.

He also felt desperately sorry for Tom who, though he didn't know what the problem was, certainly sensed that there was something very wrong and had been tearful and clingy in a way that he had never been before. Jamie had managed to persuade him to go to a friend's house for tea so that he wouldn't be here when Martha came home, in case his worst fears were realised and world war three erupted. Jamie craned his neck to peer up the street, willing her to return. He needed her. He didn't know how to cope on his own.

Just then, her little white Fiat came into view, turning into the street. Jamie's spirits lifted immediately. Regardless of their difficulties over the past few months, he had missed her desperately. He just didn't function well without her.

She parked on the drive in front of the house and climbed out. Jamie watched her through the window, struck by how beautiful she looked. Different, somehow.

As if she sensed him watching her, Martha looked up and locked eyes with him. He loved her eyes. They were so expressive and he could read them so clearly. He knew instantly what they were telling him now and he felt a sudden urge to scream, but instead he made his way to the front door and opened it. He walked towards her with a sense that he was wading through water; his legs didn't seem to work properly.

Martha stood stock still, frozen in one spot. She tried to smile but the corners of her mouth seemed determined to move in a downwards direction. 'Hi,' she murmured, unsure whether to kiss him or to hit him.

Jamie reached out and cupped her face in his hands before bending to kiss her tenderly on the lips. 'Welcome back,' he said. 'You have no idea how much I've missed you.'

He watched as the blood raced to Martha's cheeks. 'Have you?' she stuttered, suddenly unable to meet his eye. Any remaining doubts he had completely evaporated. He could sense it. She had been with Charlie.

They looked at each other without speaking, neither of them knowing what to say.

Eventually, Jamie broke the silence. 'Mimi knows.' As soon as the words had left his lips he felt a small sense of release. The burden had been too heavy for him to shoulder alone.

Martha looked up at him sharply. 'What? How?' A look of panic skittered over her face.

'She heard us arguing, the night before you went.'

Martha groaned. 'What the hell did she hear?'

Jamie shook his head and put his hands on his hips, not knowing what else to do with them. 'Everything. She heard everything.'

Martha looked as if she might be sick. 'And . . . how has she been?'

'Awful.' Jamie wanted to reassure her but he couldn't. She would know the truth as soon as she clapped eyes on Mimi.

'And Tom?' Martha had straightened up and her eyes kept darting towards the house with frightened glances. 'Does he know too?'

'He knows something's not right. He just doesn't know what.'

'Oh those poor little babies!' Martha murmured, drawing herself up to her full height as if steeling herself for a fight. 'Well, we need to talk to them. Tell them that everything's going to be alright.'

She stepped around Jamie as she headed for the house, but he gripped her arm, harder than he'd intended, to stop her. 'Wait!'

Martha frowned and rubbed her arm surreptitiously. 'What?'

'I don't want to tell them everything's OK if it's not. We need to be as honest as possible with them.'

'And?' Martha replied, still frowning in confusion.

'And I'm not sure that everything *is* OK. Only you can answer that question, Martha. So ... tell me. *Is* everything OK?'

She held his look. He could see a million thoughts running through her mind but she didn't say anything.

'Well I guess that answers my question, then,' Jamie said, surprised that he sounded so much more coherent and together than he felt.

'I didn't ...' Martha began, then stopped.

Jamie waited for her to continue. He was vaguely aware that it had started to rain. 'What?' he prompted.

'I came home. To you,' Martha said, finally dropping her gaze.

Jamie nodded slowly, looking up at the steel grey skies and saying a mental prayer of thanks. Whatever had happened, she had come home. She had made her choice.

'Let's go inside,' he said, grabbing her bag off the back seat and following her into the house.

Mimi was coming down the stairs as they walked in through the front door. 'Mum!' she cried, throwing herself at Martha and wrapping her arms around her neck, before violently bursting into tears.

Jamie dropped Martha's bag and stood to one side as she embraced her daughter. Mimi was nearly as tall as Martha and almost pushed her over as she cried into her mum's hair. Mimi was as blonde as Martha was dark but they were still so alike it was breathtaking, as if they were the yin and the yang of each other.

When Mimi's tears had subsided slightly, Martha gently pushed her away so that she could look at her. 'We need to talk to you, darling.'

'I don't want to talk to *him!*' Mimi growled, shooting a look of disgust in Jamie's direction, as wounding as if she had stabbed him with a knife.

'Come on,' said Martha, guiding Mimi firmly towards the kitchen. Mimi resisted at first, but finally she surrendered and allowed herself to be propelled forward into a chair. Jamie followed, cursing his weakness and helplessness.

He and Martha took a seat either side of Mimi and looked at her carefully. Jamie was struck by how scared he felt of her, despite her youth. She was like a ticking bomb, ready to explode at any second.

'I don't know how you can even look at *him!*' she spat, addressing Martha. Despite his guilt, Jamie felt a flash of anger at Mimi's aggression.

Martha reached out and took Mimi's hand. 'Listen, Mimi. I know that you heard us arguing and I'm sorry that you found out that way. But Dad and I have done a lot of talking and we are getting through it. I'm not going to patronise you and say that everything is hunky dory because it's not ...'

Jamie looked at Martha, alarmed by what she might be about to say.

'But it *is* OK,' she continued.

Mimi wiped her eyes with the back of her hand. 'How can you possibly forgive him?' she whimpered.

Martha shrugged. 'I don't know, darling. I just know that I have.'

Mimi turned her head haltingly so that she was looking at Jamie. As she stared at him, he could see her whole life in her face, from the first moment she was born and put straight into his arms, all through her toddler years and her early school-days, to this moment now. He felt overcome with gratitude towards Martha, who even in her darkest moments would put her children's feelings before her own.

'I am so, so sorry, Mimi,' he said, tentatively feeling for her hand and feeling gratified when she allowed him to take it.

'I know that, Dad,' she replied, her voice still wobbling. 'But if I was Mum, I would still throw you out.'

'Mimi!' Martha scolded her, but Jamie put his hand up to stop her.

'No, no it's fine,' he said, aware that it wasn't fine at all, that Mimi was right.

'I bet you wouldn't forgive her quite so easily if she did the same to you!' Mimi continued, her eyes blazing. She was spoiling for a fight and wasn't going to stop until she got one.

Jamie didn't reply. He had asked himself that question so many times and he still couldn't answer it. All he knew was that Martha would never have started an affair with someone unprompted, as he had.

'Mimi,' Martha said, her voice a little gentler. 'You're a bit too young to understand this right now but every relationship has its problems—'

'You've only got problems because he had another girl-friend!' Mimi interrupted, her eyebrows knitting together as her face contorted with the pain of not understanding how this could be happening to her.

Jamie put his elbows on the table and his head in his hands. He wasn't sure how much more of this he could take. It was like having open-heart surgery without anaesthetic. Debra had never been his girlfriend. She was just someone to have sex with. He had absolutely no feelings for her whatsoever, except that he wished desperately that he had never met her. But how to explain that to an eleven-year-old? It was impossible. In Mimi's young mind, everything was black and white. There were no shades of grey.

'The point is,' Martha continued. 'That I have chosen to forgive your dad. In life, everyone makes mistakes ... even me.' She paused and glanced up at Jamie. He locked eyes with her for a second, understanding her meaning, and gave her a tiny nod.

Martha acknowledged his gesture before continuing: 'He says he's sorry and I'm going to give him another chance. But it's his only chance, Mimi, and he knows that. If he ever does anything like this again, that will be it.'

Mimi bit furiously at her thumbnail and Jamie had to resist the urge to bat her fingers away from her mouth the way he usually did. She looked scared and terrifying at the same time. It felt as if all three of them were holding their breath, the only sounds the ticking of the kitchen clock and the sluggish whirring of the fridge, as they waited for her to say something. Anything. Eventually Mimi pushed back her chair and stood up. 'OK,' she said, looking at Martha but pointedly avoiding looking at Jamie.

Martha stood up and reached out to pull her into a deep embrace. 'We both love you very much you know,' she said, pushing back a strand of Mimi's blonde hair from her face. 'You and Tom.'

Mimi nodded uncertainly.

'Please don't tell Tom about any of this,' Martha said, her voice catching slightly at the mention of his name. 'He's too young to understand and it would just scare him.'

Again, Mimi murmured her assent. She pulled away from Martha and turned as if to leave the room, but Martha kept hold of her hand. 'Mimi? Will you do something for me?'

Mimi turned. 'What?'

'Will you give your dad a hug?'

Jamie's eyes filled with tears of gratitude. He didn't deserve Martha and they all knew it. He stood up on shaky legs and made a movement towards Mimi. She hesitated, looking as if she might bolt at any minute.

'Please, Mimi?' Martha added.

Jamie opened his arms and Mimi allowed him to pull her towards him. He closed his eyes as he clasped her to his chest, desperate never to let her go again. 'I love you, darling,' he said into her silky hair.

Mimi nodded, and he could feel that his little girl had somehow stepped over a threshold into adulthood during the past two distressing days. 'I love you too, Dad,' she echoed, her voice barely audible.

As she left the kitchen to return to the sanctuary of her bedroom and her blaring music, Jamie took Martha's hand in his and bent to kiss her. 'I'm glad you did what you did,' he murmured, stroking her hair. 'And I'm so, so glad you came back.' His words were loaded with meaning that only the two of them would ever understand. Jamie suspected that she had come very close to leaving him and the prospect filled him with terror.

Martha's eyes darkened as her pupils dilated like tiny black flowers of sadness blooming. She looked as if she wanted to say something and Jamie waited for her to speak, but she seemed too choked to get the words out. He felt weak with relief. She had come back. It was the best he could hope for.

Chapter 49

Charlie drove his Range Rover up Liv's twisting driveway, a familiar feeling of dread making his chest tighten and his stomach swirl, the way it always did recently when he collected Felix. He had been staying at the hotel ever since Liv left rehab; somehow it didn't seem right for them to be living together when they were about to go to war over their son. But it had meant that the wall between them had been steadily rebuilt, brick by brick.

Martha had broached the subject on their last night together, gently suggesting that maybe he should drop his custody bid. But Charlie still felt bruised by the past and wanted to make up for what he considered were the 'lost years', when he and Felix had lived on different continents. It felt to him like he was due some payback.

Juanita opened the door and gave Charlie a curt nod, while making no move to let him into the house.

'Hi,' Charlie said, smiling despite the ominous feeling that was creeping over him. He was due to take Felix on location for a couple of days and had carefully made the arrangements with Liv, letting her know what time he would be picking him up. Surely she wouldn't have deliberately taken him out somewhere? 'I've come to collect Felix?' he told Juanita, whose face was impassive, with a slight hint of hostility.

'He not well,' she replied, and made as if to close the door.

Instinctively, Charlie reached out and put the flat of his hand against the huge wooden door, forcing Juanita to open it again. 'I'd like to see him,' he said, stepping up and into the hallway, not caring if he seemed rude.

'Oh! But Miss Mason said . . .' Juanita began, but Charlie didn't hear the rest of her words as he stalked through the cool, tiled space, heading for Felix's room with a mounting sense of dread.

The door to Felix's room was closed. It was the first time he had ever seen it closed and Charlie's heart was thudding furiously as he came to a halt outside the door. He pressed his ear to the wood and listened carefully, trying to steady his erratic breathing. He couldn't tell if there was anyone in the room; the only thing he could hear was the air conditioning.

He put his hand on the pewter doorknob and twisted it slowly and silently. He knew, even before he opened the door, that they wouldn't be there. That Liv had taken him.

'Oh!' Liv murmured in surprise as the door swung open. She was sitting on the floor beside Felix's racing car bed, rhythmically stroking the sleeping boy's forehead. Even in the half-light, Charlie could see that his skin looked clammy and flushed.

'I thought . . .' he began, putting the palm of his hand to his chest and feeling his heart race beneath it. 'I thought you'd gone ...'

Liv frowned slightly. 'Gone where?'

Charlie shook his head. 'Nothing,' he said, feeling foolish. He walked over to the other side of Felix's bed and peered in at him. 'What's wrong?'

'He's got an ear infection. We've been up all night.'

Charlie tore his eyes away from Felix's sleeping form and looked at Liv. Under her eyes, blue-black shadows hung above her apple-shaped cheekbones. The healthy glow that her skin had sported recently had been replaced by a grey pallor that confirmed her story.

'I'm sorry,' she whispered, looking up at him with tired eyes, 'but he's not going to be coming on location with you today.'

Before Charlie could stop himself, his eyes filled with tears.

Liv watched him with a puzzled expression as she got up off the floor and rubbed her back. 'Look, it's no big deal. There'll be other chances,' she said, before bending over Felix once more. Charlie watched as she smoothed his curls to one side of his forehead and kissed his hot cheek. Even though he was in a deep sleep, Felix smiled at her touch and moved his face a few millimetres towards her hand.

'Come on,' she said to Charlie, motioning to him that they should leave the room.

'Just give me a minute.'

Liv looked at him for a few seconds, then left, closing the door gently behind her. Charlie knelt down beside the bed and looked at his son, sleeping soundly in the bright red racing car bed that he loved so much.

Something inside Charlie seemed to crack and he wondered distractedly if it was the sound of his heart breaking.
This child meant everything to him, and all he wanted – all
he had ever wanted – was to be a proper father to him. But he
couldn't do it.

Yes, he could buy a huge house himself and recreate Felix's
fabulous bedroom. But the truth was, he already had one.
Here. At home with his mum. Where he belonged. Where he
was happy.

Charlie rested his head on the smooth painted wood of the
bed and finally gave in to his grief for all that he had lost.

A long time later he walked into the kitchen, where Liv
was perched at the island in the middle of the room,
studying a script. She glanced up at him with a look of curiosity mixed with suspicion, but something in his expression
must have alarmed her because she quickly looked down
again.

'Not long 'til you start shooting?'

'No,' Liv replied, biting on her thumbnail nervously.

Charlie took a deep breath. 'Liv, I've come to a decision
about Felix.'

The script dropped out of Liv's hands and landed with a
heavy thwack on the floor. 'Oh no! Please, Charlie, please
don't . . .' she began, her eyes suddenly haunted. 'I'll do anything. Just please don't take him . . .'

Charlie closed his eyes, hating what he had done to Liv.
Making her beg as if she was pleading for her life.

'I'm not,' he whispered, unable to speak the words any more
clearly. Then he crouched down and buried his head in his

hands, thinking that he couldn't bear another moment of this agony.

After a while, he felt a hand on his back. 'Charlie?' said Liv, her voice shuddering and tremulous.

He looked up, feeling hollowed out with sorrow. Liv's own face was a reflection of his. 'What did you mean?' she whispered.

Charlie shook his head, suddenly feeling bone-weary and wrung-out. 'I can't do it. I so wanted him to be with me ...' he said, standing up unsteadily and gripping the island for support. 'But I can't do it.'

Liv's bottom lip wobbled dangerously. She closed her eyes and wrapped herself around him, pressing her damp face to his. Charlie inhaled her scent and thought about a half-remembered moment many years ago when she had done the same. 'Thank you,' she murmured into his ear. 'Thank you.'

As he left, promising to return later to check on Felix, Liv smiled at him in a way that he hadn't seen for many years. It lit up her face as surely as if she had taken a magic cloth and wiped away all the guilt, worry and sadness that had become etched into her skin.

'I meant what I said, Charlie.'

'About what?'

'That if there's anything I can do for you ...'

Charlie shrugged. 'I don't think anyone can do anything for me ... I'm a hopeless case.'

'You're referring to Martha, I presume?'

Charlie stopped and gave a short, bitter laugh. 'She's gone. It's over. End of story.'

'I'm sorry.'

'Me too.'

'Will it make you feel better or worse if I tell you that she really did love you?'

Charlie smiled. 'But not enough to stay with me. Story of my life,' he added.

The blood raced to Liv's cheeks. 'You'll find the right woman, Charlie. One day.'

Charlie looked back at her with a sad gleam in his eye, as he climbed into the car. 'I thought I already did,' he said through the open door. 'Twice.'

Chapter 50

Jamie leaned back in his chair and contemplated the little black recorder sitting on Martha's desk on the other side of the office. Martha had been busy earlier in the day transcribing her interview with Liv Mason, when Jamie had walked in unannounced to bring her a cup of tea. Martha had snatched the recorder up with suspicious haste and turned it off abruptly.

Ever since, Jamie's mind had been whirring with possibilities of what might have been said. He got up and opened the door to the office, listening out for signs of life in the house and confirming that Martha had, indeed, gone out with Lindsay and that both children were fast asleep in their beds.

He swallowed guiltily and picked up the recorder tentatively. Almost in slow motion, he pressed the 'Play' button. At first he could just hear rustling, as someone, presumably Martha, turned the pages of a notebook, followed by the scratch of a pen on paper as she wrote something.

Then he heard Liv Mason's unmistakably upmarket voice: 'So, how are things?' she said. 'You know, personally?'

Jamie put a hand over his mouth and considered switching off the recorder. One of his mum's favourite sayings had been that prying eyes were liable to see things they didn't like. But, he reasoned, as he waited for Martha's reply, she never said anything about prying ears.

'Um, good.' Jamie could tell from the tone of Martha's voice that she didn't want to be drawn into this conversation.

'I'm glad,' Liv said, followed by: 'He's a lovely man, Martha.'

Jamie's heart swelled and he smiled to himself with relief as he heard Martha's reply: 'He is.'

'I really appreciate what he did for me,' Liv continued. 'I don't know what I'd have done if it wasn't for him that night . . .'

Jamie sat up, suddenly alert. He hadn't told Martha what had happened that night because Liv had asked him not to. He was suddenly worried that she would be cross that he had kept something else from her.

'The night you went into rehab?' Martha asked, and Jamie groaned slightly to himself.

'No,' said Liv. 'That was the next day, after Charlie found out what had happened.'

'I thought you were talking about Charlie?'

Jamie stared at the recorder in shock. So Martha hadn't been referring to him when she'd agreed that he was a great guy. She had been talking about Charlie. The realisation hit him like a punch in the stomach.

'No,' he heard Liv say. 'I was talking about Jamie.'

'Jamie?' came Martha's response. 'My Jamie?'

'Yes, Martha, *your* Jamie! Didn't you know what happened that night?'

Jamie put his head in his hands as a feeling of dread swept over him. He should turn this off now but he couldn't.

'I can't believe he didn't tell you!' Liv's voice echoed through the room. 'He was such a hero.'

Jamie listened in grim silence as Liv relayed the story of Felix's disappearance, ending with, 'He's a really special guy.'

Jamie waited for Martha to agree, but there was silence. He shook his head and rubbed his face as Liv continued: 'Martha? Please tell me you guys have worked through your problems?'

'You mean him cheating on me?' he heard Martha snap, and he shrank a little further into his chair, unable to listen to any more but equally unable to turn it off.

'Well, yes. I did know about that but he seemed genuinely sorry, Martha. And he really seemed to love you very much,' came Liv's voice.

Martha's reply was barely distinguishable but he thought she said, 'And I loved him.'

Past tense, he thought.

'Past tense?' said Liv on the recording, echoing his thoughts.

'No, not really. I still do love him. But . . .' said Martha, as Jamie tensed in readiness for what he suspected was coming next.

'But you also love Charlie?' said Liv.

'I think maybe I do, yes.'

Jamie started to shake as the recording continued.

'Have you seen him again?' asked Liv, verbalising the question that was on Jamie's own lips.

'Yes,' murmured Martha after an achingly long pause. 'Yesterday. He came and found me.'

The bile rose in Jamie's throat and he had to swallow hard to stop himself throwing up.

'What are you going to do?' he heard Liv ask. He closed his eyes as Martha's answer reverberated through the room and through his brain. 'I'm going to stay with Jamie! What else can I do? I have no choice because of the kids . . .'

Jamie leaned forward and with a trembling hand switched off the recorder. He had heard enough.

Chapter 51

It was early November and Jamie had taken Mimi and Tom to their school fireworks display while Martha wrote up a profile interview she had just done with a British TV presenter who was enjoying a resurgence in his career. Normally she could find some sort of connection with her interviewees, but this one had been difficult because she had decided almost immediately that she couldn't stand the guy. He had been charming and friendly towards her but there was something about him that made her think he was essentially a bully who was used to getting his own way; he had what Lindsay would describe as 'bad karma'. She had tried really hard to hide her dislike, but transcribing the interview, she realised that she hadn't been very successful. The only answers she had been able to get from him were bland, boring and pat.

She sighed and stood up to look out of the window. The inky night sky was dappled with smoky trails, which looked like skinny ghosts when illuminated by each explosion. She used to love fireworks when she was a child, but as she got older and had her own children they had started to scare her.

She couldn't enjoy them without worrying about what might happen if one exploded in the wrong direction, so although Jamie was desperate to buy his own and have a mini display in the garden, Martha had always stopped him.

There was an almighty crack as a huge firework exploded into a cascade of white stars, like a waterfall of diamonds against the wide black sky. Martha thought about Jamie and the children, wrapped up against the cold in their brightly coloured coats, scarves and boots, huddled together as they peered up at the spectacle above their heads.

She was worried about Jamie but she couldn't put her finger on exactly why. He had been behaving oddly, almost shiftily, as if he was up to something. Whenever she tried to ask him about it, he would simply reply that she was free to check his computer, his emails, his phone if she didn't trust him. There was an eagerness about his urging that puzzled her.

In the beginning, when she had first discovered his affair, she had taken to checking up on him anyway, but as time went on she had realised that if they were to stand any chance as a couple, she had to stop. She felt pretty sure that she wouldn't find anything incriminating because Jamie was a whizz with the computer, and if he had anything to hide, she knew he would make sure to cover his tracks this time. And it made her feel horrible about herself, reading through his private emails and texts, so she hadn't checked up on him for a long time.

The fireworks display was reaching its crescendo and Martha sat back down at her computer, listlessly re-reading what she had written already and deleting most of it. Behind her, from Jamie's computer, came a sort of electronic grunting sound, which was the signal that he had a new email.

Martha glanced over at the screen. Jamie was downloading some photography tutorial and had set it running before he left. In the dock at the bottom of the screen, a little red circle appeared, with a '1' in the middle, signifying that he had one new email.

Bored with her interview, Martha rolled her chair over to Jamie's computer and casually pressed on the email icon. At the top of the list of emails was the new one. The sender's name was *Debra Steele*.

Martha frowned as her heart began to race and a fine sheen of sweat broke out on her face. It couldn't be.

Her eyes moved to the subject line, which read: *Hi Sexy!* The jauntiness of the greeting seemed grotesquely inappropriate, considering that they were the two small words that would finally bring an end to her marriage.

The screen blurred in front of Martha's tears and she tried to blink them away as she read the rest of the email, only confirming her suspicions that he had resumed his affair.

It wasn't the same as before, when the shock had almost killed her. This time it was a seeping sadness that there was no way back. She closed the email and stood up, brushing herself down as if that would somehow help. For a few seconds she wondered if she might faint, and she gripped the back of her chair for support. Gradually, the light-headedness passed and her balance returned.

Slowly, as if in a trance, she walked to the window and looked out. The pavement outside was full of people leaving the fireworks display. In amongst them were Jamie and the children, who peeled off from the crowd and turned into their drive.

As she watched, Jamie looked up and met her eye. The look on his face told her everything. She pressed her hand and her forehead to the glass. It felt cool under her hot palm.

Without losing eye contact with her, Jamie said something to the children, who took the key he proffered and let themselves into the house. He nodded and gave her the saddest smile she had ever seen, before he turned and walked away from their house, from their marriage, and from their life together, with his back straight and his chin lifted.

Epilogue

Dear Mimi & Tom,

By the time you read this I will be gone from your lives forever. But before I go, there are some things I want to tell you.

Firstly (and most importantly) I cannot begin to express how much happiness you have both brought me.

Mimi, from the moment you were put into my arms, all red and scrunched up, your fists flailing and your perfect little mouth opening and closing as you bawled, I fell in love with you. We had such a wonderful time together, those first few years, but it wasn't until you, my gorgeous Tom, were born that the fun really started. It seems to me like you were born smiling and you have smiled ever since. You made our family complete and we loved you instantly and passionately.

I want you both to know that none of what happened is your fault. There is only one person to blame and that's me. I did something very wrong and there hasn't been one single moment since that I haven't regretted it and wished fervently that I could turn back the hands of time and make it not have happened.

But I can't go back and change anything. And that is why I am writing this letter to you now. Now that your mum is with Charlie, I think it would be best for everyone concerned if I was no longer here.

Losing your beautiful mum was very hard, but losing the love and respect of my two darling children has made me feel that I don't want to be in this world if I can't see you and spend precious time with you, having stupid debates over the breakfast table and going out exploring on our bikes like we always used to do.

I can understand why neither of you have wanted to see me or have anything to do with me, but the truth is, without you in my life, I have no purpose and no future. Don't blame yourselves. Blame me.

So, goodbye my beautiful children. I love you to infinity and beyond.

Dad

xxx

'And the Oscar goes to . . .' There was an overly long pause, as the dark-haired actress in the emerald green sequinned dress tried to build the tension. '. . . Charlie Simmons!'

On the TV set, Charlie could be seen beaming with delight as he stood up and gave a half-wave to the applauding audience around him, before striding towards the stage at a pace that suggested he couldn't wait to get there.

He kissed the girl in the green dress on both cheeks and

took the small gold statue she was holding out to him. Then he walked towards the microphone, his eyes shining and his smile wide. 'Thank you!' he cried. 'Thank you so much! I really am overwhelmed with gratitude for this honour.

'If you'll forgive me for bumbling through this like an idiot,' he continued, prompting a polite but generous ripple of laughter from the auditorium, 'there are some people I need to thank.'

He took a deep, steadying breath before beginning by thanking the cast and crew. 'Next,' he said, clearing his throat slightly, 'I'd like to thank my ex-wife, Liv Mason ...' A murmur of surprise went through the crowd, causing him to pause momentarily with a slightly raised eyebrow. 'Liv gave up her life here in Hollywood to move back to the UK with me, so that I could be nearer to our beautiful son, Felix. It was a big sacrifice for her to make, but I'm happy to say that her acting career hasn't suffered as a result. In fact, I'd be willing to bet that she's standing on this very stage next year, when she wins the best actress Oscar!' There was another low hum of laughter.

'I'd like to thank my parents, Mike and Jo, for their unstinting support ...' he continued. 'And of course, my darling Felix, who is such an inspiration to me.'

There was another pause, and Charlie's smile shrank as he seemed to struggle with his emotions. 'But most of all I'd like to thank my beautiful wife, Martha, who can't be here tonight because our baby is due imminently and she wasn't able to fly out from our home in England.'

A wave of 'aaahhhh's washed over the auditorium.

Charlie's eyes glistened as he looked into the TV camera in front of him. 'But, darling, I know you're watching with Mimi and Tom and I just want to say thank you, from the bottom of my heart, for giving me a reason to live. I love you.' As he finished speaking, he broke into a wide smile once more and held his Oscar statuette aloft in a gesture of victory.

Jamie reached for the remote control and pressed the 'Off' button. For several moments he stared at the black screen in which he could see his reflection, sitting alone in the middle of a worn-out sofa, surrounded by bits of screwed-up paper. It seemed apt, somehow, and gave him a sense of grim satisfaction. A sense that justice had been done.

He looked down at the letter in his hand. He had found it earlier while tidying out one of the drawers in his small flat and had slumped down onto the floor, feeling shaken by its contents and trying to remember how he had felt the night he wrote it.

He had fully intended to end it all, but during the dark night of the soul that followed, he had sat up for hours crying, imagining the effect it would have on Mimi and Tom's lives forever, knowing that their dad had killed himself. By the time dawn broke, he knew that he couldn't do it to them.

And, in a twisted quirk of fate, it was that morning that Mimi chose to ring him for the first time since he had left, to tell him that she and Tom wanted to see him. He had expected their first meeting to be stilted and peppered with recriminations, but as soon as they saw each other they fell into each other's arms, crying with relief and happiness. It was almost as if they sensed how close they had come to losing him forever. Since then, the children had kept him strong, and they had developed a new depth to their relationship now that the anger and hurt had abated.

The way their lives had worked out meant that he could take some comfort from knowing that he had done the right thing. He couldn't have lived with the knowledge that Martha was only staying with him because of the children, while deep down she was in love with Charlie. But Martha would never have ended their marriage if he hadn't set up a false account and sent himself that email, supposedly from Debra. He had given Martha the reason she needed to find happiness with someone else. Someone who deserved her.

Jamie got up and went to the tiny kitchenette, which was sectioned off from the living area by a small breakfast bar. He opened the fridge and took out the bottle of non-alcoholic fizz he had bought earlier. Charlie Simmons wasn't the only one with something to celebrate that day. He opened it with a practised pop and took two glasses out of the cupboard. They weren't champagne glasses but they would have to suffice.

As he filled the second glass, the intercom buzzed. Jamie smiled to himself and picked up the handset, which was mounted on the wall beside him. She was coming to help him celebrate the fact that he had finally secured a deal to write two children's books, realising a life-long dream of his.

'Hi,' she said, the sound of her voice making his insides flutter for the first time in a very long while. 'It's me, Liv.'

Acknowledgements

I simply wouldn't have had a clue where to start in Hollywood if it wasn't for the help of Vickie White, Nigel Stoneman, Carla Romano and Natalka Znak – thank you all for your valuable insights.

I am also indebted to Sharon Osbourne, who was as *"fabulous"* as ever in LA and generously shared her experiences as a Brit living the high life in Tinseltown.

The biggest thanks goes to my old friend Jacqui Moore, who flew in from New York to act as chauffeur, chaperone, tour guide, running buddy and dining companion. I don't think I've ever laughed as much as I did during our time in LA. Thanks Jaqs!

Heartfelt thanks to Maxine Hitchcock, who was at her usual brilliant best when editing this novel and to Clare Hey and the whole team at Simon & Schuster for their continued support.

Huge thanks to my wonderful agent, Sheila Crowley, who is always there for me and to everyone at Curtis Brown.

Thank you also to Alex Bowley, who has supported me in so many ways for so many years now.

Nothing would be possible without my amazing family. It's been a difficult year (RIP dad) but we've come through it stronger than ever. Thank you all.

And finally, extra-special thanks to Alice, Paddy & Rob, who make it all worthwhile.